Tempting Rafe

"So now that you've found me out, will you toss me back on the street, denounce me for the reward money?"

"Good Lord, woman, what kind of man do you take me for?" Rafe spoke sharply. "If I was the kind of man who would turn you over to those murderers on the so-called committee for public safety, don't you think I would have left you on the street with those animals today?"

"Forgive me," she said quietly. "I find it difficult to judge people these days."

Rafe rose and walked over to the bed.

Alix looked up, searching his eyes. "Will you help me?" Her voice was steady, her face pale, but proud. "I can pay for your services."

It struck Rafe that the only payment he wanted was to press her back against the mattress, to cover her slender body with his own and to kiss her soft lips until the desperation and fear were gone from her eyes. He started to reach for her, his hand moving slowly toward her face, and suddenly he realized what he was doing. Good God, he thought with a shock, what on earth was he thinking? He was a gentleman with an almost fiancée, and Alix was a woman in need of assistance, not seduction.

Don't miss the next novel from Joanna Novins

Souvenir of Love

THE SOUVENIR COUNTESS

JOANNA NOVINS

BERKLEY SENSATION, NEW YORK

THE SOUVENIR COUNTESS

A Berkley Sensation Book / published by arrangement with
the author

PRINTING HISTORY
Berkley Sensation edition / January 2004

ISBN: 0-425-19387-X

BERKLEY SENSATION™
Berkley Sensation Books are published by The Berkley Publishing Group,
a division of Penguin Group (USA) Inc.,
375 Hudson Street, New York, New York 10014.
BERKLEY SENSATION and the "B" design
are trademarks belonging to Penguin Group (USA) Inc.

PRINTED IN THE UNITED STATES OF AMERICA

10 9 8 7 6 5 4 3 2

*For my sister Dana Eve whose advice enriches my work
and whose love and friendship enrich my life*

Chapter One

❦

"Please let it still be here," Alix prayed as she ran her hands frantically over the floor. Her fingers at last grazed the rough cloth of the sack containing supplies she'd stored several weeks ago. She reviewed the items by touch: the wool clothing, the flask of water, the parcel of dried fruits, the porcelain chamber pot. Fumbling with trembling hands, she found a candlestick and a stub of candle. She didn't dare light it, but knowing she had it made the darkness more bearable.

No light penetrated this airless room behind a false panel, but Alix closed her eyes anyway. So many nights she'd lain awake thinking about this hiding place, tucked beside the mantle in one of the château's many guest rooms, but she'd never truly believed she'd have to use it. Her father had been so confident that the trouble in the village would pass, that the people would see reason and release the king. She'd almost begun to believe him. She pressed her back against the rough wall and hugged her knees tightly. Every nerve ending screamed with fear. It seemed as if the quick intakes of her breath and the whisper of her silk gown were the only sounds in the world.

And then the monstrous symphony began.

The peasants stormed through the grand entranceway of the château screaming for the blood of the de La Brous. Catcalls and jeers, bits of martial songs and the shuffling stomp of many feet penetrated the secret room. The people were moving through her home, up the grand staircase and down the long portrait gallery. The sounds became sharper, clearer, and Alix heard the clang of pitchforks and scythes against wood and glass, the crash of furniture falling and the tearing of fabric as the villagers entered the grand salon, nearing her father's library.

She'd begged her father to flee or at least to conceal himself.

"Alexandre Charlotte, don't be ridiculous. De La Brous do not scurry off, or crouch in dark corners like rats." His lips thinned in distaste. "But if it suits your delicate nature to hide away from our people, you may."

By then the sounds of the angry villagers outside had become distinct in the grand salon, the hoarse shouts of the men, the screamed curses of the women and the relentless pounding of thick-soled shoes against the wide gravel drive.

"Papa *please* . . ." she tried a final time, but he didn't bother to rise from his chair or even close the book he had resting on the knees of his satin britches. Waving a lace-draped wrist in her direction, he said simply, "Go hide, Alexandre. When the fellows come up the drive, I'll treat with them."

They were his last words to her.

Even to the end, her father had not believed the peasants would harm them.

The din from below lulled. It could only mean one

thing—the mob had found her father. As clearly as if she were standing by his side, she imagined him confronting them, his thin shoulders thrown back, his powdered head as proudly erect as if he were attending the king at Versailles. He'd address them as if they were children, as he had so often spoken to her, patiently explaining that he was their lord, their master, the Comte de La Brou, descended from a family that had defended them for centuries.

There was a swirling howl, a sound more terrible than any she had ever experienced. Her blood seemed to freeze. Then she heard a roar of indignation she recognized as her father's. A single animal scream. The people's voices rose in triumph. The villagers had cut her father down as if he were nothing. She knew this with awful certainty.

Crouching in the stifling darkness, she felt she could no longer breathe. The floors and walls were vibrating with the orgy of looting and destruction just beyond, and she lost all sense of time. At one point the sounds were so clear she realized that people were just beyond the thin barrier of the false wall; she thought she might even recognize some of the voices. Was it hours or days that she lay curled in this little passage, her hands vainly pressed against her ears? Gradually she became aware again of the sounds of her breathing, the rustle of her skirts and the soft scrape of her own foot against the floor.

The Château Valcour, always so full of voices, movement, and music, was as still as death.

She pressed her ear to the panel beside the mantle, straining for any evidence that she was not completely alone. When she heard nothing, she quickly began to unlace her gown, dropping it to the floor. She rolled down her silk stockings and tossed them in a heap, along with her satin flowered garters. Reaching into the cloth bag, she pulled out a pair of cotton stockings and a coarse wool gown, donning them with damp and shaking hands. She raked her fingers through her stylish coiffure, twisting her tangled hair into a thick bun at the nape of her neck, topping it with a cotton mobcap.

Willing her hands to be still, she unlatched the panel and pushed it open. Porcelain and glass shards popped and scraped beneath her plain leather shoes as she walked slowly through the once elegant sitting room. The portable furniture was gone, the larger pieces gouged and slashed. She knew she shouldn't look, couldn't linger, but as she hurried out of the room small things caught her eye and seared themselves into her memory.

A book she had been reading the night before lay in a doorway, the charred crescents of its pages fluttering. A silver hand mirror her grandmother had given her, its glass gone, was bent and battered on a stair. Things, just things, she told herself, trying not to think about where and how her father's body might lie.

She crept down a back staircase, reminding herself with each step to concentrate on reaching her mother in Paris. If she could just find Madeleine, she told herself, everything would be all right. She hadn't heard from her mother in over a year, but the post had become notoriously unreliable since the revolutionary government had taken over. All she knew for certain was that after the royal family had been imprisoned in the Tuileries, her mother had moved to an apartment in the Faubourg St. Honoré area. She'd found the address when she'd gone through the center drawer of her father's desk, where he kept his most important papers.

Her foot bumped the remains of a Sèvres vase, and it rolled down several steps and shattered. She froze against the wall, waiting to see if she would be discovered. But the only sound was the rocking of the curved shards of porcelain as they settled into place. She exhaled slowly and continued down the stairs, her mind still on her mother. She hadn't seen her in three years, not since she'd lived with

Madeleine at Versailles in preparation for her marriage to the elderly Marquis de Beincourt.

The Marquis had died of smallpox and Alix's father had demanded her return to Valcour, complaining loudly about the collapsed betrothal and hinting darkly that Madeleine was somehow responsible. He'd made no efforts to arrange another marriage. She grimaced; her father probably thought he'd have plenty of time to find her a husband. He'd refused to consider death the way he'd refused to consider the consequences of the overthrow of the king.

She unlatched a small side door and stepped outside.

"*Hisst*, mademoiselle, over here."

Alix spotted Solange and David Chaumier standing by a tall hedge that banked the formal gardens. She exhaled slowly; she hadn't allowed herself to think what she would do if her maid didn't come to find her as they'd planned.

"Come, mademoiselle, lord knows what scum might be watching the place or roaming the grounds. David's got the horses waiting on the other side of the garden." When Alix didn't move, Solange reached out and tugged her sleeve. "There's nothing for you to do here now."

Alix turned for a final look at the château, its circular towers and long rectangular wings wreathed in smoke. She wanted to howl, she wanted to scream, to roll on the grass and gouge at the earth. But it wouldn't change anything. It wouldn't bring her father back, and it wouldn't restore Valcour.

Tearing her eyes away, she reminded herself that nobility didn't lie in buildings or fortunes, but in blood. She was the last of the de La Brou line, and she would prove that the strength of the ancient warrior dukes still ran in her veins. She would survive and return to reclaim her heritage. Wrapping her arms tightly around her corseted waist, she felt the reassuring rustle of her father's property titles against her chemise. Feeling armored against the uncertain future, she hastened to join David and Solange.

Robert Lamartine stood in the copper light of late afternoon, looking out the tall windows of the Comte de La Brou's grand salon. A movement below suddenly caught his eye. A footman was holding apart branches of the thick garden hedge for two housemaids to pass through. All three had cloth sacks slung over their shoulders. He chuckled, thinking he was not the only faithful servant collecting long-overdue rewards from the comte. But as the last woman ducked through the hedge her mobcap caught on a branch and a wealth of dark hair tumbled down her back. She turned and a ray of fading sunlight caught her face.

"Why Alix, you naughty little minx," Lamartine muttered unpleasantly, "wherever do you think you are going, and what do you have in that bag?"

He shrugged. It made no difference to him where the comte's daughter thought she was headed. Without the proper identification papers, there was little chance she would make it very far without being arrested and executed. She might just as well have died with her father.

He caught his reflection in the fractured remains of a gilt-framed mirror and smiled. It had been so easy to arouse the peasants. He'd simply spread a few rumors that the Comte de La Brou was raising money to send to supporters of the imprisoned king. Then he'd paid an orator to stir things up with a lovely speech detailing the comte's efforts to betray the new republic. The villagers had been incensed, spilling out of the market square, grabbing up pitchforks and pikes, and marching up to the château demanding vengeance. He really was quite gifted when it came to planning and coordination.

Not that his master had ever truly appreciated him. No,

the ridiculous old man had been too busy prancing about in his powdered wigs and painted heels. Making tiresome speeches about the noble history of the warrior de La Brous. When all along it was he, Robert Lamartine, who was responsible for Valcour. His work as steward—collecting the rents and duties, overseeing repairs, keeping an eye on the staff—had made the château a showplace and enabled the comte to live a life of comfort and ease.

Lamartine crossed the grand salon, the crackle of broken glass beneath his feet sending shards of pleasure up his spine. When he reached the doorway at the far end of the room, he stopped and the head of a small porcelain milkmaid came to rest against his buckled shoe. He knelt to pick it up. A shame it had been broken; he'd rather liked the little piece. It reminded him of his sister Marie, though her clothes had never been as lovely as this figurine's. Nor had they been warm enough to protect her from the consumption that had taken her life. Robert opened his hand. The head rolled off and shattered.

Straightening, he sidestepped the remains of a paneled door and entered the comte's private library. The comte had never thought fit to thank his steward properly, so Lamartine had been thanking himself, skimming generously from estate accounts. He smoothed the front of his simple olive and brown striped waistcoat and patted his old-fashioned bagwig. From his modest appearance no one would ever guess he was really quite a wealthy man. However, a man of wealth should have property. As soon as he found the comte's titles, he'd have that, too.

The foolish comte had relied upon him to sign all his papers. Lamartine doubted anyone could tell their signatures apart. Which was how he'd convinced a registrar of deeds to notarize papers transferring the de La Brou estates to one Robert Lamartine, in the unlikely event of the comte's own demise.

Eyeing the headless body splayed across a delicately in-laid desk, Lamartine reflected idly that some might raise questions as to why the comte hadn't left his property to his wife or to his daughter. He had little doubt they could be laid to rest. After all, the comte had frequently been heard to say that the only responsibility a woman could be entrusted with was birthing a man's heir.

With effort, Lamartine rolled his former master's battered corpse onto the floor. Grinning, he drew a fine linen handkerchief from the comte's waistcoat pocket and wiped the desk drawer's lock free of gore. Then he inserted a fine gold key. It turned with a satisfying click, and he slid the drawer open.

His smile was short-lived.

It was empty. His hands scrabbled wildly, like crabs trying to escape a box, searching the corners, the back of the drawer, behind the drawer. Nothing! Enraged, he turned to the body on the floor and kicked it. "You stupid, useless old man . . . *What have you done with those papers?*"

Chapter Two

❧

"You'll never believe this, Captain," Jervis Jones said, wiping his mouth on his greasy sleeve. "The Frogs have definitely gone crazy on this one. I'm over at the Place de la Grève last Saturday, and I see this great gaggle of people. Well, they don't seem to be killing anybody this time, so I stroll over to get a closer look. And can you guess what they're doing, Captain?"

He didn't wait for an answer and Rafe Harcrest knew his participation wasn't required to keep the conversation going.

"They're getting married, the whole bloody lot of them. There's this little wizened clerk lecturing at them, and when he finishes up he says, 'All right, do you folks agree to be married?' and they all shout, 'Yes.' And that's it, the thing's done, everybody cheers and goes home. Can you imagine, Captain, English women getting married like that, no fancy dress, no flowers, no celebration?"

"None of the women in my family," Rafe agreed absently.

"Course when you marries Lady Anne, I suspect you'll have your fill of flounces and folderol."

Rafe, who had no interest in discussing Lady Anne Dinsmore, pushed the soup tureen across the table to Jervis who ladled out a bowl of dubious-looking brown lumps.

"Course," Jervis rambled on, "guess it would be fine to go without all the display if you could get the missus to agree. But no drinking and no dancing? No question, Captain," he said, smacking his lips over the stew, "these Frenchies have gone round the bend. Do you think it's even legal?"

"I believe our French neighbors' concepts of law are a little unusual these days," Rafe said delicately. The inn was crowded and while it was unlikely anyone could hear their conversation over the din of clattering silverware and vigorous luncheon conversation, he wasn't willing to risk attracting any undue attention.

Jervis loudly spit out a piece of bread having discovered, Rafe speculated, either straw or stones in it, flour now being in short supply in Paris. Hard times had come to France, and from what he and Jervis had seen, things were only going to get worse. The sooner they concluded their business here, the better. Rafe cursed the impulse that had brought him to Paris in the middle of a bloody revolution.

"Yes sirree, Captain, this is just like the squirrel stew I used to fix you when we was in the army, except that I think they may be using cats." Jervis glanced over at Rafe and said abruptly, "You're drumming again."

Rafe raised an eyebrow. "I beg your pardon?"

"You always do that you know, drum your fingers when you get restless and your mind's going wandering off somewheres. So what is it, the silks or Elizabeth?"

"Both," said Rafe lying through his teeth. He had no intention of confessing to his manservant that the real reason he'd dragged them both off to France was because at the last moment he'd lost his nerve and found himself unable to propose to Lady Anne Dinsmore. When they returned, he had no doubt that she would be waiting with considerably less patience for him to make his offer.

"Don't know why you're worrying so much about them silks. The cargo would have gotten loaded fine without you running over here to check on it. You've done a fine job setting up this business; it practically runs without you."

As well it should, Rafe reflected, his fingers continuing to beat a noiseless tattoo on the rough table. With Jervis's help, he'd established a lucrative trade cloaked in a level of secrecy that would have made a first-rate spymaster weep with envy. Not that there was anything underhanded about importing French fabrics into England, but it would have been the scandal of the ton had it been discovered that the Earl of Moreham was engaged in trade. He smiled grimly. Better that he and his family decline gracefully into poverty, with their aristocratic virtues intact and their hands unsoiled by work.

His fingers stopped drumming and curled into a fist. He hadn't intended to become involved in trade anymore than he'd expected to become the Earl of Moreham, but he'd be damned if he allowed his stepmother Louisa and his half sister Elizabeth to suffer the consequences of his father's and older brother's extravagant spending and insatiable love of gambling. Both had died within a few years of each other, leaving him with heavily mortgaged estates and a mountain of debts. Rafe had been a soldier, and with a soldier's sense of order and discipline he'd mounted a campaign to bring his family back to financial security.

Most of the ton believed his frequent visits to Paris were to satisfy a fondness for French women. Over tables at White's, men speculated over the identities of his conquests, while ladies seemed eager to discover what "foreign" techniques he might possess. He'd had to remove more than one maidenly hand from his thigh, though never, he reflected, Lady Anne's.

Unbidden, an image of Anne Dinsmore took shape in his head, tall and elegant, with ash blond hair and pale blue eyes. She was not beautiful, her face was a trifle too long, her nose a bit thin and sharp, but she carried herself with all the grace and composure one would expect of a duke's daughter. Rafe looked down and realized he was drumming again; he forced his fingers to be still.

"You worry too much about Elizabeth, too, you know. She's young yet, but give her time, she'll settle down." Jervis chuckled and spooned a bit of stew into his mouth.

Anne Dinsmore's grace and charm, not to mention her impeccable standing among the doyennes of high society, were precisely what he needed to help him manage his spirited young sister. Elizabeth had barely been out of leading strings when their father died. His stepmother was an absent-minded creature who spent most her time puttering about the gardens at Moreham Hall, leaving Elizabeth's upbringing to a string of governesses and Rafe. There were times when he felt more like a father to Elizabeth than a brother. He shook his head; he found it hard to believe that the gangly girl with the knotted curls was on the verge of coming out into society.

If she would just pay more attention to his advice, Rafe thought, unconsciously tapping his fingers on his thigh. She needed to learn to conduct herself with the decorum befitting an earl's daughter. She needed to be more responsible and stop haring off on impulse. He'd told her that repeatedly, and each time she'd look up at him, eyes full of tears, lip quivering, and promise to do better. Rafe had a notion he was being shammed, but he always relented.

Jervis's voice interrupted his musings. "What does last month make, two or three governesses she's run off?"

"I believe it's three." It wasn't that he wanted to kill her spirit, just curb it a bit. Rafe knew all too well where impulse could lead.

"You could do with bit of high spirits yourself my lad," Jervis said, wagging a spoon at him.

Rafe's lips tightened. He'd heard that argument before and he mistrusted it; it only led to disaster. It was impulse that had taken his father over a jump too high for his favorite horse, leaving the earl with a broken neck and the horse with a shattered foreleg. It was impulse that had led his brother to wager the family fortune on the turn of a card. And it was impulse that had brought him here to Paris instead of coming up to scratch with Anne. Rafe made up his mind; as soon as he returned to England he'd speak to her.

As if sensing the direction of his thoughts, Jervis broke in. "I hear they've finally reopened the gates of the city. The cargo's nearly all been delivered to the ship, so when do you think we might be getting out of here?"

"Another day or so and I think everything should be signed and delivered."

"I tell you, Captain, I'll be glad to see the last of this place."

"Well, the city seems to have settled down."

"Yes, it's almost eerie. People going about their business as if there weren't rotting corpses stacked like cordwood the next street over. In all my years, I never seen anything like it."

Rafe nodded. In his late teens he'd fought in the colonial wars in the Americas; it was where he'd met Jervis. He'd experienced hand-to-hand combat in the forests of New England, fought at the disastrous battles of Saratoga. But in all those years, he'd never seen such horrific killings. He found it hard to believe that only a week ago, mobs had broken into the jails of Paris, slaughtering the inmates. For days after, thugs known as sans-culottes for their distinctive baggy pants, roamed the streets looking for "counter-revolutionaries" and "traitors to the state." He would never forget the sight of these men, their clothes spattered with blood and their wrists swollen from their labors, swaggering about boasting of their murderous deeds.

Jervis pushed his bowl away, patted his stomach, and emitted a satisfied belch. "Where to now, Captain?"

Rafe spun the stem of his spoon between his long elegant fingers. "Jervis my man, I believe it's time to fold our cards and quit the game."

Chapter Three

⁂

Alix stood in the open ground floor of a butcher shop on a muddy side street in Paris, picking chicken feathers out of her hair. "You know," she said to David Chaumier, "I think this idea was better in the planning." They both cast their eyes to the street where a cart with a false bottom was parked.

"Well, the crates of chickens did keep the guards from checking the wagon too closely," David pointed out. "Nasty things though, chickens. Hate the way they're always staring at you with them beady little eyes, probably thinking how to peck your fingers off with them sharp little beaks."

"It wasn't the birds that frightened me. It was the fear that I might expire from the odor. I wish I'd had my vinaigrette with me."

"Here now," David said in a whispered scold. "We told you. You can't go waving fancy silver boxes under your nose like you're too good for the barnyard or the streets. People will think you're putting on airs, or worse."

"I know, I know," Alix replied quickly. "Don't worry so. I haven't as much as a lace handkerchief among my things. Speaking of which . . ." Alix swept a hand across her dress. It was spattered with detritus from the chicken cages.

David gestured toward an alleyway. "Henri says you can change your clothes in the room behind his shop, through the door over there."

Alix picked her way carefully through the refuse-strewn passageway. Pushing open a rough wooden door, she entered a small dark room. From the light of a grimy window she could make out a bed, a table, and two crudely hewn wooden stools. The smell of butchered meat permeated everything, and her gorge rose. She willed her stomach to be still.

It had been a rough trip, but it was almost over. It was a stroke of good luck that one of the château's former cooks, Henri, had set up a butcher shop near Les Halles, not far from the Rue de l'Université where her mother was living. More fortunate still, he had been willing to offer his assistance, though Alix understood the gesture was out of friendship to the Chaumiers rather than to her.

She pulled off her kerchief and began to unlace her dress, eager to shed the clothes she'd been wearing since she fled the château six days ago. She wished she could have changed her chemise, but without assistance she could not remove the stays that overlaid it. She recalled Solange arguing that she should wear a corselet, a shorter garment that laced in front, or forgo them entirely since they were currently out of fashion in Paris. Alix thought she would feel naked without her stays and so had refused. Besides, they had proven a useful hiding place for her valuables. She ran her hand along the lumps of papers and jewels sewn into the garment's lining. Heaving a small sigh, she wondered whether her linen would look less grimy if she folded under the lace of her chemise.

Henri, she saw with relief, had left a pitcher of water and a basin on the table. Using the skirt of her yellow wool dress, she sponged her face and body as best she could. Then she opened her cloth bag and pulled out her carefully chosen costume: a clean petticoat, cotton stockings, a white muslin dress sporting a print of gay red, white, and blue posies, and a waist-length red jacket. At the bottom of the bag lay a lace cap and a somewhat crushed straw hat trimmed with red, white, and blue ribbons. Clad in this attire, she should be able to pass as just another patriotic citizen attending to her business in the city.

She emerged into the alleyway, transformed, or at least so she hoped. She performed a graceful pirouette for David and Henri, and asked, "So, citizens, am I not a vision?"

Henri pursed his lips, uncertain of how to respond to his former mistress, but David crowed with laughter. "Oh, mademoiselle," he gasped, "you're a vision all right. I'm just not sure a vision of what."

Alix eyed him. "I was given to understand such outfits are all the rage in Paris. Are you suggesting my attire is less than à la mode?"

"Well," David offered, "maybe if you could do something with your hair?" He plucked off her hat, picked a pin-feather out her hair, and tried to smooth her tangled waves into a semblance of order. Tucking in as many of the errant strands as he could, he replaced the hat, stood back, and surveyed his handiwork. "I suppose if you walk with a purpose, don't look anybody in the eye, you could make it to your mother's without attracting too much attention." David's voice grew serious. "I tell you, Mademoiselle Alix, I'd feel better if you'd let me take you there. And you know Solange would agree with me."

Alix looked at him, her gray eyes softening. "David, I

can never thank you enough for everything you and
Solange have done for me. You've gotten me this far, and
I can't bear to ask any more of you. If I'm picked up by a
district patrol, and you're with me, you'll be accused of
aiding a fugitive aristocrat. And we both know what that
means." She cast a look at Henri, and he nodded in assent.

"She's right, you've no idea of the awful killing that's
been going on here. Those sansculottes will string you up
on a lamppost as quick as twisting a chicken's neck. And
no one will stop 'em."

Alix continued in a rush, afraid that if she didn't get the
words out at once, she might reconsider and ask him to
stay. "David, you know Solange and I practically grew up
together. I could never look her in the face again if I were
responsible for making her a widow. You must return to her
now." She stepped forward and took his broad callused
hand. In it she placed her maid's identity papers and a roll
of notes and coins. She closed his fingers gently around the
bundle and kissed them.

Looking up at him she said, "Every day without her
identity papers puts Solange in danger. You both have
risked so much for me, I only wish I had more to give you.
This should be enough to see you safely home and perhaps
to give you a fresh start." Tears began to fill her eyes, and
she wiped them fiercely away, "Go now, David, *now*."

David looked down at the bedraggled figure before him.
He straightened her straw hat and tugged the cap underneath it down. "I'll go, mademoiselle, for Solange's sake,
not for the money, though I won't be saying I'm not grateful for it. You've got a good heart miss and a brave one."
He paused, unsure of what else to say, then cast a look at
the thickset butcher. "Henri, my friend, you see she gets to
her mother safe."

With a last reluctant glance, David clambered up onto
the seat of the chicken wagon, clicked his tongue at the

bony nag waiting in its traces, and drove off. Alix watched him go till he was lost among the traffic of horses, carts, and carriages.

Henri cleared his throat nervously, and Alix turned. "Beggin' your pardon, mademoiselle, I mean citizeness, would you like a bite to eat or would you like to set out?"

Alix's stomach growled an eager response, but she could see by the way the butcher's eyes darted to the street and the way his hands tugged at the wiry hairs of his balding head that he was anxious to have her gone. "Citizen," she said, "I thank you for your kind offer, but I think it would be best if I were on my way."

The butcher's face visibly relaxed, and he rubbed his thick hands together. Barely able to conceal the spring in his step, he said, "I'll go harness up Agnes. Whyn't you step back into the shop and rest yourself, and I'll let you know when she's ready to go."

Alix made her way through the piles of crates and baskets, some with squawking or grunting inhabitants, past the hanging haunches of meat, and into the darkened interior of the shop. A small door behind the counter led to where she had changed her clothes, and Alix reluctantly ducked back into the fetid little room.

After a mercifully short time, she heard a soft knock at the window and peering out saw Henri waiting in the passageway, holding the reins of a dust-coated mare so thin she looked more like an anatomy lesson than a horse.

"Here," Henri said, biting back the *mademoiselle*. "Here, citizeness, I'll give you a hand up." He seated her sideways on the generous sway of the animal's back and mounted up in front of her. Henri flicked the reins, and Agnes set off at a slow roll. "Hold on tight, citizeness," he said over his shoulder. "These streets are narrow and people just come dashing through on them fancy horses and in them big carriages." He shook his head in disgust.

As they turned onto a larger street, Henri continued talking, and Alix had to lean close to hear him over the din of horses' hooves and carriage wheels jostling and squelching through the mud. It seemed to Alix that everyone on the streets was speaking as loudly as possible, competing with the street vendors in an effort to be heard.

From the words she could catch, Alix understood Henri was talking about the route they would take. "Been here fifteen years . . . still get lost among these damn twisty little streets . . . think you know where you're going and then, heh, you're stuck in some cul-de-sac." He spat perilously close to an elderly couple walking their dog. "Taking you across the Pont-Royal would get you closer to your mother's but then we'd have to ride along the Place du Carrousel and that mess around the Tuileries . . . ." He muttered something about thieves, whores, and politicians and spat again.

Alix heard his voice take on an apologetic tone, caught bits and pieces about crossing the Pont Neuf. "Have to pass Saint-Germain-des-Prés . . . using the abbey as a prison . . . terrible killings there, bastards using bodies for tables, dipping their bread in the blood." Henri shook his head and continued. "Should be cleaned up by now. . . . Still, don't look away if you see a bit of body or blood . . . might be taken as unpatriotic."

Alix slowly absorbed the essence of the butcher's disjointed dialogue. There had been killings in Paris again and recently. Black spots danced before her eyes, and there was a flat metallic taste in her mouth. For a moment Alix wondered whether she might slip off Agnes' swayed back and be trampled.

Desperately, she tried to battle back mounting waves of fear. What if her mother wasn't home? What if she had gone into hiding? What if . . . what if she was dead? She dug her nails into her palms, willing the pain to overwhelm the gibbering voices in her head. Easy, Alexandre Charlotte, easy, she intoned and felt calm creeping along the edges of her panic.

Her mother was too fierce a spirit to have been imprisoned or killed. She'd have seen and understood what was going on in Paris and found some way to escape. Hadn't her father always complained that his rebellious young bride would be spending his money long after he was gone? Her father was gone, Alix thought digging her nails more deeply into her hand; she wouldn't believe that her mother was, too.

And then they were caught in the traffic of the bridge, a crush of vehicles, animals and people so thick Alix had to clutch the butcher's wide hips to keep from being swept off Agnes. From her place in the crowd, she could barely see the dark waters of the Seine flowing beneath them. People yelled and whistled in an effort to move forward, and, at one point, there was a great roar of laughter as a cow, riding sideways in a wooden cart, lifted its tail and splattered the red-and-blue-striped stockings of a passing dandy on a high-stepping bay.

After what seemed a noisy eternity, they crossed and turned west toward the Rue de l'Université. The streets widened a bit, easing the press of traffic, and Alix loosened her grip on Henri's waist. Her eyes lingered on the tops of the burgess houses with their peaked roofs, ornate dormer windows, and tall chimneys. As Agnes carried them further west, the house fronts became increasingly ornate, with fanciful arches, classical columns, and elaborate stonework. So many ordinary sights, she thought; a group of children were playing in a garden in front of one of the larger homes. A couple strolled arm in arm. A group of young men engaged in a heated debate in front of a bookseller's stall.

Then up ahead, Alix could see the familiar pointed

porch tower of Saint-Germain-des-Prés high above the abbey walls. And then they were passing the grounds of the monastery, the church, the cloisters, and the famous library. How odd, she thought. If it hadn't been for the armed guards at the gates with red, white, and blue cockades stuck boldly in their hats, one would never have known that the place was now a notorious prison.

It was clear from the stiffening of his shoulders that the stories of the gruesome killings that had taken place behind those walls made Henri anxious. Shortly after they passed the abbey, he said curtly, "You best get off here, citizeness." He gestured toward the side of the street with his head and sat waiting, making no move to help her. Alix slid off the horse's back. When she turned to thank the butcher, she saw that he was already guiding his nag's bony head into the swirling traffic.

She stood for a moment, her head swiveling about to take in her surroundings. She felt lost, abandoned as people pushed past her, jostling her with their elbows. She'd been in Paris before, but most often she'd viewed it from the comfort and safety of a cabriolet or a carriage. The few times she'd walked the streets she'd been accompanied by servants and her father or mother. Alix felt a sharp stab of grief as she thought of her father and the pain propelled her forward, reminding her of why she'd come to Paris; she needed to find her mother.

As she wove through the crowded street, Alix tried to look beyond people's faces, fearing if she caught someone's eyes she might wonder if this man or this woman was among those who wished her dead. Their clothes caught her eyes instead, the fashions another unwelcome reminder of how much had changed. She had heard that Parisians were rejecting any fashions that smacked of the old regime—the jewels, wigs, and wide skirts—but she was unprepared for the bizarre styles and garish displays of red, white, blue that met her gaze.

A woman strolled by wearing a thin gauze dress and what looked to be nothing under it, and Alix fought the urge to stare. She heard David's voice in her head: "Look like you belong, mademoiselle. Don't be gawking about. Don't be stopping, neither. Keep walking. It makes folks think you've got places to go and people waiting on you." Thinking of David, she tried to imagine he was with her walking a few steps behind, just out of sight.

A tantalizing aroma rose from the waffle vendors' carts, tickling her nose, and reminding her she hadn't eaten in nearly two days. She smelled butter and eggs, a hint of vanilla, and her mouth flooded with the imagined taste of a crisp waffle dusted with powdered sugar. For a moment she considered stopping; then she fueled her steps by thinking about what she would ask Madeleine's chef to prepare.

Alix glanced at the buildings on either side of the street. She was fairly certain she was going in the right direction, but it was not always easy to find numbers on the façades. In one of the few letters she had received from her mother, Madeleine had described a bas-relief of frolicking nymphs over the front door. Surely such a distinctive feature would be easy to find.

With increasingly anxious eyes, she scanned the elegant façades, seeking the distinctive frieze among the columns and ornate brickwork. From time to time she would linger in an archway in front of a shop window, pretending to examine the display, but really using the reflection in the glass to examine the buildings around her. At one point, as she struggled to make her way through a crowd seated at an outdoor café, her heart leapt with certainty that she had found it, but the relief turned out to be a grotesque series of gargoyles. And then, just as she was beginning to fear her tired feet could take her no further, she saw it.

"*I like the* way her hips roll when she walks," said the heavyset man in the red, white, and blue striped trousers.

"I dunno," said his companion, who had been scratching vigorously beneath his red woolen liberty cap. "With them bum rolls on their backsides and the padding in their tits, it's hard to know what's woman and what's horsehair. That's why I likes my women fleshier. When you gets their clothes peeled off, you still got something to squeeze." He threw his beefy arms around an imaginary woman, and his companions laughed.

The three men had been following Alix for several blocks, ever since they'd noticed she was unaccompanied. They'd admired her figure and speculated coarsely on her availability. Alphonse, the man in the striped trousers, felt certain she was a *femme du monde*. Fraze, his friend in the red cap, was less certain. Gerard, a scrawny young fellow with a spotted complexion and greasy yellow hair, was simply hungry.

They watched as Alix climbed the stairs of an elegant home and knocked on the front door. "Looks like she's got business there; now can we get something to eat?"

"Quit your whining, Gerard," Alphonse snapped, never taking his eyes off Alix. "Now what's she doing? Nobody's lived in that house for months."

"So," said the red-capped man shrugging, "maybe she's a thief, not a whore."

Chapter Four

❧

" 'Ere, citizeness, we're just after a bit of fun. No need to act so high and mighty."

Striding along the Rue de l'Université, his mind on the final shipment of silks, Rafe heard the man's taunt. He glanced across the street, his gaze following the harsh sound of the voice, and saw three men in the baggy pants and red wool caps of the sans-culottes looming over a young girl. They'd backed her up the front stairs of an elegant home. The sleeve of her jacket hung by a thread and her gown was torn. In a twisted parody of the seminude women dancing along the frieze on the building's façade behind her, she was clutching the front of her jacket with one hand and trying to fend the men off with the other.

Walk on Harcrest, walk on, he told himself, as his legs crossed the distance between them. It's not your city; it's not your business. You can't save every poor soul you see. Someone else will come along and stop this, he said to himself, even as he saw people on the street quickening their pace to bypass the unfolding drama.

"Come give us a kiss sweetheart," one of the men said, "a kiss for the heroes of the Republic."

"And then perhaps a bit more," his friend said, crudely thrusting his hips at her.

The girl dodged the largest of the men and another man circled behind her and slipped a hand under her skirt. She slapped at him and backed against the heavy paneled front door of the home. She made no sound but her eyes scanned the street in a desperate cry for help.

When her gaze met his, Rafe caught a glimpse of wide-set gray eyes, a straight nose, and firm full lips beneath a tangle of dark curls and crushed ribbons. For a moment, he had the oddest feeling they had met before, and that her face was somehow as familiar as his own. But that was ridiculous he thought, as her eyes were torn from his.

One of the men snickered. "Don't worry little one, you'll see Alphonse knows how to treat a woman."

A few more steps, a thrust of his shoulder past a brawny arm, and Rafe found himself standing between the girl and her attackers. It occurred to him as he surveyed the reddened eyes and bristling faces of the men, that he needed to come up with a plan of action and fast, but before his mind could manufacture an idea, the girl swept the initiative from him.

"Darling," she said, seizing his arm in a death grip, "you're late, you naughty devil, and what's worse, you've given me the wrong address." She burst into a tirade that made his ears burn, and Rafe wondered whether he was falling prey to some bizarre street scam. He raised his elbow to shake her off, but as he did so he looked down and saw the look of defiance on her delicate features and his body stilled. And then it was as if the rest of the world stilled. He was once again swept by the odd feeling of familiarity; he was keenly aware of how her slim form fitted against his body, her heart racing against his chest and the rapid rise and fall of her breasts. She was dirty and she smelled as if she'd been rolled through a barnyard, but he could see what had drawn the men.

"She yours then, citizen?" said one of the men, breaking the spell.

Though the man was nearly a foot shorter than Rafe, he stuck his face in so close Rafe could smell the sweat staining his woolen jacket and the wine he'd had for breakfast. He was seized by the strong desire to break the man's jaw; he knew he could take all three. But then there would be the problem of the French authorities. These were, after all, revolutionary heroes. He'd have to play along with the girl.

He smiled pleasantly at the unshaven face abutting his, "Why yes, this sharp-tongued baggage is mine. Though why I put up with her is sometimes a mystery to me." Drawing the clutching girl close to his chest, he swept his other arm around her slim waist. With a knowing wink over her head to the three men he added, "And so I find I must constantly remind myself."

Slanting his mouth forcefully against hers, he swept his tongue along her plush lower lip and into the determined bar of her clamped teeth. Rafe's eyes flew open to meet a gray glare of shock. He had meant it to be a forceful kiss, a kiss of possession that would leave no doubt in the men's minds the girl belonged to him, but to his surprise her soft full lips remained resolutely closed. He found himself sharply reminded of when he was fifteen and had attempted to kiss a fourteen-year-old chambermaid.

"Monsieur," she whispered sternly, "let me assure you I am not the type of woman who kisses strangers in the street."

He was not the only one who noticed the girl's awkward reaction to his kiss.

"Here now, citizen, it don't look like you and the citizeness are as familiar as you say," said the largest of the three men in a leering tone. "Or perhaps she needs a more experienced teacher." He elbowed his friend in the red cap, and they both laughed like dogs growling in their throats. The yellow-haired man with the pocked face stepped closer and made a grab for the girl's skirt. She shrank closer into the circle of Rafe's arms, and he felt oddly protective.

"What can I say, citizens?" Rafe inquired with mock sorrow. "The little one is shy. She prefers to display her talents in private rather than on a public street." He heaved her up and over his shoulder, then turned as if he'd forgotten something. "But I thank you for taking such good care of her." Reaching into his pocket, he scattered a handful of gold coins in front of the men. As they scrambled to pick his largesse out of the mud, Rafe carried his wriggling cargo off down the street.

The girl immediately began pounding his back with her fists. "I am not a baggage, I am not your little one, and I demand that you put me down this instant."

Rafe ignored her outbursts. "Ungrateful wretch," he said in a low tone. "Have you noticed whether your friends are following us? I haven't got eyes in the back of my head, though from your position you might do the job." She quieted, and he felt her elbows against his back as she maneuvered into a different position.

"They're still looking for money," she answered and then added in a strained voice, "Thank you for coming to my aid, citizen."

Rafe acknowledged her thanks with a nod. "I would put you down, but I'm afraid that clad in your current attire, with no chaperone in attendance, I'd only have to come to your rescue again."

The girl lay stiff and silent and Rafe imagined he could

feel the heat of her frustration through his coat. Then there was a sudden wild motion, and she cried, "My hat, my hat!"

"Dreadful piece of millinery anyway, my dear," Rafe responded without stopping his stride.

"But I haven't got another," she said in an exasperated tone. Her body fell limply against his, and he found himself acutely aware of the warm curves and slender legs draped against his chest.

"May I ask where you are taking me?"

"I confess," Rafe said, "I'm not in the habit of rescuing damsels in distress, and so I haven't thought this all the way through. But as your gown is rather in disarray, and my lodgings are not far from here, might I suggest that you come with me and see what can be done? Unless of course you've got somewhere else to go."

And that, of course, was the crux of it, Alix thought bitterly. She'd been overconfident and sent David home and now she had nowhere else to go.

"Very well, but I warn you, I am a lady, and I will not submit to any discourtesies." Even as she said the words, she knew how ridiculous they sounded. She was draped across this strange man's shoulders like a sack of potatoes, her clothes were in tatters, and chickens had been nesting in her hair. If the Chaumiers could see her now, she thought wryly, they'd have a hard time arguing that she looked too much like a gently bred lady.

Then again, she doubted she could pass as a courtesan either.

She closed her eyes as he carried her bouncing along the street. It was humiliating, but it was better than remaining behind with the sans-culottes. Her rescuer spoke a cultured, if oddly accented, French. Perhaps she could appeal to his gentlemanly sensibilities . . . .

"Ah, here we are."

From her position Alix could see nothing, but she was aware that he was turning and that she was being carried through a large, carved doorway. The pungent smell of cooked meats, unwashed bodies, and wood smoke filled her nose as they entered the common room. A break in the general hum of conversation followed by catcalls and scattered laughter told her that their entrance had not gone unnoticed. She flushed and buried her face in the man's dark blue coat, feeling the fine quality of the wool against her cheek and the hardness of muscle beneath. As he took the crooked stairs two at a time, she was forced to grab at him to keep from falling. Her hands scrabbled around his waistcoat, finding little handhold on his taut waist and belly.

Kicking open the door Rafe called loudly, "Jervis, tea for the lady," strode through the small sitting room past his astonished manservant, kicked open a second door, and slid her to her feet.

Alix took measure of the room in a glance. It was modest and clean, with two windows overlooking the courtyard and stables below. Two armchairs flanked the hearth where a small fire was burning. A three-legged table was set between them and on it sat a silver chamberstick and several books. But it was the large four-poster bed that caught and held her attention.

She whirled on Rafe. "While I am grateful for your aid, sir, you should know that I have no intention of, intention of . . ."

"Sharing my bed?" Rafe finished helpfully. "Well," he said, leaning against the mantle and stretching out his long legs, "there's a mercy. While I don't doubt you're a pretty young thing underneath all that dirt,"—he gestured an elegant hand in the general direction of her face and hair—"I make it a rule never to bed women who smell like chicken runs."

For a moment, Alix thought she might take offense, but

then the absurdity of the situation struck her and she began to laugh. Rafe swept off his hat and made her a courtier's bow. "Rafe Harcrest at your service, mademoiselle."

Alix, echoing his exaggerated courtesy, sank into a deep curtsy. "Alix Rabec." He extended a hand to help her rise, and for the first time, Alix got a good look at her rescuer.

Why he's lovely, she thought, the words sounding so clearly in her head that for a moment she feared she might have said them aloud. When he'd removed his hat, he'd loosened his queue and a few strands of tawny-colored hair fell softly across his high forehead. His eyes were an amazing shade of greenish brown, like sunlight and shadow on a country stream, and they tilted down at the outer edges in a roguishly charming way. They lent an odd softness to his face, which a deep crease between his brows suggested frowned more often than it smiled. Indeed, she thought, as she took in his aquiline nose and strong chin, it might have been a dauntingly severe face, had it not been for those eyes and sensual mouth.

She'd known he was tall and muscular when he'd hefted her over his shoulder as if she weighed no more than a child, but seeing him up close—the broad shoulders, the slim hips, and the long legs encased in cream colored-britches and dark leather boots—was distinctly unsettling. She was relieved when his manservant announced his entrance with a rattling tray.

"They got less and less in the kitchen, these days. Certainly nothing you could rightly call tea. But I brought you some cheese, some dried apples, and a bit of wine. Just something to wet your whistle."

Alix blinked in surprise at the familiarity with which Rafe's manservant addressed him, and Rafe gave her a crooked grin. "My servant Jervis hails from the Americas and is still acclimating himself to the ways of European service."

Jervis snorted. "Been with the lad fifteen years . . . ac-climating my . . ." But the words were lost amongst the clatter of dishware.

Alix smiled back at them both. "It looks delightful to me." As if to underscore her point, her stomach growled loudly. She bit her lip in embarrassment. "I'm afraid it's been a while since breakfast."

"How long?" Rafe asked conversationally.

"Oh, just a day," she replied lightly.

Jervis caught Rafe's eye. "Thought I saw some more of that cat stew," he muttered as the door banged loudly behind him.

Rafe gestured toward a chair next to the tray, and when Alix was seated, he took his place across from her. Staring at her intently he said, "So Mademoiselle Rabec, you haven't eaten in a day, you've only one hat, and you were wandering unchaperoned on a Paris street. You've made it clear you're not a working girl, so what in heaven's name were you doing?"

"I was *not* wandering." She paused for emphasis. "I have but recently come to town, and I was unaware the streets were so dangerous. I was on my way to find my mother who I assumed, quite naturally, would supplement my wardrobe." She frowned, uncertain whether to continue, then added, "But her house appears to be empty."

"Empty how? As in perhaps she stepped out for a stroll along the boulevard, or empty as in packed up and gone?"

"I knocked for some time, and then I went round the windows and looked in. There was no sign that anyone was living in the house."

"I see," Rafe said quietly. He sliced some cheese and offered it to her. "You are aware that a great number of people in Paris have gone missing recently." She nodded. "Could your mother have been among them?"

Alix took the cheese from him, her fingers brushing

lightly against his. Studying his face, she answered carefully, uncertain how much to reveal. "It's possible, I suppose, but I won't believe it until I've looked around a bit more."

"And how will you do that?"

"I don't know," she answered, "but I'll think of something."

Alix chewed slowly, staring pensively into the hearth fire. There was no one in the city who might help her, but could she confess this to him? He'd saved her today, but that had been an impulsive gesture. Would he risk his neck to save a woman he didn't even know? There was something about his face, his voice, that made her want to trust him, but was she simply seeing what she wanted to see?

The door banged open again, and Jervis reentered carrying a steaming tureen, a bowl tucked under one arm. He set them down and pulled a spoon from his pocket. "This'll warm you up miss. And if you don't mind,"—Jervis paused and sniffed loudly for effect—"I've taken the liberty of ordering you up a bath. You'll pardon my manners, mademoiselle, but you smell like chicken squat. And if you'd like, while you're soaking, I'll take a look at that dress and see if there isn't something I can do to fix it up for you."

"That sounds like heaven." Alix couldn't decide if it was the smell of the stew or the mention of the bath that won her over more. If she wound up on the guillotine, she thought wryly, at least she'd go clean and well fed. She leaned forward for another piece of cheese and a discreet rustle reminded her of her stays. How would she get them off without Solange's help? She'd just have to manage, she told herself resolutely. After days of riding along dusty roads, hiding in barns and filthy back rooms, the lure of a bath was simply too difficult to resist.

Lamartine stepped into the small room off the château's great kitchen. In contrast to the kitchen itself, which looked as if a party of cannibals had feasted and then been abruptly called away, the barren room furnished with a simple desk and chair was undisturbed. He smiled; people were so easily fooled by appearances.

He carefully dislodged a loose brick from the wall and slid out a stack of books and papers. He felt for, but did not withdraw, the carefully wrapped bundles of money that lay pushed to the back, reassuring himself his fortune remained intact. He dropped the books and papers on the desk and slid into the chair. Closing his eyes he tried to imagine what was going on in the mind of Alix de Rabec de La Brou. Where would she have gone?

Deep in thought, he reached out a soft white hand and caressed a small stack of correspondence. Such a shame Madame la Comtesse's letters had failed to reach her daughter. So much valuable information they contained: fascinating tales of confusion in the court, violence in the city, entreaties to Alix and her father to flee France, and a most touching farewell letter written seven months ago before Madeleine left for England. Lamartine grunted. If the foolish girl was trying to reach her mother in Paris, she was in for a surprise.

For a moment, he imagined Alix helpless and alone in Paris, pictured himself coming to her aid, convincing her to let him safeguard her father's property. Then he shook his head. A sheltered, well-bred young lady like Alix would have no idea how to get to Paris on her own. Most likely she was hiding somewhere nearby. All he had to do was figure out where.

He picked up a quill and drew the estate payroll book close.

Stroking the neat columns of names with the quill's feather, he muttered into the silence. "I need those titles. As long as they remain in de La Brou hands, Alix or some other relative can reclaim the estates." A dreamy expression flickered across his smooth pale face. "I suppose I could denounce you. Ah, but then the state might claim the château and put it up for auction." He stabbed the desk with his quill, loudly snapping the point. "I will not spend good money on properties that should be mine."

He returned his attention to the book, his eyes circling restlessly like a hawk scanning for prey. "Alix, Alix, Alix, you have no close family, so whom would you have turned to for help?" The list of names was long and it was some time before he found what he was looking for. His pale eyes lit with pleasure.

Solange.

"So careless of me not to have thought of her sooner! I will pay the Chaumiers a call. And if you're not there, Alix, I'm sure I can persuade them to tell me where you've gone."

Chapter Five

Rafe sat before the fire, idly twirling the thick stem of a wineglass between his long fingers. The plates had been cleared, and his unusual guest had retired to take her bath in the antechamber. There was something curious about her, he thought. She spoke courtly French and carried herself like a lady, and yet she was dressed like a woman of the streets. He found himself intrigued to see what she looked like underneath the dirt.

The wind rattled the panes of the room's long window and set the curtains fluttering. Jervis rose and stoked the fire, which had begun to sputter from the draft. "Weather's beginning to change captain. If we don't get started for Calais soon, it's for sure the *Xanthus* will sail without us." He gave the fire a strong poke. "I don't relish the thought of being stranded in another French inn, waiting for the next available passage to Dover."

Rafe placed his near empty wineglass on the table. "I'd

like to make sure those cargoes of silks reach London in time for the opening of the season."

Jervis nodded and sat down across from him. "The troubles here have been driving prices sky high. With the right timing, you stand to make a pretty profit." He tapped a finger along his long nose and his dark eyes twinkled. "And I'll be betting you'll need to keep a sharp lookout on Miss Elizabeth, this being her first season and all."

Rafe frowned; Lord knew what trouble his sister would get herself into with only her mother in tow.

"So what about the little baggage next door? She's not exactly your style, Captain."

Rafe explained how he'd found her.

Jervis frowned. "Those sans-culottes are a bad lot. I've heard all kinds of stories about them attacking women on the streets and no one lifting a hand to help." He shook his head. "Still it seems odd that the girl was wandering about alone. You think it could be some kind of a set up? Maybe she's part of a gang and they play along until somebody rescues her and then she sets the poor sod up for robbery."

"She claims she was looking for her mother."

Jervis raised an eyebrow. "You're sure it wasn't her madame?"

An erratic bumping followed by a loud crash interrupted their debate. "What in hell's . . ." Rafe muttered as he flung himself from the chair and burst through the antechamber door without stopping to knock.

Alix was sitting on the floor, her face flushed beneath the tangle of her hair, her hands twisted around her back. She looked up at him and grimaced.

"I appear to have knocked over the table while trying to unlace my stays."

A small three-legged table lay on its side along with a now-dented candlestick, a lump of soap, and a hairbrush.

Jervis, peering around Rafe's shoulder, gave a whoop of laughter. Rafe motioned for him to step back.

Alix mustered a tone of great dignity. "Perhaps you might send someone up to assist me with my toilette?"

A smile playing at the corners of his mouth, Rafe held out a hand and helped her to her feet. "I have some experience in these matters. Perhaps I might be of service." When she hesitated, he spun her about, hooked a finger in the laces of her stays and pulled her toward him. Ignoring her sputter of protest, he deftly unlaced the rose satin ribbons and slid the heavy garment off.

Alix gasped both from the unexpected familiarity of the gesture and from the fear that he might examine the stays too closely. Turning to face him she said in her most imperious voice, "I'll take back my stays if you please."

"I've told you I'm not interested in taking you to bed," he responded, amusement in his voice. "At least not in your current state. But no doubt you'll agree with me that all of your garments are in serious need of a wash. If you'll hand out your chemise and petticoats, I'll find you something to wear until we've got your clothes clean and mended. In the meantime, I suggest you get into that bath before the water grows cold."

The door closed with a snap.

Alix stood frozen in place. What to do now? She'd look ridiculous if she went storming into the next room with nothing on but her shift demanding the return of her stays. Moreover, a heated argument over undergarments was bound to raise questions. She glanced at the hipbath by the fire, steamy tendrils beckoning like phantom fingers from the surface of the water and caught a whiff of lavender. She relaxed her body with effort, then slid her shift over her head and eased into the soapy water, feeling the warmth embrace her tired body.

She'd just have to trust that she could get her stays back

before Rafe or anyone else had a chance to examine them too closely.

She picked up the washcloth. Things were happening too fast. She shouldn't have sent David back before she'd reached her mother's. She began vigorously scrubbing her hair and skin, rinsing away layers of grime. She and David had passed through so many checkpoints, been searched and questioned, but still they'd managed to get through. She glanced at her hands; David had made her scrape them along rocks so the skin wouldn't look so smooth and unaccustomed to labor. Her nails were broken and dirty. There were long scratches on her arms that she'd gotten from crawling between the boards of the chicken wagon. She scrubbed harder. The distance to her mother's had been so short, and she'd been so *sure* that Madeleine would be home. She'd gotten overconfident.

Alix shuddered, thinking of the three men who'd attacked her on her mother's doorstep. She wished she could scrub hard enough to erase the memory. They'd grabbed at her, their eyes hungry and their mouths loose and wet. She wasn't naïve; she'd seen and heard enough at Versailles to know what they wanted. She thought of how she'd struggled and no one had come, how people on the streets just kept walking. Until the man Harcrest came along. Her hands clenched the washcloth. She wondered what he would he expect in payment for his services.

Men always expected payment, her mother said.

She closed her eyes and forced herself to breathe. He'd *said* he wasn't interested in taking her to bed, she reminded herself. Yet he knew she was alone and unprotected. She cursed herself for telling him too much, but what else could she do? She could go back out on the streets, or she could somehow convince this man to help her. Alix thought of the gems in her stays. Perhaps she could buy his protection, promise him more when she found her mother?

There was nothing else to be done, she thought as she ran her fingers through the worst of the tangles in her hair. She needed his help. She'd have to go back to Madeleine's apartments and see if there was anyone or anything there that might tell her where the comtesse had gone. She couldn't bring her mind to accept the idea that her mother might be imprisoned or killed. She *must* have fled, but where? Italy was too far, the way to Austria cut across a war zone. England was the most likely choice.

How could she reach Calais by herself? She splashed water on her face. She was so tired, it was hard to think. She gazed longingly at the low rope bed against the wall, and yawned. The threadbare linens and the rough wool blanket looked as inviting as any eiderdown. Maybe if she could just rest her head for a few moments, the fog that enshrouded her brain might clear and it would come to her what she should do.

"Mademoiselle Alix seems to be a bit awkward for a *femme du monde*," Jervis remarked as he dropped back into his chair. He eyed the stays Rafe still held in his hand. "And that's some fancy looking lingerie she's sporting."

Rafe turned the elegant stays in his hand examining not only the satin laces, but the rosebuds delicately stitched in pale shades of silk thread. He flipped them over and his eyes narrowed as he recognized the label of one of the most exclusive stay makers in Paris. Handing them to Jervis he said, "Not exactly the stays of a working girl."

Jervis whistled in appreciation. "Not to mention a bit too hard wearing for the job." Then running his hand across the fabric, he frowned. "Here, what's this? There's something sewed into this thing."

Knowing Rafe would stop him if he asked first, Jervis slipped a small knife from his boot and began cutting the tiny stitches. A pile of tightly folded papers tumbled into his hand. "Eh, papers, can't read 'em," he muttered thrusting them at Rafe. "Ooh, but I definitely speaks the language of these gents," he said as a small trove of jeweled earrings and rings spilled out of another section of the lining.

Rafe glanced at the glittering gems in Jervis's lap and said sternly, "Put them back."

Jervis chuckled. "The gents and I was just visiting, not planning a lasting friendship. So what's the story? What's in them papers?"

Rafe unfolded the sheets and smoothed them out. Leafing quickly through them, he said, "Titles for several large estates south of Paris, residency papers." He glanced up at Jervis, his eyes thoughtful. "I think the lady and I need to have a talk. In the meantime, make yourself useful and stroll back down to the Rue de l'Université. See if you can find out who's been living at the house with the dancing nymphs on the front, but do it quietly."

"You don't have to worry about me none, Captain," Jervis replied, retrieving a battered tricorne from the window ledge. "I am the soul of discretion." He paused at the sitting room door and glanced back at Rafe. "We're still leaving Paris on Friday, aren't we, Captain?"

Rafe nodded reassuringly. "I'm sure there's a simple explanation for all of this. We'll find the girl's family and be on our way. You'll be back on English soil with a good pint of ale in your hand by week's end."

Jervis turned back to the door and rapped lightly. Receiving no response he tried again, knocking more loudly. When there was still no answer, he pushed the door open. Rafe heard him chuckle. "Here now, Captain, come look at this. I told you she was a thief. The little baggage has stolen my bed, see if she hasn't." Shaking his head he said, "She's a pretty little thing, I'll give you that, but this is no time to be tasting the French pastries. And you, don't you want to

be hurrying on back to Lady Anne?" Without waiting for
an answer, he went cackling off down the stairs.

Rafe frowned at the fading footsteps of his manservant,
then crossed to the room to kneel beside the low rope bed.
The girl must be exhausted, he thought, as he pushed aside
a damp curl that had fallen over her face. She had been
brushing her hair when she fell asleep; his silver-backed
hairbrush was still tangled in her dark tresses. He drew it
out, feeling the silken strands slide free across his hand.
Her hair was as not as dark as he'd thought when he'd first
seen her. It reminded him of polished mahogany, richly
threaded with russet and gold.

He studied the pale oval of her face, the dark lashes ac-
centing the olive rings of fatigue beneath her shuttered
eyes. She flailed suddenly and as Rafe bent close to prevent her from falling off the narrow cot, she mumbled
about fire and death. She had titles for several estates sewn
into her stays. How far had she come to reach Paris? How
had she gotten here and had she traveled alone? And if not,
where were her people now?

Alix tossed again. "Please, Papa, *please*," she begged.

He smoothed her forehead and shushed her as he'd done
with Elizabeth when she'd been small and had bad dreams
after their father died. Her skin was so soft, he thought, allowing his finger to trail along the downy curve of her
cheek. She muttered incomprehensibly, flailing with her
arms as if to push someone away, and the thin sheet covering her slid down exposing the upper half of a creamy
breast. A feeling that was far from brotherly swept through
Rafe, and he quickly pulled his hand away.

He cast a glance around the room to see if he could find
something more substantial to cover her with and she
flailed again, throwing her body half off the cot. At this
rate, he worried, she was going to wind up on the floor.
Telling himself it was for her own protection, he slid one

arm beneath her shoulders and another beneath her knees and carried her into his room. Her body was warm and sweet, and he tried to ignore the arousal unfurling in his belly as he tucked her into his bed.

He stood for a moment looking down at her, sleeping more calmly now, and wondered again who she was. Her skin looked like she hadn't spent much time in the sun, and her hands and arms, though scratched and bruised, looked too slim and smooth to have spent much time at heavy labor. He thought of the papers Jervis had found. Was she a thief, as Jervis had suggested—perhaps a ladies' maid run off with her mistress's gems and papers? He frowned. The stays were much too elegant for a ladies' maid; her chemise, though soiled, too fine. Could she be some former lord's mistress? The furrow between his brows deepened. Or a fugitive aristocrat?

Rafe thought of the house-to-house searches the National Guard and the sans-culottes had conducted the week before. He recalled the stories he and Jervis had heard downstairs in the inn's tap room; people laughing over tales of aristocrats caught in outrageous disguises: a marquis discovered dressed as a fishwife; a comtesse garbed as a prostitute. He thought of Alix's silly hat and the imperious way she'd informed him that she didn't kiss strangers on the street, her elegant curtsy. He shook his head as he turned and stoked up the fire. He should have known that his impulse to rescue that little waif would lead to trouble—impulses always did. He lit a candle on the table and drew the curtains, casting the room into soft golden shadow. Jervis was right. She was a pretty little baggage, but they needed to send her on her way. As soon as he found someone to take care of her, that's precisely what he'd do. Pulling off his jacket and unbuttoning his waistcoat, Rafe settled back in an armchair to wait for Alix to wake.

Alix was back in the dark passageway in the château, watching with paralyzed horror as peasants brandishing pitchforks and torches burst through the false wall and spilled into the narrow hall. She turned to run, but was blocked by her father who frowned down upon her. "Don't be a coward Alix; treat with the fellows."

"Treat with them?" she screamed in frustration. "You tried to treat with them and look what happened. They killed you."

"You think you know better than a man how to handle these things?" He shook his head disapprovingly.

Alix glanced back at the mob, so close now she could reach out and touch their weapons, then back at her father, his arms crossed over his chest and his eyes dark with disapproval.

"Alexandre Charlotte, you're just going to get yourself into trouble. Women always do."

Alix turned to face him. "I won't get myself into trouble, I won't."

"Look at the mess you've gotten yourself into already. You need a man to take care of you."

She felt the mob lifting her, carrying her away from the figure of her father, and she twisted back to see him. "I'll save myself and the titles, you'll see."

She was still screaming, or so it seemed, when she woke.

Clutching the sheet to her chest, her heart pounding and her breath coming in gasps, she tried to make out where she was.

She didn't remember the room or the bed. She remembered being so tired after her bath, stumbling to the low cot, wrapping herself in a sheet and . . . Alix glanced down. It was the same sheet but a different bed. A four-poster bed.

His bed.

She surveyed the room, the fear and frustration she felt

from her dream roiling and melding with shock and anger, finding focus on the tall figure reading in the chair by the fire.

He'd looked up, marking his place with his finger when he'd heard her stir.

"You filthy degenerate, you couldn't even wait until I woke to put your hands on me. . . . You're worse than those men in the streets. . . . You're . . ." She paused, desperately seeking the words to describe his outrageous behavior. "A beast."

Rafe interrupted her tirade. "I suppose I could have left you to thrash about in Jervis's bed. You were half-naked and half on the floor when I found you. He'd have appreciated it, but I've quite a lot of things for him to do before we leave Paris, and I'd rather he not be distracted."

He rose. "As for your clothes, well, perhaps you should pack better when you run away from home, Madame la Comtesse."

"Madame la Comtesse is my mother," Alix snapped, then hastily covered her mouth as if to recapture the words.

Rafe raised an eyebrow. "That answers my first question, Mademoiselle de La Brou." Feeling oddly pleased to discover Alix was unmarried, he rummaged in a trunk near the bed and pulled out one of his nightshirts and a shawl he'd purchased for Elizabeth. Tossing them on the bed he said, "I'll turn my back so you can put those on."

Alix eyed his broad shoulders balefully. "You won't turn around?"

"On my honor as a gentleman."

"Who knows what that's worth?" she muttered.

"A very ungracious response to a man who saved your life," he chuckled.

Alix scrambled into the shirt, her mind working as furiously as her fingers. How much did this man know, how did he know? God, she thought as she pulled her hair free from the shirt's collar and reached for the shawl, she knew nothing about him and here she was trapped in his bed-chamber, clad in little more than his nightclothes. What had he done? Had he touched her? She shook her head. Grow up Alexandre, she told herself, at this point your virtue is the least of your worries. Folding the cuffs over her hands, she decided frankness was the best approach.

Straightening the shawl over her shoulders and folding her hands in her lap, she said, "You may turn around now."

Rafe, who'd been leaning against the mantle, turned and cast an appreciative eye over her. "You do clean up nicely," he said, thinking that she looked most appealing in his nightshirt, her small frame lost in its loose folds, her tou-sled hair tumbling about her shoulders.

She met his eyes with a piercing stare. "So, Monsieur Harcrest, what do you think you know about me?"

Rafe considered her for a moment then lifted the papers that had been sewn into her stays off the table. He tossed them into her lap along with the jewels and money.

Alix's eyes grew large. "What kind of man searches a lady's *unmentionables*?" she demanded in an outraged voice.

"Jervis," he replied helpfully. "Jervis thought you might have sticky fingers, but I thought your hands looked a bit too smooth. Have you been denounced?" he asked with studied casualness.

The room was silent for a long moment.

"I don't know. My mother is missing, so maybe she . . ." Alix let the words trail off. "My father is dead. Killed. I took his papers because I thought . . . someday . . . some-day . . ."

"Someday you might come back for your land," he said softly. She nodded.

"Is there anyone who can help you? How did you get

this far? And why, in heaven's name, are you traveling alone?"

At the last question, her chin jutted defiantly. "I wasn't traveling alone. I had a servant with me, but I sent him back as soon as we reached Paris. I thought I could reach my mother's on my own, and I didn't wish to put him or his wife, whose identity papers I was using, at any further risk."

Rafe shook his head in disbelief. "Didn't you know about what's been going on in Paris? About the massacres?"

"We haven't had any had any word from the city in months. I thought perhaps the trouble was only in the countryside, as it was in '89, and that I'd be safe in the city." She took a deep breath. "My mother is so well-connected, I felt sure she'd know what to do." She stared at her fingers tangled tightly in the fringes of the shawl, and when she spoke her voice was bitter. "I misjudged."

After a moment she looked over at him, certain she would see her father's disapproval mirrored in his face, but Rafe had settled back in the armchair and in the dim light of the room his features were too shadowy to read.

"So now that you've found me out, what will you do?" Her fingers tensed in the tangled fringe. "Will you toss me back on the street, denounce me for the reward money?"

"Good Lord, woman, what kind of man do you take me for?" Rafe spoke sharply, his voice filled with anger at what she'd suffered and disgust that she might think he'd be party to it. "If I was the kind of man who would turn you over to those murderers on the so-called committee for public safety, don't you think I would have left you on the street with those animals today?"

"Forgive me," she said quietly. "I find it difficult to judge people these days."

Rafe rose and walked over to the bed.

Alix looked up, searching his eyes. "Will you help me?" Her voice was steady, her face pale, but proud. "I can pay for your services."

It struck Rafe that the only payment he wanted was to press her back against the mattress, to her cover her slender body with his own and to kiss her soft lips until the desperation and fear was gone from her eyes. He started to reach for her, his hand moving slowly toward her face, and suddenly he realized what he was doing. Good God, he thought with a shock, he was like one of his father's stallions racing for the hedges. What on earth was he thinking? He was a gentleman, a gentleman with an almost fiancée, and Alix was a woman in need of assistance, not seduction.

He caught her hand instead and brushed the back of it with his lips. "What else is there for a proper English gentleman to do?"

She studied him curiously. "You're English. I suppose I should have thought as much from your appearance and, of course, your accent."

Rafe raised an eyebrow in mock horror. "My accent? Mademoiselle de La Brou, you shock me. I have it on authority that my accent is impeccable."

"This authority," she said smiling, "would be a woman?"

He dipped his head. "A gentleman never kisses and tells."

Glancing at his wickedly curved mouth, the thought occurred to Alix that he must have kissed a number of ladies. She found herself suddenly annoyed. He might have swept her off the street, but he was not going to sweep her off her feet. "And is it the ladies that bring you to Paris?" she asked.

Rafe considered how to respond. Womanizing had always been his explanation for his travels back and forth to France, but he didn't want to leave Alix with the impression that he was a libertine. If he was going to help her, he reasoned, she needed to trust that she would be safe with him. On the other hand, he didn't like anyone knowing too much about what he did in France. Rumors had a nasty way of floating back across the English Channel. He shrugged noncommittally. "I have some unfinished business in France. I am simply here to tie up some loose ends."

So it was a woman, she concluded. Well, what difference did it make if he was a womanizer or married she thought, as she freed her fingers from the elegant shawl. This man Harcrest was offering his help. And she badly needed it. Fate had thrown them together in unusually close quarters, but there was no need to become familiar. Once she'd found her mother, she would probably never see him again.

"Do you speak English?" he asked.

Alix paused. She did, actually, and quite well.

"Oh no, I'm afraid I have no ear for languages."

At dinner parties with foreigners, she'd found they had a tendency to say the most amazing things in front of her when they thought she couldn't understand. Fluttering her lashes and putting on her worst accent, she added for emphasis, "The quill of my aunt is on the table of my uncle."

Rafe gave a mock shudder. "I think things will progress far better if we continue in French."

Alix's gray eyes twinkled, and she lowered her lashes to hide her amusement. "As you wish."

Good Lord, Rafe thought, had she batted her eyelashes at him? His eyes traveled over her face, the wide gray eyes, the high cheekbones, the slim nose and full soft mouth caught in a slight smile. Unable to stop himself, he traced the curve of her neck, the graceful arch of her collarbone down to where her pale skin disappeared in the shadowy V of his nightshirt. He felt his groin tighten as his mind continued where his eyes could not follow.

Breaking his gaze and shifting in his chair, he inquired. "About finding your mother . . . where should we start?"

Alix explained that her mother had been staying at the house where he had found her. "I've given it a lot of consideration," she concluded, "and I think we ought to break in."

"I beg your pardon," he said, trying to keep his voice level. "Did you say break in?"

"Well," she said, "it's not as if I have a key. And it's not as if we can go door to door inquiring about the whereabouts of former members of the court. So the way I see it, if I can just look around a bit, perhaps I'll find some clues as to where she's gone."

Rafe found himself fervently praying that Jervis would be able to ferret out some information that would enable him to avoid becoming involved in a burglary.

"I've sent Jervis to have a look around," he said. "When he returns, we'll see what he's found out and proceed from there." Silence fell between them, and Rafe cast about in his mind for a way to change the subject from the prospect of committing a crime in a city that currently was far too sensitive to suspicious behavior. Something too that would keep his mind off what lay covered by his nightshirt.

"Chess," he said hoping his voice didn't reveal the disquiet he felt. "Do you play chess?"

The rasping breath of the woman on the floor was disturbing his concentration. Lamartine stepped over her writhing figure, pushed aside a tumbled chair and went outside. He glanced back briefly, not at Solange Chaumier, but at the neat farmhouse. The Chaumier's single-story stone home was not much different from the one he'd grown up in. Except for the yard. Lamartine's eyes surveyed the well-kept vegetable garden and the plump chickens and geese roaming about the house. His father had been too busy drinking and beating his mother for their yard to ever have been so well tended.

He shook his head as he picked his way through the noisy clusters of foraging fowl. He had explained in his most pleasant manner that he needed to find Alix de La Brou, that it had been the comte's wish that he look after her. Solange had not believed him, had kept insisting that she knew nothing about where Alix had gone. The moment she'd opened her mouth, he'd known she was lying.

So he then suggested the local revolutionary tribunal might be interested in searching the Chaumier home, said he hoped the citizeness had all her papers in order. Solange had turned as white as her mobcap. It had been an idle threat; he'd never dreamed she'd have been so foolish as to lend her identity papers to Alix.

He reached the tree where his horse was tied. Solange had not wanted to tell him where Alix had gone, but he knew how to get answers. He flexed his small hands, re-membering the feel of her throat, her skin, the flexible cords, the way her eyes had bulged and her mouth had gaped. She'd resisted, held back details, but in the end, she'd told him what he needed to know.

Alix had gone to find her mother.

He sincerely hoped she hadn't been hauled off to prison or executed yet. That would be most inconvenient.

He unknotted the reins of his horse and drew them back over the gray's head. He supposed it might be possible to send someone else to retrieve her. But no, he thought, as he climbed into the saddle, if you wanted something done right, you had to see it through yourself. Lamartine brought his crop down with a sharp crack across the gelding's flank, and set off in the direction of Paris.

Chapter Six

Rafe tapped the black pawn lightly. "I believe, Mademoiselle de La Brou, your king is in check."

Alix was staring at the board, her brow furrowed, a look of intense concentration in her eyes. Suddenly she stiffened and looked towards the door. "Did you hear something in the sitting room? Is that Jervis?"

Rafe released the piece and turned his head toward the door, listening. It had been three days, and they hadn't heard a word from Jervis. "I don't hear anything."

When he glanced back at the board his bishop had been moved and his pawn was nowhere in sight. Alix's gray eyes were twinkling.

Rafe raised a brow at her. "Mademoiselle, this is no way to win at chess." He held out his hand. "My pawn please."

She laughed. "Ah, monsieur, I fear you have gravely underestimated your simple pawn." Then she forced her face into a serious expression. "He is, in fact, a noble in disguise, a loyal servant of the white king, and when you so foolishly looked away, he leapt upon his faithful steed Hermes and raced to warn the king of your evil plans."

Rafe looked down at the board; his knight was missing too. "Alix," he said warningly.

She sighed. "You English, no sense of romance."

He laughed. "You French, no sense of discipline."

Alix leaned over the table to replace the missing pieces, but as she did so her shawl trailed across the board and swept the remaining pieces to the floor.

Rafe shook his head. "You do hate to lose don't you?"

He smiled at her, a now familiar smile, a smile that made her heart race and her skin grow warm, made her want to reach out and trace the sensuous curve of his mouth. Alix's hand stole unconsciously to her own lips as she thought of the way he'd kissed her so unexpectedly that day in front of her mother's house. She'd been kissed before, cold wet kisses stolen by the Marquis de Beincourt, breathy damp kisses from a few bold suitors at court, but never had she felt more than a faint curiosity to kiss anyone back.

Now every time Rafe smiled at her she wondered what it would be like.

She turned to look out the window, trying to hide the flush she could feel spreading across her face. In the street below, vendors hawked their wares and horsemen jockeyed for position with carriages while the people on the sidewalks tried to avoid being splattered with mud. In short, life in Paris was continuing as usual while she was locked in a room with Rafe Harcrest waiting for Jervis to return. She should be out looking for her mother, she told herself, not playing chess and flirting with Rafe, and certainly not mooning over his smile.

She heard the rattle of chess pieces and glanced back to see Rafe picking scattered pieces up off the floor. "Here, I should really be doing that," she said, bending to help.

"I'm wretched company, I know. It's just that I wish I could be doing something, anything beside waiting and worrying."

"And playing chess?" he suggested.

"And playing chess," she agreed. "Though I did beat you four out of six times."

"Seven," he said with his crooked smile. "If not for that little accident."

"We shall never know shall we?"

"I could set up another game," he offered, his hazel eyes gleaming.

Alix waved her hands in surrender. "Cry peace, no more chess."

She retrieved a bishop that had rolled under one of the chairs and reached out to hand it to Rafe, her fingers brushing against his. Rafe fought the urge to pull her up and against him, to press her teasing lips to his. He felt the ivory curves of the chess piece in his hand and thought of how he'd like to stroke the curves of her body. He abruptly dropped the piece into the box where it settled noisily amongst its companions. Three days in this room with Alix and even the game pieces were making him think of bedding her. Where in hell was Jervis?

He stood up quickly. "I'm sure Jervis will return soon."

Alix turned back toward the window, her fingers restlessly tracing shapes on the glass. Rafe poured himself a glass of wine and admired the play of the late afternoon sun on her hair. She reminded him of an exotic bird he'd seen in a marketplace once, thrumming its wings against the wires of its cage. She was so small and colorful, so full of energy. So different from Lady Anne Dinsmore, he thought, the taste of the wine turning acid on his tongue.

The pale blond image of Lady Anne took shape in his head. He'd grown up with Anne. Their parents had country estates in the same county. Over the years they had met at supper parties and country dances and, as they'd grown older, at the more elegant social gatherings in London. She should have been snapped up in the first season, he mused, but she hadn't, in her first, her second, or even her third. Despite the distinguished title, the family was impoverished and the estates heavily in debt. And there was an edge to Anne, a sharpness to her tongue that made men uncomfortable. It was her ability to wield her tongue like a fish knife, deftly removing the backbones of social climbers and foppish posers, he reflected, that had made her the darling of the matrons who ruled the *haut* ton.

Rafe found making the rounds of the social season tedious, but useful for keeping abreast of the trends in fashion and, when it amused him, dropping remarks that spurred the purchase of his silks. His presence at the season's gatherings, however, made him a target for every giggling and fluttering young girl and her matchmaking mama. He'd found refuge in Anne's acerbic wit. As their friendship had grown, she'd chided him about using her as shield against the husband-hunters.

"You aren't getting any younger, Moreham," she said, tapping him with her lace fan. "One of these days you are going to have to choose one of these girls and set up your nursery. Elizabeth is nearing marriageable age; she'll need more guidance than Louisa will offer when she comes out. And once she's married, what will you do? Rattle around your estates and play gentleman farmer?"

Rafe realized Anne was right. He hadn't looked beyond seeing Elizabeth securely married off. He thought of the great house silent, bereft of his sister's laughter and mischief. Louisa was quiet company. She rose and retired early so that she could spend her time puttering about her gardens. Perhaps it was time to consider finding a suitable companion and filling his home with children.

Gradually, he began to notice the spaces in his life, the

time not filled with business or spent drinking and playing cards in his club. He began to think of what it would be like to have someone to ride with in the mornings, to dine with, to share his bed. Still, surveying the ruffled confections that littered the ton, he found no one with whom he could imagine sharing his life.

One evening at Devonshire House, as he watched Lady Anne weave gracefully through the crowd, it struck him that they would do well together. They shared a similar background, and he found her company comfortable. With him, she sheathed her famous tongue, never argued, keeping silent if she disagreed with him, but more often complimenting his opinions in her softly modulated voice. Smiling wryly, he considered how Anne's impeccable connections among the doyennes of the ton would put an ironclad seal of approval on Elizabeth's introduction to society.

Riding in the park the next morning with his closest friend, Cole Davenport, he'd broached the subject. They'd grown up together, fought in the Americas together, and spent most of their holidays together. Though they were as different as night and day, Rafe valued Cole's opinion.

Reining in his snorting bay, Cole had turned to stare at him. "Are you completely addled? Marry that stuffed goose? Whatever for? I mean surely you haven't developed a *tendresse* for her?"

Rafe shook his head. He had to admit he wasn't physically attracted to Lady Anne. "Let's be serious, Cole, most men of our class don't marry for love; they marry to beget heirs. I'm not getting any younger."

Cole's dark eyes narrowed. "Good Lord man, you're even beginning to sound like her."

"Well," he replied dryly, "not all of us can be so fortunate as to have our future wives hunt us down with muskets and hold us captive."

Cole laughed at this reference to his first encounter with

his wife Phoebe, but quickly grew serious. "Rafe, don't settle for Anne. She may suit, but that's not enough for you. When you find love, it fills every corner of your life, it gives everything meaning, a purpose."

He shook his head. "I sound like one of those blasted romantic poems Elizabeth reads. What I'm trying to say is, wait a bit longer. Find a woman who takes your breath away, who you can't live without, not simply one who suits."

He looked hard at Rafe. "You don't want to wind up one of those men who spends his life avoiding his cold fish of a wife, wasting his time at his club or in the arms of his mistress, pretending the passion that he's paid for is real."

Spurring his horse into a canter, Rafe signaled an end to the discussion. Privately, he'd dismissed Cole's words. Davenport was passionate, impulsive; he always acted before he thought and damn the consequences. Rafe, by contrast, believed a man was better served by taking a cautious, well-planned course through life. He wasn't the sort who'd be swept up by passion. Hell, he wasn't even sure such a thing existed. Slowly, he'd begun to court Lady Anne, spending more and more time with her, monopolizing her dance card. Nothing had been said between them, but all was understood.

Three weeks ago, when he'd known his stepmother's handiwork would be at its finest, the gardens lush and beautiful, he'd invited Anne to his country estate. News of her visit had spread through the summer-dulled ton like wildfire and betting in the clubs was not on whether he would propose, but on the precise day. And he had intended to propose.

On the last Thursday of Anne's stay, shortly after lunch, he'd sought her out, a fine sapphire that had once belonged to his grandmother in his pocket. The air was heavy with the fragrance of sun-sated roses. As he strode along the winding path through the garden, he'd caught the sound of Anne's voice on the other side of the hedge and his steps inexplicably slowed. It was, he told himself, not because he had any doubts about asking her to marry him, but because she sounded to be in deep conversation with her brother James.

"Do stop your incessant whining about your debts, James. You've become positively tedious."

"I wouldn't have to be so *tedious*, if you'd just get on with it and bring Moneybags Moreham up to scratch. Can't you trap him in the library and tear your bodice or something? At this rate, the creditors will have clapped me in irons before the fellow makes his offer."

"Don't be so vulgar, James. I have neither the desire nor the intention to invite Moreham to paw at my bosom."

"Well, that should make it rather difficult to beget the earl's heir."

"When the time comes I shall do my duty, just as I will do my duty to the family by marrying Moreham."

A flat metallic taste filled Rafe's mouth, and he swallowed hard. What had he expected, to hear Lady Anne declaring her love for him? He wasn't in love with her. Why should he be surprised that she viewed marriage with him as anything more than a convenient arrangement?

"So if you're not offering up your maidenly charms, sister dear, how do you intend to bring him round?"

"He's nearly there," Rafe heard Anne respond coolly. "But should he continue to drag his feet, I'll simply suggest what a dreadful season his little sister is likely to encounter without my experience to guide her. Then I'll make certain that things become very bumpy for Lady Elizabeth Harcrest."

"Why Anne, you wicked puss, I believe your claws are showing." James's laughter was lost in the crunch of gravel as he led his sister farther down the path.

Rafe told himself he was no young buck, crushed to discover his ladylove had played him false. He was a mature man who had chanced to see his partner's cards. And yet he wondered, why did he feel as cold and empty as if he'd found her cheating? Lady Anne was the most suitable bride he was likely to find, the right choice for the house of Moreham, and the right choice to help Elizabeth pilot the dangerous currents of London society.

But the sapphire ring had remained in his pocket that afternoon and was in his desk drawer when he'd left for France the next day, apologizing profusely for having been so suddenly called away.

"Well, it appears that my refusal to play chess has struck you quite dumb." Alix's voice interrupted his unpleasant recollections. "So what'll it be, twenty-one, philosophical debates, pantomimes? If we had music we could dance." She cocked her head at him, her long hair sliding over her shoulder. "Though I suppose in your life you might not have had much opportunity to grace the dance floor."

Rafe had told Alix that he was a cloth merchant, involved in importing French silks into England. "I'm afraid my dance skills are limited, mademoiselle," he said offering up a silent apology to his dance master.

"Well then, monsieur, what do you propose we do to pass the time?"

He stared at her slim form, still garbed in his nightshirt and a suggestion that had nothing to do with dancing swept through his mind. But he was saved from having to answer by Jervis's entrance into the room, preceded by a ragged ginger cat that streaked through his legs and leapt onto the chair beside him.

Jervis glared at it. "Damn cat, nearly broke my neck. Worthless fleabag," he added as the cat flexed its claws and regarded him complacently.

Rafe stroked the cat beneath its chin. Cutting short Jervis's threats to the animal, he inquired, "What have you discovered?"

"I was going to tell you before that creature tried to kill me. See if I don't take him to the cook yet." He eyed the contented feline balefully. "Well, I went round to the house and watched it for a while, no one coming in, no one going out, windows completely dark. So then I took myself off to the café down the street and had a cup of coffee and bit of a chat with the locals. Word is that no one's been living there for a couple of months." He glanced meaningfully at Alix. "Since before the killings last week."

Alix, who hadn't even realized she was holding her breath, exhaled sharply. "Did anyone say where the inhabitants of the house had gone?"

Jervis shrugged. "There was plenty of speculation that the lady had left the country, but no one seemed to know whether she'd emigrated to England or Austria. One man swore he'd seen her selling ribbons on the street."

Alix fixed her gaze on Rafe. "So we have to break in."

Jervis swung around to face his master. "Here, this sounds interesting."

Rafe frowned at them both and said sharply, "If we need to enter the house illicitly, *we* will be Jervis and I. You, Mademoiselle de La Brou, are going nowhere."

Alix crossed her arms tightly across her chest. "That's ridiculous. Neither of you knows a thing about my mother. How will you even know where to begin searching?"

Rafe nodded agreeably. "It's true I have not had much experience breaking into people's homes, but no doubt Jervis and I can manage adequately without your help." "Besides," he added with a twinkle in his hazel eyes, "I believe you'll have some difficulty conducting a burglary in my nightclothes."

"And whose fault is it that I'm in your nightclothes?"

"You know, that's an interesting question, and one I suspect we could debate for some time. *After* Jervis and I conduct our inspection of your mother's home, I will contact some friends in the city about acquiring some new garments for you." Disregarding her efforts to protest, he said, "I think you'll find I'm quite a good judge of style." He eyed her slender figure appreciatively adding, "And fit."

"In the interim, I will let it be known below stairs that I don't wish to be disturbed. If anyone comes in, well, I suppose we could hide you in that." He gestured towards a fair-sized trunk in the corner of the room. Alix looked at the trunk and then back at Rafe, disbelief clearly sketched in her raised brows.

Rafe pointedly ignored her expression, picking up one of the papers from the pile on the table. "Is this the only residency paper you have for Paris?" Alix nodded. He turned to Jervis. "Do you think any of our friends can improve the contents of this document for us?"

"For a price, Dubois can draw up papers proving she's Marie Antoinette's long lost sister."

Rafe smiled. "That's not exactly what I had in mind. I think we're looking for something with a bit more of the common touch." He reached into his waistcoat pocket and pulled out a sack of coins. "This should be ample for Monsieur Dubois." He tossed it to Jervis who promptly pocketed it.

"Now about this evening's activities."

"Yes, about them," Alix interrupted, feeling very much as if she'd already been shut into the trunk.

Rafe politely dismissed her efforts to be included. He rose and began to pace in front of the fire, the cat following him. "Tell me everything you noticed about the layout of the house."

"From the street there's two rectangular buildings joined in the middle by this long wall with an arched *porte cochère* in the center large enough to admit carriages. It's usually closed, but there's a door cut into it that's unlocked. Just behind the wall there's a garden and some service buildings that Madame de La Brou shared with the neighbors. See, turns out she only rented one wing, the one with the dancing nymphs over the door. Anyway, it's three stories, if you count the upper floor with the dormers, which, for this job I don't. The ground floor has a gallery that opens onto the garden, and a couple of salons that overlook the street. The bedrooms are upstairs. The way I see it, our best bet is to go in through one of the street side windows." Jervis rubbed his nose. "I'm pretty certain I noticed that one of windows was open."

Alix dropped into an armchair and fumed. She'd led a sheltered life, it was true, and she'd always followed the dictates of her father. But something inside her had changed over the last several weeks. Just like the rest of the country, she thought wryly, she'd had a taste of freedom. If Rafe Harcrest thought that she was going to stay quietly in the room while he made decisions that affected her life, he was sadly mistaken. Jump into a trunk if anyone came in, what a ridiculous notion. As they continued to discuss their plans as if she weren't there, Alix studied Rafe's manservant. Jervis was broader, but not much taller than she was. Like Rafe, he wore English-style boots, but his britches were baggy and his waistcoat was unfashionably loose and long.

She eased her shoulders against the chair to relieve the tension that had built up in them and the cat, intrigued by the motion, leapt up to investigate. She scratched him behind the ears and he settled in against her purring loudly. As she stroked his bony spine, her eyes focused on Rafe. The firelight shone through his full cambric sleeves clearly outlining the muscular curves of his arms. His cream-colored waistcoat fit smoothly across his broad chest and slim waist. She couldn't help noticing how it lay flat against his taut belly and her eyes wandered lower.

He caught her looking at him and came over to stand by her chair. Running the side of his finger along the curve of her cheek, he smiled reassuringly. "We'll get you out of this mess."

Get her out of this mess, indeed, she thought, as if the revolution was something she'd inadvertently put her foot into, as if traveling alone through France was some whimsical choice she'd made. But her annoyance was tempered by the gentleness of his touch.

It was confusing how he seemed to arouse so many conflicting emotions in her.

Rafe turned back to Jervis. "See what you can do about fetching up a light supper. We'll dine and then leave before dusk. I want to make sure there's enough light in Madame de La Brou's apartment to look around without having to light any candles. And when we leave the place we'll have the cover of darkness to hide our movements."

Rafe turned toward Alix. "Would you care to join us, or shall we set up in the sitting room where we won't disturb you?"

Alix gestured toward the table. "I'd be grateful for your company." She wasn't hungry, but she wanted to be sure she knew exactly when they left.

Jervis returned shortly with some soup, a bowl of haricots, and a cold chicken. As Rafe pulled a chair out for her to sit, it crossed her mind that she should have been uncomfortable eating alone with him, but they'd spent so much time together, he'd begun to feel like an old friend. A sometimes moody and often imperious friend, but a warm and caring one as well. As he took his seat across from her, Alix stared at him pensively. He was risking his life for her, a woman he hardly knew at all. It was a sense of honor her father had talked about at length, but she had never seen among the nobles at Versailles.

It was hardly something she would have expected from a simple English cloth merchant.

Pouring them some wine, Rafe raised his glass. "To your safe return to your mother."

They drank, lost for a moment in their separate thoughts. Her mother, she should be thinking about her mother, Alix berated herself. A warm fire, good food, and a handsome face, and she'd nearly forgotten why she'd come to Paris. She could almost hear her father laughing; saying how typical of a woman to become distracted and forget what she was about. A sharp knot of pain drew up in her stomach and twisted around her heart. Her hand unconsciously stole to her waist where she'd carried the titles sewn into her stays. She hadn't been able to save her father, but she wouldn't fail to save the de La Brou name. She'd find Madeleine and somehow they'd figure out a way to restore Valcour.

Rafe, seeing the shadows cloud her eyes, felt a fool for reminding her of the danger surrounding her. "You remind me of my sister," he said. And she did, he thought, young and full of spirit. Though, he mused wryly, he'd never had such a fierce desire to kiss his sister.

"Tell me about her," Alix asked.

Rafe detailed Elizabeth's unruly encounters with her governesses, as if with his talk of everyday events he might weave a protective spell around them, holding back, if just for an hour, the violence and chaos in the city outside.

Gasping with laughter, Alix exclaimed, "She kissed her dancing instructor?"

"Ah yes," Rafe said, wagging a chicken bone. "But her excuse was that it was a scientific experiment. He was simply a control subject so that she would know when the right man came along."

"Well," said Alix, daubing her mouth with a napkin, "at least she's applying some discipline to the matter."

Rafe chuckled. "I hadn't thought of it in that light."

"But I've talked too much about myself, tell me about your family," he said, leaning forward and fixing her with a sympathetic gaze.

Alix told him about her parents, how she lived mostly with her father, describing in wicked detail the stuffy old couples who frequently dined at his table. But as they both laughed, she couldn't help wondering what would become of her father's elderly friends and their families. Her face sobering, she told him about her father's insistence on remaining in France and his final hours.

Rafe said nothing, only reached out and covered her hand with his. They sat like that for several moments, the only sound in the room the crackle of the logs burning in the fireplace.

It was Jervis's return that startled them apart. Bustling about, he quickly cleared the room so that there would be no reason for any of the maids to come calling. Alix bit her lip to keep from laughing as Rafe emptied his trunk to make certain there was ample room to conceal her. As he tucked her up in bed, she wondered if they would ever leave. After what seemed hours, the two men departed, exhortations for her to remain hidden still on their lips as the door closed behind them.

Alix immediately threw off her shawl and raced into the sitting room, making for the trunk where Jervis kept his clothes. Rifling through the contents, she pulled out a pair of britches, a cambric shirt, and a waistcoat. A stale odor rose from them and Alix sniffed, thinking he'd had a lot of nerve telling her she smelled.

She pulled them on, augmenting the outfit with her own cotton stockings and shoes, and surveyed her appearance in a mirror over the mantelpiece in the sitting room. Not bad, but she'd have to do, something about her hair. Too bad neither gentleman wore a wig, though, she mused, she rather liked Rafe's tawny mane.

Casting her eyes about the room, she saw a large tricorne lying under the bed. Tying her hair in a semblance of a queue, she tucked the length under her collar and topped it with the hat. Lumpy, but it would have to do, she thought, giving herself a final check in the glass. Listening to make certain no one was in the hall before she slipped out, her eye fell on the closed chess set. Alix smiled.

It was time to move on to a new game.

Robert Lamartine was having a bad week. Thinking back over the events of his journey to Paris made him positively livid. It seemed as though every half-witted yokel calling himself a patriot had stopped him, demanding to see his papers and questioning his reasons for traveling. He had wasted precious time while erstwhile farmers, who ought to be tending to their crops, argued about whether he might be an Austrian spy or an aristocrat in disguise. He shook his head. Those oafs probably would have held up their own grandmothers.

Everything was fine now, he told himself. He was in Paris, in Madame de La Brou's apartment, and now all he had to do was wait for Alix to show up. Leaning back in a silk armchair, he drew a meat pastry wrapped in a linen napkin from his pocket and unfolded it carefully on his knee. He took a small bite and began chewing slowly, soothing himself by reviewing the events of the day that had gone well.

It had been simple to find the place since he'd arranged for the rental after Madame had moved from Versailles. He had used his knowledge of the property and its owner to gain entrance. He'd told the neighbors that he was employed by a second-hand furniture company and had permission from the landlord to evaluate the contents of the house across the courtyard. Spreading his hands and giving them his most piteous look, he'd explained that he hadn't been able to locate the landlord and his employer would be sorely distressed if he returned without completing his estimate.

The neighbors, a family of newly wealthy industrialists, had taken one look at his finely tailored suit and neatly powdered wig and led him straight over. They'd even insisted on giving him a tour of the rooms. Rattling on about Madame de La Brou and her dinner parties, they'd followed him from the vestibule into the antechamber, the small salon, then into the grand salon and on upstairs into Madame's boudoir. From their covetous glances at the furnishings, he suspected they were more curious about Madeleine's interior decorations than in keeping watch on him.

Well, he thought, for what she spent on a monthly basis, the comtesse should have style. The anteroom, where the footmen waited, was a relatively simple room, but the rest were decorated in the latest styles and colors. The small salon was paneled in light wood with raised garlands of roses over the doors and windows. Green silk curtains draped the two long windows that overlooked the garden, and the gracefully rounded armchairs were upholstered in matching fabric. The large salon was decorated in sky blue, the walls hung with rows of expensive art, mirrors were set in the corners and over the white marble fireplace, and the floor was covered with an Aubusson carpet. Madame's bedchamber was all in yellow.

Though appreciative of their naiveté in admitting him to the house, the neighbors' incessant gossiping wore on his nerves. And so he had pulled out a sheaf of papers and begun cataloging in excruciating detail every chair, sofa, and table, until at last, barely disguising their yawns, the neighbors were beaten into retreat. After they'd left, he'd wandered back through the rooms eyeing the fine porcelain and silver pieces lining the mantles and table tops. His fingers itched to take a few of the smaller pieces, but he reminded himself that if he remained patient these things would come to him.

He debated where to await Alix's arrival. The footmen's antechamber was the nearest room to the front door and had views of both the garden and street, but he disliked the idea of sitting in the servant's quarters. The wild thought crossed his mind of positioning himself in Madame's boudoir, waiting in the shadows with his feet stretched out on the comtesse's damask-covered chaise longue. But in the end, he decided the small salon was just right.

He'd pulled the curtains overlooking the street and the room was cast in shadow. It really was quite comfortable. Finishing his pastry, he refolded the napkin and whisked the crumbs off his dark wool britches. Settling his feet on a delicately embroidered footstool he yawned. He hoped she didn't take long.

Chapter Seven

◆

Rafe found a foothold in the stone work and swung himself over the sill and into Madame de La Brou's grand salon. As he swept a bit of crumbled mortar off his sleeve, he wondered what the gentleman at White's would make of the Earl of Moreham breaking into fashionable homes in Paris. Cole would certainly be amused.

A moment later, Jervis heaved himself headfirst through the window. Catching himself with his hands, he scrambled upright. His satisfied grin was reflected in the corner mirrors of the room.

"Told you I'd noticed one of the windows was unlocked," he said. He ran his hand over the polished finish of a mahogany side table, pulling out the single drawer in its curved front. "That's nice work." He picked up a silver candy dish and hefted it in his hand. Noticing an ormolu clock on the mantle, he put the dish down and walked over to the fireplace. "Now," he said, glancing back at Rafe and rubbing his hands together, "where do we start?"

Rafe looked around the salon, tastefully decorated in pale blue, and pondered Jervis's question. Where should they start and what on earth were they looking for? A floorboard creaked, and he heard a door swing open.

"I think you should start by explaining what you're doing in this house," said a voice from across the room. The slight figure standing in the open door frame walked calmly towards them.

Rafe noted with interest that the man hadn't lit any candles to dispel the growing afternoon shadows. He had a strong suspicion that the man had no more business in the comtesse's apartments than he and Jervis did. And then a stronger suspicion crossed his mind. Perhaps they were all here on the same business. He waited until the man was standing a few feet away and said, "I think it's important to exchange introductions before launching into conversation. Don't you, monsieur?"

"Names are unimportant, *monsieur*, between passing acquaintances. And in these troubled times, they can even be dangerous." The slight man did not take his eyes off of Rafe. "So I repeat my earlier question, what are you doing in this house?"

Rafe held the man's stare. "I am here on an errand for a friend."

"How curious," Lamartine replied. "Perhaps it is the same errand that draws us both here." He paused, appraising Rafe's features carefully. "Despite the look of your companion, you seem rather well-dressed for thievery . . ." He swept a hand over his own simple but well-cut suit. "As you will notice am I. A young friend has gone astray, a young woman who was, shall we say, attached to this house. I am looking for her."

Rafe considered the smooth-talking little man. There was something oily about him, as though the truth would slide right off his skin. "A young woman, you say. Are you her lover?"

Lamartine stiffened, as if offended. "I am an *emissary* from her *father*. He is gravely ill and desperate to have her at his bedside."

"Why would a young girl leave her sick father and come here?" Rafe asked, stepping closer.

"Ah," said Lamartine, his hand fluttering dismissively. "You know how young girls are, they have a tiff with their parents and go galloping off into the night. Then when they run into trouble, the silly things make up wild stories to escape proper punishment."

"Wild stories? What kind of wild stories?"

"Ah, monsieur, who can say what might arise in the imagination of a young girl? A simple maid working for a wealthy employer might perhaps take some things that did not belong to her and claim them as her own."

"So we have gone from a tiff to a theft. But you have not explained why, monsieur, the girl would have come here."

Lamartine ground his teeth. He had already admitted he was an emissary from the girl's father, but if he said the comte sent him, the tall stranger might denounce him as a royalist sympathizer. "Perhaps to bring her ill-gotten gains to a lover amongst the staff?" he suggested as quickly as he could manage.

Rafe weighed the possibility that Alix was a runaway maid, then dismissed it. Alix was far too imperious, far too comfortable being served to be a maid. Moreover, he thought wryly, how many French maids played chess? And why send him on this wild goose chase to find Madame de La Brou? Odd, too, that an emissary from a dying father would seem so calm, would not immediately demand to know if Alix was unharmed. No, whatever Alix's story, it held together better than this little man's.

"Now," Lamartine continued, clutching his hands behind his back to conceal his mounting frustration, "if the girl has perhaps come under your care, has somehow taken you in, you could turn her over to me and I could return her safely to her father." He smiled a tight smile. "And no one need ever know about her unfortunate indiscretions. Eh, monsieur?"

Thinking about the papers and jewels sewn into Alix's stays, odds were the little man was far less interested in her well-being than in something she carried with her. A cold finger of suspicion ran up Rafe's spine.

Perhaps the man was seeking out Alix to denounce her.

Rafe closed his fingers around the stem of a heavy silver candlestick. Jervis, who'd been watching the conversation carefully, detected the movement and edged over to stand beside him.

"You have proof of your connection with the girl?"

Lamartine grimaced. He didn't have any documents. Who was this man? Why was he getting in the way? His mind began racing like a rat in a maze. He was so close to getting Alix! He could certainly forge a note from the comte beseeching her to come home. That would work.

He opened his mouth to speak, but was interrupted by a loud scrabbling noise from outside the open window at the other end of the salon. As he turned toward the disturbance, Rafe swung the candlestick. Lamartine's bagwig padded the blow, but the force was sufficient to knock him unconscious. As he slid to the floor, Rafe knelt to check that he was still breathing. Glancing up at Jervis he hissed, "Put him in the room next door and tie him up with whatever you can find."

Jervis hurriedly dragged Lamartine's limp form through the doorway while Rafe raced back across the room and slipped behind the blue silk curtains. As the rich fabric settled around him, he cursed silently; Madame de La Brou's salon was fast becoming more popular than the Tuileries.

Alix pulled herself into a sitting position on the sill and jumped down into the room. Silently congratulating herself on having found the open window, she inspected her surroundings, finding no sign of Rafe or Jervis. She suspected they were searching upstairs. There'd be hell to pay when she caught up with them, but why should men always have the last word just because they wanted it? For that matter, why couldn't a man ever admit a woman might have something useful to offer?

In the case of her mother, Alix speculated it would require another woman's eye to detect any clues left behind. Madeleine de Rabec had grown up with a great name, but no fortune. She had told Alix about her childhood: how things around her were always disappearing, paintings, furniture, jewelry, and trinkets. Since her grandmother forbade mention of the missing items, Madeleine had never known whether they had been sold to pay her father's gambling debts or stolen by the servants. She'd learned to paste things of value behind the furniture with candle wax and pomade and, she confessed to Alix, even after she'd married the wealthy Comte de La Brou, she'd continued the habit.

Alix cast an eye over the grand salon, thinking that her mother's boudoir would be the best place to start. But as she stepped forward, she was grabbed roughly from behind. A muscular arm held her tight, while strong fingers clamped around her mouth. Thrashing wildly she managed to kick her foot backwards, connecting solidly with a booted shin.

"Alix, you little hoyden, what the hell are you *doing* here?" From the moment he'd grabbed the intruder, Rafe knew exactly whom he had caught. He'd recognized the fragrance of his own expensive Bond Street soap, and the armful of uncorseted breasts only confirmed his knowledge. He spun her around to face him and his eyes narrowed as he caught sight of her costume. "Are those *Jervis's* clothes?"

Jervis, just reentering the grand salon, gasped in indignation. "Here now, that's my best waistcoat!"

Rafe interrupted. "If I might repeat my earlier question Mademoiselle de Rabec de La Brou, *What the hell are you doing here?*"

Alix raised her chin and looked him straight in the eye. "I told you earlier I wanted to help."

"And *I* told you to stay at the inn."

"You are not my guardian, monsieur. You may not tell me when or where I have leave to go."

"Obviously."

"So are you going to stand here arguing with me until it's too dark to search?"

Rafe stared at her sharply. A maid would never take that tone. He released her. She was right about the light. "Well, mademoiselle, where do you suggest we start?" He would definitely have more to say about her outrageous behavior when this misadventure was over.

Alix bit back a real smile, knowing she'd won, and quickly explained about her mother's habit of hiding important items. "Have you checked her bedchamber yet? I think it would be the best place to start."

Rafe gave a negative shake of his head and started to ask why she hadn't told them this back at the inn. Then Alix started across the salon towards where the unconscious man was stowed.

Jervis quickly stepped in front of her. Pointing back across the room he said, "Through those doors to the gallery, then upstairs to your right. You and the captain can start there, and I'll check the rooms down here."

She nodded. "Be sure and run your hands behind all the furniture." She glanced toward Rafe. "*Well*, are you *coming?*"

"Hoyden," he muttered under his breath and followed.

As they left the grand salon Rafe wondered whether to mention the unconscious man. No, he thought, watching her sashay up the stairs in Jervis's britches, he'd see how the rest of this little adventure played out before he raised it with her. If she had lied, he'd catch her out. And if not, then why alarm her with the news that she was being pursued?

Alix moved quickly down the gallery, peering into one room after another, trying to decide which bedchamber might have been her mother's. When she opened the door to a pale yellow sitting room her heart leapt. Madeleine loved yellow. Crossing the thick carpet woven in pale yellow and blue, she caught the lingering fragrance of lilac, her mother's scent. And then it was as if signs of her mother were everywhere, not just in the bottles of perfume and jars of powder and cream scattered over the dressing tables, but in the books by the nightstand, a trace of ribbon on the floor. Alix picked up an ivory-handled hairbrush, threaded with long dark strands and called softly, "Monsieur Harcrest, I've found her room."

When Rafe entered the bedchamber, Alix turned her speculative gray eyes on him and said, "Run your hands down the backs of the furniture and see if you feel anything pasted there. I'll check underneath." Then she slid down next to the bed, an elegant confection crowned with hangings patterned in birds and flowers, and began running her hands along its base.

She has lovely legs, he thought distractedly as his eyes followed the undulating curve of calf to thigh protruding from under the bed. Then he shook himself mentally. Oh no, the little hoyden is attractive, but she is definitely *not* what you need in your life. Lady Anne, he reminded himself, was waiting for him in England. He turned and began vigorously searching the drawers of a delicate pear wood writing desk.

Alix poked her head out from under the bed. "Don't bother, Mother would never be that obvious."

Rafe had the distinct feeling that there was nothing obvious about de Rabec de La Brou women. It also occurred to him that while he'd been in many ladies' bedchambers, he'd never searched one before. He rifled through papers, noting scraps of poetry, a series of letters to a friend debating the nature of man, some bits of lace, but nothing that would tell him where Madeleine de La Brou might have gone. He pushed the drawer closed, feeling more like an intruder than he had when he'd climbed through the window. He was beginning to think it was all a ridiculous exercise, when he heard Alix's triumphant cry.

"There's something behind this painting! I just knew she'd leave something behind."

Rafe saw that she was waving a small piece of stationery, its corners stained with wax. He walked over to Alix and read over her shoulder.

Dearest Tartine,

I pray that you will find this letter. Our departure has had to be conducted in such haste and secrecy, that I fear there was no time to speak with you. It has become far too dangerous for me to remain in France and so I leave tonight for England. My dear friend Lady Melbourne has offered to take me under her wing when I arrive and has invited me to stay with her in London until I might find a more permanent residence. Although it has been several months since I have had news of the Comte or my daughter Alix, I foolishly hope that they will find me there.

Rafe barely took in the remainder of the letter detailing how Tartine, apparently a chambermaid of long standing, might obtain her wages. Rafe's head felt as if it had tumbled off and been tossed beneath a horse hooves, knocking all sense clear out of it. Alix's story was true. Her mother had gone to London. And if she had made it safely there, then the Comtesse de La Brou was now living under the patronage of one of the most influential ladies of the ton.

He could only imagine the scandal when he arrived in London with Alix in tow. If Lady Melbourne truly was a boon companion of the Comtesse de La Brou, and there was no reason to doubt she was, they'd have him married before anyone could say "publish the banns."

Alix's voice intruded. "You see, I *told* you there'd be something here that would help. And I *told* you I could be of use. Now all I have to do is figure out how to get to London."

How indeed, Rafe was thinking, when Jervis slipped into the room.

"Hope you found something useful, because we've got company."

"We did," said Alix beaming. Then her face grew serious as she registered what Jervis had said, "Is it the watch?"

"Not yet, but the neighbors are downstairs, squawking about all the activity over here." He cast a meaningful look at Rafe. "Seems they let a furniture appraiser in earlier in the day, and now they're having second thoughts about whether he might have been a thief. I think we'd better get out of here in case they find anything amiss."

"Where are they now?" Rafe asked.

"Downstairs gallery."

Rafe went to the window and looked down into the garden below. There was a flimsy looking drain spout and a tall tree within reach. "Ladies and gentleman," he said swinging open the window frame, "I believe it's time to climb. Jervis, you first, then Alix, and I'll follow."

Jervis wasted no time in swinging out over the sill and into the tree. Alix paused on the sill, studying the distance to the nearest branch and the two-story drop down. She looked dubiously back at Rafe. "Perhaps there are some trunks about?" she asked half-heartedly, glancing about the room for a place to hide. "I haven't climbed a tree since I was little."

"Nothing you can't handle, my little hoyden. Now out you go." He held her hand as she reached a foot toward the branch and clutched with her free hand toward the tree. Fragments of bark rained down and they heard Jervis swear. "See," he whispered as he released her, "nothing to it."

Voices were rising up the staircase. "Well, I don't see anything missing, but I wonder if we should send word to the landlord."

That was encouraging, Rafe thought. The neighbors apparently hadn't discovered the man downstairs yet. He swung himself out and into the tree. He could hear Alix just below him, scrabbling at branches and muttering. He watched her drop the last few feet into Jervis's waiting arms, and heard him grunt, "Hey, that's me best tricorne you're wearing!"

"I'll buy you a new one," she snapped.

"Children, this is no time to bicker," Rafe interjected as he dropped softly down beside them. As they crossed the geometrically landscaped garden toward the *porte cochère*, a woman's scream rent the air.

"We can't run, it'll look too suspicious," Rafe said, lengthening his stride and pulling Alix close. "Let's just get to the street as quickly as we can, then split up. Alix and I will go back to the inn. Jervis, you need to find Dubois and get those papers. Have him make up a set of Paris residency papers and a passport with the necessary seals for travel to England. And tell him the faster he can get them done, the more appreciative I'll be."

"What about clothes?" Alix said quickly.

"And stop by our friends and see if you can arrange for suitable traveling clothes for the lady."

"You got it captain."

As they stepped through the *porte cochère,* Rafe caught sight of a group of men carrying pikes and swinging lanterns, heading down the street. He dragged Alix into an alleyway between the houses. Jervis quickly crossed the street and disappeared in the opposite direction, whistling a tune that sounded suspiciously like "The World Turned Upside Down."

Chapter Eight

❧

Rafe grabbed Alix by the elbow and hauled her swiftly down the alley. Her foot connected with something repellently smooth and she slipped. "You don't have to drag me," she insisted, "I can follow on my own."

"You, follow?" Rafe snorted. "That would be a first."

"Well, I'm sorry that I'm not as obedient as your troops, *Captain*," she said in an irritated voice.

"No more so than I. In the army, disobedience is a flogging offense."

"Why do we have to walk so fast anyway? The watch didn't see us, and we didn't take anything . . ." Her voice trailed off and she gasped, "Or did you?"

Rafe stopped in mid-stride and swung round to face her, his hazel eyes hard. "I beg your pardon, mademoiselle. You are the one who insisted, no *demanded* that Jervis and I break into your mother's house. Are you now implying that we stooped to theft?" He loomed over her, his face a study in sharp angles.

"I'm sorry, I didn't mean to suggest you'd stolen anything," Alix said, taking a step back. "But," she added defensively, "you must admit it was a bit peculiar the way the neighbors came by all of the sudden. And why on earth did that woman scream?"

Rafe resumed walking and Alix had to run to keep up with him. His brows were drawn together and his eyes narrowed as he turned to look at her. "Jervis and I left a man trussed up in the small salon of your mother's apartments; a gentleman who said he'd been sent by your desperately ill father. The gentleman claimed you'd stolen something valuable and that you were bringing your ill-gotten gains to a lover who worked in Madame de La Brou's household."

"And you believed him?"

"If I had," Rafe responded dryly," I never would have hit him with the candlestick."

"Hit him with a . . ." Questions filled her head. "But why would someone make up a story like that . . . ?" And then a horrible thought: "You don't suppose my father could be *alive*?" Her blood turned to ice. "I never saw his body. . . . I heard the people yelling, the screams, and what sounded like blows. But Solange and David wouldn't let me look for him." Her voice dropped to a strangled whisper. "David told me . . . the mob . . . cut his head off." She grabbed Rafe's arm and looked beseechingly up at him. "What if they were wrong? What if he's badly hurt and he needs me?"

Rafe hadn't believed the man's stories and seeing the anguish in Alix's face, he refused to let her travel down that road either. "I think the man was lying, Alix. I think you have something he wants, or he is seeking some sort of revenge against your family." Seeing she remained tense, he added, "Unless, of course, the treasures in your lingerie were stolen and you do have a lover waiting for you somewhere in Paris?"

"Don't be ridiculous," she said, her eyes widening. "If I were planning to take the jewels and papers to some mystery lover, wouldn't I have run to meet him, instead of following after you?"

"Perhaps you expected to find him waiting at your mother's. Perhaps the man in the salon was your lover. Although, he did seem a bit old," Rafe added teasingly, trying to lighten her mood. "But then there's no accounting for tastes."

Her eyes narrowed and her jaw set, "I would appreciate it if you would stop impugning my virtue. I am, a, a . . ."

"Virgin?" he supplied helpfully.

"Yes." Her face flushed and she was grateful he couldn't see it in the shadows of the alleyway. Their conversation had become as twisted as the route they were taking back to the inn. Then another thought struck her. "The man in the salon, what did he look like?"

Rafe paused to remember. "Slight, middle-aged, dark suit, powdered wig."

"Did you notice anything else, anything distinctive?"

Rafe shook his head.

"Surely you must have noticed something, eye color, scars, blemishes, anything?" He shrugged.

"You've described half the men in Paris, including Citizen Robespierre." She shook her head disgustedly. "Men, no eye for details."

"Well," he drawled sarcastically, "if I'd known you were going to come scurrying after us, I'd have arranged a proper introduction before I hit him."

The two fell silent as they entered a well-lit street. The sidewalks were full of people out for an evening stroll. A group of young men heatedly debating politics parted to let them through. Two old men passed by complaining about the rising price of wine. A group of chattering young women, trailed by a scowling chaperone in an enormous lace cap, cast admiring glances at Rafe. Alix, feeling suddenly chilled and vulnerable, hunched her shoulders, pulled Jervis's hat down over her face, and kept walking.

At last, Rafe turned and led her down a small muddy street. He stopped before a grated door and pushed it open. Its rusted hinges squealed in protest.

"Hey, who's there?" a startled groom called out, curry comb in hand.

"Evening Bernard," Rafe responded.

"Oh, Citizen Harcrest. Jervis. Good evening." The horse the groom had been brushing nipped at his arm. "I'll get you to your feed bucket, just have a bit of patience boy," he said turning back to his work.

Alix followed Rafe across the rutted stable yard, up a set of worn wooden steps and into the inn's kitchen.

A sturdy woman, perspiration dotting her flushed face and dampening her blond hair, stood before the wide fireplace washing dishes in a steaming iron kettle. Two other women sat at a scarred wooden table, sleeves rolled up, fichus draped over the backs of their chairs, peeling potatoes. Blackened pots and pans hung from the low ceiling, along with bunches of dried herbs. The room was warm and smelled of broth and sautéed onions.

Rafe drew two bottles of wine from a rack beside the table and took two freshly washed glasses from the woman by the fire.

"Here now," one of the women began. But he cut her off. "Put it on my bill."

As they mounted the narrow back stairs, one of the women called after them, "If you're having a party citizens, let us know if you'll be needing any company," and the other two crowed with laughter.

A party, Rafe thought, that's what he was going to have, a bloody engagement party. The bottles clinking as he mounted the back stairs to his room, he wondered how many more he would need to get drunk. Not excessively drunk, just oblivious enough to ask this French termagant to marry him. It wasn't that he would mind bedding Alix, he reflected, desire snaking through his loins as he thought of how Jervis's britches left little of her slim legs and rounded buttocks to the imagination. But he hadn't reckoned on spending the rest of his life with her when he'd come to her aid on the street.

Still, he reflected as he booted the sitting room door open, he'd made that decision and he was man enough to live with it. He'd given his word as an English gentleman that he'd help her. Certainly, he thought as he glanced over his shoulder and saw Alix taking the steps two at a time to catch up with him, he couldn't live with the consequences of leaving her to fend for herself in the killing fields of Paris. An image of Lady Anne in the garden with her brother crossed his mind and he frowned. He'd find some other way to protect Elizabeth, he told himself.

Rafe strode into the bedchamber dropping the bottles and glasses resolutely on the three-legged table. He tossed his jacket into a corner of the room, loosened his stock and unbuttoned the top buttons of his waistcoat. Pouring two glasses of wine, he offered Alix one, then took his, and dropped heavily into one of the armchairs by the fire. He motioned for her to join him and took a deep draught of his wine, nearly emptying the glass. "Sit, my little hoyden, we've got a great deal to discuss."

Alix studied him carefully as he leaned back in the chair, his long legs stretched out before the fire.

"Sit," he repeated, seemingly fascinated by the play of the firelight on the crimson liquid in his glass.

Alix perched gingerly on the proffered seat and took a sip of her wine; it was surprisingly good, she thought absently, and took another swallow appreciating the warmth it brought to her chilled body.

Rafe refilled his glass. "Let us talk of how we are going to get you to London."

She took another, deeper sip of her wine, her heart pounding in her ears. She couldn't believe her luck. Despite the increasingly odd turn of events, he still seemed willing to help her reach her mother. She leaned forward anxiously. She'd given her escape to London some consideration, and she didn't want him to think she was entirely without resources.

"I've plenty of money," she assured him, "so you needn't worry about paying my way."

Rafe finished his glass and topped hers off as he filled his again. "Believe me my dear, finances are the least of our worries."

She ignored the sarcasm in his voice and continued. "I was thinking that I might travel with you under the guise of a governess for your sister."

He looked at her and snorted. "You're too young and too pretty. There isn't a man from here to Calais, leastways not one with blood flowing through his veins, that would believe that one. Try again."

He took a long swallow of wine, and Alix found herself following suit. He topped off her glass again.

"Well then, I could travel as your maid."

He swirled the remaining contents of his glass, staring intently at the small red whirlpool. "No one would believe that either."

Alix drained her glass, trying to quell her rising annoyance. It was as if he had already worked out how he was going to get her to London and was testing her to see if she could come up with the correct answer.

"I suppose, I might continue dressing in Jervis's clothes and pose as a footman or a groom." The wineglass in transit to Rafe's mouth arrested. How had she ever imagined his eyes looked like a sun-specked pool, she thought as she poured herself another glass of wine. They looked more like a swirling torrent as they swept the length of her body. Moving slowly at first, they roved across her face, lingering on her mouth, then picking up speed raced down her neck, paused at her breasts, sped the length of her waist and her long slim legs. When he raised his eyes to meet hers, her skin burned and her heart pounded as if she had been caught up in a raging current.

"No," he said softly, "that definitely won't do."

Though Jervis's clothes were by no means tight or revealing, Alix suddenly felt as exposed as if they had been painted on. She crossed her hands on her lap, pulling at the full sleeves of the shirt as if they might hide the jointure of her thighs from his probing gaze. Rafe, still watching, said nothing. She took another swig of wine, the heat of her body flaming into anger.

"You clearly don't approve of any of my ideas," she finally snapped, "so pray, enlighten me. What's your brilliant plan?"

Rafe's glass dropped with an abrupt *thunk* onto the table and wobbled precariously. Ignoring the teetering glassware, he stared fiercely into her eyes. "Marriage."

A strangled noise, something between a gasp and a laugh, escaped Alix's throat. "You're mad," she managed to choke out. "No, you're drunk. No, drunk and mad."

"Not nearly drunk enough, my dear," he responded dryly. "You see, it is understood that I come to Paris to pursue certain, ah, discreet pleasures. Should it become known that you arrived in London travelling under my auspices, whether as my sister's governess, my maid, or"—he added, amusement in his voice—"my groom, the conclusion would be the same. Everyone would believe that you had been my mistress. You would be ruined. Completely."

Rafe poured more wine for them both, tossing his quickly back. "Moreover, your mother is not the only one acquainted with Lady Melbourne. She and my stepmother share a passion for roses and gossip. If Lady Melbourne were to take into her pea-sized brain the idea that I had taken advantage of you, then cast you off, she would make certain my disgraceful behavior was published in every fashionable drawing room and ballroom in London. It would be, quite simply, disastrous. So you see, my dear, there's nothing for us to do but marry."

"That's absurd, there's no reason for us to pay such a heavy price simply because you were gentleman enough to rescue me."

"Thank you," he said. "I think."

Alix continued. "My future has been uncertain for some time. If I have to live in England with a ruined reputation, so be it. It's better than winding up on the guillotine."

"A dramatic statement, though I doubt you'll feel the same way in a year's time, when you are shunned by society and the proposals you are offered are far less respectable than mine."

Feeling emboldened by the wine, she continued. "What difference will a little scandal make to you? You're a man. The ladies will call you a rake and rap you with their fans while slipping you their room keys, and the men will hail your conquest. I've seen it happen dozens of times at Versailles."

"Ah, but London society is definitely not Versailles. Even if I were the type of man to despoil and abandon a young girl, which, I might add, I am not, think of the others who might be harmed by such a scandal—your mother, my sister. I, for one, have worked too hard to ensure Elizabeth has a bright future on the marriage mart." His voice sounded suddenly tired. "Come now, *mademoiselle,* it's not as if people in our position marry for love anyway. Marriage is about responsibility."

It crossed Alix's mind that she should ask him exactly what his position was, but then he might infer that she was considering his crazed proposal. She rubbed her temples with her fingers, her head beginning to ache. She heard him rambling on about position, responsibility, and marriage. Such familiar themes, she could almost hear her father's voice chorusing in. And the way he talked about marriage, so dull, so dry, he might have been discussing new methods of irrigation.

She had the insane urge to throw something at him.

Why was it that men became so pompous when they thought they were in the right? And why on earth did they have to go on and on about it? She was well aware she was in desperate straits. She needed to get out of France, she needed to find her mother, but she didn't need to be straight-laced into marriage with a man she'd met on the street. A man, who, however, attractive, seemed to have far too many opinions on what was best for her. She took a long swallow of her wine and scowled at him. Finishing off her glass, she said sharply. "If you're quite finished, would you please stop?"

Rafe looked taken aback, and she was satisfied to see that he did, indeed, stop.

"Well," he said finally, "you see my point."

"Yes," she responded, refilling her glass. "I see your point. But I don't want to get married." Silence fell on the room. Rafe gave Alix a look that made her feel like some exotic species of livestock. Finally he asked, "Don't want to get married at all or don't want to marry me?"

"You'll forgive me if my mind isn't on courtship," Alix said with deceptive calm, carefully enunciating her words. "But right now I am mourning the death of my father, trying to find my mother, and trying to escape France with my life." She took a long swallow of her wine and studied his face. "I suppose I'll marry sometime, but not here, not now, and not you."

Rafe was astonished. He'd expected protests, tears, gratitude, perhaps some soothing of maidenly fears. What he hadn't expected was to be so adamantly refused. She was being ridiculous. As he saw it there was no other way out. He couldn't help asking, "Why ever not?"

Alix ran an exasperated hand through her hair. It was almost as if she were back at Valcour arguing with her father. He just wouldn't listen, and she was suddenly past tired of being told what was best for her. Her father had thought remaining in Valcour was best for her and look how that had turned out. Now Rafe was telling her marriage was best for her, and she could just imagine how that would end. He wanted a reason she wouldn't marry him, well then she'd give him several.

Rising from her chair she eyed Rafe as if he were a horse up for auction. "You're attractive enough, well-built, not too old, and you have all your teeth." She began to circle his chair and noticed how the firelight played across his tawny hair, casting softening shadows on the harsh planes of his face. He turned to follow her movements and it struck her as unfair that a man should have such long lashes. Her eyes swept the length of his body, lingering on the cream colored britches molded to his muscular thighs, and the bulge between his legs, and her thoughts trailed off and her mouth went dry.

"Well?" he prompted an eyebrow raised.

"I barely even know you." It was a lame excuse, and she knew it even as the words formed themselves.

The corners of his mouth twitched slightly. "That's certainly never been a problem for one of your class before. Try again."

"How do I know that this isn't some sort of trick to bed

me, and that you won't abandon me as soon as you've had your way with me?"

"Alix," he said, shaking his head and taking another sip of wine, "if I wanted to have my way with you, I doubt that I should have to resort to marriage."

What an incredibly arrogant and overbearing assertion! She straightened to her full height and pointed a finger at him. "You, sir, are an ass."

"And you," he growled, rising to tower over her, "haven't the good sense to know what's best for you."

She stared up at him with clenched fists. "And I suppose what's best for me is being carried through the streets like a sack of washing, being ordered about, and told to hide in a trunk."

"It's a damn sight better than breaking into fashionable homes in the Faubourg Saint Germain dressed like a man."

"It served its purpose didn't it?" she demanded.

They stood glaring at one another.

It struck Rafe that this proposal was not going at all as he had planned.

"Alix," he said, lowering his voice with effort and touching her arm. "Don't you understand the seriousness of your situation?" The room fell silent again, and he stared at her, willing her to understand.

"You know how my father died, how can you even ask me that?" she finally whispered. His fingers were rough and warm against her skin, and she felt suddenly overwhelmed by the heat of his body. The scent of leather and soap, sun-dried linen and his flesh was dizzying. "I can't make a decision like this, a decision that might save my life now only to destroy it later." She stumbled backward and he followed. "I can't marry you."

"Oh yes you can, and you will."

Alix opened her mouth to refute him and found it covered with his own. Rafe's lips were rich with the taste of wine. She tried to twist her head away, but his mouth persisted, his tongue dancing and darting along her lips, then plunging into her mouth. And suddenly it was as if sparks were flying along her nerve endings.

She ought to push him off, she thought as the pounding in her blood raced through her chest and reverberated in her head, drowning out all coherence. His hands swept up her waist to cup her breasts and her nipples jutted their response. It's the wine, she told herself, too much wine, unable to stop her hands from tangling in his hair, drawing his face closer. One more kiss and she'd demand that he stop, she instructed herself, as his mouth burned a path down her neck. His hands were working at the buttons of Jervis's waistcoat, and he pushed her gently back to release the lower ones—then suddenly he stopped.

Alix's eyes flew open, smoky with desire and confusion.

"No," he said, closing her shirt so he couldn't see the flush of passion across her skin, the rapid rise and fall of her breasts. "Not like this. We've both had too much wine." He found the discarded nightshirt she'd worn earlier in the day and handed it to her. "Put this on, and get into bed."

Turning on his heel, he left the room.

With trembling hands, Alix stripped off Jervis's clothes. The warmth of the hearth fire was nearly unbearable against the heat of her aroused skin. She slipped the nightshirt on and scrambled into the big bed, grateful for the coolness of the linen. She breathed deeply, trying to calm the pounding of her heart and found her nostrils filled with the scent of him. She could not let desire cloud her judgement, nor, she thought as her head spun dizzily, wine. There had to be some means of getting to London without marrying Rafe Harcrest.

She was still trying to come up with one when her eyes closed heavily in sleep.

Rafe sat in the adjoining room staring into the dying fire, the wineglass and bottle long emptied. It had been some-time since he'd heard any movement from the bedcham-ber and he hoped Alix had found sleep more easily than he. He'd known as soon as he'd seen Madame de La Brou's note that he would have to propose marriage. It was the responsible thing to do, and the only way he could think to get Alix safely out of France. He hadn't been able to sway her mind, he mused wryly, but he'd come unex-pectedly close to convincing her body.

Rafe thought of the warmth of her lips, the pressure of her firm young breasts against his chest, the way her arms had wrapped around his neck to draw him closer, and he groaned involuntarily. Alix would come around to his pro-posal, she had no other choice. And neither, he reflected, suddenly grim, did he.

Jervis stumbled wearily into the room just before dawn, a bulky package tucked under one arm. "You sleeping here?" he asked the lean figure sprawled in the chair by the cold fire.

Rafe passed a hand across his eyes. "Not exactly."

Jervis dropped down on the rope cot and began pulling off his boots. "I got everything done," he said, dropping one mud-encrusted boot onto the floor. "Cost you a right penny, but I got the identity papers, the passport, and the visa. And,"—he said patting the package—"some new clothes for the lady." He yawned, dropping his other boot. "So what time are we leaving tomorrow, or is it today?"

"We leave," responded his master, "right after the wed-ding ceremony at the Place de la Grève."

Chapter Nine

~≈~

Alix swam slowly toward wakening, trying to make out where she was without lifting her eyelids. She could feel soft cotton against her cheek and her body seemed to be ensnared in yards of fine linen. She was, she realized with a start, in a bed. For a fleeting moment she hoped her flight from the château had been a dream and she moistened her lips to call Solange for some cocoa and buttered rolls.

The stale taste in her mouth reminded her of the previous evening.

She'd been drinking wine with Rafe, quite a lot of wine it seemed. And now it was morning, and the painful feeling across her eyes must be sunlight slicing through partly opened curtains. She tried to turn her head away from the brightness, and immediately wished she hadn't. Pain radiated through her head like a giant hand clasped over her scalp. If someone could promise that they'd remove her head that very instant, she thought bitterly, she'd welcome the guillotine.

Why, oh why had she drunk so much? Her mother had always told her to pace herself with water. "A drunken woman is an unappealing sight," the comtesse would say, pacing the room and rapping her hand with her fan for emphasis. "Wine loosens the tongue, coarsens the manners, and swells the eyelids the following morning." Why did mothers always have to be right? She comforted herself that at least her mother hadn't seen her performance last night.

Alix winced. She'd called Rafe an ass.

Then she cringed. Had she also told him he was attractive?

And he'd kissed her.

An agony of embarrassment swept through her more painfully than the hangover as she remembered how she'd kissed him back. Drinking and carousing, what would her father have said? He'd have said it was typical female behavior, she thought sourly. Instead of keeping her mind focused on escape, she'd been distracted by a man. An experienced, womanizing man, judging by his kisses. Well, there'd be no more of that, she thought, nodding firmly and sending waves of pain ricocheting around her skull. She groaned out loud.

"Ah, I see you're finally ready to rise, mademoiselle," piped a cheery voice. Gingerly raising her head, Alix peered across the room. Jervis was sitting in front the fire, vigorously shining her shoes. When he saw her look up, he put them down and rose. As he did so, Alix noticed a smart navy blue walking dress draped over the chair next to him, along with several neatly folded white bundles that she took to be undergarments.

"Care for a bite to eat? Lisette in the kitchen can whip

you up a nice fluffy omelet if you'd like, or would you prefer a bit of cold ham?"

The thought of food sent an unwelcome undulation through her stomach. "No, thank you, monsieur," she said weakly.

"Ah come now, that's no way to start your big day." Jervis eyed her stricken state thoughtfully. "The captain warned me you might have a bit of a hangover. I've taken the liberty of mixing up a bit of something that should help. Here, try this," he said, thrusting a large crockery mug filled with a brown liquid under her nose.

Alix eyed the cup suspiciously. "What is it?"

He ignored her question, urging, "There's a good girl, just toss it back, one big swallow."

Suspecting she couldn't feel much worse, she tried tossing it back. A thick cool slime, with a slightly bitter taste slid down her throat, nearly rebelling before it reached her stomach. "Good Lord, Jervis," Alix grimaced, "what was that awful stuff?"

"Raw egg, rosemary, and ale," he responded proudly. "A traditional Jones family recipe. Should have you feeling better in just a bit."

"If I don't die first," she moaned.

Jervis chuckled. "You won't die. Besides you've got too much to do today. Hurry up then, up and out of bed, get yourself dressed." Taking the emptied mug from her hand, he left the room before she could inquire just what exactly was planned for the day.

She lay back on the pillows, Jervis's home remedy weighing heavily in her stomach. At least, she thought grimly, it seemed to have stopped her belly from lurching about. Slowly, very slowly, she sat up, cradling her head as if it might unexpectedly detach. Let this be a lesson to you Alexandre Charlotte, she berated herself. And then another memory from the previous night skittered across her brain;

she'd actually congratulated him on having all his teeth. She shuddered. She must keep her mind on the task at hand. Madeleine was in London; she must get to London. If she made it to London, she reassured herself, surely her life would resume its normal, steady course.

Swinging her feet over the side of the bed, she wobbled over to the washstand like a toddler testing her legs. She filled the basin with water and and splashed some over her face. Peering through the droplets hanging from her lashes, she spotted the navy traveling gown. She needed to get dressed. Crossing to the chair, she lifted up the gown and examined it more closely. The material was a fine quality. The style was understated and elegant. Undoubtedly, this was not the first time Monsieur Harcrest had selected garments for a woman's wardrobe.

Alix slid the chemise over her head, then looked around for her stays, locating them on the mantle. She picked them up and examined them, saw that someone had clumsily stitched her papers, money, and gems back in. She wrapped the garment around her waist and tried in vain to tie the strings in the back. It was no use, she was in too much agony to twist around. She could either wear them slipping and sliding about, ask for assistance, or do without. Deciding to do without, she pulled some money out of the garment, then tossed it into Rafe's trunk. She pulled the fine wool dress over her head and tied the burgundy and blue sash tightly about her waist. She had just finished arranging the lace fichu over her shoulders and was smoothing the tight-fitted sleeves when she heard a light tap at the door.

"It's me, mademoiselle," Jervis said, "just checking to see if you need anything."

Alix cast a look about the room then called back, "Have you a hairbrush? My hair's a knotted mess." She heard Jervis rustling about, then he knocked again and entered, a silver-backed hairbrush monogrammed with the letter *M* in one hand and a steaming cup of mocha in the other.

He looked her up and down. "There now, mademoiselle, you've certainly made a good start of it. I knew my tonic would do the trick. If you'd like, I could fix your hair for you. Used to do it all the time for my mother when I was little."

It was strange, but reassuring to think of this sharp-eyed little man as a child. Alix accepted the cup and his offer and sank into an armchair by the fire.

Jervis began gently tugging at the tangles. "You've got lovely hair, mademoiselle," he said. "I was born and raised in the Americas, you know." He worried at a particularly snarled knot. "So I understand how hard it can be, packing up and leaving everything familiar behind." He resumed brushing. "But sometimes a fresh start is just what you need."

Alix took a sip from the steaming cup and allowed herself to relax under Jervis's ministrations, barely listening to his chatter. A stray thought flitted through her brain and she frowned. Had Jervis said something about a "big" day? She considered asking him, then thought the better of it. It was inconceivable that Rafe Harcrest could get a license, post the banns and find a priest all in one day. Marriage, what an absurd idea. This was neither the time nor the place for a marriage.

Jervis put down the brush and began to twist and pin her hair. "There's a lot you can learn about yourself when you plunk down someplace new."

Distracted, Alix picked up the brush, noticing for the first time the *M* engraved on the back. "Jervis," she asked, "what does the *M* stand for?"

Jervis paused, then replied in a rush, "The *M*? That's for the captain's father, the brush belonged to him."

Alix noticed his stumble, and pursed her lips. Rafe's father indeed. More likely a pretty remembrance of some woman, Margot, Marguerite, Marianne. No doubt, some common hussy. Monsieur Harcrest was mistaken if he thought she was going to blithely join their ranks. Thinking of Rafe reminded Alix of a question that had been niggling at her. "And just where is Monsieur Harcrest this morning?"

"Oh," said Jervis breezily, "he's gone over to the Hotel de Ville to get the marriage license."

Alix jerked forward so suddenly that one of the tresses Jervis had been pinning slipped loose. "A marriage license?" she yelped, her head feeling as though it would split. "But surely he can't get a marriage license on such short notice?"

Jervis chortled and recaptured the stray lock. "Oh, mademoiselle, welcome to the *new* France. It's an amazing thing, wouldn't have believed it myself if I hadn't seen it with my own eyes. All you have to do to get married in Paris these days is walk into the municipal offices at the Hôtel de Ville, announce your intentions, fill out some forms, get some stamps, then show up for the ceremony at the Place de la Grève."

Alix put her aching head in her hands.

"The captain figured you wouldn't be too comfortable going to the Hôtel with him, it being the meeting place for all them government committees and all. Not that you should have any trouble with your new identity papers," he added reassuringly. "Dubois is a master. It's just that he thought, being who you are, you might not want mingle with all them National Assembly members."

She needed to think of a plan, if only her head would stop throbbing!

"Said he'd be by later this afternoon to pick us up for the ceremony and that I should have you dressed, packed, and ready to go. Soon as I finish here, I'm going to check on the coach arrangements to Calais. I tell you, I'm not much of a sailor, but the sooner I've got the boards of a ship bound for England beneath my feet, the better."

"But is such a marriage even legal?" she managed, finally lifting her head. Her queasiness was fast turning into fury. Rafe had moved ahead without discussing things further with her.

"I dunno," Jervis admitted, scratching his head. "But," he added brightly, "it is in France and that's the important thing."

Perhaps she could have it annulled as soon as they reached London, Alix speculated furiously.

"There now," Jervis said, stepping back to admire his handiwork, "you look fine."

"My thoughts exactly," said a voice from across the room.

Alix turned to see Rafe leaning indolently against the doorframe. "You," Alix said rising to her feet, "You and I, monsieur, need to have a serious talk."

He cocked an eyebrow at Jervis. "Why is it that when a woman says that a man immediately knows he's in trouble?"

"I think I best be checking on those travel arrangements," Jervis muttered. He snatched up his jacket and tricorne and sped out the door.

"Because you *are* in trouble," Alix snapped. "How *dare* you fetch a marriage license without my consent?"

Rafe dropped into a chair and regarded her questioningly. "You've come up with a better idea since we last spoke?" He continued without pause. "It's simple really. I've booked passage for us on a ship leaving Calais in three days time. With valid papers proving you're the wife an English citizen, we should have no trouble reaching the port. No hiding in barns, no crouching among chickens, no pretending to be someone you're not."

"And when we reach England?" she asked.

"I will settle a suitable allowance on you, and you can choose to live either in the city or countryside, whichever pleases you best. I will place few demands on you and, in return, I shall expect you to comport yourself with dignity and discretion."

"And that is all you will require of me?"

"I will occasionally expect your attendance at certain social functions, and of course, your assistance in getting an heir."

He stood watching her, waiting for her response. He was making her a generous offer, saving her life, and setting her up comfortably. It was an offer most women of the ton would have leapt to accept, but not, it seemed, Alix.

He felt an odd twisting in his chest as she turned away from him, staring out the window as if fascinated by the activity in the stable yard. His eyes roved over the slim line of her back, the slender waist, the stiffly held shoulders. Sunlight drifted across her hair, making it look like polished mahogany, richly threaded with russet and gold. Rafe was seized with the desire to unpin Jervis's painstaking coiffure and feel the silken strands slide across his fingers.

Instead, he rose and stood behind her, his hands clasping her upper arms. "Alix," he said gently, "if I could think of another way to help you out of France I would. We've managed pretty well so far. Would it really be so awful, being married to me?" It occurred to him that he could dangle his title in front of her, tempt her with life as a countess and yet, brushing unpleasant memories of Lady Anne from his mind, he wanted to hear her say yes to Rafe Harcrest and not to the Earl of Moreham.

"It's not you Rafe," she said softly.

"Then what is it Alix?"

"I don't know." She gave a shaky laugh. "This isn't exactly how I imagined my wedding day."

He stroked her arms. "Alix," he said, "in a few hours, just across the Seine, the tumbrels will begin to roll and people will die." He felt her shudder but continued, his voice insistent. "You know what their greatest mistake was?" She remained unmoving. "They couldn't imagine that times were changing and they couldn't change with them. You understand that, Alix, it's the reason why you didn't remain at Valcour to perish alongside your father. Its what's brought you this far. You can't stop now. Take another step forward, Alix, come with me."

She turned and looked up at him, her expression emotionless, but her gray eyes glistening. "This marriage at the Place de la Grève, will it be legally binding?"

He frowned. "I don't know."

"I'll marry you." Alix spoke stiffly. "I'll move forward, but it will be my choice. I won't be swept along like so much jetsam."

A small breath of relief escaped him. Jetsam indeed, he thought, more like lost treasure.

After a moment, she added, "But I want it annulled as soon as we reach England."

Somewhere deep in his heart he felt a sharp stick of disappointment, more painful than when he'd overheard Anne in the garden, and he wondered at it. It was the long night, he told himself, the anticlimax of convincing himself that marrying her was the right thing to do. He thought of Lady Anne waiting for his proposal and her threat to Elizabeth. Alix was right, he reflected, an annulment would be best for them all.

"Very well, I will seek an annulment as soon as we reach England. In the meantime," he said, "shall we go see about being united in wedlock?"

The coach was a ridiculous affair, Alix thought wryly, probably the gift of some wealthy lord to his mistress. The exterior was painted a sapphire blue and the door handles and wheels were guilded gold. Handing them up into the coach, the driver cheerfully explained how he'd bought the vehicle for a song from a desperate aristocrat. He'd considered purchasing a fleet of coaches, he said, but with the rising price of grain, the damn horses cost too much to feed.

Inside the seats were upholstered in blue velvet, and gaily-painted shepherds courted coy shepherdess around the windows and roofs. Atrocious, she thought, but at least it was more comfortable than the lumbering old berlin her father used to travel between his estates. Her eyes blurred as she pictured the comte, great curled wig slipping to one side as he gestured out the window, enthusiastically pointing out historic sites of interest. She wondered what he'd think of this coach, and, as Rafe slid into the seat across from her, what he'd make of her husband-to-be.

She stared listlessly out the window, recognizing the route she had come with Henri only two days ago. At least now she knew her mother was alive, she reminded herself as they passed the massive walls of L'Abbaye. They crossed the Pont Neuf, and turned west, in the opposite direction of the Tuileries where the guillotine had been set up. She reminded herself, as she stared at a particularly insipid shepherdess, that at least she was not traveling in a tumbrel.

The coach moved slowly through the traffic of the Rue Saint Antoine, pulling up shortly before the Hôtel de la Ville. Rafe, who'd respected her silence during the trip, helped her out. "We'll meet you back here as soon as the thing is done," he said to Jervis, who was sitting up on the box with the coachman. Taking her elbow, Rafe led down the street toward the Place de la Grève.

She looked at the fashionable crowds coursing up and down the street. "It's amazing," she whispered, "the carriages, the people showing off their finery, greeting each other as if nothing has changed."

"Don't let appearances fool you, Alix," he said softly.

They entered through the arched doorway of the municipal building and joined a line of couples waiting to have their papers stamped. Alix hadn't cherished any romantic illusions about the marriage that her parents would some day arrange for her. Still, she reflected, as they shuffled toward a table where a clerk was waiting with a heavy seal and wax, she hadn't imagined anything quite so drab. She glanced up at Rafe who stood quietly by her side and wondered what he was thinking. Her father had anticipated marriage would bring him a dutiful wife who would wait on him hand and foot. Rafe had said only that he required an heir, but what else did he expect?

Alix knew a moment of fear when the clerk examined her papers; Jervis and Rafe had assured her the forgeries were perfect, but still she waited for him to denounce her. Instead, he asked if it was their intention to be married, and if they understood the seriousness of such a commitment. It wasn't a commitment, she told herself, as she signed the marriage license, it was just a temporary arrangement. Intentions and expectations had no place at this ceremony.

As she watched the clerk stamp the papers with the seal of the new republic, she wondered for the first time what *she* would want from a marriage. Her father was dead. Perhaps when she arrived in London her mother would permit her some choice in a husband. Or perhaps she wouldn't ask her mother for permission at all, perhaps she would demand it. She'd find a husband who wouldn't bully her, who'd listen to opinions and allow her to make up her own mind, a husband who would respect her. She wanted a man who would see her as more than a body in his bed or a vessel for his children. And when they married, she told herself, it would be on a fine sunny day with lots of music and flowers.

Rafe led her back outside and they joined the couples standing about the Place de la Grève. The sky above the Hôtel de la Ville's peaked roofs and ornate dormers looked sullen and gray. A chill breeze rippled off the dark waters of the Seine, and Alix tugged the folds of her cloak closer. She stole a glance at her husband-to-be. The wind fluttered the capes of his greatcoat and teased strands of golden brown hair from his queue. As if feeling her gaze, he turned to look at her, a questioning look in his hazel eyes.

She flushed and looked away. Beside her a young couple stood holding hands, heads bowed together whispering and giggling. Training her eyes forward, she noticed the man in front of her running his hand down the waist of his bride-to-be and patting her backside familiarly. Feeling like an actress who'd walked into the wrong scene of a play, she feigned intense interest in the muddy toes of her shoes.

Rafe studied the downcast figure of his bride. Her face was pale and grim, a sharp contrast to the heated gazes and warm blushes of the rest of the women in the crowd. While he hadn't expected her to be thrilled about the wedding, he hadn't anticipated she'd look quite so miserable. Was she disappointed the ceremony wasn't more festive? He eyed the colorful bunches of flowers and ribbons held by most of the other women. He thought Alix looked sleek and elegant in her dark wool traveling dress, but now that he thought on it, perhaps he should have brought her a small gift or token.

He looked at her slender hands folded stiffly in front of her, and it struck him that she ought to have a ring. He grimaced. He'd make this up to her; the family vaults were full of gemstones. Would she prefer an heirloom or should he have something designed for her? he wondered. He glanced down at his own hands. His signet ring would have to serve until he could give her something more permanent. Drawing it off his finger, he reached for her hand. Alix looked up, surprised as he slipped it on. The enormous gold band dangled loosely. She closed her hand around it and gave him a thoughtful stare.

Rafe tucked a hand under her arm and drew her close as an official in a navy redingote with a great red, white, and blue sash across his chest, mounted the dais in front of the crowd and began to speak. The wind, growing stronger, whipped the speaker's long gray hair around his face, and he clutched at his cockaded bicorne with one hand as he shouted the words of the ceremony. Most of what he said was lost on the wind, but Alix thought she heard something about fidelity and trust, then more about dedication. After a surprisingly short speech, the man cried out, "Do you all agree to be married?" And the crowd answered back with a vigorous, "Yes." The air was filled with hats and flowers and spatters of applause as he pronounced them men and wives.

The couples around them began embrace enthusiastically and Alix felt suddenly awkward. As if sensing her discomfort, Rafe drew her toward him and with his free hand tilted up her chin. His kiss was gentle, reassuring, and Alix found herself responding to the warm insistence of his tongue. She leaned in closer, and the hand under her chin slid into her hair. "So soft," he whispered as his tongue plumbed the depths of her mouth.

The sound of a throat being loudly cleared interrupted.

Alix was suddenly aware of a cold rain misting on her cheeks and Jervis at her elbow.

"Begging your pardon, Captain, but the coach is waiting." He glanced balefully up at the sky. "We best be getting on our way before this rain turns the roads into a muddy mess."

They hurried back up the street to the corner. Rafe handed Alix inside the carriage and slipped into the seat next to her. Alix gave a start, then realized they were man and wife, and that it would look odd if he sat across from her now. She heard Jervis clamber up alongside the coachman, heard the crack of the whip, and then the coach lurched suddenly forward, throwing them together. She felt goose bumps play across her skin where it brushed against his. Damn appearances, she thought and said, "I think it would be better if you sat across from me."

Rafe tipped his tawny head in acquiescence, "As you wish."

This, though, was much worse, as she could now take in his wind-loosened hair and the pensive swirl of his hazel eyes. Dropping her gaze was no better, as she found her eyes then confronted the span of his chest in his finely embroidered waistcoat and the muscular line of his thighs in his form-fitting britches.

Rain began to spatter against the roof.

"Wouldn't Jervis be more comfortable riding inside with us?" she suggested, annoyed at a betraying quaver in her voice.

Rafe shook his head. "Jones hates riding in coaches more than he hates the rain."

So, she thought, no rescue there. Well then, she'd just have to face the issue dead on. "Monsieur Harcrest."

"Rafe," he corrected, "we are husband and wife."

"For the purposes of this journey only," she amended. She cleared her throat and began again, "Rafe, I would appreciate it you would stop looking at me that way."

"What way?" he inquired innocently.

"As if you would like to . . . to . . ." words failed her.

"Kiss you?" he offered.

She nodded. "You agreed we should have this, this arrangement annulled as soon as we reached England."

She flushed but continued, "So I think it best that we avoid . . . touching one another."

What was it about him that she found so unappealing? he wondered, a surge of anger rising in his chest. He thought of how Alix had kissed him the night before, her hands tangled in his hair, her skin flushed with passion. He realized there was something he needed to know. He leaned forward and slid his hands around her waist.

Alix's breath caught and she felt desire trip up her rib cage. She wished suddenly that she'd chosen to wear her stays, because she knew from the triumphant gleam in his eyes that he'd felt every nuance of her response.

He brushed a tendril of hair off her forehead and smiled. "I'll do my best sweetheart, I promise."

Chapter Ten

❧

Lamartine ran ink-stained hands over his bristled pate and frowned at a crack in the plaster running down the wall in front of him. The room was dank and smelled of cabbage and unwashed bodies. A candle flame cast a spidery light over the crumpled wads of paper on the scarred wooden desktop where he sat. He gave a delicate shudder as he thought of the fleas infesting the low rope bed behind him. Hopefully none of them would find a home in the bagwig packed in its worn leather traveling case on the grimy washstand.

These miserable lodgings were all Alix de La Brou's fault, he thought, angrily scratching at a fleabite on his scalp. If she had just stayed put and died at the château, he wouldn't have to be wasting his hard-earned money on rented rooms and public stables. He grimaced as his fingers traced the small lump at the back of his head. He'd like to find the man who'd struck him as well.

He'd had a rough time of it when the neighbors had

found him in Madame de La Brou's small salon. He'd had to whine and cringe his way past the district constable. It had been humiliating and that too was Alix's and the strange man's fault. Once he'd gotten those titles, he'd denounce them both and gladly watch them die.

But first he had to find them.

His eyes narrowed thoughtfully. They'd only met once, but he'd recognize the tall stranger if he ever saw him again. The long nose, the arrogant smirk, the elegant English-style riding boots. Too well dressed to be a thief, but almost certainly not a friend of the comte's. He prided himself on remembering the names and faces of every noble visitor to the estates.

And yet, recalling the man's evasive responses to his questions, he could have sworn the stranger knew something about Alix, perhaps even had the girl hidden away somewhere. Could he have been a friend of Madame de La Brou?

The sounds of vigorous commercial lovemaking disturbed his thoughts, a woman repeatedly groaning, "You're the best." Lamartine slammed his fist against the wall. A man's voice answered with an obscenity and a bottle crashed against the wall. He scowled. The place was disgusting, but in overcrowded Paris, having a room, much less a bed to himself, was a luxury.

The people here lived like rats. Each district in the city was a warren, with people crowded in on top of each other, marrying, producing children, growing old, and dying all in the same neighborhoods. But, he mused, their closeness did have its advantages. If Alix or her protector were in the area, or went near the apartment on the Rue de l'Université, the filthy urchins he'd paid to watch the place would let him know.

He took a battered gold pocket watch out of his waistcoat and flipped it open. The comte's watch no longer ran, but it still had its uses. Inside it was a delicate miniature of a dark-haired girl with wide gray eyes, an impressive likeness of Alexandre de Rabec de La Brou. He'd shown the portrait to every little street beggar he could find, along with the coins he'd pay for information concerning her whereabouts. It would work, he reassured himself, and he would find her.

He took a sip of wine from the glass at his elbow, ignoring the vinegary bite as it slid across his tongue, and resumed his practice of the drafting notes in the comte's hand. The shadow of a smile played about his thin mouth. Wouldn't Father Bonheur be proud if he could see Robert Lamartine working so diligently at his lessons? If there was one thing the village priest had beaten into him after his parents had died, it was the importance of hard work. He dipped his quill into the ink and wrote out a few sentences. He had to get the tone of the letter just right, the correct balance of command and sentiment.

After a few moments he crumpled his draft and tossed it into the pile on the desk. Command was easy; it was the sentiment that gave him trouble. He dipped his quill again. He'd stay another week in Paris. If Alix didn't turn up, then perhaps he'd pay a visit to Madame la Comtesse in London. And when he did, he reflected, reaching for a fresh piece of paper, he'd be well prepared.

Darkness was falling and the street lamps had been lit. As the coach passed them, their flickering light would briefly illuminate its shadowy interior. Lying back against the velvet cushions, Rafe used these moments to study the face of his sleeping bride. She'd discarded her hat and lay slumped against the side of the carriage, her head pillowed in her cloak. A frown creased her brow and there were smudges of fatigue under her eyes.

Bride. New wife. He considered the words thoughtfully.

Not his to keep he reminded himself, his fingers drumming softly on the coach door. She didn't want him; she'd made that clear. He'd said he'd give her an annulment, and a gentleman should stand by his word. Besides, he told himself, she was not the sort of wife he ever would have chosen. Unpredictable, argumentative . . . he felt the increasingly familiar surge of heat that occurred whenever he spent too much time thinking or looking at Alix . . . passionate.

He turned his eyes away from Alix and stared sightlessly out the window. Lady Anne's voice echoed coldly in his head, *"I have no desire to invite Moreham to paw at my bosom."* He frowned; there had been such revulsion in her tone. He'd never considered whether passion would be a feature of his marriage to Lady Anne; now he wondered if he could bear a lifetime without it.

And yet, he reflected, his fingers ceasing their beat, it had been Anne's cool composure that had drawn him to her in the first place. He needed her calming influence on Elizabeth, didn't he? And what if she took her revenge at his failure to come up to scratch out on his sister? Elizabeth might be wild and impulsive, but she had a good heart. A season laced with social barbs and vicious gossip would destroy her. Rafe tried to recall his feelings for Lady Anne before he'd overheard her conversation in the garden, tried to superimpose her pale blond features over Alix's sleeping ones.

Alix's tumbled hair remained resolutely dark, and Rafe forced his gaze back to the window. Dark masses of trees rose up, took shape and then blurred in passing. He knew that Paris was behind them. He checked the gold watch that hung from a fob beneath his waistcoat; they were making good time. Just before they'd left the city, they'd exchanged the sapphire blue coach for a sleek black post chaise.

He'd known the expensive hired vehicle would attract

the attention of the national guards as they passed through the various checkpoints on the road to Calais, but he'd reasoned that since their papers were in order, they'd have no problems. Rafe smiled wryly. What he hadn't anticipated was the interest the newly minted marriage license would invite. At nearly every stop he and Alix had been subjected to a wealth of ribald advice and demands to see the newlyweds embrace.

Not that his own manservant had been much help. As soon as they neared a checkpoint, Jervis would wave his hat in the air, calling out that they were the newlywed express. When he'd drawn Jones over and suggested he stop, Jervis had smiled broadly. "That's the beauty of it, Captain, these Frenchies can't resist a handsome young couple in love. Distracts 'em from asking too many nosy questions." He poked Rafe in the chest. "So you two just keep playing it up." He chuckled. "By God, the kiss at the last stop nearly had me convinced."

Rafe nearly groaned at the memory. His eyes were drawn irresistibly back to Alix's sleeping form: Playing it up, indeed—more like playing with a bed of smoldering coals. The first kiss flared like tinder, the second flamed like kindling, and the third roared through his veins with the heat of seasoned wood well caught. And when Alix trembled beneath him, he could swear she felt it, too. God's breath he was a man, he thought as he checked his watch again and wondered how he would last out the trip without making love to her.

His ruminations were cut short by the lurching stop of the coach. The horses whinnied, and he heard the coachman trying to calm them. Sliding back the window he peered out, saw lanterns mounted on an overturned wagon in the road, and a group of men clustered around it.

Alix sat up, rubbing her eyes and pushing wayward

strands of hair out of her face. "What is it?" she asked with a yawn.

"I believe it's an accident in the road, seems to be an overturned wagon." But his speculations were cut short by a pounding at the coach door, and a man's raised voice.

"By order of the Senlis Revolutionary Tribunal, we demand you stop and show your papers."

Rafe and Alix stepped out of the carriage into a pool of lantern light. Jervis and the coachman were standing among a group of young men, all wearing blue jackets with red epaulettes and red, white, and blue cockades in their hats. All, Rafe noted grimly, were armed with an array of sabers, pistols, and rifles. He pulled their passports and identity papers from his coat pocket and a sturdy young man with dark hair stepped forward to take them.

"I am Anton Doret, captain of the Senlis Guard Nationale," he said, studying the papers carefully. "You are English citizen?" he inquired, frowning at Rafe.

Rafe nodded.

Anton beckoned to several of his companions to join them. "An Englander," he heard the young man mutter. "Bastards," he heard one of them say, spitting harshly on the ground, and another man growled, "English spy."

"Search the carriage," Doret ordered.

One of the national guardsmen climbed into the carriage and began thumping the cushions, sliding his hands between them, and peering under the seats. As he stepped out of the chaise, Alix's beribboned hat fluttered out after him, settling onto the rutted road, where it was promptly stepped on by one of the nervously stamping horses. The guardsman swung up into the coachman's seat and began searching there. A moment later they heard him call down, "Anton, I've found a pistol here."

The postilion protested. "I got papers showing I'm employed by Citizen Pascal, carriage builder on the Rue

Guengaud in Paris. I'm a loyal citizen, I am, and I need that pistol for protection."

Doret answered roughly, "You'll have it back when we've settled this matter. It's not you we're interested in, it's these possible English spies." He gestured for the guardsman searching the carriage to inspect the rear of the coach. The man climbed down and unstrapped the trunks fastened in the back. Dropping them into the road, he began rifling their contents.

Rafe saw Alix tense as the guard lifted out her stays and waved them appreciatively at his mates. They laughed and he tossed them, along with several of Rafe's freshly laundered shirts onto the road.

Stepping forward to block Alix's view of the searchers, Rafe addressed Captain Doret. "You can see, Captain, we carry no weapons. As our papers clearly state, we are cloth merchants on our way back to England. My understanding was that your new government was encouraging a continuation of trade between our two countries. However, should you require some contribution to demonstrate our support for your revolutionary cause . . ." He let the words trail off suggestively.

The young man wheeled on Rafe and snapped, "You are mistaken in thinking we are like the corrupt officials of the old regime. You cannot buy us off. You will stay with us overnight and in the morning, if the revolutionary tribunal decides that you are indeed what you say, then you shall be permitted to continue on your way."

"But, citizen, my papers," protested the postilion.

"You," Anton responded, "are free to go." Then turning to the men guarding Rafe, Alix, and Jervis, he directed, "Huget, put these three in the storeroom."

Rafe balked. "Our property citizen, my wife and I would appreciate it if after you've searched our clothes, your men would return them to the trunks."

Doret nodded, then motioned for Huget to take them away. Huget, a massive figure armed with a bayonet, motioned for them to follow him across the road. Rafe could make out a row of steep-roofed houses, candles flickering in the windows and smoke curling from their chimneys. As the passed between two of the houses, he caught the sound of laughter, and the clink of plates and glasses.

Rafe scanned their surroundings with a soldier's eye, finding nothing that would aid their immediate escape. There were guards in front and behind them; he glanced at Jervis whose hand had crept to his boot where he kept a throwing knife hidden. Catching Jervis's eye, Rafe shook his head warningly. He and Jervis might be able to take the guards, but he was unwilling to risk Alix's safety should the soldiers start firing their muskets. Better to see what prospects for escape the storeroom might hold.

Huget led them across the courtyard toward the stables. The ground was uneven and muddy, and Alix had to lift her skirts to keep them from becoming sodden and filthy. The guardsman behind her whistled admiringly at her ankles. When they reached a small curved hut adjacent to the stables, Huget held his lantern high and gestured with his rifle for them to enter. Jervis swung open a crude wooden door and they filed into a dusty, windowless room.

"Can we at least have a light?" Alix asked.

The man who had whistled at her ankles snickered. "Can't risk you burning down the place." And the door banged shut behind them.

Rafe immediately began feeling about the corn cob and mud-daubed walls; they were surprisingly solid and the room was without windows. He could hear Jervis moving about in a similar inspection, heard him drop down and utter a disgusted sigh.

"Nothing but feed sacks and buckets, not a nice stick or sharp implement in the place." Jervis sneezed. "And hay, damned hay, makes my eyes itch. Why couldn't they have put us into a cell like normal jailers? No, it had to be a stable." He sneezed again.

Alix slid to the floor and leaned against the crude stucco. "Forgive me for my lack of sympathy Jervis, but I think I prefer this to a prison." Her voice rose questioningly. "Surely they wouldn't have put us in here if they anticipated keeping us for a long time?"

Jervis blew his nose loudly into what Alix hoped was a handkerchief, but Rafe suspected was his sleeve. "Do you think the ship will sail without us, Captain?" he asked.

"Williams is paid good money to wait," Rafe's voice cut assertively through the darkness. Rafe knew that if the weather changed, it wouldn't matter what Williams had been paid to wait, he'd sail to protect his ship and cargo; but he didn't want Alix more worried she already was.

"Yes, but how long? We could be here for days, that is, if we're able to leave at all." Alix's stomach had contracted. Until then she'd been worrying about whether they'd escape the local revolutionary committee; now she worried that they might miss the packet altogether.

"She's right," Jervis sniffled. "I say we break out of here."

"How do you suggest we do that?" Rafe asked.

"Well, we could tell the guard that the lady is sick, then you could hide behind the door and conk him a good one when he comes in to check."

"An original plan," Rafe said dryly, "but after I've conked the guard, how do we get past the rest of the armed men out there? Do we steal the horses before or after we've overcome the guards? And as Captain Doret is holding our papers, how do you propose we make our way to Calais without them?"

"Details, you've always got to be so caught up in the details, Captain," Jervis grumbled.

"Might I remind you that this is the French countryside, not the wilds of the colonies. It's not as if we can just slip away amongst the trees and live off berries and deer meat."

Alix cut in. "Well, what do you suggest Monsieur Harcrest?"

"Rafe," he corrected. "I suggest we get a good night's sleep. In the morning I will show these gentleman the bills of lading in my luggage that prove you, Jervis, and I are exactly what we say."

And if that doesn't work, he thought grimly, he would insist word be sent to the English ambassador in Paris. Relations between France and England were deteriorating, but, he speculated, they had not eroded to a point where the fledgling French government was ready to risk the political and economic repercussions of harming a British peer. His business operations would be exposed, and there would be a scandal, but at least Alix would be safe. It struck him that Lady Anne would be most displeased to discover the source of the fortune she was seeking to marry.

Jervis sneezed again and the room fell silent. Alix lay back against the wall, listening as Jones's congested breathing gradually slipped into a snore. Her fingers worried at the bits of dry straw covering the floor and she wished that sleep would come as easily to her. Rafe's argument made sense and he seemed so sure that the papers would get them through, but she wished wildly that they'd followed Jervis's plan. Fighting their way out seemed better than patiently waiting to die.

Rafe listened to Alix's restless stirrings, wondering that after all she'd been through she hadn't swooned or broken down in tears. Such a tough exterior for the gently bred daughter of a French aristocrat, and yet he knew she was afraid. She'd be a fool not to be, and that Alix de Rabec de La Brou was not. He wished he knew how to comfort her, to reassure her in some manner that would not ring false. He thought of the nights he'd spent before battle with his men, breaking the tension by swapping insults and bald-faced lies.

Alix heard Rafe draw closer, felt his shoulder bump against hers, then his breath warm against her neck.

"Are you really merchants?" she asked.

"Are you disappointed we're not English spies?"

"Don't be ridiculous," she retorted.

"So tell me, little Alix, are you a snob? Are you disappointed you've married beneath yourself, married a man who earns his living rather than living on what he can inherit or gamble off others?"

She inhaled sharply. "You do have an amazingly low opinion of me, Monsieur Harcrest."

"Rafe," he corrected once again.

"I've lived among enough titles to know they're no guarantee of a man's quality."

"So," he teased, "you're beginning to think I'm a man with qualities."

"Are you fishing for compliments?"

"Are you avoiding answering, Alix?"

"You are persistent."

"Is that a quality?"

"Yes," she whispered, laughter mingling with the annoyance in her voice.

"See," he said, "I knew I'd begin to grow on you."

He pulled her close, tucking her head into the crook of his shoulder. "I also make a fine pillow."

Rafe seemed so certain that everything would be all right. Alix wanted to believe him, wanted to absorb a little of his strength and confidence, she told herself as she leaned back into the cradle of his arms. "I only asked because I wanted to know if you really thought it would convince them to let us go. What you do for a living makes no difference to me," she murmured, "I still want my annulment."

He dropped a kiss on the top of her head. "Goodnight wife."

Was she a snob? she wondered. *Was* she disappointed that he wasn't a man from her class? No, she mused, there was something inherently noble about Rafe. Not just in the way he was risking his life for her, but in the way he carried himself, the proud line of his shoulders, the arrogant turn of his jaw, his ease of command. The way he swept in and tried to take charge of her, she reminded herself sternly. She shook her head, her cheek brushing against the solid wall of his chest. She was done with letting men decide the direction of her life.

His long elegant fingers curved around her hand, one finger caressing her palm. A languorous warmth purled up her arm. She felt his lips wandering across the side of her face, then capture her ear, his tongue tracing the sworls and she shivered.

"Rafe," she started.

"Ah," he chuckled, "you've finally learned to use my name."

"What do you think you're doing?" she whispered sharply.

"I thought I might demonstrate some of my other qualities."

His mouth found hers in the darkness, and his tongue slid in, toying with hers, leading it back into his mouth and claiming it for his own.

Alix struggled to free her mouth. "We are not alone."

"True," he sighed against her neck. "But when Jervis isn't on duty, I've known him to sleep through the opening shot of a battle." As if to underscore his words, a sputtering snore drifted from the corner of the storeroom.

"This isn't right. You promised you wouldn't touch me."

He hadn't meant to touch her, not in this musty storeroom, with guards at the door and Jervis sleeping several feet away. But when she'd leaned against him and he'd felt the silk of her hair and smelled the fragrance of her skin, he'd been swamped by the need to possess her.

"I promised I would try." Rafe trailed a line of kisses across her jaw, pausing at the line of her neck and settling to play at the hollow of her throat.

"You mustn't . . ." Her voice wavered as his hand slid inside her fichu, found the curve of her breast and began to massage its way to her nipple.

"Mustn't what, Alix? Touch you here?"

She moaned softly.

Rafe untied her fichu then reached behind and unloosened the laces of her dress so that his hands could roam more freely. The soft flesh of her breast filled his hand and he kneaded it gently, catching the nipple between his fingers. "Or here?"

Alix felt the night air prickle against her nipples, felt the nip of his teeth, then the warm wetness of his mouth settle around them swirling and suckling. Desire spiraled through her body, and she arched against him even as she whispered, "No."

"No?" he murmured questioningly against her breast. "It is not enough?"

His free hand caught at the hem of her dress and slid sinuously up her ankle, stopping to caress the back of her knee and the warm flesh above her garter. Her skin rippled with arousal. In the darkness it seemed as though his hands and mouth were everywhere, riding her thighs, caressing her belly, brushing the damp curls between her thighs. She was like a candle burning at both ends, Alix thought wildly, her core slowly turning molten. Then his finger dipped between her moistened folds.

Alix whimpered and Rafe caught her cries in his mouth. All she could think about were the fingers between her legs, sliding up, around and down, and his tongue in her mouth matching its rhythm. She closed her eyes and gave herself up to the sensations. Her body ached, and burned, and *needed*. In the darkness, Alix reached for Rafe, tangling in his clothes, searching for skin, and when she found him, the moans that filled her mouth were not hers alone.

Even as she knew she should pull away, demand he stop, she pressed against his hands and mouth. His finger slid more deeply inside and Alix arched against him, begging for a release she barely understood. He lifted her hips and one hand quickened the pace, while his thumb slowly, achingly teased the sensitive nub that seemed to be the volcanic peak of all her sensations. And then her passions seemed to spill over, sluicing through her body like a mad river of heat, searing beneath her skin and exploding in red stars against her closed eyelids and Alix clung to Rafe as if she were drowning. And she was drowning, she thought, drowning in the taste and feel of him, swept away from her common sense. She couldn't allow this, she wouldn't.

"Sweet, sweet Alix," he murmured against her hair, rocking her trembling body.

"This is wrong," she muttered, "I never should have let you touch me."

"No, it's not wrong," he insisted, kissing her damp forehead. "You're my wife."

"In name only," she said, fumbling for the hem of her dress in the dark.

He reached out to caress her. "You feel the attraction, too, Alix. Why fight it?

"And what is that attraction based on?" her voice quavered. "Is it fear? Is it gratitude? Is it simply the desire to bury myself in something that will take this nightmare away, even for a moment? Can you tell me that, Monsieur Harcrest, can you? And if I give myself to you, how do I know you won't abandon me as soon as we reach England? Or sooner, for that matter," she said, straining to keep her voice composed. "I don't want to be married to you. I just want to find my mother. I want my life back."

His hands fell to his sides, and he lay silent against the rough stucco wall. He didn't know what he could say. He only knew that he'd never felt such a fierce desire for a woman before. She felt it, too; he'd known it even before he felt her body surge against his as he'd given her pleasure. Rafe nearly groaned aloud when he thought of how she would respond when he came inside her. What was it about this girl? He'd agreed to this farce with every intention of giving her an annulment, hadn't he? Now every time she mentioned it, he had the irresistible urge to put her under lock and key.

She was driving him to madness, he thought, his body taut with unresolved hardness. He never should have taken things this far. The musky scent of Alix lingered on his fingers, and his erection strained uncomfortably against the fabric of his britches. He heard Anne's distaste for his touch echoing in his head, and he could well imagine her lips pursing in displeasure at the very thought of the intimacies he and Alix had shared. He could almost hear Anne's mocking voice, *"You're behaving like some randy schoolboy, Moreham."*

Chapter Eleven

❧

Alix awoke to the sounds of horses stirring impatiently in their stalls. The air was redolent with the aroma of hay, horseflesh, and manure, and as awareness of where she was returned, she snapped her body straight, coming up hard against Rafe. Her hands flew to her clothing and she found her bodice and fichu disarrayed; she flushed recalling where and how his hands had touched her. Quickly she pulled away from the circle of his arms. He made no move to hold her, and she stumbled backwards, tripping over Jervis.

Awakened, Jones floundered, issuing a string of muffled curses through the coat he had wrapped about his head, until at last, face freed, he sneezed loudly. "God's blood, I hope they come for us soon, my head feels like it's been split open and stuffed with straw." He blew his nose noisily and sniffed. "And if they're going to kill us, I hope they offer us a last meal first. I'm so hungry I'd even welcome some of that grit-filled Parisian bread."

"Well if it's going to be our last meal," Rafe said pleasantly, "I think I'd like something more substantial, perhaps a bit of eggs and some ham."

Alix shook her head, looking from one to the other. "We may be led out of here and shot, and you two are worrying about your stomachs?"

Rafe's mind was, in fact, far from breakfast, but if they were to try for an escape, he wanted Alix to remain as calm as possible.

"First things first, focus on the simple problems before throwing yourself at the larger ones."

There was a rough pounding on the door. "I certainly hope that's the ham and eggs," Jervis said.

"All right, you three step outside," a voice barked.

The door swung open and Alix threw up an arm to shade her eyes from the sudden glare of sunlight that filled the room. Rafe whispered in her ear, "Alas, not a coffee pot in sight."

That was certainly true, she thought as she stepped out into a circle of uniformed men, bayonets at the ready. Blinking and brushing bits of straw from her skirts, she assessed the results of the evening spent in the storage shed. She was stiff and dust-covered but, she reflected, at least she had fared better than Jervis. Jones's dark eyes were swollen like walnuts and his long nose was reddened and dripping. Rafe, she noted with some annoyance, looked unruffled.

"Right," he said, picking a stray bit of straw from his sleeve and turning to the earnest looking guards, "shall we go and straighten out this misunderstanding?"

The guards ignored him. "You," one of them said jerking his chin at Alix, "come with us." The guard reached for Alix and, without thinking, Rafe's fist flew up and connected with his chin. The guard went down and Rafe whirled to face the next man, but as he did so was met by the blinding pain of a rifle stock across his head. Staggering back he heard the distinct click of four rifles being cocked and Alix screaming as they dragged her struggling across the courtyard, "You bastards, you bastards!"

"Easy now, Captain, let me look at your head. Nasty bit of work, but it doesn't feel like anything's broken. Four against one, whatever were you thinking?"

Rafe, coming to, groaned. "I didn't want them to hurt Alix." He raised himself onto his elbows, ignoring the pain ricocheting through his head. "Where have they taken her? Could you see?"

"No, Captain, there's a tree and a broken cart blocking my view. She hasn't been gone too long."

The two men strained to capture any untoward noises, but all they could hear were the sounds of normal stable yard activity. A young maid stood eyeing them curiously as she tossed table scraps from her apron to a flock of noisy chickens. A stablehand wheeling a cart full of manure stared as he passed, nodding to the young soldiers who stood self-consciously shifting their feet, guns at the ready. Then the guard who had hauled Alix off reappeared—Alix at his side.

Rafe scanned her appearance anxiously. Her fichu was missing. And she wasn't meeting his eyes; she was staring above them, at his head.

"Bloody fools, you might have told him you were taking me to the privy." Glaring angrily at the guards she continued scolding. "Just *look* at what you've done! You could have killed him."

One of the guards, a young man with spotted skin, shifted his rifle uneasily. "Didn't give us a chance; crazy Englander attacked us before we could say anything."

Alix sniffed, turning her attention to Rafe. Taking a clean end of her fichu, which she'd used as an impromptu washcloth and was still holding in her hand, she began to dab gently at the bloody crease across his forehead.

"So Jervis and I played heroes to prevent them from hauling you off to the jakes?"

She bit her lip. "Apparently so. Most gallant, but not, I'm afraid, too well thought out."

Rafe laid back and closed his eyes. "Madame Harcrest, you seem to have a disconcerting effect on my most well-laid plans."

The guard who had led Alix off now cleared his throat and said gruffly, "Perhaps the gentlemen would also appreciate the opportunity to freshen up before they appear in front of the revolutionary tribunal."

Alix watched as Jervis and Rafe followed the guard across the stable yard. Wringing out her damp fichu, she attempted to smooth the lace triangle. Her hands were shaking and the fichu was filthy, smeared with Rafe's blood. She'd been so frightened when she'd seen him fall under the butt of the guard's gun. She shuddered at the notion that he might have died trying to prevent them from taking her to the privy.

Drawing the ends of the fichu across the front of her bodice, she couldn't help recalling the feel of his hands and his mouth on her breasts the night before. She shuddered again, but this time not from fear. She needed to get away from Rafe Harcrest, she told herself, as much for his safety as for her own.

Huget, the massive guard from the night before, joined them a short time later. Frowning at the lump on Rafe's head he said, "Mayor de Poix, the head of the Senlis Revolutionary Tribunal is ready to see you." Addressing the guards he added, "Make sure these English dogs don't try anything." In silence, interrupted only by the sounds of Jervis trying to clear his nose and throat, they marched across the yard and around to the front a well-kept stucco and stone house. A tri-colored flag hung over the doorway, snapping lightly in the cool morning breeze.

Huget knocked at the front door and Captain Doret opened it. "I am reporting with the prisoners, sir."

It struck Alix that they were almost like boys playing soldiers, though she well knew that this was no game. A wave of fear washed over her as strongly as when the guards had dragged her away from Rafe, but she schooled herself to remain calm. Never show people what you feel, her mother had always cautioned, it will give them too much power over you. Well then, vowed Alix, squaring her shoulders, these men would see nothing more than the face of an honest French citizen unjustly detained.

Captain Doret led them through a well-furnished vestibule and into a dining room where several people were seated around a table, enjoying their morning meal. There was an array of cold meats on a platter, a steaming tureen of eggs, and a silver mesh basket full of freshly baked breads. It was with an effort that Alix raised her eyes from the food to face the stout man in the neatly curled wig seated at the end of the table.

"Well, Doret," the man said, putting down his coffee cup, "what have you brought us this morning?"

"Mayor de Poix," Doret said saluting, "we believe these individuals may be English spies."

De Poix dabbed at his mouth with a fine linen napkin, then impatiently motioned the captain forward. "Let me see their papers."

Doret handed him a packet that Alix recognized as their identity papers, visas, passports, and marriage license.

De Poix drew a pair of spectacles from his waistcoat and adjusting them on his broad nose studied the papers carefully. He glanced up. "Tell me Anton, what was it about this threesome that aroused your suspicions. Apart from the fact that the gentleman and his servant are English?"

Doret answered smartly. "They were travelling in an expensive hired chaise at a high speed late at night. With all the aristocrats trying to smuggle funds out of the country, and reports of foreign interference, I thought it would be best if you inspected them before they were allowed to pass."

"I see," de Poix said, stroking a roll of loose skin beneath his square chin. "And did you search their coach?"

"Yes, sir, we did."

"What did you find?"

There was a pause. "Nothing suspicious, sir. But this morning they attempted to attack my men and that one"— he gestured toward Jervis—"had a knife concealed in his boot."

Alix bit back an indignant response to the captain's skewed description of the morning's events.

Doret continued. "I didn't want to disturb your family, knowing that your son had just arrived." He inclined his head toward a slim young man with fine blue eyes and a wealth of blond curls. The young man, who was wearing the red, white, and blue sash of a government official, nodded impassively.

De Poix grunted. "Well, yes, I see." And for the first time he looked directly at Rafe and Alix. "And what have you to say to these charges?"

Rafe stepped forward. "First let me apologize for the unfortunate incident with the captain's soldiers. I thought they meant to harm my wife. And, as I am sure you understand, Your Honor,"—he nodded meaningfully toward a stout woman seated to de Poix's right—"my only thought was to protect her." The lace cap atop the woman's gray curls bobbed appreciatively.

De Poix nodded and Rafe continued. "I respect the ef-

forts of your government to protect itself against its ene-
mies and quite understand the civic zeal of young Captain
Doret. However, our hurry last night was to meet a packet
in Calais that is loaded with fabrics for the English market."

Drawing an additional packet of papers from his jacket
he said, "Perhaps these receipts will put your mind at rest
that our interest in your country is purely commercial.
Should you have any further questions, may I suggest you
contact the British embassy in Paris? You will find that I
am well-known to His Lordship."

De Poix perused the additional papers. "I don't think it
will be necessary to trouble the ambassador. These seem to
be in order . . . but," he added, fixing his eyes on Rafe, "I
believe the gentleman is not telling us the whole truth."

"Indeed, citizen?" Rafe inquired, raising a brow.

The mayor gave a wheeze of laughter and waved a hand
toward Alix. "Surely she is not a purely commercial interest."

Rafe smiled. "Indeed not, though I might protest that if
anyone were guilty of a crime it would be she, for stealing
away my heart."

Alix threw a furious glance at Rafe before dropping her
lashes and wishing desperately that she could kick him in
the shins. Did the man take nothing seriously? she wondered.

De Poix gave another puff of laughter. "Spoken like a
newlywed." He turned in explanation to his seated family.
"It appears the Englishman took some time out from his es-
pionage to get married yesterday." He gestured around the
table. "Allow me to introduce my family." Nodding
proudly at the fair-haired young man he said, "This is my
son, Victor, a representative of the National Assembly, who
to our good fortune is passing through on business today;
my wife, Citizeness de Poix; and my daughter Henriette."

Waving his napkin at Doret, he said, "A fine job young sir, but I think the nation will be safe in letting them pass."

De Poix's son spoke for the first time. "I do agree father, though it will be a shame for France to lose such a lovely maid."

"Too late for your flattery young buck, she's taken." Then, encompassing the meal with a sweep of his plump hand, De Poix said, "Come, join us for breakfast, I doubt they fed you well in the stables."

Victor de Poix rose and drew out a chair to his left, smiling at Alix. Rafe guided his wife to a seat next to Henriette and took the proffered chair.

The mayor chuckled, then motioned to Doret. "Captain, why don't you take Citizen Harcrest's man around to the kitchen and see if you can find him something to eat." As the slightly flustered-looking Doret led Jervis away, de Poix said, "I would apologize for the inconvenience Citizen Harcrest, but in these troubled times, one cannot fault the guardsmen for being too careful."

Rafe inclined his head. "I fully understand."

The men fell to discussing politics as a servant brought round extra plates of food. Before Alix could put a bite of eggs into her mouth, Henriette began to ply her with questions. "So tell me," she said, her curls bobbing and her blue eyes sparkling, "is it true that in Paris the women have abandoned their stays? Are they really wearing gauze dresses you can see right through? Parading half-naked in the Tuileries? Have you been to the Tuilieries and the Place Royale? You must tell me all."

Alix tried to respond, all the while straining to catch bits and pieces of the men's conversation. They seemed to be discussing proposed legislation to change the inheritance status of émigrés.

"It's disgraceful," she heard Victor say. "Those damned aristocrats robbed the people blind for centuries and now they think they can leave the country and take their stolen wealth with them. We'll put a stop to that, you see if we don't."

Alix tilted her head toward the conversation.

"Indeed," de Poix said, motioning a servant to bring him more eggs, "what is the Assembly planning?"

Victor leaned forward. "They're talking about confiscating the land of those émigrés who refuse to return to France by the first of next year."

Alix unconsciously put a hand to her chest, thinking of the titles now hidden in Rafe's trunks. If she left the country they would become worthless.

Henriette abruptly ceased questioning Alix about which shapes of hat she favored. Dropping her voice, she whispered conspiratorially. "You must really be in love with your husband." Alix threw the young girl a startled look and Henriette giggled. "You haven't taken your eyes off him throughout this entire conversation. Not that I blame you; he's really quite handsome."

Out of the corner of her eye, Alix noticed the corner of Rafe's mouth twitch; he was eavesdropping. She ignored the question and the comment.

"How long have you been married?" Harriet persisted.

"Since yesterday."

Henriette gasped. "And you spent your wedding night in our stables? How terrible."

Alix saw Rafe turn his head ever so slightly toward their conversation. Raising her voice so that she was sure he could hear, she said, "Rest assured, citizeness, I have put all thought of it right out of my head."

Henriette clasped her hands together dramatically. "Look at those blushes, I knew it, a love match, I can always tell. You look just like my older sister did when she met her Antoine. You must tell me all the details of how you met."

Alix abandoned all hope of following Victor's descriptions of the planned legislation. Smiling at Henriette she searched for an answer that would be closest to the truth. "We met at a small private gathering and he quite swept me off my feet."

"How romantic," Henriette sighed.

Alix saw Rafe's shoulders quiver as he turned his attention back to Victor and Mayor de Poix.

Henriette sighed again. "You are so fortunate. The men here are so dull. I fear I will never meet anyone suitable. I would love to go to Paris, but mother says it is far too dangerous. After breakfast you simply must come upstairs with me. You can freshen up in my bedchamber and tell me more about the city."

Alix dabbed at her mouth. "It's an enticing offer, but I am certain that mon . . ." she caught herself. "My husband . . . will be anxious for us to be on our way."

"Oh but you can't," Henriette said. "Your postilion has gone back to Paris."

Alix turned to stare at her. "He's gone back to Paris," she repeated dumbly. Henriette nodded.

Alix struggled to keep her voice calm. "We must meet a packet that is sailing from Calais in two days. Is there a public stable that might help us make new arrangements?" Henriette shook her head.

Alix looked across the table at Rafe, desperate to catch his attention, but he was deeply absorbed in his conversation. She frowned. Perhaps they could rent horses and ride to the next town, have Rafe's and Jervis's trunks sent after. She felt a hand on her sleeve, and turned to see Henriette smiling mischievously at her. "I have an incredible idea."

"Victor," Henriette called down the table. "Victor, cease discussing your dull politics for one moment and listen to me." He stopped mid-sentence and looked at his younger sister. "The Harcrests's postilion has returned to Paris without them and they must meet a ship at Calais. You're traveling in that direction, and there's plenty of room in your carriage. Why don't you take them up with you?"

Rafe frowned. "It's a kind offer, but we wouldn't want cause your brother any inconvenience."

Victor smiled. "It would be no inconvenience at all. I'd be glad for the company. If anyone objects, I shall simply say that I doing my part to further trade between our two countries."

"We're on a rather tight schedule," Rafe persisted.

"And so am I. We can leave as soon as you're ready."

"Well, then it's settled," Henriette said smiling. She waved a hand. "Very good gentlemen, continue as you were." Turning to Alix she said, "Why don't you come upstairs with me. I have a fichu you might have and we can see what can be done about freshening your clothes while my maid dresses your hair."

Descending the stairs a half an hour later, her ears ringing from Henriette's artless chatter but her appearance considerably refreshed, Alix encountered Rafe. He'd changed his shirt and shaved, and someone had bandaged his head.

He held out a hand. "Walk with me a moment, Alix." Tucking her hand under his elbow, he led her out of the house into the de Poix's small flower garden.

It was a far cry from the elaborate gardens of Valcour, Alix thought, a simple diamond framed by low hedges with a centerpiece of rose bushes, the few remaining flowers straining to retain their petals against the stiff September breeze.

When they had walked a safe distance from the house, Rafe stopped. Drawing Alix up, he said, "I can't allow you to travel with Victor; it's far too dangerous."

Alix raised a brow. "You can't allow me?"

Rafe ran a hand through his hair, "Alix, he's a National Assembly member."

"You thought I hadn't noticed?" A slight smile curved her full lips.

"You are the most damnably frustrating woman." In more ways than one, he thought.

Alix squeezed his arm. "If you think about it, it's a perfect arrangement. No one would ever imagine an aristocrat would be riding with a government representative."

"I still don't like it."

"You and Jervis keep telling me my identity papers are a work of art and all our other papers are in perfect order. Victor's father has approved them. There shouldn't be any problem."

"But what if you accidentally let something slip?"

She tossed her head, the red and blue ribbons of Henriette's borrowed bonnet fluttering in the wind. "And what is there to let slip, citizen? I am the newly married wife of the upstanding English merchant Rafe Harcrest. A man who is willing to defend his bride's honor, even to the jakes."

He looked down on her, his brow furrowed with concern.

Alix felt an odd desire to smooth the deep indentation above his aquiline nose. "We both know this is our best chance of meeting the packet."

He started to speak, and she pressed a finger to his lips. "I can do this Rafe. I made it from Valcour to Paris and I won't founder now. Trust me."

Chapter Twelve

~~

They left Senlis shortly after breakfast. Victor de Poix's berlin was not as sleek or swift as the hired post chaise, but it was comfortable, and his status as a representative of the National Assembly ensured that they moved easily through the many checkpoints along the road to the coast. Jervis had ridden ahead to reserve food and lodging for the night and a carriage for the ride to Calais the following day. Tucked in his waistcoat was a note Victor had written placing them under his protection.

For a short time they made polite conversation, but Victor's eyes kept sliding to the leather satchel on the seat beside him. When Rafe suggested he might like to do a bit of work, Victor apologized for being such poor company and confessed he was anxious to complete a report he was preparing for one of the National Assembly's many committees.

The road to Calais was well traveled, deeply rutted by the wheels of thousands of carriages, wagons, and horses hooves. Clouds of dust billowed past the windows of the coach. Alix tried to sort through the twisted strands of emotion in her head. Each turn of the carriage wheel reminded her that she was closer to her goal of escaping France and reaching her mother. It was both exhilarating and depressing; the de La Brou titles would be safe, but there was no way of knowing when the revolutionary madness would pass and she and Madeleine could return.

What would it be like to live with her mother? Her year at Versailles was the longest they'd been together, and Alix remembered it as a time of cumbersome clothes, uncomfortable hairstyles, and relentless criticism.

"Stand up straight, shoulders back, can't you wear those stays any tighter? Glide when you walk, Alix, don't trot like a carriage horse. Hold your head still, just a gentle incline of the neck when you talk, you don't want your dinner companion dodging showers of your hair powder. Puce, puce, never wear puce Alix, it makes you look as sallow as a plucked chicken."

Madeleine, Alix reflected, had a way of making her feel like an unpolished stone under a jeweler's loupe. Her mother rarely doled out compliments. By year's end, when she'd learned to glide through the long corridors of Versailles and to avoid catching her panniers in the doorways, the criticisms eased and Alix suspected Madeleine was pleased with her progress. Surely her mother would be impressed at how she'd matured since then, and managed to escape Valcour with her father's papers?

As she stirred restlessly, her arm brushed against Rafe's and a sick feeling that had nothing to do with the rocking of the coach snaked through her stomach. How would she explain him to Madeleine? She could just picture her mother, dark eyes snapping with disapproval, tapping a slippered foot and demanding to know how on earth she could have been so foolish as to marry a complete stranger. Alix knotted her fingers together. Perhaps she and Rafe could have the thing quietly annulled and her mother would never need be told.

It might work, if nothing like what had happened last evening in the shed ever occurred again.

She could not give way, not if she wanted an annulment. And yet, there was something about Rafe, something about the warmth in his eyes, about his body. Ever since they'd left Senlis she'd tried to avoid looking at him. She knew her eyes invariably would be drawn to his hands, or his mouth, and that the memory of how he had touched her would come rushing back as vividly as if he were still holding her in his arms. He's just a man, Alexandre Charlotte, she scolded herself. It was the prospect of leaving France, and all that was familiar, that had weakened her defenses. She willed herself to turn and look at him.

He was absorbed in a book Victor had lent him; his hazel eyes moving intently along the text, a slight frown settled above his long straight nose. As always, Alix found herself wanting to smooth the worried crease. No more of that, she warned herself. She forced herself to focus instead on the bulky white bandage above his brow, a reminder of the trouble she'd brought him. He'd nearly gotten his skull caved in trying to defend her honor. Heaven knew what damage she'd caused his business. And his life, what plans had he made for his life that might be destroyed by his taking on the burden of a wife whose fortune was entailed in France?

Closing her eyes resolutely, she leaned against the side of the carriage, absorbing its rocking sway, and tried to clear her mind of Rafe, her mother, and France. Gradually, she fell into an exhausted sleep.

The rustle of Victor's papers woke her several hours later. Alix looked up and saw him sliding his work back into his satchel, closing his lap desk with a snap, and pulling out a simple silver watch from a fob beneath his waistcoat. "Goodness," he said, "it's nearly two o'clock and I've been so absorbed in my work I haven't thought whether you two might be hungry and wish to stop for lunch." Unrolling his widow, he leaned out and called to the driver. "Hercule, see if you can't find a place to stop, and we'll pull out the hamper and have a bite to eat."

Moments later, Alix heard the coachman clucking to the horses, felt the carriage slow and then stop.

"I'll pull out the hamper for you, citizen," Hercule said swinging open the door, "then see about getting some water to cool the horses down."

Hercule unstrapped a hefty basket from the back of the berlin, and put it down in a sunny spot near a streambed. Alix reached for the coarse woven blanket packed on top at the same time Rafe did, and his hand grazed hers. It felt like sparks sweeping over her skin. She stepped back so quickly she nearly stumbled

Victor unpacked the contents of the basket. There was a loaf of fresh bread and wrapped packages of cheese, pâté, olives, gherkins, and several bottles of wine.

"This is quite a feast," Alix observed.

"There are food shortages throughout the country, but my parents are concerned that I might starve." He shook his head with some embarrassment, his golden curls dancing about his shoulders in odd contrast to the intense look in his eyes.

The two men discarded their jackets and sat in shirt-sleeves and open waistcoats absorbing the warmth of the early September sun. Rafe patted a spot on the blanket close to his side and called to Alix to join him. Knowing it would seem odd if she refused, she sank down next to him, her dark skirt billowing around her.

"This cheese is delicious," Rafe said, "you must try it."

Victor smiled. "It's made in Senlis, the locals are quite proud of it."

Rafe held out a pale square of cheese. "It's rather soft, let me feed it to you." Alix had no choice but to open her mouth or seem churlish. His fingers brushed her lips, and she tasted the salt of his fingers. She had no idea what the cheese tasted like, but complimented it anyway.

As they dined, the men fell to discussing new methods of agriculture, the subject, it turned out of Victor's report to the National Assembly. Alix sipped her wine and studied the two through her lashes. Victor, with his golden curls and deep blue eyes, was quite handsome, and yet she felt no quickening of her pulse, no primal stir of attraction when she looked at him. Indeed, seated on the ground next to Rafe, he seemed somehow pale and immature.

Half-listening to the men's conversation, it struck her how little she knew about Rafe. For a cloth merchant, he seemed remarkably well-informed about large-scale farming. For that matter, she thought, flicking an ant from her skirt, during their stay at the inn, he had kept her entertained with lively discussions about literature, art, and social reforms.

Her father would have enjoyed meeting Rafe; the thought struck her with a sudden wave of guilt and sadness. David had promised her that he would make sure the comte's body was buried in a churchyard. When she returned to France, she told herself, closing her eyes to press threatening tears back into place, she'd find a way to make sure he was laid to rest beside his father and brothers in the family crypt.

She leaned back on her elbows, watching as the wind ruffled the leaves of the trees overhead, fluttering patterns of green tinged with red and gold. The seasons were changing, the gardens at Valcour would be full of the last flowers of fall, and she wouldn't be there to see it. Where would she spend the fall, she wondered, and the winter? London, she supposed, with her mother. She'd seen pictures of London in books, heard about its wide, paved streets and the odd yellow fog that hung over it like a great onion skin. She wondered if she'd like it, if it would ever feel like home.

Victor rose and began pulling on his jacket. "I'm afraid we need to be getting back on the road."

They quickly packed up the remainders of their impromptu picnic. Hercule, who had been watering the horses, strode back, hefted the basket on his shoulders and carried it to the rear of the carriage. Rafe held out a hand to help Alix back into the coach. Intent on ignoring the sensations she felt when his fingers brushed hers, she slipped on the step. Rafe caught her around the waist, and beneath her clothes she felt her body flare with desire. Get a hold of yourself, Alexandre Charlotte, she scolded herself as she regained her footing and climbed in.

It was dark when the coach pulled up in front of the inn where they had arranged to meet Jervis. A freshly painted sign featuring a red woolen liberty cap hung over the door, creaking and swaying in the evening breeze. Victor stepped down from the coach with them, watching as Rafe's trunks were carried inside. He reached out and clasped Rafe's hand. "Have a safe trip my friend."

"Are you sure you won't join us for dinner?"

Victor shook his head. "I thank you for the offer and for the pleasure of your company today, but I've promised an old schoolmate in the next town over that I would pass the night with him." He winked. "It saves the taxpayer's money, and he swears his wife is a better cook than any in chef in Paris." Then raising Alix's hand to his lips he said, "Do not let your new husband make you a stranger to France, citizeness." He turned and climbed into the berlin, the light of the carriage lanterns wavering across the red of his sash like coursing blood.

He'd been so kind, Alix thought with anguish, and yet, it was not Rafe but young men like Anton Doret and Victor de Poix who had made her an outcast in her own country. As if sensing her pain, Rafe tucked his hand under her elbow and led her into the inn.

Jervis met them inside. He looked travel-stained and tired, but wore a satisfied grin. "The inn's about full up, Captain, but I was able to get you and the missus a cozy little room on the third floor." He chuckled. "There's a wine merchant quite put out that he'll be sharing a common room with the likes of me, but lord, you should've seen the landlord's eyes pop when he seen all them flourishes and seals on Monsieur, I mean, Citizen de Poix's letter. There's a nice little fire going in the hearth and I've spoken to the kitchen maid about sending up some warm water for a bit of a wash, knowing how particular you are about your cleanliness." Jervis rubbed his long nose with his sleeve. "Though what harm a bit of dirt does a man, I'll never know. Would you be wanting something to eat, or would you rather wait? It's amazing, for all the talk of food shortages, they've got a lovely supply hereabouts."

Rafe raised a hand to interrupt Jervis's disconnected flow of information. "Jones, first tell me what you've been able to find about the *Xanthus*; is she still in port?"

Jervis's smile grew even broader, and for the first time Alix noticed he was missing several teeth in the back. "Indeed she is, Captain, and Williams is set to sail at ten o'clock tomorrow night. You and the missus can have yourselves a nice rest this evening, sleep in a bit, and then we'll all take a nice ride to Calais. I've got the carriage and a sweet foursome of bays hired and ready to go."

Rafe grinned back. "Good man, Jervis. We should be in London the day after tomorrow." He turned to look at Alix. "If it's all right with you, I'll have Jervis bring up a light supper in about an hour's time."

She nodded; her stomach's needs the farthest thing from her mind.

"So then, shall we go and inspect the wine merchant's former room?"

The stairs were narrow and crooked, but the walls and floors of the inn appeared clean and well kept. Reaching the top of the staircase, Jervis led them to the last door down the hall.

Jervis turned the key in the lock and swung the door open to reveal a small room tucked under the eaves. As he had promised a fire was burning on the hearth. A small settee and an armchair were set before the fire, a low round table between them. A colorful woven carpet covered the broad planks of the floor, and a bed was set into an alcove, draped with red and white patterned curtains. A fabric screen in the corner concealed the washstand and commode.

Alix stepped inside, Rafe following, and his presence seemed to fill the room. Even though he wasn't touching her, it seemed any direction she turned he was brushing up against her. Jervis was right, Alix thought, it was cozy, far too cozy. She glanced quickly about looking for a door that might lead to a sitting room, but found none.

"Well," Rafe said, stepping in front of the fire and rubbing his hands, "this is certainly better than last night's accommodations." He glanced at Alix and couldn't resist adding, "Though the storeroom wasn't completely without its comforts."

Alix flushed and Rafe wondered why he couldn't leave well enough alone.

"As you see, I've had your trunks brought up already, Captain. Is there anything else you might be needing?" He pulled the end of his nose. "There's a dice game on in the tap room, and I was doing rather well for myself before you arrived."

Rafe chuckled. "Go on then, you've earned a bit of fun."

As the door closed behind Jones, Rafe glanced at Alix. "I always have Jervis make sure there's plenty of hot water and clean towels waiting for me at the end of the day. If you'd like, you can wash up first before dinner arrives."

Alix nodded, as she untied the bow of the bonnet Henriette had given her. Hanging it on a hook behind the door, she went behind the screen. The water in the pitcher was warm and there was a thick bar of soap on top of the towels.

"After we dine, I'll need to check up on a few things with Jervis," Rafe called out to her. "If you'll pull an extra blanket off the bed and a pillow, I can make up a comfortable place for myself with the settee and the chair pulled together."

Alix squeezed her washcloth so suddenly a stream of water ran down the front of her chemise. You see, she told herself, he's being a perfect gentleman, indeed he had been all day. She draped the washcloth carefully over the bar at the side of the washstand, wondering why she felt an odd sting of disappointment. A wave of embarrassment swept over her. Perhaps her behavior in the shed last night had disgusted him. But when he touched her, she'd felt uncontrollably drawn to him, had been unable to think of anything but touching him back, running her hands through his hair, along the strong lines of his arms, his back.

Madeleine said a lady should always resist, particularly if she was unmarried. But they were married, she reminded herself. Alix stood, suddenly confused and unwilling to step from the behind the screen and face him.

"May I borrow your hairbrush," she asked, stalling for time.

"Tell you what, you give me a turn with the hot water before it goes cold, and I'll brush out your hair."

It was a simple request, he didn't wish to make do with cold water, and yet the thought of him so close, touching her hair worsened the chaos in her head. "By all means," she said more resolutely than she felt.

A serving maid brought in a light supper while Rafe washed. He'd thrown his waistcoat and shirt over the screen and Alix tried not to notice that if she looked at the mirror over the mantle she could see his bare chest.

She poured herself a steaming cup of coffee, willing herself not to look at him. The rich liquid scalded her tongue and she quickly put the cup down. Her eyes were drawn irresistibly back to the mirror. Mesmerized, she followed the path of the washcloth along the sculpted muscles of his arms and across his chest. Golden brown hair curled below his collarbone, wound around his nipples, tapered in a dark line down his flat stomach and disappeared into the unfastened top of his britches. Her skin felt as seared as her tongue.

She tore her gaze from the looking glass above the mirror and stirred her coffee, even though she knew the sugar had already dissolved, desperate for something to fill her hands. He stepped from behind the screen a moment later, in a fresh shirt and pale green waistcoat.

He served her a plate of supper and then served himself. They talked of nothing important as they ate, discussing things they'd seen during the day's travel, bits about their preparations for the morrow. When she thought he wasn't looking at her she studied his face. He seemed distant, his eyes dark, almost murky in their depths, and his fingers drummed imperceptibly on the table.

Rafe's restless fingers grazed the edge of his plate and dislodged his knife, which fell, clanging loudly against the tabletop. Startled, he stared as if the utensil were somehow unfamiliar. "Sorry, damnable habit my drumming; Jervis is always at me to stop." Placing his napkin on his plate, he said, "Well then, I did promise I'd brush out your hair if you'd save me some hot water. And a promise is a promise."

Like the annulment he'd told her he'd give her as soon as they reached England, he reminded himself.

He pulled the hairbrush from his trunk, wondering why he'd offered her this service. But he knew, knew that he needed to touch her in some way, if only by brushing out the tangles in her mahogany hair.

It was just hair, he told himself, as he drew the pins out and watched the rich waves cascade down her slender back. He lifted a silken hank, his fingers grazing the curve of her neck, and began to brush in long downward strokes. She leaned back, her eyes half closed, her lips slightly parted. Rafe felt a wave of pure lust wash over him and settle in his groin. He tied her hair back with a black velvet ribbon he used for his queue. "Perfect," he muttered, knowing he meant more than her hair.

"I think I'll go downstairs for a bit and check on Jervis's preparations for tomorrow," he said, tossing his jacket over his shoulders and picking up his tricorne. "You may take a nightshirt from my trunk if you'd like." He swallowed hard as an image of her lithe and nude slipping into his nightshirt rose unbidden into his head. He needed a walk, he thought, to breathe in the cool night air and clear his head. He needed to remind himself of Anne, and Elizabeth, and the life he had planned waiting for him in England.

It was dark outside, and torches had been lit along the main street of the little hamlet. Candlelight framed the windows of the houses in flickering squares of amber. Myriads of stars were scattered in the dark sky, caught up here and there in veiled wisps of clouds. Rafe strode briskly along as if he had some destination in mind.

Keep walking Harcrest, he told himself, unwittingly recalling the first time he'd seen Alix on the street in Paris. It was becoming a bad habit with him, he thought grimly, this impulsive walking. He'd walked away from his proposal to Anne and now here he was trying to walk away from Alix.

He stopped suddenly, finding himself nearly at the end of the village, the unlit darkness of trees and road looming thickly ahead. He could just make out the hazy gray shape of a kilometer post on the side of the road. Leaning against it, he pulled a cheroot out his coat pocket, lit it, and inhaled deeply.

Anne loathed cheroots, referred to them as a filthy colonial habit. Rafe puffed slowly, considering why he'd been so determined to make her his wife. She'd certainly fit the part of a countess, elegant and composed, adept at handling social situations. Even as a child, he recalled she'd been precise about her dress and manner, ever mindful of her position. A wry smile twisted his lips as the aromatic smoke curled around his head. He certainly couldn't picture the regal Lady Anne dressing in Jervis's clothes and climbing through windows.

She'd never embarrass him, never fight with him, or make his life unpredictable. Never, he thought, make his loins surge with passion, or his fingers ache to tear at her clothes and plunder the sweetness beneath them.

Cole's words haunted him: *"You don't want to wind up one of the men who spends his life avoiding his cold fish of a wife, wasting his time at his club or in the arms of his mistress, pretending the passion he's paid for is real."*

Rafe's eyes narrowed; Alix wanted him as much as he wanted her, he'd seen it in her eyes as wide and silver as the mirror she'd tried not to look at while he bathed that evening. But was the passion he felt for Alix real or simply overwhelming lust? He would never know unless he took Alix, made her his wife in more than name. And suddenly he wanted that, more urgently than anything he'd ever wanted before. He didn't know if would be worth throwing away the careful life he'd planned with Anne, only that he had to find out, now before he'd lost his chance, lost her. He ground the cheroot out, the sparks scattering beneath his boot and began walking back into the hamlet, back towards the inn.

Chapter Thirteen

❧

Lamartine fumbled in his waistcoat pocket, bringing out a thin leather pouch. The woman slouched in the doorway, her bodice hanging as slackly as her bosom, held out a broad hand expectantly. Shaking loose three coins, he thrust them at her. The woman gave him a tired look and shook her head. "Robbery, highway robbery," he muttered as he shook out two more coins and dropped the lot into her reddened palm.

Tucking the pouch back into his pocket, he straightened his bagwig and made his way down the twisting stairs to the street. He'd spent far too much time in Paris, with far too little to show for it. The street urchins had filled his ears with stories of former aristocrats selling their belongings, even their clothes on the streets, but they'd brought him nothing, not a whisper of where the comte's daughter had gone. During the long days of waiting, it had amused him to imagine that if Alix wasn't in prison, then she'd doubt-

less discover she had more to sell in the streets than her
fineries.

He patted his coat to make sure the letter he'd so carefully crafted was still safely tucked in his pocket. Madame
la Comtesse de La Brou would find it most convincing, he
thought. And as to why the comte had decided to deed his
lands to his faithful steward, well there would be plenty of
time to craft that story during the passage to England.

Rafe stood framed in the doorway, his eyes glittering and
his hair windswept from his walk. Alix, who'd been sitting
by the fire, sprang to her feet, eyes wide, mouth dry with
fear, certain from the urgency in his face that something
terrible must be following on his heels.

"I've been discovered," she said sharply, her mind
clutching her worst fear. What could have gone wrong?
Had she said something to Victor that made him suspicious? Perhaps someone had recognized her? Or was it the
papers? The forgeries had held up under so many inspec-
tions she'd begun to believe Rafe's assurances they were
perfect. She turned away so Rafe wouldn't see her terror;
she'd been so close to deliverance, she'd thought she was
safe. How much time did she have? Where could she go?
Trying to conceal the tremor in her voice she said, "You've
done enough for me, more than enough."

In a single stride he was behind her, close. "But I
haven't, Alix, not nearly enough." And he drew her around
and against his chest, his lips finding hers in a burning kiss.

She tried to pull away from him, "You and Jervis must
go, *now* . . . tonight."

His hands tangled in her hair, and he pulled her head
back to look at him. "I'm not leaving you Alix, not
tonight," he whispered, "maybe not ever."

She opened her mouth to protest and felt his tongue. She
turned her head and he followed, his body impelled more

closely against hers. "There's no need for you to be caught up in this," she whispered, and struggled again to free herself.

His hands left her hair, trailed her face sliding down her neck and shoulder, taking her fichu with them. "But I am caught up in this," he whispered hoarsely, "caught up in you."

Alix heard the triangle of lace *shush* to the floor behind her, heard a log pop in the fire, and stared up at Rafe in a haze of confusion. "The guard?" she asked, her voice rising in a question.

"No guard, Alix, just you and me."

"I don't understand."

"I don't understand either," he said. "I just know that you're all that I think about. I can't face another minute in a room, or a carriage, or a shed, beside you without touching you. I want you Alix. I *need* you."

He pressed himself hard against her and the heat of his body seemed to sear through her clothes. She felt her senses flare in response, her clothes suddenly seemed hot and heavy, the layers of petticoats and wool coarse and cumbersome. And she knew that she needed him, with a raw aching need that burned away all thoughts of her father, Valcour, her mother, and England. She was tired of thinking, so tired of worrying. She wanted this moment; she wanted *him*.

With an anguished sigh, she reached for him. Rafe's arms tightened around her and he murmured her name, trailing hot wet kisses across her eyes, her nose, her mouth, down the curve of her jaw into the hollow of her neck. His knee pushed between her skirts, lifting her hips against his, and his body impelled her against the wall. His tongue dipped and played along her collarbone, swirling in the hollows, his teeth lightly nipping at the delicate skin.

She closed her eyes and leaned against the cool plaster,

felt his hair brush against her chin as his mouth traveled lower. Soft fingers clasped her breast, a tongue rasped and suckled at her nipple, and a fierce wave of passion shivered through her, breaking against a thousand heightened nerve endings.

Alix didn't know if she was waking from a nightmare or walking into a dream, and she didn't care. She felt his hands working at the ties of her gown, easing it down off her shoulders, lifting her arms out of the sleeves until it fell, pooling around her knees. And then his deft fingers were at the satin laces of her chemise pulling loose the ribbons, unfastening the tapes that held it over her shoulders. The rough plaster of the wall bumped against the bones of her back as the chemise caught around her hips.

Rafe pulled her close, the thin linen of her chemise tangling around her waist, the hard shape of his erection pressed against her thigh. Its pulsing length frightened her and a soft whimper escaped her. A whimper that turned to a moan as he began to move against her, rubbing gently against the liquid ache that flooded her. Instinctively she rose to meet him, wrapping one slim thigh around his long muscular one, drawing him closer.

His breath caught against her neck. "And I thought you might not want me," he murmured. Alix moved against him and he caught her hips. "Oh, no, my little hoyden, you've rushed me into any number of things since I've met you, but not this." Rafe's arm slid to her knees and he swept her up against his chest and carried her to the bed. Alix, still with her eyes closed, felt the drapes brush against her face and flutter across her body as he laid her against the pillows.

"Open your eyes, Alix," he commanded huskily. "We'll do this together, with our eyes wide open." Alix's eyes fluttered open, gray and smoky with passion. She watched as he removed his waistcoat, untied his stock and lifted his shirt over his head, loosening his queue. Strands of gold glinted in the tawny hair that tumbled across his face and in the fine mat that curled across his chest, undulating in a chestnut V down the muscles of his belly and continuing lower. As if in tune with her eyes and thoughts, his fine long hands reached down unfastened his britches and slid them and his linen drawers away. Alix stared at the evidence of his desire that jutted thickly from its nest of dark gold hair.

He seemed impossibly large; she'd heard that it could hurt, that she would tear, but at this moment, with the exquisite sensations roiling through her body, pain seemed impossible. And besides, she thought boldly, she'd had so much pain already, how could this possibly compare? Alix raised her hands to draw him down. And then he was over her, his hands and mouth resuming their earlier explorations. He caught her breasts in his hands, their lush curves spilling between his fingers. His kisses spiraled up and around, tracing a heated path to her nipples. Her breath caught when she felt his mouth latch on to the sensitive tip of her breast, and she moaned softly as he suckled.

She knew brief moments of sanity when he lifted his head and the cool air drifted across her fevered skin. She shouldn't be doing this, giving herself to this man who had a legal right to her body, but had made no commitment to her soul. And then she felt his warm breath as he descended to take her other breast and the whirl of sensations that followed the path of his tongue and she arched upward so that his mouth could find her nipple sooner.

She heard a growl of pleasure low in his throat and then he raised his body and Alix once again felt the cool clarity of the night air. She felt a tug as he pulled her chemise down to her hips; the soft fabric draped between her legs and she wondered for a brief moment whether he might stop, if she might stop him. He sank back and began to nip and kiss the skin along her rib cage, at the same time she felt his hand begin to move along her leg, tracing the contours of her calf, tickling the back of her knee and then caressing her thigh. His long fingers prowled the skin of her inner thigh, closer and closer to the damp curls between her legs.

Alix moaned and shifted her hips, restlessly tense with desire. She felt his tongue dip below the fabric now bunched at her hips, at the same time his fingers found her moist folds. His fingers moved purposely, and she began to throb with need. Instinctively, she began to rock her hips, upward towards his hand. He obliged by sliding his finger deep within her. She moaned again, then whimpered as he withdrew his finger and stroked her sensitive nub.

Alix clenched at the sheets as her hips moved faster and tremors began to seize her skin, her body, her core. When she felt his mouth close around her nipple, and his finger thrust deep within her, she arched a final time, overwhelmed by the sensations that fizzed like champagne bubbles beneath her skin.

She sank back into the bed, unable to think, unable to move, limp with the pleasure. Rafe kissed her gently and she looked into his eyes, glowing like gypsy fires in the half-darkness of the alcove.

"Alix," he whispered. "I want to finish what we've started. I need to finish. I need to come inside you."

She shivered at the passion in his voice, at the implications of his words, at the ache that still burned deep and low between her thighs. Tomorrow she would worry about what it all meant. Tonight she didn't want to think anymore; she wanted him, not just his touch, but the sweet oblivion as well.

"Come," she murmured back. He stripped away her crumpled chemise and then his mouth found hers. She felt her senses begin to swim, as his body covered hers, the fur of his chest teasing and warm against her breasts. Alix wrapped her arms around Rafe, needing to feel him close, needing to explore what he was offering. She scattered kisses along his face, nibbled at his ears, teased his neck with her tongue. Then, growing braver, she traced the shapes of his back, his ribs, and his waist, her hands surprised to find the skin covering his lithe muscles so soft. Her fingers fluttered tentatively toward his flanks.

She felt his hips shift, nudge her thighs apart. Then she felt the head of his erection hot against her thigh. She felt him reach down and position himself between her slick folds, felt him nudge his thickness forward. She rocked her hips slowly wanting to feel him, but frightened. She felt him slide farther in. It was good; it was what she wanted. She arched up, felt him press deeper, then felt the stinging shock of pain.

Rafe smoothed the damp hair back from her brow and kissed the tears forming in her eyes. "Only this bit of pain, sweetheart, then it will be better." He stroked her breasts, teasing her nipples with the rough pad of his thumb, and desire set her hips in motion. "That's it Alix," he breathed, "open for me."

Rafe felt her slick and tight and he shuddered. He wanted nothing more than to plunge deeply inside her and ride her until the dark passion that roiled in his blood was exhausted. But he wouldn't hurt her. She was so giving, so trusting. A heady mix of power and protectiveness pulsed with the desire coursing through his veins.

He slid his hands down around the cheeks of her bottom, kneading encouragingly as he pushed himself inexorably deeper. She moved her hips tentatively upward and he pushed again until at last he felt her heat encompass the length of his throbbing member.

She was his, he thought triumphantly, the unique treasure he had found. He raised himself slightly to see the curves of her body, slick with sweat, her skin flushed. Alix's eyes were closed and her bottom lip was caught between her teeth. He began to move his hips slowly, determined to see her gray eyes open and filled with the same smoky passion he'd seen when he'd pleasured her with his hand. He saw her teeth lose their grip, saw the tip of her tongue leave her plush lower lip, and he began to move. Slowly at first, easing himself in and out, allowing her tender flesh to adapt to his fullness. He felt the tension in her body ebb, and her hips began to move to his seductive rhythm. He began to thrust faster, then faster and it was his undoing. He couldn't help himself, he was losing himself in her heat, and her wetness, and the music of her soft moans.

Alix's eyes flew open, locking with Rafe's as he reared back and plunged. He needed her, needed to bury himself deep inside her. He felt his body surge and he no longer knew where his body ended and hers began. Alix's arms and thighs wrapped tightly around him as they climaxed together, their bodies shuddering as if absorbing the aftershocks of an earthquake.

They lay together afterwards in a musky tangle of limbs, unspeaking. Rafe rolled off Alix, and pulled her close to his side, and she leaned her head against his chest, their breath mingling in shattered gasps. He wrapped the coverlet around them, and they nestled in the alcove, watching the firelight flicker behind the red draperies of the bed.

Towards morning, Rafe awoke, strangely pleased to find Alix's arm thrown across his chest, one slim leg draped across his. Beyond the curtains the room was gray and cold, the fire just a memory of smoldering coals. But inside the air was still redolent with the heavy warmth of their lovemaking. Rafe felt himself stirring against Alix's thigh. He smiled wryly. Last night had not cured his passion for the little hoyden.

He turned, running a finger along the underside of her arm until he reached the curve of her breast. Gently he traced the rounded shape pressed against his chest, watching with pleasure as her nipple stiffened at his touch. Her hips moved unconsciously against him and he swept his hand down to cup the cheeks of her bottom.

Rolling her onto her back, he kissed her neck, savoring the taste of her skin. He felt her arms go around him as she roused to his touch, and he heard her whisper, "Again?"

"Are you too sore, sweetheart?" he asked, concerned that she might not be ready for him so soon. He felt her shake her head, no, then felt her tongue flicker at his ear. He chuckled softly in his throat, as her hands slid down his back and fluttered tentatively on his buttocks. She was learning fast, and the knowledge that her passion had only been whetted by their first encounter was a powerful aphrodisiac.

He slid his hands back up her flanks to cup her breasts and took turns suckling at each. With his teeth he tugged gently, enjoying her shudders of pleasure. It struck him, as he trailed kisses along her abdomen, stopping to swirl and dip his tongue into her navel, that he wanted very much to give Alix pleasure, wanted to brand her with his touch the way she had branded him. He ran his tongue along the bones of her hip, then traced their gentle decline to the dark curls between her legs. She gasped and tried to sit up.

He looked up from between her thighs, to see her face flushed and embarrassed.

"It's not right," she whispered hoarsely, "you shouldn't."

"Trust me Alix," he said, "it's very right."

She lay back down, but he felt her tremble. Sliding her thighs apart, he lowered his head, inhaling the fragrance of her arousal. His mouth meandered along her inner thighs, until he found her heated core. His tongue dipped and probed her moist folds, then his lips fastened around her most sensitive flesh and he suckled gently.

Alix arched and shuddered against him, sharp cries caught tight in her throat. It was too much, it was not enough, her mind screamed as waves of sensations arced through her body. "I need, I need," she murmured and he obliged, thrusting deep within her, filling her with his heat, riding her hard over the edge of her climax and falling with her into sweet release.

He fell limply against her, and she stroked the damp tendrils of his hair.

"I'm too heavy for you," he said. But he wasn't, she thought wonderingly, and she held him close. She'd supposed she ought to feel regret for what she'd done; no doubt that would come later. But strangely, at this moment she felt more at peace than she had in months.

Alix caressed the sinews of Rafe's back and shoulders. His breathing slowed, and she felt him soften within her. An image of a tapestry that hung in her father's home came to her mind, a virgin taming a unicorn. She smiled into Rafe's hair, perhaps it was just a young girl's fancy, but that was how she felt, as if she had tamed some powerful, magical beast.

Chapter Fourteen

❧

There was a knock on the door, a pause, and then the sound of heavy boots clomping across the planked floor. "When I said you might sleep in, I never thought you'd be keeping London society hours. Lord a'mercy, it's nearly afternoon," Jervis's voice scolded.

There was a thump, a slosh, and a rattle, followed by a long silence and a low whistle as Jones apparently absorbed what had taken place within the curtained alcove. "I'll just be leaving some water for washing and some coffee. . . . But," he added, raising his voice, "if anyone here wants to be reaching Calais, they best get moving."

As soon as the door closed behind him, Rafe rose and threw open the window shutters, flooding the room with sunlight. "Up you go! We've got a ship to catch and a snappy little carriage just waiting to go. Shall I pour you some coffee while you dress?"

He was disgustingly cheerful.

Alix had never been a morning person. She winced at

the soreness between her legs and groaned an affirmative. Then, struck by a concern that had been rattling about her head she called out to him, "Can you send someone up to help me with my stays? After our last encounter with the National Guard, I've been thinking it might be best if I wore them, rather than leaving them lying about in your trunk."

"Slip on your chemise sleepyhead, and I'll lace you up." He couldn't resist adding, "Don't worry, I've had some practice with these things."

"I'll just bet," she muttered under her breath.

"What's that? Oh—you'd be *delighted* to have my help. Well then, let's get a move on."

He was outrageously blithe. And actually, Alix thought, as she slipped his nightshirt off and scrambled into her chemise, she would not be delighted to have his help. It was one thing to be swept up in the passion of the night, but in the bright light of day, she felt strangely self-conscious.

"I'd really prefer to have a maid sent up," she said as she handed his nightshirt out through the bed drapes.

"Coward," he chuckled. "This from a maid who paraded about Paris in Jervis's britches . . . Unless," he added with a devilish grin, "you've decided you don't trust yourself in a state of near undress alone in a room with me."

"Fine," she replied through gritted teeth. She climbed out of the alcove, thinking it was clear *he* felt no discomfort around *her*. Had she likened him to a unicorn last night? Well, this morning, clad only in buff-colored britches, he seemed more like a preening peacock. Turning her back to him she said, "You may lace me up."

Rafe handed her the stays. Holding them over her breasts, she inhaled deeply as she felt him begin to pull the satin ribbons tightly together.

"I think you've put on a bit of weight my dear," he said

as he tugged on the laces. She gasped sharply and he added, "Not that I mind. I like a woman with a well-rounded figure."

She spun around and he eyed the fullness of her breasts pressed up high by the tight corset admiringly. Ignoring him as best she could, she said coolly, "My dress, if you please."

He handed it to her and she slipped it over her head, turning again so he could lace up the back. He held out her stockings and garters, frowning with mock seriousness. "Do you think you'll need any help with these?"

Snatching them from his hand, she snapped, "Didn't you say something about coffee?"

"Your wish is my command sweetheart," he replied with a mock bow.

Rafe's cheerful mood continued on the ride to Calais. Alix closed her eyes and pretended to sleep, but her mind was far from restful. He seemed to take the fact that they'd made love as his due, but it was turning her world upside down. Of course, she thought to herself, he probably made love to women all the time. Why, for all she knew, he had scores of women strewn between Paris and London.

What could she have been thinking, she asked herself repeatedly. And each time the answer came back the same. She hadn't been thinking, she'd simply let herself feel; but what now? *We'll go into this with our eyes open*, he'd said last night. What had he meant by that? Had he been trying to tell her it was a moment of passion or something more?

Alix fluttered her eyes open and peeked at him. Rafe kissed the top of her head, smiling. "Go back to sleep sweetheart, we've another hour to go."

They'd consummated the marriage. Did that mean he would expect her to stay with him when they arrived in England? She hadn't thought about staying with Rafe. She hadn't allowed herself to think about it, and now, truth be told, she didn't know. She did know that she'd felt drawn to him since the first moment they'd met and that last night lying in his arms had felt wonderful and right.

Alix tossed and turned in the coach seat, and when Rafe put out a hand to calm her, she allowed herself to imagine life with him, the wife of a simple, but clearly comfortable cloth merchant. It would be different from marriage among the nobility, she thought, simpler. It wouldn't be a contract between families for the purpose of begetting suitable heirs, it would be a friendship, a partnership. She smiled as she thought of their night together. It would be a marriage without separate beds or separate homes, a union based on understanding and trust.

They reached Calais toward late afternoon, and when Rafe discovered Alix had never been to a seaport, much less traveled onboard ship, he insisted that she walk with him about the town. He bought her a licorice water and tucking her hand under his arm, strolled with along the streets leading down to the waterfront. There was a cool breeze and a tang of salt in the air and Alix found herself relaxing in spite of her concerns about the days ahead.

She was savoring the last sweet taste of her drink when Rafe suddenly stopped in front of a small jewelry shop. "Let's step in here for a moment," he said. Feeling as awkward as if he'd led her into a corset shop, Alix wandered a bit away from him admiring the shop's wares while he conversed in low tones with the jeweler. The jeweler brought out a tray of thin gold chains and Rafe selected and paid for one

As soon as they stepped outside the shop, he pressed a soft leather sack she knew contained the chain into her hand. "I wouldn't want you to lose your wedding band since it's much to large for your hand, so I thought you might keep it on this."

Alix thanked him, threading the gold chain through the massive signet ring. She lifted her hair so he could fasten it round her neck. As the ring settled smooth and cool between her breasts, she found herself wishing he had said something more. Was he simply trying to prevent her from losing a valuable family heirloom or trying to tell her something else?

Alexandre Charlotte, you're behaving like a feather-headed woman, she heard her father's voice say in her head. You've given him your body and now you're offering him your heart, she scolded herself as they turned on to a much broader street filled with the traffic of wagons and carriages. She needed to take things slowly and carefully, to stop trying to read something into his every word and gesture. Surely then, she told herself, if she kept her eyes open, she would understand what she needed to do.

As they reached the docks, the sights, sounds, and smells of Calais overwhelmed her internal debate. Piled high all around were containers of every size and kind imaginable, barrels, crates, urns, canvas-wrapped bundles, and trunks. Standing about them, lifting, loading, and arguing were an amazing assortment of people: burly fishwives with baskets on their head; ragged sailors with woolen caps; officers in glittering uniforms; a group of dusky-skinned men in crisp white turbans.

Countless aromas competed for attention: salt water and rotting fish; fresh cut timber and tar; spices and sun-dried horse droppings. And just beyond the wharves, a sea of masts and square-rigged sails, flapping and swaying in the wind. Rafe, his eyes as sparkling as the sun on the waves, raised his voice above the din to point out the different types of ships lying at anchor. His enthusiasm was infectious, and Alix found herself captivated by his descriptions of barques, brigs and snows, topsails and mainsails, mizzenmasts and jibs.

She turned to him smiling. "Rafe Harcrest, it's wonderful, but I'm sure I'll never be able to keep them all straight. Just tell me which one is the *Xanthus*."

He pointed. "It's that three-masted barque there with the British flag, the one with all its sails furled except the triangular after sail." Alix squinted. "It's right between the four-masted barque flying the white flag with the red cross of Malta, and the ship that's having its masts repaired. See that boat loaded with the long timbers tied up next to it?"

Alix cupped her hands over her eyes and looked again where he was pointing. "I see it. It looks so much smaller than the other ships," she said, a note of doubt creeping into her voice.

"Smaller, but just as safe and faster. Williams is a fine captain, been sailing since he was a cabin boy. Nowadays he mostly delivers cargo and mail between England and France. He doesn't usually take passengers, but we've known each other for a long time. He usually finds a space for me. But I warn you, it won't be luxurious."

Alix eyed the ship skeptically. "Just so long as it gets us to England without swimming."

Later that evening, just after sunset, Captain Williams hung a series of ball lights from the mainmast, signaling that he was making ready to leave, and they should come aboard. A longboat rowed them out to the *Xanthus*, making its way carefully between the other ships swaying back and forth at their moorings. When they reached the ship a sailor, his hair tucked up in a dark woolen cap, leaned down and called, "Beggin' your pardon my lord, would her ladyship be using a ladder or would she like the chair?"

As she pretended to listen to Rafe's translation of the English into French, Alix pondered which would be worse, to be raised by a series of ropes fastened to a chair up and over the side of the ship, or to brave the rope ladder fastened to its side. Concluding that with the ladder, her fate would at least be in her own hands, she answered Rafe.

He cocked an eyebrow, murmuring softly. "I should have known you'd choose the hard way. You go first and I'll follow in case you should find yourself in need of assistance."

Alix didn't respond, but as she clutched the thick rope sides of the ladder, her skirts billowing out past the thin wooden planks, she found it reassuring to know that Rafe was there to catch her if she fell.

When they were all safely on deck, she saw that half the crew was clambering about the rigging, loosening the huge triangular sails so that they could catch the wind. The captain inclined his head. "If you like my lord, there's a nice spot near the stern where you and her ladyship can watch us prepare to sail."

Rafe nodded, smiling. "Don't worry, Captain, we'll stay out of the crew's way."

As they stood watching the great sails fill with wind, Jervis sauntered up. Nodding at Alix, he turned smiling to Rafe and said in English. "Well my lord, it looks like we're on our way." He inhaled, his long nose almost seeming to twitch. "Never thought I'd be so pleased to smell salt air. The wind seems to be blowing in the right direction. Looks like I'll be raising a pint in England tomorrow."

Rafe laughed. "You've earned it, my friend, but I've a few more things for you to do before you wander off to a tavern."

Jervis nodded. "Will you be wanting me to tell Ferguson to get off his starchy arse and open up the house in town, or will your lordship be heading straight for the hall?"

"I think we'll stay in town for a bit." He inclined his

head slightly towards Alix. "I daresay her ladyship will require more than a traveling gown."

Studying the activity in the rigging above, Jervis said, "You told her yet that you're a tad above an English silk merchant?"

"I'm waiting for the right time."

Jervis chuckled. "I'm thinking you'd better find it soon, my lord, or you'll have your own French rebellion on hand."

The ship began to come around and the first mate strode up to them, doffing his woolen cap. "Pardon my lord, but the captain has asked me to let you know your cabin is ready and to inquire whether there will be anything further you or her ladyship might need."

Rafe turned to translate to Alix. Though her eyes had been fixed on the flickering lights of Calais for much of Rafe and Jervis's conversation, she hadn't missed a word. Nor had she missed the mate's deferential manner toward Rafe and his reference toward them both as lord and lady. It was with an effort that she kept her face blank as she assured Rafe that she was quite comfortable for the moment.

Answers to odd questions she'd been too preoccupied to ask before tumbled like dominoes in her mind: how a simple merchant could afford a single room in the crowded inns of Paris, or a post-chaise; how he had been able to reserve passage on a packet and seem so certain that the captain would wait for them. Various comments Rafe had made came flooding back to her. His assurance that he was well-known to the ambassador in London, his reference to "people in our position." Her stomach lurched as she recalled his explanation of why it was imperative that they marry to avoid scandal. *"Your mother isn't the only one acquainted with Lady Melbourne. She and my stepmother share a passion for roses and gossip."* Merchants' stepmothers didn't associate with duchesses.

Alix felt an almost hysterical urge to laugh. Here she'd spent the day wondering what her life might be like married to a simple English cloth merchant when she was married to an English lord. But the laughter stuck in her throat. She didn't have to imagine what her life would be like, she knew exactly what it would be. Indeed, Rafe had told her already; he'd set her up with a suitable allowance and she could chose whether she would like to live in the country or in town.

Just like her parents, they would lead discretely separate lives.

Her hand closed on her corseted chest as she thought of the titles sewn into her stays. If what Victor had said was true, that the National Assembly was planning to confiscate the land of those émigrés who refused to return to France by year's end, then she and her mother would be nearly penniless. She felt light-headed. She supposed she should be pleased with the way things had turned out; she'd stumbled into the perfect marriage of convenience. Wouldn't her father have been delighted? She could almost hear his laughter in the flapping of the shrouds.

A reason for their lovemaking she hadn't considered before now occurred to her. Rafe had wanted to avoid a scandal. *"I've worked hard to ensure Elizabeth a bright future on the marriage mart,"* he'd said. Then he'd given her his word as an English gentleman that she could have an annulment. Well, she thought, her stomach twisting, he'd found a neat way of keeping his word and getting what he wanted. He must have known that it would be difficult for an English lord to gain an annulment, and that even if the courts had granted it, the scandal would have been worse than any Lady Melbourne could have created on her behalf. So to make certain the marriage would stick, he'd consummated it. Alix thought about how wild he'd seemed when he'd returned to the inn last night. God, he must have been desperate to have the thing done before they reached England.

And she'd been desperate for him.

Alix bit her lower lip; she'd been a fool. Even if his motives hadn't been as devious as she was thinking, he'd lied to her and misled her. She wasn't sure what, if anything, she could trust about him anymore. She thought of the silver hairbrush with the *M* engraved on the back and fought back another wave of hysterical laughter. Good lord, she didn't even know if Rafe Harcrest was truly his name.

Rafe touched Alix's shoulder and smiled down at her. "Look at those shrouds fill with wind, watch how she swans about, Alix. We're on our way home." Alix stumbled to the side of the ship, cast a final look at the lights of Calais and vomited.

Chapter Fifteen

Alix closed her eyes tightly, listening to the hiss and splatter of the sea against the planked walls of the cabin, trying to ignore the pitch and roll of the ship. Rafe and Jervis were arguing over the best remedies for seasickness, Rafe insisting on champagne and sea biscuits, Jervis on a cold mug of seawater. She waved them both weakly away, fervently believing that an empty stomach would be the best cure of all.

The ship was noisy and Alix found herself straining to identify every squeak and thump, every shouted command, in an effort to reassure herself that the *Xanthus* was not in imminent danger of sinking. Curled up in a tight ball on the bunk, her back against the planks and her hands braced against the frame, she eyed the cabin. It was a cramped space off the officers' mess and smelled heavily of tar and broiled fish. A single lantern hung from the beamed ceiling, its light swaying over the two narrow bunks that hung from the far wall. Her stomach began to rise. It seemed even the rhythm of the waves matched the shifting pattern of questions in her mind—stay or go, stay or go. He'd said they would do this together, with their eyes wide open, but he hadn't been open about anything. She'd been a fool, Alix thought, as she closed her eyes, leaned over the side of the bunk and heaved.

But her stomach it seemed was as empty as her mind was of answers. Finally, worn out by illness and worry, she drifted off to sleep.

Toward morning she was awakened by the clatter of the officers taking their breakfast in the mess. She smelled coffee and onions, and her stomach rolled. Deciding not to attempt sitting up just yet, she lay back and listened to the voices conversing in English. Such a foreign sound, she thought, before recalling that she was the foreigner now.

Rafe entered the cabin, a steaming mug in one hand and a biscuit in the other. Leaning against the door, he surveyed her carefully. "You're looking better."

"Liar," she said flatly, "even without a mirror, I know I must look a wreck."

He grinned. "Well then, a bit less green around the edges. I've brought you some tea. Drink it down like a good girl, and then I'll take you up on deck. The fresh air will do you good, and there's something I want you to see."

Alix sipped the tea and tentatively nibbled on the biscuit, avoiding Rafe's watchful eye. She was angry and confused, yet his concern made her feel vulnerable. She didn't need Rafe Harcrest to take care of her, she reminded herself. She put the mug and half-finished biscuit on the railed desk. Lifting her chin resolutely, she said, "Lead on."

Bracing her feet carefully against the sway of the ship, Alix followed Rafe through the narrow companionway and up onto the deck. He was right, she thought, as he led her back to where they had stood the previous night. Though the air was cold and damp with the promise of rain, it felt good. She could almost feel her color returning. The ship was fully rigged with three levels of sails and they bellied out, filled with wind. Two sailors, their pants rolled up about their knees and their bare feet swinging, sat high among the spars.

Rafe followed her glance upward and smiled. "They've just finished adjusting the sails. The winds and the current have been with us, we're making good progress.

"Look," he said, gesturing toward the horizon, "you can see the coast of England."

Alix looked to where Rafe was pointing and saw in the distance a jagged line of white cliffs barely visible through the early morning fog. As the ship cut through the waves, Rafe stood by her side pointing out Shakespeare's Cliffs and other harbingers of Dover. He turned toward her and tucked a loose strand of hair behind her ear, grazing her cheek with his finger. "If you'd like, next summer I'll bring you back down the coast, show you some of the little villages. Sea bathing's becoming quite the thing."

Alix nodded, but made no answer, knowing there would be no such trip.

Within two hours they reached Dover. Alix slipped on her cloak and tied the ribbons of her bonnet, feeling somewhat dazed that her journey from Valcour was nearly at an end. She stood on the deck watching as the crew clambered about the masts like a ragged pack of monkeys, lowering the sails, and binding them loosely to the spars. There was a great clanking of chains and a splash as the *Xanthus*'s massive anchor was lowered. The crew began preparing the longboats that would take them to shore.

"Should I prepare a chair to lower her ladyship, or will she descend by the ladder?" the captain asked Rafe.

"Her ladyship will take the chair," he answered firmly. Then, turning to Alix, he translated. "The captain wishes you to take chair down to the longboat."

Alix concealed her annoyance. Her husband, it appeared, couldn't be trusted to tell even the simplest truths.

The chair swayed precipitously as they lowered her down to the longboat and Alix clutched the arms, her knuckles showing white, as she inwardly cursed Rafe's high-handedness.

They rowed through a heavy mist to reach the wharf and, as Rafe helped Alix up, he explained that they would stop at a little inn just up the street for some tea while Jervis arranged for a coach to take them up to London. As they walked, the mist began to turn to drizzle and Alix tugged her cloak more closely about her. Glancing about the busy streets she saw others do the same, men pulling their hats more firmly down around their ears, ladies with umbrellas opening them and those without drawing their shawls around their heads. Rafe pointed out the sign for the inn, just as the drizzle turned to a steady driving rain.

The hem of Alix's skirt became sodden from the grimy water sluicing past her along the cobblestones. She watched enviously as people ducked into the doorways of their homes, or climbed hastily into the their carriages, wondering if it was possible for her to look or feel any more bedraggled. As if in answer, two elegantly clad women with a small boy in tow dashed into a doorway. Casting a charming smile at Alix, the little boy quickly turned and stamped his foot in a puddle, splattering the front of her skirt with mud.

"Oh, darling, look what you've done to your stockings," she heard one of the women fuss, as the door closed behind them.

Rafe glanced down at Alix's once-smart traveling gown. "It seems we'll need to visit a seamstress as soon as we reach London," he said reassuringly. "But for now, let's see if we can't get you warm and dry. As luck will have it, this is our destination." He held open the inn door through which the women and the boy had passed.

The walls inside were white, the ceiling beams low and darkened by decades of smoke. A fire burned in the large stone hearth and groups of people sat around tables covered in good linen, talking and laughing over plates of food. Rafe whispered in her ear, "This place is famous for its scones, people come from London just to try them. I'll make certain they have a plate waiting with our tea."

As she surveyed the room, it struck Alix that the customers seemed more upscale than she would have expected in a busy seaport. Though there were a number of men who looked to be sea captains and merchants, there were a quite a few more dressed in the fine wool and silks of the quality. Groups of tastefully clad women, who appeared fresh from a day's shopping, chatted over tea, exclaiming over the contents of prettily wrapped parcels.

Rafe cast a worried look at Alix, then at the dining room, then back to Alix, as if noticing for the first time how truly travel-worn her gown appeared. He hadn't seen any familiar faces among the shoppers, but that didn't mean he hadn't been recognized. This was not the way he wanted society to meet his bride, he reflected grimly. "I'll see if I can't arrange for a private dining room for us," he said.

He's embarrassed to be seen with me, Alix thought as Rafe stepped away to speak with the innkeeper. She found herself wishing she could disappear between the cracks of the wide planked floors. Even the serving girls, in their crisp white aprons and mobcaps looked more reputable than she.

"Sweetheart, you may have your soldiers after you've had your tea."

"But I want them now," Alix heard a child whine. She turned and saw the little boy who'd splashed her staring defiantly at a heavy-set blonde in a red brocade gown that was too formal for afternoon.

"After tea, dear," the woman cooed in a tone of strained sweetness.

"Now!" the boy demanded in a voice that threatened to become louder.

The woman glanced around with some embarrassment to see who might be listening to the exchange and as she did so, her eye fell on Alix. She studied Alix briefly then dismissed her with a sniff that suggested a disreputable odor had somehow made its way across the dining room.

The woman turned back to the boy and Alix heard her say, "Very well sweetiekins, you may have your soldiers, there's a good boy; now let mother and Auntie Harriet enjoy their tea." She cast another look about then demanded in a piercing tone, "Where is the serving woman with our tea?"

A young girl in a crisp white apron slipped past Alix carrying a tray laden with tea things. Placing the tray down, she carefully but quickly set out cups, saucers, and plates heaped high with cakes and scones. Alix couldn't help staring, not at the women, but at golden brown scones and the delicately iced cakes. She was, she realized suddenly, ravenously hungry.

As she turned to see whether Rafe had returned for her yet, an overly loud whisper from the woman in the brocade dress reached her ears. "Look at the shabby looking creature that's come in with Moreham."

Her companion, a pinch-faced brunette in a canary yellow dress, turned her sharp eyes toward Alix. "Who do you think she is?"

"Well, I haven't the slightest idea, and I doubt Lady Anne does either," the blonde said, leaning toward her companion but raising her voice so her words clearly carried. "They say the earl invited Lady Anne to his country estate and was all set to propose when *poof*, he hied off to France without a word. The ton is buzzing with the news; everyone was certain his lordship was finally going to come up to scratch. Of course Lady Anne, being the quality that she is, hasn't said a word, but you know she must be fit to be tied. She isn't getting any younger."

Both women were staring openly at Alix now. "Do you think she's the reason the earl didn't propose?" the woman in yellow asked incredulously.

The heavyset woman stifled a snort of laughter. "Well, they do say he likes his French pleasures. Perhaps he's decided to import them now that they're having all those troubles over there."

The yellow clad woman tittered. "Well if he did, then the price couldn't have been too dear. She looks like something the rag vendor cast off." Both women snickered into their handkerchiefs.

"Oh Georgie sweetheart, don't eat all those cakes so fast, you'll get a tummy ache." The woman in the brocade turned her attention to the boy who was now busily stuffing his face with sweets, and the conversation shifted away from Alix to the importance of a healthy appetite in the young.

Rafe reappeared and led Alix to a private room that had been set with a light repast. She followed, her brain chattering with this latest piece of information about Rafe Harcrest. Or was it the Earl of Moreham? She glared at his broad shoulders as he pulled the chair out for her. All the time he was making love to her he had a fiancée, or something quite close to it, at home. The man was a perfect cad.

He poured her some tea and held out a plate. "Would you care for some cakes, or perhaps some scones with jam?"

What she wanted to do, she thought fiercely, was to

upend the jam on his head. Instead, she smiled politely and took a slice of cake.

They ate in silence for a moment, and Alix wondered when and how Rafe would reveal the truth.

"You know," she said sweetly, "you've told me about your sister Elizabeth and your stepmother, but you've never spoken about your home. Do you live in London?"

Rafe busied himself with his plate. "I have a place there."

"Oh," Alix said, "is it above your shop, or are your living quarters separate?"

"Separate," he said. "Would you care for more tea?"

"And didn't you mention something about a country home? You must do quite well with your trade." His face was expressionless, but Alix noticed the muscles tense around his jaw. "You know, I think it would be fascinating to see your warehouse and your place of business," she continued.

He glanced up at her. "I think you'd find it all rather dull," he said quickly. "Not at all the thing a lady of your position would find interesting."

Alix toyed with her napkin. "But that is all behind me now. I've fled my home. I've married a merchant. I must forge a new life for myself here." She waited to see how he would respond, whether he would offer her even the smallest bit of truth.

"Well," he said at last, "if you're going to start a new life, I think you could use some new clothes. And I know just the modiste near Leicester Square to get you started." He smiled. "Soft colors, I think, and for God's sake, no red, white, and blue."

No pastels; no red, white, and blue; and definitely no *you,* she decided as she bit into her scone.

As they left the inn, Alix looked towards where the two women and the boy had been sitting, but they were already gone. She found herself fervently hoping that young Georgie and his mother both got terrible stomachaches from the scones.

They rode for the next several hours in a driving rain that made conversation in the coach difficult, if not impossible. Alix stared through rain-spattered windows as scrubby seacoast gave way to rain-drenched pastureland and then to the dense hamlets that marked the outskirts of London.

Rafe watched Alix, her eyes as overcast as the skies and her hands fisted tightly in her sodden skirt. It must be overwhelming for her, he thought, to be wrenched from her homeland and transplanted among strangers. He would make it all right, he told himself, starting with a fresh new wardrobe.

A smile crossed his lips as he pictured her dressed in silks and satins, in soft shades of blue and sea green to compliment her eyes, rose to match her skin. He imagined her hair, clean and lustrous, falling free past her shoulders and the fantasy quickly moved from dressing Alix to undressing her. He closed his eyes, recalling the taste and feel of her skin. Then he opened them abruptly as he felt the familiar desire for her begin to settle in his groin. Now, he reflected, was neither the time nor the place to be thinking about making love to Alix, and yet, she was like a melody that had become trapped in his head; he couldn't seem to break free of her.

He drummed his fingers lightly on his knee, as he recalled her questions about his residence in London. She'd be annoyed, he speculated, when he revealed his little deception, but he had no doubt that he could win her over. She hadn't mentioned an annulment since they'd made love in Calais. He took her silence on the matter as acceptance of the reality that she must remain with him. Even now she might be carrying his heir. The thought broke over him in a surprising wave of pride and pleasure. Perhaps, he thought with an inward chuckle, he should limit his dress order at Madame Guenard's.

The traffic became heavier as the reached Tyburn Road and made their way toward Oxford Street. Rafe drew the shade on his window. The season would not be officially begin until the end of October, but it was impossible to know who among the ton had already arrived in town. There were endless arrangements to be made before the season could begin, homes to be opened, horses and carriages to be ordered from Tattersalls, clothes to be fitted for the endless whirl of parties, suppers, and dances. Rafe told himself that he was not yet ready to be seen around town with Alix. There were too many explanations and introductions to be made first.

It was a marvel, he thought, that they'd been able to slip in and out of Dover unnoticed. One benefit to the troubles in France, he thought grimly, was the decrease in young aristocrats touring the continent. It was regrettable, he thought, but he'd have to take Alix into Madame Guenard's through the side entrance reserved for the demi-reps and their patrons. He'd explain to the modiste what was required, then leave Alix in her capable hands. He'd slip over to Lombard Street, meet quickly with his man of business about the cargoes he was having brought into London, and return to pick her up. With any luck, the seamstress would work her magic, and Alix would be ready for her introduction to Moreham House.

Alix found herself amazed at London's wide cobbled streets, the elegant shops with bow windows, the neatly painted signs hung discreetly over the doors. Rafe handed her down from the coach in front of a lovely shop, with an array of elegantly plumed hats and leather gloves displayed in the window. She cast a desperate look down at her navy traveling dress, now crumpled and stained from the rain and days of wear. He took her hand and patted it reassuringly.

"Madame Guenard is the soul of discretion," he reassured her. "No one need see you like this. And if they do, when she's done with you, no one will believe you're the same lady."

"Madame Guenard, is she French?"

Rafe chuckled. "Actually, she's Maggie Gunnert, born and bred in Spitalfields. She changed her name to impress her clientele. You'll see, once she finds out you're French, she'll find some reason to step out and help someone else before you can test her grasp of the language. She doesn't know much beyond *oui, non,* and *mon Dieu.*"

Taking her arm, he guided her into a discreet side entrance to the shop. A young shop girl, in a simple, but well-cut plum gown immediately glided up to Rafe. "May I be of some assistance, my lord," she murmured.

"The lady requires a complete wardrobe in the height of fashion. Simple, elegant, nothing too low-cut or revealing. Shades of pastel, I think, not too much lace. Yes, and she will also need undergarments, preferably in silk, stockings, gloves, shoes, and hats to match. Expense is not an issue. The bills should be sent my address on Curzon Street."

The lady in plum inclined her head gracefully. "If . . ." She paused, waiting for Rafe to supply Alix's name. When he did not she continued smoothly. "If Madame will come this way."

Rafe turned to Alix and spoke softly in French. "Everything is arranged. I have some business to take care of, but it should take no more than an hour or two." He raised her hand and kissed it. "And then I shall take you home."

Alix smiled at him, a smile that disappeared as soon as his tall frame could no longer be seen through the windows of the elegant dressmaker's shop.

"Well," said the woman in plum, "shall we begin?"

Alix, lost in thought, did not immediately respond. A second, smaller woman dressed in plum, a cushion full of pins in her hand and a tape measure draped over her arm, tittered. "I don't think his lordship's mistress speaks English."

The taller woman sniffed as she began to unroll bolts of fine silk. "The likes of her don't need to speak. Still, she must do something special; it's a rare thing for him to come in here with anyone besides his sister. And he's never been so ready with his purse."

Alix lifted her chin and turned to face the two shop girls. Speaking in clear precise English, she said, "I am not his lordship's mistress. Nor do I have any need of a wardrobe from this establishment. If you will kindly arrange a conveyance for me, I will be leaving."

The two girls blushed and stammered apologies, but Alix ignored them. Finally, comprehending that Alix would not be swayed, the taller woman went out and arranged for a hackney cab.

"What address should I give him?" she asked Alix.

Alix froze. Her mother's note had said she would be staying in Mayfair, but there had been no address given. That left her with only one option, "Tell him I would like to be taken to the home of the Duchess of Melbourne."

Chapter Sixteen

She'd left him. Rafe shook his head as if unable to contain the thought. He'd been gone for less than two hours and when he returned, the shop girl had primly informed him that the lady in question had left in a hackney shortly after he had departed. Unwilling to cause a scene in the dress shop, he had stood momentarily dumbfounded outside Madame Guenard's. How could she have gone, without a word, without a note? He'd scanned the street as if he might catch sight of her, as if, he thought with rising annoyance, she might have changed her mind and come running back to him.

He could guess where she'd gone, haring off after her mother. Though how Alix thought she'd find the comtesse without a proper address was beyond him. Unless, the unpleasant thought crossed his mind, she'd gone to Lady Melbourne's. His lips tightened at the prospect. One couldn't walk into Lady Melbourne's drawing room without stumbling over half a dozen leading politicians, a smattering of playwrights and poets, and the devil alone knew who else her ladyship found entertaining. He could just imagine the reaction should he storm into Melbourne House demanding they hand over his wife. He'd be the butt of the season's jokes, a column in half the broadsheets in town and probable inspiration for some new, interminable play. And for all he knew, Alix might very well deny they'd ever been married.

Women, he thought, as he started down the street, were outrageous, irrational, incomprehensible creatures. How was it that they found their way under a man's skin, winding their way around his brain and his heart until he could no longer think straight nor function without them? As he strode along, it seemed the streets were filled with women, ladies, maids, servants, and shop girls, everywhere chatting and strolling, going about their business. They looked so innocent, so inviting, who knew what havoc they could wreak on a man's life. As he turned the corner, he knew where he was headed, a bastion, a haven, a place where no woman ever stepped foot—White's.

Rafe swept up the marble staircase of White's and stepped into the gaming room. The murmur of deep voices, the rattle of dice, and the shuffling of cards was like a soothing balm. He surveyed the occupants of the green baize tables with grim satisfaction. Groups of men clustered about the room sporting all manner of odd gambling dress. Some wore straw hats or leather visors to protect their hair from the candle flames, many had their lace cuffs tied back, and a few wore their coats turned inside out for luck. Rafe's lips tightened in a parody of a smile.

Not a woman in sight.

It was well after three in the morning when Cole Davenport found him. His dark eyes flitted restlessly from table to table, narrowing as they came to rest on Rafe, coat cast aside, sleeves rolled back, deeply engaged in a game of solo whist. From the detritus on the table, Cole surmised the game had been going on for some time; the candlesticks were thick with wax and empty bottles of wine and half-filled glasses were scattered about the table. Cole was not surprised to see an unused glass at Rafe's place and a large pile of notes and coins spilled carelessly at his elbow.

Rafe, he knew, never played cards unless he was stone cold sober and extremely angry. From the pile of winnings at his elbow, Cole judged his friend's mood was black, indeed. Rafe looked distant, almost bored, and his long fingers drummed softly on the baize tabletop. A single man, whom Cole recognized as Viscount Fallsworth, was continuing to play against Rafe, while the other men at the table, having folded their hands leaned back in their chairs and watched intently.

Fallsworth was vainly striving to emulate Rafe's bored expression, but his mouth looked tense and the candlelight picked out glittering beads of sweat just beneath the crown of his gray wig. Cole saw him surreptitiously wipe his palm against his buff-colored britches. Fallsworth forced a laugh and then spread his cards on the table. "I'm done in, Moreham," he said. "The play's too deep for me."

Rafe didn't reply, simply swept the viscount's losses into his pile and raised a brow inquiringly at the two men to his right and left to see whether they were interested in another round.

Cole strolled over to the table, bent low, and murmured into his friend's ear. "My, my, aren't we in a foul mood." Rafe stiffened but didn't look up. He folded Rafe's hand and placed the cards down on the table. "Gentleman," he said, "I believe this game is over." Cole could have sworn he heard a collective sigh of relief from the earl's gaming companions.

"I could call you out for that," Rafe said dryly.

"Indeed, you could," Cole agreed pleasantly. "But you won't. Besides the fact that I am the better shot, dueling is far too impulsive, and you, Moreham are never impulsive." He motioned for a servant to collect up Rafe's winnings and bring a bottle of brandy to a table in the corner. "Come, stop fleecing the lambs and have a drink with me."

Rafe glanced at the servant sweeping his winnings onto a silver tray. As he stood up to follow Cole, he paused and plucked a note from off the top. Tossing it back across the table he said, "Take this back Fallsworth. I never play for a man's home, particularly when his family's still in it."

The viscount paled. Mumbling his thanks, he awkwardly stuffed the note into his pocket.

Cole poured several fingers of brandy into a snifter and slid it across the table as Rafe joined him. Rafe accepted the glass but did not drink. Casting Cole a curious glance he said, "What brings you here?"

"Jervis suggested you might be in need of company," Cole responded, pouring himself a brandy.

Rafe swirled the liquor for a moment before raising it to his lips. "Did he now? And what exactly did he tell you?"

"Nothing more than that. When it comes to your personal affairs, Jones is remarkably tight-lipped." Cole sipped his drink. "So would you care to tell me what is going on?"

Rafe drummed his fingers lightly against the glass. "I don't think so."

Cole nodded amiably. "I see. Then I suppose I will have to guess why the Earl of Moreham, who abhors gambling, is wreaking havoc at the gaming tables." He frowned. "Let me see, the ton is buzzing with the news that you're preparing to offer for Anne Dinsmore. So, I would surmise, you offered and are now having second thoughts."

Rafe, sipping his brandy, shook his head slightly.

The furrow between Cole's dark brows deepened. "Don't tell me she turned you down?"

Rafe shook his head again.

"Well, then," Cole said smoothly, "I am prepared to stay by your side until I have it out. For the good of the lambs, you understand."

"Don't you have a wife who is likely to come seeking you?"

"Phoebe trusts me implicitly," Cole answered with a smile. "I am all yours until you decide to talk."

Rafe glared at him.

Cole ignored his friend's hostile response. "I know it's not Elizabeth. She's safely tucked away in the country. And Louisa never angers anyone. So," he said tapping his lips with his finger. "What could it be?" He glanced at Rafe. "I suppose I could take you over to Gentleman Jackson's and pound it out of you over the course of several rounds."

Rafe's eyes glittered in the candlelight. "It would be my pleasure. Though I suggest that all you would gain for your troubles would be bruises."

"That may very well be," Cole responded. "Though I doubt you would come off completely unscathed. Moreover, I shall be soothed by Phoebe's gentle ministrations, while you shall be forced to put up with one of Jervis's ghastly colonial remedies." He cast an agreeable smile at Rafe. As he did so, he caught the merest flicker of pain in his friend's eyes. Cole ceased his teasing and said softly, "It's a woman, isn't it? And you can't tell me Anne Dinsmore stirs this depth of feeling in you. Who is she, Moreham?"

They sat in silence for several moments sipping their brandy. Finally, Rafe said in a low tone, "My wife."

Cole knit his dark brows together and leaned more closely over the table. "Excuse me," he said, "but I could have sworn you just said your wife."

"I did."

Cole let out a whoop of laughter and several tables turned to see what had occasioned his outburst. "Forgive me," he gasped, "but that's rich. Anne will be irate. She's got tradesmen all over town extending her credit in anticipation of spending your money. So, when do Phoebe and I get to meet the lady who's swept you off your feet?"

"You don't," Rafe said acidly. "She's gone."

Cole stifled another laugh. "You're here destroying the fortunes of the British peerage because you've lost your bride?"

Rafe glared at him and Cole fell silent. "Forgive me," he said after a moment. "I can see that my humor is misplaced. Would you care to tell me about it?"

Rafe drummed his fingers on the table, pain and anger warring in his expression. "Very well," he said finally and proceeded to explain how he had met and married Alix.

When he had finished, Cole shook his head wonderingly. "She left you without a word? Do you have any idea where she's gone?"

Rafe answered tersely, "Lady Melbourne's."

Cole whistled softly. "You have got a devil of a problem."

Rafe nodded. "I hadn't planned on a major scandal for my sister's first season." He briefly considered telling Cole about the conversation he'd overheard between Anne and James Dinsmore, then dismissed it. He had enough problems already; he'd deal with the Dinsmores later.

"Do you know if the marriage is binding?"

Rafe shrugged. "I would expect so."

"Do you want her back?"

"If only to wring her pretty neck."

Cole smiled slightly. "And then you'll grant her an annulment?"

"Not if she's carrying my child."

Cole eyed his friend speculatively. He'd lay odds there was more to this story than what Rafe had told him. He felt a keen curiosity to meet the woman who'd so disturbed the customary composure of the Earl of Moreham.

"Suppose we drop by Lady Melbourne's tomorrow and see if the lady is at home to visitors?" he suggested.

"And risk having her turn me away, or worse claim she's never heard of me? I think not."

Cole's eyes took on a speculative light that Rafe, had he looked across the table, would have recognized and instantly mistrusted. "So," he said, dropping his voice and leaning conspiratorially close, "what'll it be? Shall we wait for her to venture out, then sweep her into your carriage? Climb through her window and haul her out, tossed over your shoulder?"

"That's your style Davenport, not mine."

"A discreet letter then to Lady Melbourne's solicitor informing her she's holding a bit of your prized property?"

Rafe grimaced. "I can see the married state has not quenched your thirst for the dramatics."

Cole drew himself up with feigned offense. "Very well, Moreham, you always have a plan. Let's have it."

"I don't know," Rafe snapped, "if I did, would I be playing cards with the likes of Fallsworth or listening to your rattle-brained schemes?"

Cole laughed. "It appears as though this season may not be quite so dull after all. Perhaps I should convince Phoebe to come to town for a bit. A second honeymoon, I'm thinking."

"It seems to me you've had several honeymoons already and a son to mark each one," Rafe said dryly.

"Ah, you're just jealous. But you'll have brood of your own soon enough." Cole continued. "Unless, of course, this dark humor is how you propose to win the lady over. I've never known snarls and scowls to be an effective method of courtship, but then perhaps French ladies are different?"

Rafe shook his head. "I'm just so damn angry with her, Cole, I never expected she would leave that way, without a word, without a note . . ."

The teasing banter vanished and Cole's voice softened. "Perhaps you should take a step back before you set out to woo your wife. Some time in the country to think things through. Check on Elizabeth, make sure she hasn't talked your stepmother into letting her wear something scandalous for her come out."

Rafe smiled for the first time that evening. "Louisa's not that out of touch with fashion, but you do have a point." And he thought it would give him some time to sort out his feelings for Alix. Given time, he told himself, the desire to have her close to him would surely fade. Perhaps the swirl of emotions she stirred in him would settle, and he would discover she'd been nothing more than a passing disturbance in his well-ordered life.

"Davenport," he said, "as astounding as it seems, you just may have hit upon a sensible plan. And to demonstrate my appreciation, why don't you bring Phoebe and the boys to Moreham Hall for an extended visit?"

The hackney driver laughed as he held the carriage door open for Alix to enter. "Sure I know where Lady Melbourne lives, everybody does. She and the duke had that great big place on Grosvenor Street, then they up and swapped it for the Duke of York's house in Whitehall. They say Lady Melbourne did it because she prefers the chimes of Westminster to those of Saint James." He shook his head as he closed the coach door muttering. "Quality, they're something different, that's for sure."

About the time Rafe was striding confidently back to Madame Guenard's, Alix was standing at the elegant front portico of the Melbourne's home staring in to the forbidding face of the Duchess's butler.

"Have you an appointment with her ladyship?" he asked in a tone that suggested he sincerely doubted that she did.

Lifting her chin imperiously she said, "Please inform her ladyship that Mademoiselle Alexandre Charlotte de Rabec de La Brou wishes to speak with her. She and my mother, Madame la Comtesse de La Brou, are good friends."

Casting a dubious look at her rumpled traveling dress, the butler nodded and closed the door.

Willing herself not to fidget, Alix held herself erect; she hadn't come this far to be put off by an arrogant house servant. Her hand stole to the thin gold chain at her throat. She'd found herself touching it at the oddest times, she reflected, as if it were a talisman that might somehow protect her. The heavy gold ring shifted between her breasts and she pulled it out and examined it. A light flickered in the ruby's depths like some secret red world and Alix found herself reminded of the alcove where she and Rafe had made love. She dropped the ring abruptly, but not before catching sight of a motto in Latin engraved on the inside of the band: WHAT I CLAIM IS MINE.

Her lips tightened. Rafe Harcrest might have laid claim to her body, she told herself firmly, but he had laid no such claim to her soul. She was her own woman, she reminded herself. She'd escaped the terrors of France, preserved the precious de La Brou titles and someday she would return to reestablish the family name. If, she thought with wry amusement at the vehemence of her emotions, the butler would just open the damn door.

As if responding to her will, the heavy door swung open and the butler blandly informed her, "Her ladyship will see you now, if you will follow me."

Alix stepped into the domed entrance hall trying not to

think of the contrast her stained traveling gown made against the rich interior of the duchess's home. She willed herself to imagine that she was back at Versailles, sweeping down the long corridors in one of her lace and jewel-encrusted gowns.

The butler opened a heavy paneled door and announced, "Mademoiselle Alexandre Charlotte de Rabec de La Brou."

Uncertain what to expect, Alix stepped into the room, her skirts rustling softly against the thick blue and gold Brussels carpet. The walls and windows were draped in matching blue silk and portraits of horses and landscapes hung in heavy gold frames. Two women were seated at a tea table in the center of the room; one of them was Alix's mother.

Before Alix could say anything, Madeleine rose, moved swiftly toward her, and enfolded her in a cloud of lace and perfume.

"*Mon Dieu,* Alix," she whispered in a voice choked with tears, "it is you, *ma petite*, it really is you." Alix dropped her head on her mother's shoulder and allowed herself to be cradled like a child.

Several hours later Alix sat tucked up in a massive four-poster bed, watching the sun set though the long windows of one of the Lady Melbourne's many guest bedrooms. She sipped her cocoa, absentmindedly admiring the delicate floral design on the Sèvres cup. Her skin and hair were at last clean and smelled faintly of expensive lemon soap. Madeleine had lent her a silk dressing gown. Closing her eyes and feeling the soft fabric whisper against her skin, Alix could almost imagine that the hardships she had endured were nothing more than a terrible nightmare. Except for Rafe, a small voice whispered. Surely what they'd shared at the inn near Calais had been more like a dream.

Alix reopened her eyes, unwilling to let her mind draw her back into the pain and confusion that enveloped her when she thought of Rafe. She saw Madeleine seated in a small armchair at the foot of the bed, her small slender hands anxiously smoothing the rose-colored fabric of her skirt. She looked, Alix thought, as beautiful as she remembered, though there were a few strands of silver in her dark hair that hadn't been there before, and her skin seemed drawn a bit more tightly against the delicate bones of her face.

Madeleine broke the silence between them. "Your father . . ." she began, her voice rising in a question.

". . . is dead," Alix responded quietly.

Madeleine nodded. "I won't pretend that we were close, but I am sorry for your loss. How did it happen?"

Alix explained about the peasants storming Valcour.

Madeleine listened, the story unfolding in fits and starts. A sheen of tears glistened in her dark eyes; she could see how difficult it was for her daughter to tell the tale. When Alix finally stopped speaking, she said in a whisper, "I tried to warn Paul about the troubles in Paris, but he never answered any of my letters."

"He never mentioned any letters," Alix said, surprised. "And I saw none among his papers." She took a deep breath. "Not that it would have made any difference. Father was convinced the new government wouldn't last and that the king would be restored to the throne."

Madeleine shook her head wonderingly. "And you escaped with the Chaumiers's help. But how did you know where to find me and how did you come to England?"

Alix pleated the linen sheets, wondering what to say, where to begin. It had been painful enough telling her mother about her father's death. She couldn't begin to think of how to tell her about Rafe and what had passed between them. A log shifted in the fireplace and sparks crackled in the silence.

Madeleine rose and came to stand by her bed. Smoothing back Alix's hair, she said softly, "I can't imagine what sort of ordeals you've been through. But I can respect your wish not to discuss them further. The important thing is not how you got here, but that you *are* here and are safe. Lady Melbourne has graciously offered to let us stay for the season. Perhaps we can both put the past behind us and learn to make England our home."

Alix nodded wordlessly.

Madeleine started to leave, then stopped, one hand on the door. "Alix," she said, her teeth worrying at her lower lip. "I can't say that I'm sorry I left your father, but I want you to know that I always regretted having left you behind. When you came to Versailles, I couldn't allow myself to become close to you, knowing that your stay at court would be brief." She paused and drew in a tentative breath. "I know it's too late to be a mother to you, but perhaps . . ." Her voice trailed. "Perhaps we could become friends?"

Alix studied her mother, thinking that of all the times she had imagined finding her mother, she had never expected such an offer.

"I think I would like that," she said.

Chapter Seventeen

Three boys burst through the hedges brandishing wooden swords and wearing an odd assortment of clothes, undoubtedly scavenged from the attic of Moreham Hall.

"Stand and fight foul knave," the oldest boy, a tall sturdy child of nine, demanded. His younger brothers, waving their swords and hopping up and down in their excitement, urged him on as he engaged in battle with a slender young woman sporting an old-fashioned waistcoat over her peach-colored gown.

"I'll fight you to the death Robin Hood and see your merry men hanged from the battlements of Sherwood Castle," she said, parrying his thrusts, and the little boys giggled. The sounds of the wood swords smacking together echoed loudly through the garden. The boy lunged and the young woman caught his sword under her arm. Staggering back dramatically, and throwing her free arm across her chest, she gurgled, "You've won Robin Hood. Tell Maid

Marian I love her." Then she fell back into the grass and lay still.

The boy placed one foot on her stomach and raised his sword victoriously. "So dies the evil Sheriff of Nottingham."

The young woman suddenly sat up, grabbed him by the ankle and rolled him into the grass tickling him wildly. As the younger boys joined the fray, a plump woman in a faded brown dress and a wide straw hat looked up from her planting. "Mind the beds, Elizabeth, I've just finished putting in bulbs for next spring."

Elizabeth waved in understanding to her mother, then sprang up, and raced across the lawn with the boys in hot pursuit.

Phoebe Davenport, who'd been watching the mock battle from a bench across the garden, laughed. Her husband, who was seated next to her, shook his head. "It's hard to believe she'll be entering polite society in less than a month."

Phoebe rolled her eyes. "Just because Elizabeth enjoys a bit of fun with the boys doesn't mean she's lacking in common sense or the social graces. She'll do fine, you'll see."

Cole smiled and kissed the tip of her nose. "I know, it's hard not to see her as the gangly girl in the rumpled gown following Rafe and me about the house."

"Well, she's a young woman now, with a mind of her own," Phoebe said. "And you and Moreham would do well to remember that. Especially Rafe," she added. "If he pulls the reins in any tighter, she's sure to rebel, if only to spite him. You should see him inspect her gowns for the season; he's more demanding than a general viewing his troops on dress parade."

"He's just concerned about her future. You know Rafe,

he thinks he can plan everything ahead like a military campaign."

"I understand," she replied with a worried frown. "But lately he's been different somehow, driven, as if he were trying to maintain control over his and everyone else's life." She put her hand on Cole's arm. "You should speak to him. Find out what's troubling him."

He nodded, thinking that he agreed with her. Rafe was driving himself and everyone around him too hard. For the past two weeks, it had been on the tip of his tongue to confide in Phoebe the truth of what was bothering Rafe; Cole didn't like keeping secrets from his wife, but he respected his friend's desire for privacy as well. "I'll speak to him about easing up on Elizabeth," he said rising.

"And everyone else as well," she called to his retreating back.

Cole found Rafe in his study, a massive room with an elaborately patterned red carpet spread on the floor and towering bookcases reaching from floor to gilt-trimmed ceiling. Rafe sat at heavy mahogany desk, books piled high around him, poring over columns of figures. Cole leaned against the heavily carved marble mantelpiece, studying first the portrait of the fifth earl, Rafe's father, hanging behind the desk, then the face of his friend. At forty-seven the previous earl seemed younger than his son did now. Rafe looked drawn and tired, the habitual frown between his brows more deeply grooved.

"It's a beautiful day outside, you know. You should be out riding, enjoying the clear air while you can, before you're once again surrounded by the coal dust of London."

Rafe shook his head. "I've got work to do. Someone has to see that these estates are administered properly."

Cole dropped into an armchair in front of the massive mahogany desk. "You have some of the most well-run estates in England, not to mention a highly competent steward. Burying yourself in work and riding herd on the servants and Elizabeth is not the solution to getting to your problems."

Rafe looked up, his frown deepening. "Elizabeth will be introduced to society in seventeen days. She does not seem to understand how important it is that she dress and comport herself in the proper manner. Indeed, the more I try and explain her responsibilities, the more frivolously she behaves."

Cole stretched out his legs. "She's young. Let her enjoy her first season before she's married off and saddled with babes."

Rafe continued as if he hadn't heard. "You can't just do as you please all the time, running off without knowing where you're headed, thinking things will all fall together in the end. Life doesn't work that way. You have to think things through, plan ahead." His lips tightened in a thin line. "Impulse took my father over a hedge too high for his horse, and it drove my brother to the gaming tables thinking each time he'd win back what he'd lost."

"Listen to me Rafe, your father loved to ride and your brother loved to gamble. Perhaps their passions were misplaced, but at least they had them. You, my friend, are trying to bury yours beneath a weight of responsibilities."

He shook his head, "If I hadn't acted on impulse, I'd never have met Alexandre de La Brou; I'd be arranging my marriage to Anne Dinsmore, and Elizabeth would have someone to guide her through the pitfalls of the ton."

Cole leaned forward. "Did you ever consider that impulse might be the angel and not the devil on your shoulder? You don't love Anne Dinsmore, and I'd wager that you never will. This Alix, well, I've never met her, but she's disrupted your life more powerfully than anything

I've ever seen. You owe it to yourself and to her to find out what that means."

He massaged his temples. "It seems to me I've heard this argument from you before, and it took us gallivanting off to the colonies as if a military campaign were some kind of holiday outing."

"Yes," Cole admitted, "but we came through it, and I'd say we're better men for it." He smiled. "And I would never have met Phoebe nor had my three fine sons."

"I, however, came out of it with Jervis," Rafe said wryly.

Cole laughed. "Rafe you know what I'm trying to say. For once in your life roll the dice, take a chance."

Rafe looked at him intently. "If I were to act on impulse, I'd ride to London, storm into Lady Melbourne's fashionable home, toss Alexandre de La Brou *Moreham* over my shoulder and carry her off." He grimaced. "I can assure you, my intentions would be far from angelic." He pushed the account ledgers away and leaned back in his chair. "I tell you Cole, I don't know how I'll react when I see her. All I know is that I have to see her again."

Cole smiled. "You, my friend, are in love."

Alix lay in bed in Lady Melbourne's guestroom, staring at the intricate folds of the canopy draped overhead. Though it was mid-afternoon, she was still in her dressing gown and had yet to open the rose-colored window curtains. She knew she should get up, see the sights of London, and socialize with Lady Melbourne and her friends. But somehow she couldn't find the energy or the enthusiasm. She had the oddest sense that if she could only stay in the semi-darkness of the room she could suspend time. At this moment, she thought staring at the intricately knotted fabric overhead, she could imagine she was neither a homeless French émigré, nor the wife of a man whose touch waited to draw her into dreams of passion should she close her eyes and fall asleep.

The clattering sound of porcelain on a tray, followed by the thick aroma of coffee, and then her mother's lilac perfume signaled that Alix was no longer alone. She turned her head and saw that a maid was arranging a light breakfast on a table while her mother swept from window to window drawing back the curtains.

As the maid left the room, Madeleine approached the bed. "Alexandre Charlotte, enough is enough. I know you were close to your father and that his death has been a terrible loss for you. And since I have said I will not pry, I can only imagine the horrors you must have suffered trying to reach me." She placed her hands on her hips. "But you have been lying in this bed for nearly a week. It is time to get up and start living again."

Madeleine handed Alix a cup of coffee and began pacing the room. "I have given it a great deal of thought, and I believe we should throw ourselves into this English season. The upstart government in France has been repossessing our fortune and there is simply no way to know what will remain to us." She shuddered. "I am just grateful I was able to get out as much as I did. It should keep us in good stead for a while, but not in as good stead as a wealthy husband," she said, tapping a manicured finger on her full red lips.

Madeleine settled into an armchair and poured herself a cup of coffee. "Only imagine, Alix, this time we have no male relatives to chose husbands for us; we may decide as we like." She placed the cup down and leaned towards the bed. "Certainly in this country there must be some wealthy titled gentlemen who are not old enough to be our fathers."

"But mother," Alix interrupted, "we are in mourning."

"Oh yes," she said clasping her hands together with delight. "I've thought about that and I've discussed the problem with Lady Melbourne, and I have come up with the most delicious idea. We shall be the brave and tragic de La Brou women. I shall wear only black to express my grief at the loss of your father and the misfortunes of the Bourbons." She smiled gaily. "Black is such a wonderful compliment to my skin and hair, it will be so dramatic, and I shall never dance, or at least not for several months. The season is not truly in full swing until March anyway. You, however, are young. I think you should wear only gray, it will look wonderful with your eyes. We can trim it up with silver and black, perhaps some green or lavender for effect, but always gray. Oh we shall be such a sensation."

Alix closed her eyes, thinking of the sensation she would cause when it was discovered that a married woman was husband-hunting during the London season. She couldn't imagine Rafe's reaction, but she could guess that it would not be sympathetic. She hadn't been able to come up with a discreet way of contacting him without the servants informing her mother or the duchess, and she wasn't yet ready to face the uproar it would cause.

Madeleine was out of her chair again and rummaging through Alix's armoire. "You must get up and get dressed now," she said, tossing garments onto Alix's bed. "We have an appointment with Lady Melbourne's dressmaker this afternoon, then we have supper at Lady Albright's this evening, then cards with the Percy's. I'll have a maid sent up to help you dress and style your hair and then off we'll go."

She departed in a swirl of silk and lilac, leaving Alix stunned. A round-faced maid, freckles liberally sprinkled across her snub nose, entered Alix's room and began bustling about, her rapid-fire conversation quickly filling the vacuum created by Madeleine's abrupt exit.

"I'm Guinevere, but you can call me Ginny miss. I'll be the one helping you dress most times. And I'm good with hair, too. Lady Melbourne's hairdresser's been teaching me. You've got lovely hair, if you don't mind me saying so, miss, and a lovely figure, too. I'll just help tie your stays for you now, if you'd like."

As she pulled the laces tight, Ginny continued to chatter. "It's a good thing you're tiny like your mother, most of her dresses will fit you. Sure we may have to let the hems down a tad, but nothing that can't be whipped up in a moment. She's got lovely taste, your mother. Should you like the yellow with the flowers and the ribbons or the rose stripe?" Alix gestured toward the yellow floral and Ginny slipped it over her head.

"Course I could never wear me mum's clothes. We Potters tend to run stout as we age. My mum is the housekeeper here. You may have seen her about. Lord there's been Potters serving the Melbournes forever." She stopped and took a breath. "Forgive me miss, I tend to rattle on when I'm nervous and I do so want to do a good job for you."

Alix smiled, a slight smile, but the first genuine one since she'd discovered Rafe was an earl. "It's quite alright Ginny. Indeed, you remind me a bit of my maid Solange Chaumier. We practically grew up together." Alix fell silent, wondering whether David had made it safely back to Solange and how she'd fared without her identity papers. She looked up at Ginny. "I'm sure we'll get along fine."

Alix emerged two hours later, dressed and ready for her mother's series of appointments. As they rode in Lady Melbourne's coach to the dressmaker's (not, Alix breathed a sigh of relief, Madame Guenard's) her mother continued to chatter excitedly about her plans for their entrance into London society. Alix began to think that perhaps Madeleine had the right idea. She did need to get out more, see what the world had to offer. Moping about in the dark certainly wasn't going to change anything.

With this in mind, she found herself enjoying their shopping spree. Madeleine offered advice, but did not dictate Alix's choices. It was a novel experience for Alix. She'd never had much interest in clothes before, since someone else had always decided the cut and color. Assessing the look of a large gray hat with a deep green plume in the looking glass, she considered that her mother was right. Grays tinged with just the right shade of blue or green suited her well. It felt good, she thought, as she tilted the hat at a rakish angle, choosing styles that reflected how she saw herself, rather than how others wanted her to appear.

She wasn't an innocent young girl anymore, she mused as she waved away the modiste's suggestion of adding more flounces to the bottom of one of her gowns. Not that she considered herself a woman of the world, but she liked the idea of appearing a bit more sleek, a bit more elegant, a bit more daring than a pink gown smothered in rosebuds might suggest.

As the footman piled their purchases onto the back of the coach, Alix considered that perhaps things would turn out all right. She didn't have to think of the season as "husband hunting." She could think of it as a time to learn more about English society, to meet some new people, to learn her own mind. And if she encountered Rafe, she told herself as her heart began to pound at the mere thought of his name, the new Alix would greet him cordially. Perhaps they would dance, exchange a few words, agree that it was all a strange adventure that should best be put behind them. She shifted uncomfortably in her seat as her skin recalled the hot traces of his touch. Surely if she threw herself into her mother's planned schedule of activities, this longing to see him, to touch him, to be with him would fade.

She glanced out the window, still amazed at how wide and well paved the streets of London were, and studied the mass of expensive coaches moving smoothly, two across on Oxford street. Perhaps she would stop this endless searching among the crowds for him, and her heart would stop lurching about every time she saw a man with a similar walk or color hair. She shook herself so firmly that Madeleine, who'd been describing a particular style of gown she admired, stopped abruptly and inquired if she was cold.

"Not at all mother," Alix replied, patting her hand. "It's been a perfectly lovely day, and I agree, a black redingote would be striking."

After all, she continued musing, he'd made no effort to contact her; he'd probably been relieved when she'd left him. Scandal had been averted. Her stomach tightened. For all she knew he'd hurried back to the woman he'd been courting before he'd met her and was even now planning how to arrange a new marriage. She straightened against the cushions of the coach. One thing was for certain, when and if she encountered Rafe Harcrest, or Moreham, or whatever it was he called himself, he would not find her mooning in the darkness over him.

"Mother," she said, "tell me more about what you think we should wear to the Kensington's assembly next month."

Exercising Rafe's gelding in St. James Park several days later, Jervis Jones was startled to see a familiar figure clad in a smart gray riding habit and seated on a spirited bay, chatting animatedly to a dark-haired woman all in black. Pulling his tricorne down over his eyes, he reined Rafe's gelding in to get a better look. It was Alix all right. He watched as the two women disappeared down the path, frowning his displeasure as two young bucks who'd been watching the women's progress spurred their horses to follow.

According to the groom who'd brought his lordship's horses to town in anticipation of the opening of Moreham House, Rafe was more out of sorts than a bear who'd been disturbed before the spring thaw. Alix didn't look like she was pining a bit. Jervis pushed his hat back up thinking that while he had great respect for the captain as a gentleman, a leader, and a businessman, the man had no sense about how to treat women. If you sweet-talked them, said the right things, they didn't go tearing off to their mothers. He shook his head. He'd never seen Rafe as happy as he'd been in Calais. But if he knew the lad, and after fifteen years, he had a pretty good notion that he did, he'd probably tumbled the girl and then never said a word to her about how he felt.

They were married, Jervis reflected, and even if the ceremony had been most peculiar, they ought to stay that way. Alix was a damn sight better for his boy than any stick-up-her-arse Lady Dinsmore.

"You know," he said companionably to the black, who was tossing his head, urging Jervis to pick up the pace, "I do believe things are going to get very interesting when his lordship returns to London this week."

Jervis noticed several grooms wearing the livery of the Duke of Melbourne trotting across the park and urged the black to join them. When Rafe had left for the country, he had chosen to remain in London. Not only because he enjoyed the alehouses and the women, but because he thought it might be handy if he became familiar with the Melbourne servants, perhaps discover if any fancy French ladies had taken up residence in the house. His timing in exercising the gelding this afternoon was no accident. Nor was his cultivation of a certain freckle-faced maid. Jervis smiled as he thought of Ginny Potter, a sturdy woman with breasts like two freshly risen loaves of bread and a rump like a packhorse.

That, he thought clicking to the black, was how a proper woman should be built.

Once he'd discovered Ginny was Alix's personal maid, he'd wangled an introduction from Jake, a downstairs footman. Now he sometimes joined her on her errands. She was a good-natured, talkative sort, a bit like his first wife. Last Sunday he'd even accompanied Ginny to church. He had to admit it made him feel a bit guilty. He wasn't a praying man, but he had enough faith to believe the creator knew exactly what Jervis Jones was up to. But then, he reassured himself, it couldn't be too much of a sin if a man's intentions were good, could it? And he intended to make sure that Alix and Rafe stayed together.

He liked Alix, even if she did have the bad habit of stealing a man's clothes without asking. She had heart, gumption; she was a survivor. Coming from the New World as he did, he respected that. And Rafe, well, Rafe was too burdened down with his responsibilities, always thinking he had to look out for everyone else. He was becoming an old man before his time. He needed a woman to shake him up, to keep him guessing, get the juices flowing. The new Lady Moreham was just that woman.

All he needed to do was make certain the two kept crossing paths.

Chapter Eighteen

✦

Lamartine crouched in the fetid hold of the French smuggler *La Chance* cursing the de La Brous and all their ancestors. He thought he'd struck upon a good thing when he'd bribed two of the ship's crew to bring him aboard, but he was beginning to have his doubts. He'd been hiding among barrels of brandy for four days, while the ship's captain skulked along the coasts of the English Channel searching for a safe landing spot and trying to avoid the notice of revenue cutters.

He was sick of the smell, sick of the incessant pitch and roll of the ship, the constant noise of ropes and chains and cursing sailors. His traveling suit was stained beyond repair, and he had a suspicion that fleas had taken up residence in his bagwig, which was stowed along with a clean suit of clothes in a canvas bag at his side. Removing what had once been a pristine linen handkerchief from his waistcoat, he mopped at the oily sheen of perspiration on his brow. He didn't feel at all well, his head ached incessantly, and at night he dreamed that his father and the comte stood over him, arms linked, laughing at his failure.

He tucked the handkerchief back into his pocket and pulled a sea biscuit one of the crew had given him out of his jacket. Grimacing at the taste of stale dough, he thought angrily that he had not failed, he would not fail. He was on his way to England with a perfectly forged letter in his pocket. He would find Madeleine de La Brou and convince her to turn the titles over to him. It was a pressing matter, he would assure her, at any moment the government might claim possession of Valcour.

He clenched his hands; it would be *his* Valcour. The woman would trust him, just as the comte had trusted him. After all, what did women know of business matters? And if she did not see things his way, well then, there were ways to make her understand. As the remainder of the sea biscuit crumbled unnoticed in his fist, Robert Lamartine smiled for the first time in many days.

He would enjoy bringing Madeleine de La Brou around to his way of thinking.

For the first time in his life, Rafe Harcrest found himself grateful for decades of dancing masters and tedious balls. He moved through the dance without a thought for the steps, his eyes restlessly scanning the guests at the Kensington's assembly for a familiar mahogany mane. It was early in the season, but everyone who had arrived in London thus far seemed to be crammed into the Kensingon's public rooms. Voices rose above the sawing of violins, satin and taffeta rustled in the crush, and feathers and hair turned and nodded beneath the blaze of dripping chandeliers.

Jervis had assured him that Alix and her mother would be attending the party, but he'd yet to catch sight of her. It had been nearly four weeks since he'd last seen her, four weeks of sheer hell. He glanced at the ebony clock on the mantle across from the dance floor. It was fashionably late.

"If you're going to dance with me, at least you might pretend to make conversation," Elizabeth whispered.

"Have I told you that you look lovely this evening?" he asked without taking his eyes from the sea of bobbing heads.

"Several times, I believe."

Rafe glanced down at his sister. Elizabeth was dressed in a cream-colored satin gown, intricate patterns of flowers and birds embroidered in rose and pale green throughout. Flowers were artfully arranged in her chestnut curls, and a strand of pink-hued pearls encircled her slender throat. "You do, you know, look lovely," he said.

"I appreciate the compliments, especially since you chose the dress, but could you perhaps contribute something further to the conversation so that I don't appear to be mindlessly chattering to myself? While I do appreciate that intelligence is not a prerequisite to social success, I hope not to appear a total addlepate."

Rafe chuckled. "So, sister dear, what do you think of your first assembly thus far?"

"It's amusing." Casting a mischievous glance through her lashes she added, "And of course I am adhering to your lordship's rule of twos." In a mock stern voice she said, "No more than two glasses of champagne, no more than two dances with any gentleman, always at least two people with me at anytime, especially if one of them is a male."

"Well," he said as they began to promenade, "it's comforting to know that you have been paying some attention to my lectures."

"I pay attention to a great many things that might escape another person's notice. For instance, you have been distracted ever since you returned from France. I've discussed it with Phoebe and we've concluded it must be a woman."

"Phoebe Davenport talks too much."

Elizabeth ignored him, "Phoebe says men always get a bit cross when they've been a long time without a woman. Is it some beautiful French lady, helpless in the clutches of the new Republic, waiting for your rescue?"

Waiting for his rescue, indeed, Rafe frowned. The lady couldn't even stay put.

She lowered her voice. "Only don't tell me it's Anne Dinsmore."

"You could learn a great deal from Lady Anne."

"Like how to smile and flatter with one face, and how to savage a person's reputation with the other?"

"I think you're being rather harsh."

"I'd lay odds I'm not, only you never bet."

He was still considering Elizabeth's comments when Anne glided up to him. She looked as elegant as ever, he noted absently, dressed in pale blue and lace, a row of bows down the front of her gown and an arrangement of lace and pearls in her hair. Anne smiled at him as he took her hand and kissed it

"Moreham," she said in reproving tones, "I haven't had a chance to thank you for inviting me to visit you in the country. It was lovely, so restful, and Lousia's gardens are a wonder. My only disappointment," she said with a slight smile, "was your unexpected departure for France. I do hope your affairs there have all been successfully concluded."

Rafe thought he detected an emphasis on *affairs* and *concluded*, but decided to ignore her jibe. She was, he supposed, entitled to be a bit annoyed with him. He looked quickly around the room; still no sign of Alix. He offered Anne his hand. "May I lead you in a minuet, my lady?"

"I would be delighted," she said, her smile widening.

As they moved through the forms of the dance, Rafe continued to search the crowd for Alix. Where could she be? Had the prospect of facing a large social gathering with her limited English skills proven too daunting? He dismissed the thought almost as quickly as it came to him. His Alix had faced far worse.

His Alix, Rafe mused, it was the way he had come to think of her. Cole thought he was in love, but he doubted it. Love was an emotion for impulsive men like Davenport. What he felt for Alix was . . . he paused unsure of how to describe what he felt for Alix. It was, he decided, an urge to wring her neck for leaving him and then to kiss her senseless so that she never would again.

Anne drew close, speaking archly about the goings-on among the ton. He nodded politely as she related who had come to town and who had yet to arrive.

He wondered if Alix had fallen ill. She'd looked pale that last day he'd seen her. The crossing, he knew, had been rough on her. He thought of all she'd been through before, her father's death, the flight from France. If she'd fallen ill, it might explain why he hadn't heard from her.

But then Jervis had said he'd seen her riding in the park.

Anne took Rafe's hand as she turned. "I suppose all the gatherings this year will be littered with émigrés seeking to bolster their impoverished fortunes with a bit of English lucre. It's disgraceful. Not that I'm unsympathetic to their misfortunes, but still you'd think a more sensible people would have been able to keep a better rein on their commoners."

Lady Anne, he noticed idly, had changed subjects.

"And their sense of fashion, well, I know it's supposed to be wonderful, so much more dashing than the English, but I think it's a tad vulgar. Take Lady Melbourne's friend, the Comtesse de La Brou."

Suddenly Anne had his complete attention.

"The woman wears black to everything, and while she may, indeed, be in mourning, those necklines seem to be plunging with something other than despair." She gave a mock shudder. "And her daughter, well, you can judge for yourself." Anne tilted her neck almost imperceptibly towards a couple dancing to their left.

Alix was gracefully circling her partner just a few feet away from him. She was wearing a gown that matched her smoky eyes, a shimmering blue-gray trimmed in silver. Her hair was unpowdered and the lights from the chandelier danced along its russet waves. She wasn't ill. She showed no signs of decline. She looked, Rafe thought with a strange sense of outrage, absolutely beautiful.

She was laughing and smiling up at a man whom Rafe immediately recognized as Lord Rothwell. He frowned; Rothwell was old enough to be her father and had buried two wives already. The man no doubt was on the lookout for a third to mother his brood of unruly children. Rafe fought the urge to reach out and pluck the man's thin fingers from Alix's slim waist.

Only experience kept him moving through the final steps of the dance. When the music ended, Anne dipped her head and murmured softly. "You seem distracted, my lord, would you prefer to stroll along the gallery?"

"Forgive me, Lady Anne, but I've promised Louisa I would keep an eye on Elizabeth. If you will excuse me." He slipped away unmindful of the waspish look Anne Dinsmore cast at his departing back.

Alix was nowhere to be seen. Rafe caught sight of Elizabeth with Louisa at her side chatting with two earnest-looking country squires and a fortune hunter. Louisa waved her red-and-black fan as if to beckon him over, but Rafe kept moving. He'd check on Elizabeth and Louisa later, he told himself, his eyes riveted on a flash of silver and blue weaving through the crowd.

Not so fast, my Lady Moreham, he thought as he quickened his pace, the beating of his heart drowning out the conversations swirling around him. He barely avoided colliding with an outstretched hand holding a glass of champagne as he mentally reviewed the speech he would give Alix. He ignored an attempt to hail him. He'd explain in a calm, rational manner that the marriage had been consummated and there was nothing left for her but to come home with him. Sidestepping the flounce of a young lady's skirt, at last he caught sight of her. She was standing with a striking woman in black, whom he had no doubt was the comtesse, and the elegant figure of the Duchess of Melbourne.

Forcing himself to slow down, Rafe took a step toward the three women and found himself trapped by a red-faced man in a gray powdered wig. "Moreham, old boy, been searching for you everywhere," said the Honorable Elias Penworthy. "Didn't you see me wave? Framingham and I were just having a debate over whether white or ecru waistcoats will be the rage this season. You simply must come and decide it for us."

The Comtesse Madeleine de Rabec de La Brou stood perusing the Kensington's guests, her black lace fan drifting idly back and forth. Her dark eyes narrowed, and she snapped it closed, wrapping Lady Melbourne lightly on the wrist. "That one, there in the apple green silk with the white powdered wig, who is he?"

Lady Melbourne followed the path of Madeleine's gaze, shook her head ever so slightly. "No, no Madame, not that one. He's terrifically dull, can't start or end a conversation that doesn't include horses. You'd have to wear horseshoes and a wreath in bed to get his attention." She twisted an elbow draped in blonde lace toward her right. "See the one in the dark blue coat with the red-and-gold waistcoat, now there's a gentleman on close terms with the Bank of England."

Madeleine frowned. "The one with the stooped shoul-

ders, who looks like he might possibly be several months
gone beneath his waistcoat?"

Lady Melbourne pressed two fingers to her lips to hold
back her laughter and nodded. "The very one."

Madeleine gave a mock shudder. "*Mon Dieu*, satin
sheets and velvet coverlets are lovely, but not when they
come with sagging flesh between them."

"You are simply awful, Madeleine de La Brou, simply
awful . . . you must promise you won't leave Melbourne
House before the end of the season."

Madeleine flipped open her fan. "*Mais certainement,* if
your season does not offer better than this, you may find
me still with you in your dotage." Her fan froze in mid-
flutter. "*Regardez-ça.* Who is that delicious man there, all
in black with the golden brown hair.

Lady Melbourne smiled. "I see you've noticed the Earl
of Moreham. Now there's a prize. Not a bit of sawdust in
his stockings, no padding in his jacket, and his fortune's
just as solid. Quite elusive though. Over thirty and never
married. Last season it looked as though the Duke of Dinsmore's daughter, Lady Anne, might finally have snagged
him." Lady Melbourne gave a slight shrug. "But before she
could reel him in, the fish slipped away . . . to France, in
fact." She cast a conspiratorial glance at her friend. "They
say, he has a taste for French ladies . . . perhaps you or
Mademoiselle Alix might have better luck."

Madeleine nodded thoughtfully, the black plumes in her
dark curls wafting in Rafe's direction. "Alix, *ma petite*,
what do you think of that handsome fellow all in black?"

Alix looked and almost dropped her glass of lemonade.
"I beg your pardon *Maman*?" she sputtered. "Did you say
something? I confess I was caught up in the music."

"Alix, don't be ridiculous, the violas are quite out of
tune; they sound like cats with their tails cut off. How can

you possibly be distracted by them when such an attractive gentleman is looking our way?"

Alix looked again and saw that Rafe Harcrest was, indeed, looking at them over the heads of two stout gentlemen who looked to be in the midst of a heated debate.

"Well, what do you think, my dear, isn't he positively delicious?"

"I suppose he's handsome enough," Alix conceded, thinking there ought to be a law against a man looking so sinfully attractive.

"Handsome enough," her mother sniffed. "That must be your de La Brou half speaking. No appreciation for things of beauty. I don't like to speak disrespectfully of the deceased, but your father was the type of man who'd look at a sculpture of a Greek god and wonder why they didn't put more clothes on the fellow."

Thinking like a de La Brou, indeed, Alix thought. Rafe could be wearing a great coat and still the image of his body, bronzed in the firelight, would rise up before her eyes. Her mouth went suddenly dry.

She looked again and saw that Rafe was striding toward them. She hastily swallowed the remainder of her lemonade, wishing desperately it were something stronger.

"Lady Melbourne," Rafe said, "you are looking radiant as ever."

"Moreham, how pleasant to see you." They exchanged the requisite pleasantries. "I might flatter myself that you have come to visit with me." Lady Melbourne gave a mock sigh. "Alas, I suspect like all the other gentlemen tonight you wish to meet my friends, the Comtesse de La Brou and her daughter, Mademoiselle de La Brou. Comtesse, mademoiselle, may I present His Lordship, Rafe Harcrest, the Earl of Moreham."

"Delightful to meet you, my lord," Madeleine said sweeping her skirts into a graceful curtsy.

"My lord," Alix murmured dipping, her gray eyes watchful.

Rafe addressed Madeleine in French. "I would be honored if your daughter would join me in a dance."

The Comtesse de La Brou smiled at him. "Your command of our language is admirable, my lord, but so long as we are guests of your gracious King George, we speak only English. I believe you will find my daughter's knowledge of your tongue is impeccable."

So the little hoyden spoke English!

He shot a glance at Alix, and she blushed. He should have known, what well-educated French aristocrat would not? What conversations had she overheard during their time together, he wondered, and why hadn't she told him?

He held out his arm. "Mademoiselle, shall we dance?"

Alix's silver fan fluttered unsteadily. "If His Lordship will excuse me, I find myself too warm to dance at this time."

He wouldn't let her slip away that easily. "I think you'll find the portrait gallery much cooler than the dance floor, Mademoiselle de La Brou, and Lord Kensington's art collection is quite impressive." Rafe tucked Alix's hand under his arm, before she could protest.

Smiling warmly at Alix's mother, he said, "Madame, with your permission?" The Comtesse de La Brou nodded her approval.

"I have no desire to go anywhere with you," Alix insisted through a clenched smile as he guided her through the crowded ballroom

"We traveled through France together and now you're refusing to cross a dance floor?" Rafe shook his head. "We need to talk."

"You couldn't have sent a card round in the morning, instead you must abduct me?"

"There's the rub sweetheart, I wouldn't have known

how to address a card, to Mademoiselle de La Brou or to Lady Moreham."

"Mademoiselle de La Brou would be fine."

"You see, that's where we disagree, and that's precisely why we need to talk."

Rafe spotted what he had been looking for, a drape of velvet that concealed the doorway to a small sitting room. Glancing about to see that no one was watching them, he opened the door and pulled Alix inside. Two small candelabras burned on the mantelpiece, illuminating the dark green walls and matching armchair and chaise. He closed the door and turned to face her.

Cole's admonition to speak calmly drifted through his head. How could he speak calmly to her when she stood looking at him like that, her mahogany curls tumbled around her shoulders, her face rosy with anger and her eyes like silver flames? He had a wild desire to laugh. It was all he could do not to take her into his arms.

"You left me," he said, "without a word, without a note."

"Indeed, *my Lord Moreham*," she said frostily, "I would have thought with a fiancée anxiously awaiting your return, you would have been pleased to have found yourself unencumbered."

"I do not have a fiancée," he growled. "I have a wife."

"A wife in name only."

His eyes widened in surprise that she would say this after what they'd shared in Calais. "Oh no, my dear," he said stepping closer, "a wife in a great deal more than name."

"We had an agreement . . ."

"An agreement that was breached when I breached your maidenhead."

She flushed. "There's no need to be crude . . ."

"I'm not being crude, Alix," he said quietly, "I'm being honest."

She studied the delicate sticks of her fan. "It doesn't have to change anything."

"Alix," he said firmly, "I think you know it changes everything."

Her hand fluttered at her throat and Rafe noticed a thin gold chain entangled in her pearls. He drew nearer, lightly touching the shimmering links. "You wear my ring Alix," he said softly. "What else do you have of mine?"

She turned her back on him and said fiercely, "Nothing."

"Do you carry my child, Alix?" he whispered against her ear.

"No. Does that satisfy you? I'm not carrying your precious heir. There will be no scandal to sully the Harcrest name. You can return to courting Lady Dinsmore . . ."

Rafe caught her wrist and swung her around to face him. "It's not Anne Dinsmore that I want."

Alix stared into the green and gold of his eyes. Seared by their intensity, she dropped hers, fixing her gaze instead on the silver embroidery on his waistcoat. "We should forget that we ever met . . ."

"Can you do that, Alix?" Rafe tilted her chin up. "Can you forget?" He stroked her lower lip with his thumb. "Because I can't."

"I can."

"Liar," he murmured as his lips descended and consumed hers. She shuddered as his tongue plunged into her mouth, seeming to draw her resistance as it withdrew, then thrust again. Her body cried out for his, for the heated caresses it had only begun to know and had so desperately missed these last weeks. She closed her eyes and felt his mouth move against her eyelids, her cheeks, the length of her nose. He took her mouth again and Alix wondered distractedly if bones could melt.

"Anne Dinsmore was right," he whispered, as he drew his hand down her satin-covered breast, his thumb trailing behind to tease the hardened nipple. "Your neckline is too low."

"Anne Dinsmore was right," the words spread like ice on her flaming senses. He'd discussed her with Anne Dinsmore. They'd discussed her décolletage, no less. What else had he said about her to his fiancée? Had they laughed at what a fool she'd been, how easily she'd succumbed to his seduction? And here she was, about to give way again. Alix stiffened. She didn't know what Rafe Harcrest wanted from her, but she knew she didn't trust him.

"I can forget you, Rafe Harcrest," she gasped, thrusting him away. "I can, because you lied to me and you deceived me. You gave me your word and then you broke it."

Rafe stepped back as if he had been slapped. "I never lied to you Alix . . . I saved your life."

"But that doesn't mean you own it."

But she was his, Rafe thought distractedly. Didn't she realize that? Didn't she feel it when they touched? "Alix, be reasonable I . . ."

But Alix already had her hand on the doorknob. "This talk is over my Lord Moreham. Go back to your blond duke's daughter."

She slipped out the door, resisting the urge to run. She'd jeopardized her reputation enough without bolting through Lord Kensington's portrait gallery. She walked swiftly toward the marble staircase, not daring to look back. She couldn't face Rafe. She didn't want to see him or talk to him, or think about him. It was too confusing and too painful. And though she could think of a dozen reasons not to stay married to him, when he touched her they melted into a meaningless slush. Descending the stairs and melding into the crowd, Alix searched the sea of feathers and lace for her mother's black ostrich plumes, feeling as desperate to find Madeleine as she had in France.

Rafe stood in the silence of the empty room, inhaling the lingering fragrance of Alix's perfume. The evening had not gone at all as he had planned. He had imagined they would talk. She would see reason and come home with him. How could he have known she would believe he was engaged to Anne Dinsmore?

Lady Anne. She would never have left him. He would never have had to stalk her through London ballrooms, stealing moments with her like an illicit lover. But then Anne would never have melted in his arms as Alix did. A smile played across his lips. He wondered if Alix had seen the motto engraved on the ring she wore around her neck: WHAT I CLAIM IS MINE.

Anne Dinsmore stood in the portrait gallery concealed behind the bust of a long-dead cavalier. She watched as Rafe stepped through the curtained door, then disappeared quickly down the stairs. Her eyes narrowed thoughtfully. So the rumors were true, Moreham did have taste for things French. The earl had made quite the direct line for the girl once she'd pointed her out. She wondered if there was a connection between this slut in silver and the harlot her friend Edina Silverton had seen him with in Dover.

Whether there was or not, it made no difference, she still needed to handle the situation. Moreham could pursue all the French pastries that he liked, but only after they were married. She'd been so certain he was going to come up to scratch when he'd invited her to Moreham Hall. Yet now, since his trip to France, he seemed to be slipping farther and farther from her grasp.

That just would not do.

Anne Mary Frances Dinsmore was not going to spend another season entertaining the ton and pretending she was unmarried because she chose to be. She wanted a husband and Moreham met all the requirements: wealthy, not too old, and perfectly respectable. She descended the stairs to the ballroom, considering the indiscretion she had just seen. She could noise it about that the French girl was of questionable virtue and encourage people to cut her. But that ran the risk of offending Lady Melbourne and encouraging Moreham to step forward to protect the girl's reputation. No, she'd have to save this juicy morsel of scandal and see what else developed. Noticing Elizabeth Harcrest dancing with Lord Portsmouth, a smile flickered across her thin lips. Heaven only knew what pitfalls might lie before a naïve young girl in her first season. Anne's smile widened as she caught sight of her brother leaning lazily against a column in the ballroom sipping champagne.

Perhaps it was time for Elizabeth to become better acquainted with James and his ... interesting ... circle of friends.

Chapter Nineteen

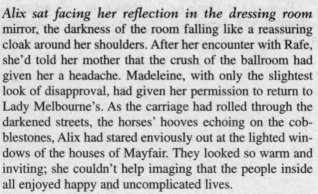

Alix sat facing her reflection in the dressing room mirror, the darkness of the room falling like a reassuring cloak around her shoulders. After her encounter with Rafe, she'd told her mother that the crush of the ballroom had given her a headache. Madeleine, with only the slightest look of disapproval, had given her permission to return to Lady Melbourne's. As the carriage had rolled through the darkened streets, the horses' hooves echoing on the cobblestones, Alix had stared enviously out at the lighted windows of the houses of Mayfair. They looked so warm and inviting; she couldn't help imaging that the people inside all enjoyed happy and uncomplicated lives.

It was a ridiculous fantasy. She knew those walls concealed their share of unhappy marriages, ailing family members, and financial insecurity. It was just that she seemed to have made such a mess of her own life, she thought, as she unclipped her pearl drop earrings and let them fall carelessly into a velvet-lined jewelry box. Ginny had been up earlier to help her into her nightdress, but she had been unusually quiet, and when she'd complained of stomach cramps, Alix had willingly sent her off to bed.

Alix began to pull the pins from her hair, the heavy tresses snaking softly down her back. How had she ever imagined she could pretend she and Rafe had never met, or that she could behave as if they were vague acquaintances? When he'd looked at her it seemed as if his eyes saw into her very soul and when he touched her . . . Alix scattered the pins, she didn't like to think about how her body betrayed her at his touch. She picked up an ivory-handled brush and, as she did so, heard the bedroom door open.

"Ginny, truly there's no need to trouble yourself; I can get myself into bed without help." The door closed, and she heard footsteps too heavy to be the maid's cross her bedchamber floor.

"But I want to help you," Rafe said in low tone, taking the hairbrush from her motionless grasp. As he had done that afternoon by the fire in Paris, he began brushing her hair in long, slow strokes. Alix sat mesmerized by the sight of him reflected in the mirror, standing so unexpectedly behind her. He was still dressed in his evening clothes, black velvet and crisp white linen. His tawny hair was unpowdered and the candlelight made it look like it had been threaded with gold. His hazel eyes were cast in shadow, unreadable as they locked with hers in the mirror.

"How did you get in here?" she asked, breaking the silence.

Rafe smiled slightly, "Jervis has a way with locks and women."

"Ginny?"

He nodded.

The thought crossed Alix's mind that she should complain to the duchess, then vanished almost as quickly as it had come. Revealing that the Earl of Moreham was in her bedchamber would cause more trouble for her than it would for the maid.

"I could raise an alarm," she said.

"You could," he agreed. "What do you think we should tell the duchess and her staff? I could say I was taking a stroll and decided to pay a call on my wife."

"What of the scandal?"

"Damn the scandal."

Alix pulled the hairbrush out of his hand. "What do you want Rafe?"

His eyes darkened as he turned her chair to face him. "I want you to stop running and listen to me Alix. I want to finish the conversation we started this evening." He ran his finger gently down the curve of her face. "And most of all, I want you."

She moved to push his hand away. "When you look at me like that I can't think straight, and when you touch me, I do things I know I shouldn't . . ."

Rafe understood. She created the same havoc in his head. "Why do you fight so hard against something that feels so right, my love?"

"Because I'm afraid that it's all that we have between us. What happens if you no longer want me, and you begin to regret you didn't marry the woman you had planned to be your countess?"

Rafe's eyes swept down the curves of her body, barely hidden by her thin nightdress and he wondered if his desire for her would ever fade. "I won't Alix."

The words seemed to echo in the room and resonate in her soul. *Don't you understand, she wanted to scream at him, I can bear it all, the loss of my father, the loss of my home, my titles and fortune, but I cannot bear to give you everything that I am, body and soul and lose you, too.*

"But you can't promise that can you?" she said quietly,

instead. "And even if you did, how do I know that I can trust you?"

"I've never lied to you, Alix."

He'd never lied to her, it was true, but she couldn't forget all the deceptions he'd practiced. "Why didn't you tell me when we were wed that you were an earl?"

How could he explain to Alix what he'd felt when he'd heard the revulsion in Anne Dinsmore's voice as she talked about bedding him? That when he'd kissed her that night in Paris before they were married, somehow even then, he'd known they were meant to be together? He'd wanted to be sure that she desired him as a man and not a title.

"Would it have made a difference Alix? And why didn't you tell me you spoke English?"

"Because I didn't trust you . . ."

They sat in silence for a moment, aware of the chasm that suddenly yawned between them.

"So what do *you* want Alix?" he said finally

"An annulment."

"The time for that has passed," he said softly. "I can't restore your innocence and I don't believe you're the kind of woman who would go to another marriage bed pretending your virtue was intact." He saw her stiffen at the impact of his words. "I'm sorry Alix, but neither of us can put things back they way they were."

"So what do we do now?"

"There will be no annulment, but I won't rush you into living with me. I will give you two months to become accustomed to the idea of becoming my wife, the Countess of Moreham. In the meantime, I will ask your mother for permission to pay court to you. We will go riding together, and we shall dance together, and we shall go into supper at parties together. And in December we will announce our intention to wed. We can go through with another, more appropriate ceremony if you like then, with flowers and a

gown and"—he lifted the signet ring between her breasts—
"a proper ring."

As he toyed with her wedding band, Alix wondered
how Rafe felt. He hadn't mentioned Lady Dinsmore. Was
Anne for him, like Valcour was for her, a part of the painful
past that now seemed lost forever? She wasn't sure she
wanted to know. Because she knew that Rafe was right, the
time for an annulment had passed, just as she knew she
would want no other husband than the man whose hazel
eyes were focused so possessively on her. She would be the
Countess of Moreham.

"Very well my lord," she said. "I will remain in the marriage."

It was the answer he been waiting to hear, but somehow
he felt cheated. Was she happy?

He brushed his misgivings aside. He'd *make* her happy
he swore, as he took her face between his hands and gently kissed her. Her lips warmed and softened beneath his
kiss. The familiar heat flared between them, and in that
moment, Rafe realized he'd do anything to keep her from
slipping away from him again. He would draw her with his
body, and then he would bind her with his heart.

He sank to his knees in front of her, his hands around
her ankles. He began trailing teasing kisses around the inside of her foot and along the curve of her ankle. Alix giggled and tried to pull her foot away. He held it fast, his lips
nipping at her calves and the back of her knees. He caught
the hem of her nightdress and slid it up. As his hair brushed
the inside of her knees and his lips and tongue traced lan-
guid trails along the soft inner flesh of her thighs, he heard
her laughter change to a gasp. Alix caught his head between her hands. "Rafe, I don't know . . . this seems . . . it
can't be right."

"Sweetheart, it was right before and it will be again . . ."

He flashed her a wicked grin. "Consider it a simple test of my trustworthiness."

Alix shifted nervously as his hands slid up to her hips, pulling her firmly back down into the chair. His thumbs moved in gentle, ever-widening ovals down around her hipbones and as his tongue meandered upwards to meet them. And then his hands left her hips, his fingers parted the folds of her moistened cleft and his mouth settled on the sensitive flesh within.

"Oh God, Rafe," Alix moaned softly, her body flushed with embarrassment and desire.

His soft chuckle vibrated against her skin, his breath hot within her. "Trust me again Alix," he whispered.

Her last coherent thought was that there was nothing simple about the way he made her feel. She pressed against him, her fingers clasping the muscle of his shoulders, as he licked and teased. His mouth drew her relentlessly toward climax, waves of pleasure rippling through her and surging upward. She flung her head back against the chair, her eyes closed, her teeth gripping her lower lip, fighting to restrain the cries welling up in her throat.

Rafe lifted his head and pulled her off the chair and down onto the thick woven carpet. As he did, her nightdress caught and twisted upwards and his mouth quickly followed its path, nipping and sucking at each measure of newly exposed flesh.

Alix grasped his hair, dragging his head up, kissing him and tasting herself salty and sweet on his lips. She fumbled with the buttons of his waistcoat, pulling the linen of his shirt from the constraints of his waistband and pushing the tangled mass off his shoulders and out of the way. Her hands gloried in the remembered feel of the hair on his chest, the smooth skin tight across his ribs and the muscles of his back.

His mouth found her breasts and together they struggled

to open his britches and drag them down his tapered hips. Alix felt his member fall heavily against her and she moved anxiously against him. She heard him groan, "Alix you drive me to madness," as he positioned himself between her thighs. She opened herself to him and this time there was no pain, only pleasure. Alix wrapped her legs around his flanks, needing to feel him strong and deep within her, satisfying the yearning only he created and only he could quell.

Her hands clenched the hard curve of his buttocks, urging him on. Rafe thrust and withdrew, circled and teased, and Alix arched upwards eagerly following his movements. He tried to control the pace, to lead her slowly into climax, but she pressed against him, the heat of her desire urgent against his manhood, and he was lost. They climaxed together, their bodies seeming to fuse with the heat of their passion. Alix whispered, "Yes, yes, yes" to unasked questions: Was it good? Was it right? Did they belong together?

Afterwards they lay slick and spent like newborn birds in the scattered nest of his clothes. Rafe drew Alix close and kissed her gently, murmuring her name. They fell asleep enmeshed in each other's arms, enjoying the first dreamless sleep either had known since they'd arrived together in London.

When Alix awoke she saw a thin blade of sunlight cutting through the curtains and she knew that it must close to noon. Rafe had woken her just before dawn with gentle caresses, carrying her to the bed and making love to her one final time before Lady Melbourne's staff was up and about. She stretched out her arms and pulled the pillow where his head had rested close, inhaling the lingering scent of his body. She was going to be his wife, she mused and smiled. The thought no longer seemed frightening. As she stroked the indentations where his body had lain, it seemed more like a challenge. She'd heard the Earl of Moreham rarely gambled and then only played to win.

Well, so did she. If he thought he'd won Alexandre Charlotte de Rabec de La Brou for his wife, then he find he would have to pay with his heart.

Alix sat up in bed, noticing as she did that her night-dress had been carefully folded at the foot of her bed. Pulling it over her head, she hopped purposely to the floor and drew back the curtains. Immediately the dark room was flooded with rich golden sunshine. It was a beautiful day, she thought, and she had lots to do.

Ginny bustled in shortly, a tray of steaming cocoa and a basket of warm bread and muffins in her hands. Putting the tray down on a table near Alix's bed, she went first to the fire, which she stoked up until the flames crackled noisily on the hearth. She stood for a moment, admiring her hand-iwork, brushing her hands off on her apron. Then she began rattling about the breakfast tray. It seemed to Alix that she spent an inordinate amount of time arranging the silverware and the breadbasket.

Finally Ginny turned, offering Alix a cup of cocoa that rattled noisily in its saucer. Carefully fixing her eyes on a spot beyond the bed she said, "Would you like some por-ridge, mademoiselle? Because we've got some lovely por-ridge in the kitchen. I know you French folks don't care for it, but it's really quite good. We've got some kidneys, too, and some nice eggs if you'd prefer . . . ."

Alix frowned. Ginny knew she didn't like to begin the day with a heavy breakfast. "No, thank you, Ginny."

"And we've got ham, some fine country ham, sliced lovely and thick. There's a bit of kippers . . ."

Alix interrupted, afraid if she didn't Ginny would pro-ceed to offer her the contents of Lady Melbourne's larder. "Really, Ginny, this breakfast is fine." She smiled reassur-

ingly. "Are you feeling better this morning?" The maid
flushed nearly as bright as her strawberry-blond hair, and
Alix understood the reason for the expansive breakfast
menu.

"Ginny," she began, "about last night."

The maid looked up her skin surpassing strawberry and
shifting to a shade Alix thought might be described as
tomato. "I'm sorry, miss, if I've done wrong, but Jervis
said . . ."

"I can just imagine the stories Jervis told you," Alix
said, trying her best not to think about what Rafe's manservant had told her maid. "Jervis could probably talk his way
into King George's bedchambers if he had a mind to."

Ginny nodded eagerly. "Right you are, mademoiselle.
The man's a marvel with his tongue. When I'm with Jervis,
sure he could convince me day was night even with the sun
shining clear as anything in the sky. When he explained
why I should step out last evening, it all seemed to make
perfect sense." She pleated her hands in her skirt. "It was
only later that I began to think I might have done something wrong." Ginny bowed her head, her hands fisted.
"I'd understand, mademoiselle, if you'd told her ladyship
to turn me out."

Alix stared at the maid aghast. "Oh Ginny, I'd never do
that. No young woman should be left to fend for herself on
the streets. There's no harm done, really there isn't."

Ginny looked at Alix, her blue eyes intent. "Jervis said
you was a good one and you are mademoiselle. He said we
were only doing what the good Lord intended. And he's a
godly-man Jervis is, goes to church with me every Sunday."

Alix had some difficulty seeing Jervis as one of the
Lord's right-hand men, much less as a regular churchgoer,
but she could sympathize with Ginny's confusion.

"I'm sure that whatever forces were moving Jervis, he

meant well," she said carefully, thinking she'd better have a talk with those forces before they led anyone else astray.

"Oh right you are, mademoiselle," Ginny agreed hastily, "right you are. Can I draw you a bath while you're taking your breakfast?"

Alix smiled. "That would be lovely."

Ginny rushed off to comply, grateful the discussion was over and that Alix wasn't angry with her. Perhaps Jervis had been telling the truth when he'd said mademoiselle was the earl's wife and that they'd had a misunderstanding. Certainly her mistress looked happier today than she'd ever seen her and word downstairs was that a servant in his lordship's livery had arrived early this morning with a letter for the Comtesse de La Brou. Still, it was mighty queer, a man and wife pretending they weren't married. Ginny shook her head as she started down the stairs for her buckets. For people who were supposed to be her betters, the quality sure could make simple things complicated.

Alix was sunk deep in her bath when her mother swirled in, a vision in a yellow day dress scattered with nosegays of violet. Madeleine might wear black in public for dramatic affect, but in private she adored color.

"Alexandre, *ma petite*, I knew you would take after the de Rabecs and not those dull de La Brous, I knew it."

Alix cast a puzzled glance at her mother.

"Don't look coyly at me, young lady," Madeleine continued. "In a single evening, you have made one of the greatest conquests of the season. The Earl of Moreham has sent word that he would like to speak to me this afternoon to seek my permission to pay his addresses to you." She clasped her hands together, her face glowing. "He is not old, he is not ugly, and her ladyship tells me he's quite well off. Indeed, the duchess was quite surprised when I told her the news. She says his lordship has been quite elusive on the marriage mart, though there had been some speculation he might marry the Duke of Dinsmore's daughter Lady Anne." She waved a hand dismissively. "I think we may have met her, a long-faced girl who speaks deplorable French."

"But back to the earl," she said, regarding Alix intently. "I will not arrange a marriage for you without your consent as your father did with that awful Marquis de Beincourt." She shuddered delicately. "With those terrible bony roaming fingers."

Alix glanced quickly at her mother, surprised that Madeleine had known about the marquis's unpleasant tendency to grope her bosom when they were left unattended and wondered what else her sharp dark eyes had observed. Schooling her face to appear no more than mildly interested she nodded. "It is all right, Mother, you may tell him I will consider his suit."

Madeleine clapped her hands together. *"Eh bien,* I will tell him." She turned back for a moment before she left the room. "I have a good feeling about this one," she said.

Alix's fingers touched the heavy gold ring hidden beneath the bubbles of her bath, and thought, So do I mother. So do I.

Chapter Twenty

Rafe entered the Melbourne residence with a jaunty step, and left two hours later, feeling as though he'd run one of those gauntlets Jervis was so fond of describing. Only there hadn't been two lines of Iroquois women tearing at his flesh, only one delicate, darkly-clad Frenchwoman who'd battered him with questions.

She'd been working at some piece of embroidery when he arrived, some doleful sampler commemorating her late husband. Pushing her needle full of black satin thread into the frame, she'd risen gracefully and extended a small white hand. Rafe had kissed it, remarking that it was a pleasure to see her again, and thanking her for receiving him so promptly. They'd continued to exchange pleasantries as she'd offered him a seat by the fire, and poured him some tea, circling conversationally until they finally settled on the purpose of his visit.

He had been prepared for her to ask about his lineage, his family, and his potential heirs, and he'd expected her to

inquire into his land holdings and financial status. However, after an hour and a half of discussions into how he
planned to provide for Alix's upkeep and possible widow-
hood, he began to wonder if he might have been better
served by sending a solicitor in his place.

Offering him a final slice of lemon cake she had set
down her teacup, turned her gaze full upon him, and said,
"My Lord Moreham, my daughter has but recently been returned to my care. I am her sole remaining relative and I
take my responsibility to ensure her happiness very seriously, so I hope you will understand if some of my questions seem a trifle probing.

"Your request to court my daughter seems . . ." She
frowned. "Ah . . . what would be the right English
word . . . precipitous? Is this love at first sight, my lord?"

"Perhaps not at first sight," Rafe answered, a smile
flickering in his eyes as he recalled that at first sight Alix
looked like she'd spent a week in a chicken coop. "But
there is something about your daughter, Madame la
Comtesse . . . that stirs me . . . that makes me feel that if I
let her slip away I will regret it for the rest of my life."

Madeleine nodded. "It is a good start. Would you like
some more tea, my lord?" When he shook his head, she
poured herself a cup. "And what about this Lady Anne
Dinsmore? I have heard that you and she were considered
practically affianced. You do not seem like the kind of man
who plays fast and loose with a woman's affections, and
yet . . ."

"I have known Lady Anne since she was a child and I
will admit I had begun to consider asking her to become
my wife. But life is full of surprises, is it not Madame de
La Brou?"

She nodded. "Indeed, my lord, if life were always as we
planned it, I suspect neither of us would be having this conversation today. It is just such surprises I am seeking to

guard my daughter against in her marriage." Madeleine carefully dropped a lump of sugar in her tea. "Do you plan to keep mistresses?"

It was with difficulty that he kept his jaw from dropping. "I suspect, madame, that any man who invites de La Brou women into his life will soon find there is no place for other women."

"Just so my lord." She smiled and stirred her tea gently. "I lived for a long time at Versailles, and while the gossip surrounding our foolish queen was never true, there were plenty of men who kept women or had other, shall we say, unusual pursuits."

"I can assure you, Madame de La Brou, my only unusual pursuit is your daughter."

Madeleine laughed. "Touché, my lord. It is only that when a man has lived without a wife for as long as you have, one begins to wonder . . ."

Rafe's brows rose. "I believe I am not in my dotage yet. However, I will explain. When I was young I had no interest in marriage. As I grew older and became more interested, I was a less-than-eligible second son. Now, as the Earl of Moreham, you might say women have found me far too eligible. It has taken me some time to find just the right woman to suit."

Madeleine cast him a scornful look. "Ah bah, my lord, horses suit the carriage, oxen suit the yoke, but a man and a woman in a marriage should do much more than suit."

Rafe inclined his head politely. "Perhaps I have chosen the wrong words, madame. Alix and I . . ." He paused, considering how to describe the way he and Alix got on. He reflected that he couldn't say to her mother that she made his blood burn in his veins and his body ache to be with her. "Alix and I get along quite comfortably."

"Then you've met my daughter before?"

Rafe studied Madeleine, but her dark eyes gave nothing

away; he didn't know how much Alix had told her mother about how she'd reached London. "Madame," he answered smoothly, "when I looked into your daughter's eyes, I felt as if we had met before. And when we strolled along the gallery we fell into conversation as naturally as old companions." Old sparring companions, more like, he thought, glancing at the comtesse to see how she responded to his answer.

Madeleine straightened. "Old companions—now that is a basis to establish a marriage, for after the passion fades the friendship must remain. You have my leave to court my daughter." But, she said, admonishing him with a slim white finger, "The final decision is hers."

"Gray," he said, eyeing Alix critically as he handed her up into his chaise two days later, "you're wearing gray again."

"My lord is very observant," Alix responded as she smoothed out the skirts of her charcoal gray walking dress.

"I don't like gray."

"Well, then it's a good thing you're not wearing my clothes," she replied. "Madeleine feels that for a young girl it expresses mourning appropriately, and that it makes a dramatic contrast with her black."

Rafe snorted.

"I don't believe I've had any complaints from my other suitors," she added. "Would you care to see the notes I've received?"

Rafe frowned. He'd seen the flowers filling Lady Melbourne's sitting room, and he didn't appreciate the idea of other men courting his wife.

"Lord Minton is taking me to the theatre this evening. I hear the play is quite good. Shall you be there?"

He hadn't planned on it, but supposed now he'd need to go, to keep watch on her. His frown deepened.

"Are you always this grouchy in the afternoon?" Alix inquired.

"No," he said through gritted teeth. "Only when my wife is squired around town by notorious bounders."

"Really?" she asked wide-eyed. "Lady Melbourne says Minton's charming and quite the catch."

"I would remind you, my lady, that you have already been caught."

Alix laughed. "Lady Melbourne was rather surprised when you came to call. She says you're quite a catch too, though she's not sure you'll come up to scratch."

Rafe's eye's gleamed golden in the sunlight. "If your ladyship will recall, I believe I have more than come up to scratch." His lips curved slightly. "However, if you feel the need for a reminder, I would be more than willing to provide one."

Alix flushed, her pulse beating quickly.

Rafe's eyes caressed the creamy expanse of her throat then meandered meaningfully down to the swell of her bosom. "Come now, Alix, why don't we give up this sham courtship and return to my home?"

Alix felt her flesh grow hot under his gaze. "What of the scandal, my lord?"

"Damn the scandal. I want you, Alix, in my home and in my bed."

"You promised me two months, Rafe, two months to become accustomed to my future as your wife." Two months, she thought, to discover if he wanted her for more than the pleasures of her body. "Does your word mean nothing, my lord?"

"You'll find my word means everything, Lady Moreham. Two months," he said, the fire in his eyes suddenly banked, "and then I shall rely upon your word."

An awkward silence fell between them, and Alix found herself almost grateful when two riders approached.

A slender blond man in a deep blue jacket hailed Rafe. He was almost handsome, Alix thought, but his looks were marred by what appeared a permanently bored expression.

"Ho, Moreham," the young man said, "lovely day for a ride about the park."

Rafe returned the greeting coolly. "Dinsmore, you're looking fit. Lady Anne," he said, his tone warming as he greeted the second rider, "as lovely as ever."

Anne smiled as she patted her horse's neck. "You flatter me, Moreham. It was good to see you last evening. I enjoyed our dance." She inclined her head in Alix's direction. "And who is your young companion?"

As Rafe introduced her to Anne and James Dinsmore, Alix studied Anne as closely as possible without staring outright. So this cool, elegant blond was the woman Rafe had intended for his wife.

"Our Rafe has always had such a fondness for things French," Anne purred. "I think it's lovely the way he and other members of society have reached out to help our poor brethren across the channel."

Alix smiled and put a hand on Rafe's arm. "Yes, his lordship has been a great comfort to me and to my mother." She noticed with satisfaction that Lady Anne looked as though she would like to reach out and slap her hand away from Rafe. Anne's brother noticed, too, and looked slightly amused.

Anne nodded knowingly. "I'm not surprised. I remember when Moreham was younger he was always rescuing pathetic little things, a half-drowned kitten, a fox kit that had been chased and chewed by the dogs."

Alix raised a brow. "Indeed, my lady, I wouldn't have thought you as old as his lordship."

Anne covered her annoyance with a brittle laugh. "We share so many interests, I quite forget that Moreham and I are not of a similar age. Although growing up, our families were so close, he seemed like a very special older brother."

Alix smiled and batted her lashes as Rafe. "I shall have to take your ladyship's word for it since I must confess, I have never seen his lordship in a brotherly light."

Sensing she was losing ground, Anne changed the subject. "Speaking of siblings, Moreham, is your charming little sister come to town yet? James and I should so enjoy her company for tea, and perhaps a visit to the philosophical society lecture."

Rafe wondered at this turn of events. Anne had never shown any interest in socializing with Elizabeth; when his sister was younger, Anne had often referred to her as "that mannerless brat." He smiled. "I wasn't aware you and James were interested in philosophy, but I will certainly pass your invitation on to Elizabeth."

Anne smiled at Alix. "One of the great pleasures of an old friendship is that we constantly learn new things about one another and find new things to share."

"I'm sure," Alix murmured.

"I say," James said suddenly, "there's Sudderby. I've been meaning to ask him about the gray Ascot's planning to race at Newmarket next week. If you will excuse us?"

Anne glanced at Rafe. "I will be looking for you to partner me at cards this evening at the Hensford's." And without waiting for an answer, she and her brother rode off.

"I can well see why you selected such a charming woman as your prospective bride." Alix shook her head, watching Anne's departing back.

Rafe chuckled. "I'll admit, Anne has a bit of a sharp tongue, but she's not so bad as all that. I admire her wit and her poise. I think they, and her father's title, have made other women a bit jealous of her and have made it difficult for her to make friends."

Alix stared at Rafe for a moment. It never ceased to

amaze her how men who were supposed to be the wiser sex could be so obtuse about women. Suddenly wanting to drop the subject of Anne, she smiled. "I suppose you could be right."

Rafe smiled. "And besides, how could I have known a French hoyden was going to sweep into my life and turn it upside down?"

Alix grinned up at him. "I believe, my lord, that *you* did the sweeping up. As I recall, I was but helpless bystander."

He laughed. "I'm beginning to think, my love, that you are never a helpless bystander."

Anne, Rafe reflected later that evening, could not have chosen a worse partner for cards. Though she looked quite lovely in her pale yellow gown and was at her most charming, brushing his arm with her hand and whispering amusing tidbits into his ear, his mind was on Alix at the theater with Minton. He'd always considered Minton to be rather shallow, but he could see, he admitted to himself, how a woman might find his easy chatter amusing. And he understood that some ladies thought Minton's blond hair and square jaw quite attractive. He had no doubt that Minton would find Alix appealing; the minx was irresistible. He wondered if he could skip the next round and make it to the theater before the play ended. He glanced at his watch. The thing must be halfway through by now. Minton was probably fawning all over Alix.

"You wound me, Moreham," Anne chided, "checking your watch. Have you somewhere else you need to be?"

"I apologize, Lady Anne, my mind was elsewhere."

She smiled. "I might have guessed. You've cost me a small fortune this evening."

"You should have chosen your partner more carefully. You know I don't care to gamble."

"Ah, but I can't resist the challenge, particularly when

the stakes are high." She gave a mock sigh, then said re-provingly. "I shall let you make up my losses by taking me riding tomorrow afternoon."

Rafe had intended to take Alix to explore the bookshops around St. Michael's alley the following afternoon. She'd mentioned in passing how she missed her books that had been destroyed when she'd fled her home, and he'd thought it might be a pleasant surprise. And yet, he didn't know how to extricate himself from Anne's invitation without appearing rude. He'd take Alix out the following day, he thought, as he assured Anne he'd be delighted to ride with her.

The next morning over breakfast Rafe discovered a de-scription of Alix's appearance with Minton in the papers. Apparently she'd caused quite a stir; the papers were dub-bing her the "silver siren." He'd been unable to make it to the theater. Anne had somehow anticipated his every effort to escape the card party. *Silver siren.* Weren't sirens the creatures in Greek mythology who lured sailors to their deaths? he thought, drumming his fingers on the breakfast tray. While there was no question his wife was bewitch-ing, he'd be the one drowning her suitors if she didn't have a care.

After breakfast, he could barely conceal his annoyance with Anne when they met for their ride. He nodded, half-listening to her tale of some mutual friends she had run into in town. His mind kept going back to that article in the paper.

Then he noticed Alix across the park.

She was riding with a much-too-dashing-looking major in the dragoons, wearing another of her damnable gray gowns, this one a riding habit trimmed in green velvet that made her look sleek and elegant. She had on a matching hat with a green feather that curled over her face, which to Rafe's eye was tilted far too close to her riding partner's.

"Oh," said Anne, following the direction of his gaze. "Isn't that your little French friend? Shall we wave them over to say hello?"

Rafe reflected that he'd like to do far more than wave and say hello, as he nodded in agreement with Anne.

"Mademoiselle de La Brou." Anne greeted Alix. "How charming to see you again, and may I say, what an elegant gray habit?"

"Lady Anne," Alix said coolly. "Lord Moreham, what a surprise. May I introduce Major Harris of his majesty's dragoons?"

"Any friend of Mademoiselle Alix is a friend of mine," the major said, a pleasant smile spreading across his broad face and lighting his deep brown eyes.

Alix. The leering clod had called his wife by her first name! Rafe wondered for a brief moment whether he should call him out.

"And how was the theater last night, Mademoiselle de La Brou?" Rafe asked.

"Quite unremarkable I'm afraid," Alix said.

"Only because Mademoiselle outshone the players on the stage," Major Harris offered gallantly. "Have you seen? The papers have taken to calling her the silver siren? I'm thinking of composing an ode in her honor."

"The silver siren," Rafe remarked dryly. "Weren't the sirens those unfortunate nymphs who drove men mad?"

"If Mademoiselle Alix drives men mad, I'm certain that it is only because of her beauty and charm," Major Harris volunteered.

"That must be it," Rafe mused.

"Why Mademoiselle de La Brou, it appears you have made a conquest," Anne teased.

"Your ladyship is reading much into a simple ride in the

park," Alix said, glancing at Rafe. "I am merely taking the opportunity to become better acquainted with one of your countrymen since it seems England is to be my home for some time."

"Forever, it is to be hoped," Major Harris said fervently.

Forever, indeed, Rafe thought with some annoyance, living in his home, surrounded by his children and far from the likes of smooth-tongued cavalry officers.

"Well, Major Harris," Anne said pleasantly, "you must be certain to show Mademoiselle de La Brou all of the interesting sites London has to offer in your effort to convince her to stay."

"I shall make it my duty," he agreed.

"Shall we continue on Moreham?" Anne asked as she urged her horse forward, an amused smile playing about her thin lips. When she had seen how Rafe fixed on Mademoiselle de La Brou at the Kensington's the other night, and then come upon him riding with her yesterday, she could have sworn he was developing a *tendresse* for the chit. But today the two looked at each other like cats that had been thrown together in a bag. This ride was turning out to be quite enjoyable.

"Quite a charming couple, wouldn't you say?" she said turning back to Rafe. "I understand you're having some redecorating done at Moreham House. I should be most interested in seeing the work. Your townhouse is so lovely, but perhaps"—she inclined her head slightly—"a bit lacking in the warmth of a woman's touch."

Rafe wondered how Anne had found out about the work in Moreham House. Nothing that occurred in Mayfair, it appeared, escaped her notice. "It's a small project, my lady, something that would, I fear, hold little interest for you." He smiled at her, and she seemed satisfied with his answer. She would have been horrified, he knew, if she could read his mind and trace the source of his smile. Because Anne

Dinsmore was the last person he would allow to see the redecorating he had planned, his wedding gift for Alix.

He had surprised himself by confessing to his stepmother his intention to marry in December. Louisa was delighted. *"Alix seems like a lovely girl,"* she'd said, but then she frowned at the prospect of a winter wedding. *"London is so dark and depressing then. Why not wait until the spring or the summer and marry at Moreham Hall?"* Shaking her head she'd said, *"I know it's silly of me, but I do love a wedding that's full of flowers."*

Louisa's words scratched at his conscience.

He found himself recalling the short, dreary ceremony at the Place de la Grève. Alix never raised the subject of their wedding being in December. Surely that was peculiar, he thought. Weren't women supposed to become excited about planning such festivities? He had found himself wanting to surprise her, wanting to make sure she remembered their wedding for all of her days. And Louisa, he had decided, was just the person to help him with his plan.

Alix might choose to lead him a merry dance, but in the end she was still his wife. He grinned and glanced at Lady Anne, grateful she'd reminded him he held all the cards. And he never gambled unless he was certain he could win.

Chapter Twenty-one

❧

"It's outrageous," Alix hissed as Ginny piled her heavy tresses high upon her head and fixed them with diamond ornaments. "For the past two weeks he's been squiring Anne Dinsmore about town as if . . ." She stopped, uncertain how much the maid knew, unable to say the words, *as if he hadn't a wife.* "As if he hadn't made certain promises to me," she finished lamely.

Ginny said nothing, simply tutted sympathetically.

"If you could see the way she puts her hands on him, calls him *Moreham*, as if he were her special possession. And he just sits there, like a great big . . . oh, what word would you use in English?" Alix glanced back inquiringly at Ginny.

"Lumpkin?" Ginny offered helpfully.

Alix shook her head.

"Dunderhead?" Ginny suggested.

"I think we must have better words for it in French," Alix concluded.

She was beginning to wonder if her request for two months to become accustomed to the idea of being married had been a mistake. At first she had enjoyed the attention of the men who courted her. She'd had far too little of that when she'd been at Valcour, and even as the fiancée of the Marquis de Beincourt. But she quickly realized that she was comparing all the men she met to Rafe Harcrest, and that they all fell woefully short.

"Why don't you just tell his lordship how you feel?" Ginny asked.

She might have been willing to admit she'd made a mistake, she reflected, if he hadn't suddenly started appearing everywhere with Anne Dinsmore. She chewed at her lip. Was he changing his mind? Had he compared her to Anne and decided that *she* came up short?

She shook her head. "He'd be insufferable. I can just imagine the pleasure he'd take in telling me what a fool I've been."

Ginny nodded. "Men do have a way of puffing up like roosters in a yard when they're in love. Still my mum says there's no harm in it."

But she didn't know whether Rafe was in love with her, Alix thought, and that was the problem. She grasped the chain around her neck, thinking that with all the lessons she'd been given in manners and deportment, someone might have provided some instruction on the ways of the heart.

Ginny placed a final ornament in Alix's hair and stood back to admire her handiwork. Alix was dressed in a gray gown with bright blue stripes over a blue satin underskirt. "Well, you can rest assured, mademoiselle, when he sees you tonight at the Beaumont's, he'll have eyes for no other. You look lovely, Mademoiselle Alix, truly lovely."

Rafe's thoughts echoed Ginny's words that evening when he saw Alix enter the Beaumont's grand salon. He couldn't resist, however, twitting her on her choice of colors. "Ah, my lady, you look ravishing this evening, and your gown . . . What do they call that color, dove gray, pearl gray?"

Alix glared at him.

"Perhaps the answer is storm gray?" he offered helpfully.

She inclined her head. "I think your lordship may have struck upon it."

"Can it be that after a mere two weeks you find yourself desperate for my company?" He leaned close and whispered in her ear. "Are you finding the prospect of a month and a half more without me in your bed more than you can bear?"

Alix felt her skin flush and she resisted the urge to swat at him with her fan. If only his words weren't so close to the truth. "It appears, my lord, that you have a rather high opinion of your charms."

Rafe shook his head in mock sorrow. "And I could have sworn that after our encounter the evening of the Kensington's assembly you did, too." His eyes gleamed with a wicked golden light. "Perhaps we should give it another try."

"You are an incorrigible rake," she breathed.

"No," he said, "I'm merely trying to seduce my wife. Unsuccessfully, it appears. Come now, Alix, what have I done wrong this time? I've given you the space you requested."

"And filled it with that blonde . . ." Alix paused searching for the correct word.

"Lady Anne," he finished.

"Not exactly the title I might have chosen, but yes," she agreed sharply.

"I see the trouble now. Alexandre de La Brou Moreham, are you jealous?" Rafe inquired with a raised eyebrow.

"I am not jealous," she insisted, "simply astonished that you would insist on holding me to our *commitment* while continuing to pursue your former fiancée."

"Anne and I were never betrothed," he said seriously. "And I am not pursuing her. I have merely been courteous to an old friend." He was about to continue when he was interrupted by the appearance of Lord Minton.

"Mademoiselle de La Brou, may I say that you look as luminous as a rare gray pearl rising from the sea this evening?"

"You flatter me, my lord."

"Not at all, mademoiselle. But you would flatter me if you would grant me the favor of a dance."

Rafe struggled to keep from rolling his eyes at this exchange.

"I would be delighted, my lord. His Lordship and I"—she cast a defiant look at Rafe—"have just completed our conversation."

Like hell they had, Rafe thought, as he watched Minton lead Alix to the dance floor. He felt a hand on his shoulder and turned to see Cole grinning at him.

"You appear to be having a damned hard time holding on to your wife, Moreham," he observed cheerfully.

"She may dance with Minton all she likes, Davenport," he said, not taking his eyes from the whirling couple. "It does not change the fact that she is my wife."

"It's a funny thing about women, Rafe; they're not like horses. It takes more than a certificate and an exchange of trinkets to make them stay put. Have you told her how you feel about her?"

"I would think that after all that has passed between us that would be understood."

"I think, my friend, it is no more clear to her than it is

to Lady Dinsmore that you are no longer an available bachelor." Cole looked up at the gallery, and Rafe followed his gaze to see Anne standing among a group of women observing the dancing.

"I've known Anne Dinsmore for a long time," Rafe muttered, "and I'm sure that she will understand."

"I watched Anne Dinsmore grow up as well and, as I recall, she was the child who would follow the game along, smiling all the while but, if she was losing, would toss a rock at your head as soon as your back was turned."

"Have you ever thought that it might have been because your head presented such an inviting target?"

A dimple appeared in Cole's cheek. "I haven't. Though on occasion I believe Phoebe might have considered a similar thing."

"Where is your charming wife this evening?"

"If you're looking for an ally then you'll have to wait. Some country squire trod on the hem of her dress and she's gone off to the retiring room to have it repaired. In the meantime, may I suggest we go in search of some of our host's famous brandy?"

Anne Dinsmore was indeed wishing she had something to throw at Rafe's head as she observed the activity in the grand salon below her. Moreham had yet to come up and greet her; as far as she could tell he'd spent all his time staring after that little French witch. She could tolerate a little flirtatious pursuit, but she was beginning to suspect that Rafe's attentions towards the girl were more serious. She'd done her best to cast herself in his way this season, to pick up where they'd left off that summer, but in spite of her efforts he seemed increasingly distracted.

There should be a price to pay for toying with a woman's expectations, she thought with rising annoyance. Moreham had failed to come up to scratch and here she was forced once again to scan the pool of men that she knew were either too short or too fat, too venal, or too stupid to make a suitable husband.

As if to rub salt into her wounds, Mrs. Hensford said loudly, "Just look at the Earl of Moreham staring at Lady Melbourne's little French protégé; he hasn't taken his eyes off her all evening. It would appear, Lady Anne, as though last season's fish is slipping your hook."

Anne purposely ignored the woman, knowing that a response would appear pitifully defensive. Instead, she languidly waved her fan and changed the subject. "You know, Mrs. Hensford, James took me to see the most marvelous play in Covent Gardens the other evening." She pretended to catch herself, as she turned to face the woman. "Oh, but then your husband prefers the ballet, does he not?" The woman flushed scarlet at this thinly veiled reference to her husband's well-known practice of keeping young dancers on his wife's money.

As Mrs. Hensford quickly found a pretense to move away from the group, another woman tapped Anne lightly on the arm with her fan. "Ah, my dear, I see disappointment has not blunted your edge."

Anne turned and smiled serenely at the elderly woman to her right, knowing that Lady Morton would not smile back to avoid revealing her missing teeth. "Moreham and I grew up together, you know. We are old friends. I'm pleased to see he's found someone to distract him from his business affairs and from the grief of losing his father and brother in so short a span of time." She sighed. "Though I do worry that in his pursuit of Mademoiselle de La Brou, he is neglecting poor Elizabeth."

"Indeed," Lady Morton said, craning her neck closer like a baby bird eagerly waiting for a tasty bit of gossip to fall.

Anne tilted her graceful white neck towards Lady Morton. "Elizabeth Harcrest is such a delightful girl, but"—she paused as if searching for just the right word—"so naïve, so careless. I fear if she should fix her attention on the wrong kind of person, she might behave in an unwise manner."

Lady Morton pursed her lips and nodded knowingly. Anne turned her attention back to the crowded ballroom, smiling with satisfaction. She knew she could count on Jemma Morton to flutter about the ton, repeating her comments with delicious embellishments. Anne's pale blue eyes came to rest on the gaunt frame of Lord Rothwell, and she glided off in his direction. Rothwell was comfortably set up, she reflected, and while he might expect her to pay nominal attention to his flourishing brood, at least he wouldn't be after her for an heir.

Alix stood before the mirror in the retiring room trying to coax a loose strand of hair back into place. Damn Rafe for the confusing man he was, she thought as the strand tumbled loose from its pin. Just when she thought she had him figured out, he'd change. Yesterday he'd had Anne Dinsmore hanging on his arm like some great pastel shawl, and this evening he'd been dancing attendance on her as if she were the only woman in the room.

When she looked into his eyes she thought she saw something that might pass for love, but he had said nothing to her about his feelings. She worried that what she saw might be simple possessiveness, or worse, nothing more than a reflection of her own emotions. She didn't want to be the one to raise the subject, and it was more than a matter of pride. If *she* asked, and he said he loved her, she'd always wonder if he'd said it only to soothe her into marriage; if he said he *didn't*, she'd be destroyed. Damn the man, she thought again, why couldn't he behave more like the swains in those poems about courtly love?

A ripple of sharp-edged laughter caught her attention. Three women stood before the mirror, patting their hair and straightening their gowns as they chattered. They were elegantly clad and coifed, and they carried themselves with the slightly bored assurance of women who had seen and experienced all that the London season had to offer. Fragments of their conversation distracted her. They were laughing at some dandy's choice of waistcoat and jacket, some other man's obsession with horses.

And then she heard them mention Elizabeth Harcrest.

"I understand the earl is going to have is hands full presenting *that* one," said a tall woman with auburn hair in a deep green gown.

"They say she's been a *terror* since she laced up her first corset," said a blonde in peach.

"Well, *I* saw her the other night at the Kensington's assembly," the third woman said knowingly and the other two turned from the mirror to listen more closely. The woman lowered her voice confidentially. "She looks sweet enough, but she was dancing just a bit too close with Lord Slane. And later, why you could hear her laughter clear across the supper table."

Alix finally pinned the rebellious strand back into place, and without looking at the women said clearly, "I've met Lady Elizabeth on several occasions. She's quite charming really, quite refined—for an English girl."

A slender blond woman, who'd been sitting in the corner of the room stitching at the hem of her sapphire gown, lifted her head. "Indeed, I know Lady Elizabeth as well. Such sweetness and beauty, I've no doubt she'll be one of the great successes of the season."

The three women drew up like a flock of startled geese. Straightening their heads, and flipping open their fans, they departed in hiss of rustling skirts and scandalized whispers.

"That should do it," the blonde in the sapphire said rising and shaking out her repaired hem. "I know I should have asked a maid for help, but I hate people fussing about me. Does it look straight to you?" When Alix nodded affirmatively she continued, "We may have laid it on a bit thick; Elizabeth is charming, but refined?" She wrinkled her nose. "Not the best description of the Elizabeth Harcrest I know."

Alix smiled ruefully. "I've never met Elizabeth, but I couldn't stand there and let those harpies tear her to shreds." She shook her head. "I confess, I used to think myself an honest person, but since I've arrived in England the falsehoods have been tripping off my tongue in frightful quantities."

"Those weren't exactly falsehoods, more like lovely embellishments," the blonde said. "Though it may have done more harm than good. The praises of a French émigré and a rustic colonial are hardly the nod from the patrons of Almack's."

As the woman joined her at the mirror, Alix noticed that she was very tall, very beautiful, and that her eyes were an amazing shade of deep blue. The blond woman laughed. "Though there's no doubt Moreham will have his hands full this season, between Elizabeth and you."

Only Madeleine's training kept Alix's jaw from dropping. Before she could think how to respond the woman extended her hand. "I'm Phoebe Davenport and you are Alexandre de Rabec de La Brou."

Alix smiled back, confused. "Alix, if you please, but how did you know my name?"

Phoebe's smile widened. "As Jervis would say, I've been tracking you. I wanted to meet the woman who breached the walls of the very-self-contained, ever-so-responsible Earl of Moreham."

"You know Rafe?"

Phoebe nodded. "He and my husband, Cole, are close

friends. We've been waiting patiently for an introduction, but Rafe seems to want to keep you all to himself." She reached out a hand. "Shall we return to the ballroom and tell him the game is up?"

Alix took Phoebe's hand, curious to get to know more about this striking woman and her husband, wondering too why Rafe hadn't introduced them.

"You should know I'm terribly forward," Phoebe said. "That's because I'm an American. Rafe was probably worried I'd corrupt you with my wild colonial ways. He can be such a stick sometimes." She leaned close to Alix as they made their way through the crowded salon. "Cole and I are so grateful you've distracted him from that awful Anne Dinsmore."

Alix took the opportunity to ask a question that had been preying on her mind. "I've heard they were nearly engaged."

Phoebe shook her blond tresses. "She's awful, simply awful. Rafe watched her grow up and I think he must have decided that since Elizabeth would be leaving home soon enough, it was time to start a nursery and that Anne would suit as well as any."

"They weren't in love?"

"Heavens no," she gave a mock shudder. "I'm not sure she's even capable of love, except maybe for her brother James. And Rafe certainly never looked at her the way he looks at you."

So Rafe hadn't been in love with Anne Dinsmore. But he had been looking for a wife. Was she simply another suitable fit? Was he one of those men who enjoyed the chase? She shivered as she thought of his hands on her body. He certainly didn't lack for experience. Perhaps the rumors she'd heard that he spent his time in France in pursuit of sexual pleasure were true. But then why had he been posing as a cloth merchant? What, she wondered with rising frustration, was the truth about the man she had married?

"So Moreham has been looking for a wife to stock his nursery?"

Phoebe chuckled. "Not exactly. It's just that Rafe has a way of thinking that if he plans his life carefully ahead everything will fall into place." Phoebe flashed a smile at Alix. "Thank goodness you came along to knock that nonsense out of him. I was beginning to worry I'd be spending our annual holidays with the Harcrests trying to make pleasant conversation with Lady Anne Dinsmore. The woman looks at me as though, at any moment, I might put feathers in my hair and dump her tea out the window."

Phoebe shrugged. "Still I suppose all his planning is understandable, when you think of all the unexpected things that have tossed his life about: becoming the earl, having to take care of Elizabeth and Louisa, to rebuild the family fortune. That's what he's really been doing in France—working—though rumor would have it he spends so much time on the continent to enjoy the women."

"He does seem rather experienced," Alix said, thinking about how skillfully Rafe's hands and lips moved on her body.

"He's no innocent, but he's no rake either." Phoebe smiled. "When you meet my husband, you'll understand that I know the difference." She turned to Alix, her blue eyes softening. "But even rakes reform when they fall in love."

Phoebe laughed. "Still, for all his reputation, it is amusing to think that a French lady has stolen his heart. There's something he never planned for, I'll wager."

Alix followed Phoebe through the crowd, admiring the advantage her height gave her in finding her way. When at last they stopped, she saw that Rafe was talking to a tall handsome man with raven-dark hair and dark eyes. He turned, his eyes sparkling when they rested on Phoebe, and his mouth breaking into a wicked grin. Alix had no doubt that the man was Phoebe's husband, Cole.

"Why Rafe, look what my very clever wife has discovered, the elusive Mademoiselle de La Brou."

Rafe murmured to his friend, "You see what I mean, Davenport, about your head being an attractive target for rocks." Straightening he said. "Mademoiselle de La Brou, may I present Cole Ashbourne, Viscount Davenport." As Cole stepped forward and bowed over her hand, Rafe added, "Don't trust a word he says."

"Ah, but you may trust me with your life," Cole said warmly as he lifted his head, and somehow Alix knew that she could. "I think that I shall dance with your lady, Moreham. I won't seek your permission, since you'll only deny it. And I do think Mademoiselle de La Brou needs a chance to discover that not all Englishmen dance like great glowering giants."

He did dance exquisitely, Alix thought as Cole led her through the steps of a country dance. He kept up a patter of light conversation, nearly putting her at ease, but she couldn't help being aware of his dark eyes assessing her every time they drew close.

"So tell me, my lord," she said as she circled under his arm, "what is it you are dying to know?"

"Many things, mademoiselle, most too impertinent to ask."

"Why do I have the feeling that's never stopped you before?"

Cole drew his brows together in as if considering her words carefully, then said with a flash of his white teeth, "You're quite right, it hasn't." They turned and circled. "I'm wondering," he said, "whether you will leave him again."

Alix nearly missed a step. "You know about us then?" she asked when they drew up.

"Ah, yes, Lady Moreham. Rafe was quite done in when you left him. Cut a vicious swath through White's. Haven't seen him that hurt and angry since his brother died and left him the title and a mountain of debts. He was impossible to live with until Jervis started reporting in on your whereabouts."

Alix glanced up at him. "And which part of him was suffering most, my lord, his pride or his heart?"

Cole laughed. "A bit of both I believe, but mostly his heart."

"Indeed," she said as the dance ended.

Cole took her arm as they finished with a promenade around the room. "So that's how things stand," he said thoughtfully, his expression suddenly serious. "Rafe's never been much of a talker, more of a planner, a doer. Even as a child, if he saw something that needed to be fixed, he just fixed it. If he saw something he wanted, he just went out and got it. Rather a contrast with the rest of his family." He shook his head. "Terribly scatterbrained bunch if you ask me. Got so everyone looked to Rafe to be the responsible one." Cole smiled ruefully. "Even me. It makes him seem . . ." He struggled for the words.

"A bit high-handed," Alix suggested.

Cole's dark eyes twinkled. "One might say high-handed."

"And arrogant," she offered.

"I think you take my point," he said. "He's a bit more accustomed to listening to his head, rather than his heart. You have him quite confused." Cole stopped just before they reached Rafe and Phoebe. "He's never been in love before, but give him time, he'll figure it out." He eyed her appreciatively. "He's a smart man, Rafe Harcrest."

Cole led Alix back to Rafe. "I return your lady to you, Moreham." He tipped his head. "I trust you will hold on to her."

"I think to make certain, Alix and I shall take part in the next quadrille. That way she will be safe from the distractions of your sort."

"Distractions," Cole tutted, "how unjust, particularly when I have been extolling your virtues to the lady."

Alix glanced up at Rafe. "Aren't you supposed to request a dance before leading a lady out?"

Rafe smiled. "I thought one of the conveniences of marriage was that one no longer had to ask." He leaned close to her ear. "So tell me what nonsense Davenport was telling you."

Alix inclined her head towards the dance floor. "Well, for one thing, he said you were accustomed to having things your own way."

Rafe grinned. "Only when I know best."

"And you think you know what's best for me?"

His hazel eyes gleamed. "Believe me, my dear, I've some very good ideas."

Chapter Twenty-two

❧

Lamartine lay in bed, his body stiff from the strain of keeping as far as possible from the snoring lace merchant next to him. A lawyer and his clerk shared the next bed, grunting and swallowing in their sleep, only an arm's length away. He'd been stranded at this inn for nearly two weeks, sharing a bed with passing strangers, inhaling their odors, and listening to their bodily functions and inane chatter. Two more days, he reminded himself, two more days until the postal carriage arrived and he could make his way to London.

He'd stumbled into the inn, his head pounding and his stomach rejecting whatever boiled slop the English passed off as food. The owner had allowed him to remain and recuperate, accepting as payment his assistance with her bookkeeping and correspondence. Women were such fools. Under her trusting gaze, he'd gradually regained his health and his fortune. He patted a corner of the mattress. People in public inns should learn to keep a better eye on their belongings. He was sleeping on a growing cache of coins, snuff boxes, and watches. And a lovely sharp knife he'd taken off a sleeping sailor.

Traveling in a strange country, one couldn't be too careful.

Several days after the Beaumont's assembly, Madeleine de La Brou and Phoebe Davenport stood watching Rafe, Alix, and Cole playing cards at a quiet party hosted by the Percys. Madeleine was standing very still, her dark eyes distant, and her fan moving in a slow methodical wave. Phoebe studied the elegant French woman wondering idly how she made mourning look so dashing.

"So Madame de La Brou," she asked, "you do not join the games?"

"Ah bah, playing cards makes me feel like an old woman. Since I am in mourning, I may not dance, but I refuse to hide myself in a backroom playing cards with the dowagers."

Phoebe eyed the comtesse in her black silk gown trimmed with purple ribbons. "I doubt, madame, that anyone would consider you in your dotage, or that one so lovely might be hidden even in a quiet card room."

Madeleine laughed and her fan swept Phoebe's emerald silk gown. "You are quite lovely yourself and most flattering. I suppose I should hold it against you that you are an American since my country was bankrupted by supporting your revolution." She shook her head. "And your dreadful republican ideas. But I confess I find you quite charming and besides, I believe one should never allow politics to spoil a perfectly agreeable evening."

Phoebe smiled. "I must agree with you madame. As my husband is English and I have chosen to make England my home, I have found it wise to eschew political debate."

"Your husband." Madeleine nodded. "He is the handsome devil playing cards with my daughter and Lord Moreham?"

"You are correct madame, on both accounts."

"That he is your husband and that he is playing cards?" Phoebe laughed. "That he is handsome and a devil."

Madeleine tapped Phoebe with her fan. "I can see by the way you two keep trading glances that you are most unfashionably fond of one another." She pursed her lips. "And your friend, Moreham, do you think he is in love with my daughter?"

Phoebe studied the card players, noting how Rafe's eyes lingered on Alix. "I think, madame, I have never seen him so captivated by a woman, nor so determined to win her. He's not a man who takes things lightly, Rafe Harcrest."

Madeleine sighed. "I have not always had a chance to be a good mother to my daughter, but now that she is in my care I would like to do what I can to see that she is happy."

Phoebe nodded. "I believe that is Rafe's desire too, madame."

Madeleine turned and smiled at Phoebe. "That is good to hear."

She might have said more, but Lord Rothwell appeared at her elbow and offered to take her for a walk along the gallery. Madeleine made her excuses and Phoebe watched her go, reflecting that there was something quite charming about the way Rothwell bent his craggy gray head to hear Madeleine's conversation. The comtesse looked like a tiny dark bird that had landed on the branch of a venerable tree, she mused.

Phoebe strolled over to the card table and rested a hand on her husband's shoulder. Cole glanced up at her and smiled.

Alix was studying her hand, her gray eyes intent; she cast a pensive look at Rafe. "I know you must have the queen, Lord Moreham."

Cole's dark eyes twinkled. "The bettors at White's have been asking nearly the same question, mademoiselle. Is his lordship holding one queen or two and which shall he discard?"

"I assure you I am holding only one queen," Rafe said to Cole. His tone warming, he glanced at Alix. "And I also assure you, I plan on keeping her close to my chest."

Alix laughed and slid several coins across the table to him. "Then I believe, my lord, you win."

Rafe murmured softly. "But of course, my lady, I always play to win."

Cole cleared his voice, "I think I shall take my wife for a stroll now." Rising and taking Phoebe's arm, he said, "You don't mind do you Moreham?"

Rafe, who was still looking at Alix, nodded.

Alix watched them go. "Have they been married long?" she asked.

"Nearly fifteen years."

"They seem like newlyweds. Like newlyweds should be." she amended.

Rafe reached out and placed his hand over Alix's. "Like we will be." He studied her face for a moment, unwilling to spoil the moment and uncertain how to begin. "Alix, I've been thinking . . . I'd like to buy you a wedding gown."

She cast a glance at his pile of winnings, "I'm not quite so impoverished as that, my lord."

He shook his head. "I'd like it to be my wedding gift to you." He smiled. "Something in a shade other than gray."

Alix laughed, teasing, "You don't approve of my mother's flair for the dramatic? I confess, yours are the only unflattering words I've heard about my gowns since I've arrived in London. Why just the other day Lord Minton sent me a sonnet entitled, *To a Silver Siren.*"

Rafe grinned. "Spare me. I've heard Minton's poetry before and it's not much better than his taste in waistcoats."

She glanced mischievously at him. "It's really quite good. I think I have it all by heart. Would you care to hear it?"

"Alix," he growled warningly.

She laughed again. "Just enjoying my last days of freedom. For all I know, after we're officially married, you'll drag me off and bury me in the countryside never to be seen in polite society again."

"Dragging you off does have a certain appeal. But I'd never bury you Alix, if that's what concerns you."

She felt his heated gaze like fingers caressing her skin and struggled to keep her tone light. "That and a pastel wedding dress with too much lace and too many rosebuds," she managed. "Rafe, I know I'm not the bride you might have chosen, but you can't remake me into a copy of Anne Dinsmore—"

"That's not what I intended," he began, but she waved a hand to stop him.

"Leaving France, leaving my father's house, was the hardest thing I've ever done. I felt so alone and I wasn't sure I could make it. With everything I'd known falling down around me, there were times I wasn't even sure I wanted to survive. But I did and I've discovered qualities within myself I never knew I had."

She could see he was listening. "My father was always going on about the warrior blood of the de La Brous. It seemed like old-fashioned fairy tales. But now I think differently. It may sound silly to you, but for the first time in my life I feel strong, even a bit courageous. I know as your wife my body and my goods will belong to you. I'm asking you to leave me some space to grow."

She reached her hand out and covered his. "I know

you're accustomed to ordering things about you, but if you'll allow me my freedom, I can be a good wife to you."

Rafe felt as if a hand were squeezing his heart. Was this how she saw him, as a dark cloud seeking to smother her light? How could she read so much into his offer to provide her with a wedding dress? His only wish was to make this second wedding day perfect, to wash away the memories of the previous ceremony, and to make a fresh start with her. He frowned, inwardly cursing the proprieties that kept them so far apart. Always a chaperone with them whenever they were together, watchful eyes making sure they did not stand too close or touch for too long. He needed to touch Alix, he thought, to feel her close. Somehow when they were skin-to-skin everything seemed much clearer, much simpler. He wondered if he dared risk another late night foray into her bedchamber.

"Well?" Alix asked softly, and Rafe realized she was still waiting for an answer to her question.

He looked up and smiled at her, "I shall await your selection with great anticipation."

Alix studied Rafe. He was frowning and his eyes were dark and unreadable. Had what she said offended him? Had she made a mistake in reminding him that he'd had little choice in this marriage? She reflected ruefully on how desperately she had wanted to escape his company in France, and now, how she would give anything to spend more time alone with him, to somehow see into the depths of his heart. There was a rustle of satin next to the table and Alix looked up to see Elizabeth regarding them thoughtfully.

Rafe glanced at her and, trying to control the annoyance he felt, and inquired lightly, "Shouldn't you be mingling with the young people?"

She threw him a look only a younger sister can give to an older brother. "The young people are dull, the lemonade is tepid, and the cakes are stale. I thought I might find more interesting entertainment here among the older crowd. Though I don't see that Alix is all that elderly." She took a sip of Rafe's champagne. "Besides, I saw that she was in danger of violating your sacred rule of two's, so I hurried over to save her reputation."

Rafe took his glass back from his sister as Alix raised a questioning brow. "The rule of two's?"

"Oh, yes," said Elizabeth slyly. "There should always be two women to every single man, and since Louisa's talking fertilizers with some dowager or other, I thought I might do the service."

"It's amazing," Rafe said, "how you can remember your lessons when it suits you, and other times they seem to bolt straight from your head."

Elizabeth shrugged. "What can I say? Careless youth. . . . So what were you two discussing before I arrived?" she asked, as she pulled up a chair and began reshuffling the cards.

"Marriage," Rafe replied as Elizabeth dealt him a hand. "And no slipping aces into your sleeve."

"I wouldn't dream of it," she said, spreading her cards in a fan and widening her eyes in mock innocence. "Dreadful institution, marriage. Man owns the woman, lock, stock, and barrel. I think I'd rather have a bit of freedom to explore the world. What do you say, Alix?"

"About marriage? Or about exploration?" Alix asked, studying her hand.

"Both."

"I think that undertaken with the right person, for the right reasons, both can be quite exciting and productive."

Elizabeth discarded a card. "But how do you know you've found the right person, and you're marrying for the right reasons?"

Rafe, feeling distinctly uncomfortable with the course

the conversation was taking, attempted to change the subject. "You were up early this morning, Louisa said you'd gone riding. Did you meet up with anyone interesting?"

Elizabeth cast him an amused glance. "For example, behold my brother. I'm told the ladies find him quite attractive. And I've heard he's quite the . . ."

"Elizabeth," Rafe said in a warning tone.

She left the sentence unfinished, shaking her head. "But you see how he always has to have his way, to control everything. I can just imagine the lectures his wife would have to put up with, why she'd have to have the patience of a saint."

"One might say the same for the man who chose you for his bride," Rafe muttered under his breath.

"So whose marriage were you discussing before I arrived?"

"My marriage to your brother," Alix said.

"Oh." Elizabeth looked genuinely surprised. "I have put my foot in it, haven't I?"

"Indeed," Rafe agreed.

"Forgive me, please, and let me be the first to extend my congratulations." She gazed at the two of them consideringly. "Does Lady Anne know about this?"

"We're keeping it quiet for the moment. When the time comes, I shall tell Lady Anne myself."

"May I come with you?"

"No brat, you may not."

"I'd give up my voucher for Almack's to see the expression on her face when she hears your news."

"I'm sure Lady Anne will wish us only the best."

"And I'm sure she'll eat the feathers on her hat."

Alix struggled to keep a straight face during this exchange; she agreed with Elizabeth and added the silent prayer that Anne Dinsmore choked on them.

"So," Elizabeth said brightly, "did you know each other in France?"

Alix glanced at Rafe. It was a question both had dodged before. Rafe drew a card and, without looking at his sister, said, "Alix and I met in Paris quite by accident. It seems she was most taken by me."

Alix shot a glare at him. "At our first meeting, His Lordship seemed almost a different man, as if cut from a simpler cloth."

"And yet she nearly threw herself into my arms."

He was incorrigible, she thought, as she smiled sweetly across her cards. "I must admit, he outshone my companions at the time."

Rafe's shoulders shook slightly. "Mademoiselle, you flatter me."

Elizabeth stared at them both. "Why is it," she asked in a wondering voice, "that when people become betrothed they start speaking utter nonsense?"

Lord Minton and James Dinsmore strolled up to the table. "Come now, Moreham," Minton said. "You can't monopolize two such lovely ladies all evening." He smiled at Alix.

> *"The silver siren's haunting song*
> *Across the waves doth waft along,*
> *Mere mortal men cannot resist*
> *Lost beyond reason, dare drowning for a kiss"*

"I wrote that for Mademoiselle de La Brou. What do you think Moreham? Did you get the reference to across the waves, just as Mademoiselle de La Brou has come to us across the channel? Quite clever if I don't say so myself."

"Indeed," Rafe said dryly.

"Well, mademoiselle, Lady Percy's going to honor us

with a recital on the pianoforte. If you'd care to listen, I'll escort you to the music room."

James Dinsmore looked over at Elizabeth. "Lady Elizabeth, would you care to join us? My sister has offered to save us several seats."

Elizabeth winked at Rafe. "That would be delightful."

Sometime later, Alix stepped outside the Percys' salon for a breath of fresh air. Lady Percy had vigorously pounded her way through a prelude by Bach. Resisting the urge to rub her ears, she wondered if she might ever appreciate the piece again. She crossed her arms and gazed up at that night sky, inhaling the crisp fall air. She caught the scent of dry leaves, apples, and tobacco. But before she could register that she was not completely alone, a pair of strong arms encircled her and she felt familiar lips against her neck.

"My Lord Minton," she breathed. "We mustn't."

"Minx," Rafe growled against her ear.

Alix laughed softly and turned in his arms. Placing her hands against his chest she looked seriously up at him. "Do you dare drowning for a kiss?"

"For much more than a kiss," he said, slanting his lips across hers. His mouth was warm and soft, but as she kissed him back, it became more possessive. His tongue probed deeper, and his arms tightened around her. Alix felt the coolness of the evening melt away as she pressed against the consuming heat of his body.

"But a kiss will have to do for now," he said huskily as he drew back and planted a light kiss on her brow.

Rafe sat astride his horse outside the Duchess of Melbourne's home staring at the window he knew to be Alix's. It had been a foolish thing, kissing her on the Percys' veranda. He could still taste her sweetness on his lips and he ached for more. Minton was a fool and his poetry pure drivel, but Rafe reflected ruefully, he was right about one thing. Alix could drive a man to madness.

Jervis followed his gaze up to the lighted rectangle on the third floor. "It's not a good night, my lord," he said, shaking his head. "The house is full of people. Lady Melbourne's entertaining some of her political friends and Lord Melbourne's playing cards in the library." He touched Rafe's arm. "Cheer up. December's not so far away."

Rafe nodded but said nothing.

"Ginny'll let me know if there's anything to be concerned about," Jervis added. "She says her ladyship doesn't pay any attention to them other gentlemen what sends her flowers, barely glances at the cards before tossing them into the trash. And you know I'm always loitering about, checking on who comes and goes, making sure she stays put. A fly couldn't buzz in that house without me knowing it."

"I appreciate that, Jervis," Rafe said.

"My pleasure. Why don't you go on off to White's, have a drink and jaw with Cole."

Rafe smiled slightly. "It never ceases to amaze me, Jervis, how you seem to know what everyone in the West End is about."

Jervis smiled and tapped his nose. "Well, I do have my ways, Captain, and I does my best."

"I think a drink at White's will do me good," Rafe said, turning his horse away from Melbourne House.

"And if it doesn't," Jervis called after him, "I've got some sure-fire remedies."

Jervis began to whistle as he headed towards the Melbournes' servant's entrance. He felt sorry for Rafe. People thought the quality had it all with their houses and their jewels, but they complicated their lives something awful with all their rules. What Rafe needed to do was sweep Alix up and carry her off for a bit of a romp and a talk to straighten things out. He'd have done it in Paris, but never in London with the eyes of the ton chewing on his every move.

He swung the door open and was immediately enveloped in plump arms and a round bosom.

"You're late," Ginny chided him. "I was about to give up on you. I was beginning to think I'd be climbing into my bed alone."

He gave her lips a hearty buss. "Sorry, love, I had a few things to see to before I came by. But don't you fear, Jervis Jones is not a man to let you down."

"That's what I was counting on," Ginny said with a giggle, and she nestled her rosy head against his shoulder as arm in arm they climbed the stairs.

Rafe handed his coat and hat to a servant and made his way up the marble staircase of White's. He stood for a moment on the threshold, his eyes searching the crowded tables for a familiar dark head. Cole Davenport was leaning into group of hazard players, gesturing with his brandy glass as he recounted some story. There was a roar of laughter from the men seated at the table and he straightened, smiling. As he did so, he turned and caught sight of Rafe. Cole made his excuses to the gamblers and headed towards his friend.

"My God," he said, slapping Rafe on the shoulder. "You're positively beginning to haunt this place. Still, I daresay we should enjoy your company before you're swept from our midst by that captivating little Frenchwoman."

Rafe cocked an eyebrow at Cole. "I don't see that marital bliss is keeping you home."

Cole laughed. "I should be safe at home in bed with my lovely wife, but for the fact that her brothers are visiting."

"Which ones?" Rafe inquired.

"All of them," he answered with a mock shudder. "And though we've been married fifteen years, the sight of all those great glowering colonials in my drawing room still makes me a tad uneasy. So what'll it be?"

"Brandy," Rafe answered.

Cole signaled for a bottle and two glasses. "Are you drinking with an old friend tonight, fleecing the lambs, or . . ." He stopped, his dark eyes twinkling. "Perhaps you'd like to step over to that table,"—He gestured towards a table filled with young men in scarlet uniforms— "And hear Minton's latest ode, *To a Silver Siren*? I hear it's quite good."

Rafe glared at him and Cole laughed. "Don't despair, old boy, if it's any consolation, I hear the betting's on you to win the lady's hand, by at least three to one."

Chapter Twenty-three

❧

"It's the queerest thing, my lord," Jervis began, looking up from polishing one of Rafe's boots.

"Indeed," Rafe said absently, as he sipped his coffee and browsed his morning paper. He was sitting in the one of the guestrooms at Moreham House, trying to ignore the sounds of workmen pounding and banging down the hall, an easier task than tuning out Jervis.

"I'm leaving the Melbournes' this morning, and I sees this man skulking about, pasty fellow in drab suit and an old bagwig. And I say to myself, Jervis, that man looks mighty familiar. So I follow him around a bit. He's checking out the house you see, eyeing all the doors and windows, watching how the servants come and go. And as he's doing all this I'm thinking I *know* this fellow, I've seen him before."

Rafe regarded Jervis over the edge of his paper. "Jones I assume this story will arrive at a point sooner rather than later."

Jervis rubbed his nose, smearing a streak of bootblack across it. "My point is I do recognize him. Damned if it isn't the fellow you clocked with the candlestick at Madame de La Brou's."

Rafe put down the paper, his eyes suddenly intent. "You're certain of this?"

Jervis nodded. "I'd remember that face anywhere. And as I was watching, an old flower seller bumped into him, and he let loose with a powerful string of French curses. I followed him back to a nasty little inn. Appears he's just arrived in town; told the landlord he'll be here for just a bit."

Rafe said, more to himself than to Jervis, "I'm riding with Alix tomorrow afternoon. Shall I tell her then, or shall I keep her from worrying until we know more?"

"You want me to keep an eye on your lady?" Jervis asked.

Rafe nodded.

Lamartine sat in the pub, taking his bread and cheese with a bit of warm ale. What he wouldn't give for a good bottle of French wine, he thought, as the bitter drink washed down his throat. He'd spent the morning and much of the afternoon observing the comings and goings of Melbourne House. He'd learned a great deal about the routine of the servants, and he recalled with a satisfied smile, towards mid-afternoon, he'd seen Madeleine de Rabec de La Brou traipse down the front steps and into one of Lady Melbourne's carriages.

As soon as he'd seen the carriage disappear around the corner, he'd strolled up to the front door and rung the bell. A sour-faced butler had answered the door, looking him up and down with obvious displeasure. Lamartine offered the letter he'd prepared, saying in his most unctuous tones that he'd be most grateful if it could be delivered to the comtesse. He'd explained that he'd just arrived from

France and carried important news for Madame regarding her estates. The letter, he said, would explain further. He had seen a flicker of interest in the butler's eyes. "If Madame la Comtesse will be so kind," he had finished, "I will return later this afternoon for a response." The butler's bushy white eyebrows had risen slightly, as if he had offered to perform some improper act on the front steps. "We shall see what can be done," the butler had intoned disapprovingly as he closed the door.

Lamartine now dabbed delicately at his mouth with a fine handkerchief he'd taken from one of the previous inn's guests. Perhaps to pass the time, he'd stroll over to Oxford Street and look about the shop windows. A slow smile crept across his pale oval face. Perhaps when he had the titles in hand, he'd celebrate with the order of a new suit, even a new wig. He deserved it, he thought, as he tossed the barkeep a thin coin.

Madeleine de La Brou did not get to her pile of notes, cards, and invitations until mid-morning the following day. Sitting up among her pillows, sipping her morning cocoa, she perused her accumulated correspondence, tossing calling cards and invitations at her feet in piles she mentally labeled, *unacceptable, acceptable,* and *very interesting.* She noticed a card from Lord Rothwell; flipping it over, she saw he'd scrawled a brief note inviting her to go riding next week. She dropped it on top of the *very interesting* pile with a smile. The London season, though just beginning, was looking most promising.

She reached for a cream-colored envelope amidst the pile on the silver salver and paused, letter opener in hand. The handwriting seemed somehow familiar. She removed the letter and read quickly, a delicate frown creasing her smooth white brow. Placing it in on her tray, she reached over and pulled hard on the bell cord next to her bed.

It took several flurries of maids before Madeleine had the Melbournes' dour-faced butler standing at attention at the foot of her bed.

"This letter," she demanded, waving it about like a cream-colored moth, "how was it delivered?" He squinted across the four-poster and Madeleine impatiently thrust the envelope at him. The butler turned it over in his gloved hands then passed it back to her.

"It was delivered, Madame la Comtesse, by a low person. He returned yesterday afternoon and I told him you were not at home and suggested he try again this afternoon." He handed the envelope back to Madeleine, folded his hands behind his back and looked beyond her at the wall.

Madeleine stared at the letter distastefully for a moment, then said, "Should he appear again, you may show him in."

"Will that be all, madame?" the butler asked.

"Yes, Morris, that will be all." She hesitated as he turned to go. "Will you let Mademoiselle Alix know that I would like to see her?"

"Very good, madame," Morris responded as the door closed noiselessly behind him.

When Alix arrived she found her mother sitting up in bed, rapping an envelope against her open hand. She cast Madeleine an inquisitive look.

Madeleine gestured for her to sit. "I have here a letter from your father's steward, Robert Lamartine. It appears he is in London and has some urgent news for us concerning your father and the titles to his estates."

Alix's mind raced. "My father," she said, not daring to hope, "is he alive?"

Madeleine shook her head, "I'm sorry, my dear, Lamartine says he did everything in his power to rescue your father from the mob, but Paul is, indeed, dead."

Alix looked down at her hands, twisting silently in her skirts. It was a bit like losing him again, she thought.

After a moment, Madeleine continued. "Lamartine claims to have some information about your father's last wishes, a letter in fact, and desires to deliver it in person so that he may speak with us about its contents." She cast a look at her daughter's bowed head and said gently, "The future of the de La Brou estates concerns you, much more than I; it will be the inheritance of your children. I think it would be best if you are present when I meet with Monsieur Lamartine."

Madeleine paused, then added with studied casualness, "I understand His Lordship, the Earl of Moreham, will be riding with you this afternoon. Should you care to have him present when Lamartine arrives, I would not take it amiss."

Alix nodded, her mind at sea with questions, her hand unconsciously toying with the gold chain around her neck. What, she wondered, had brought Robert Lamartine to England? Was he seeking a job, some repayment for services to the family, or perhaps, she thought with a faint leap of her heart, he'd found a way to save Valcour.

Alix's mind was still on Lamartine's visit during her ride that afternoon with Rafe—Louisa and Elizabeth trotting a respectable distance behind.

"Come now, Alix, I have twitted you twice on your very smart, but still very gray riding habit, and you have responded without so much as a flash of your lovely eyes, much less an acerbic comment on my tastes. Perhaps I might have a better chance of attracting your interest if I were to begin declaiming in verse." Rafe paused. "Let me see, how about *Ode to a Gray Gamine*."

Alix glanced over at him, startled. "I beg pardon, Rafe, my mind was elsewhere." She gave him a puzzled look.

"Were you saying something about verse? I confess, I hadn't really thought you a poetical spirit."

Rafe smiled. "There is much you have to learn about me sweetheart, but never mind the verse, it was of no importance, a simple ploy to gain your attention."

Alix gave him a thoughtful look. There it was again, that indecipherable something in his eyes. He had been increasingly attentive lately, and she'd heard nothing about him spending time in Lady Anne's company.

"Perhaps I can help with what's bothering you," he said gently.

Trusting him, she mused, was as dangerously tempting as his body. After a moment, she gave way. "There is a servant, the steward of my father's estates, who has sent my mother a letter indicating that he has some information for her and would like to meet with us this afternoon. I can't help wondering what's brought him here and what he wants."

Rafe's mind turned immediately to Jervis's report about the Frenchman spying on Lady Melbourne's home. If he were a betting man, he would lay odds that he and the comte's steward were the same. But he didn't want to alarm Alix; perhaps it was all quite innocent. "Would it help if I were to join you when he arrives?" he asked.

Alix had been worrying over this question as well. Truth be told, since they were married, the estates were as good as his. And yet, he'd never even been there. He'd never seen the way the summer sun struck the peaked roofs of the towers, turning the worn stone the color of ripe apricots. He'd never walked its wide lawns, or seen its formal gardens in full bloom. Alix felt a pain in her chest, as if her heart had brittle edges. What difference did it make? she thought. She'd probably never see her father's lands again.

She glanced at Rafe, sitting straight and proud in his saddle, his broad shoulders accented by his close-fitting riding jacket, the sun through the trees picking gold strands out of his chestnut hair. Perhaps it would be good to meet the past with this man at her side, she thought.

"I'd like to have you there, Rafe," she said softly.

"Thank you, Alix," he said, sensing that her decision had been a struggle and that in some small measure he had won; she had decided to let him into a part of her world. Perhaps she was beginning to trust him, he thought, pleased that he hadn't had to demand she invite him as his right. He wanted to say more than thank you, he thought, as Louisa and Elizabeth reined in behind them. Rafe smiled at his sister and stepmother as he silently cursed their eyes. This was getting ridiculous. He needed to get Alix alone, he needed to talk to her, really talk with her without the constant intrusion of chaperones.

As they turned back toward Melbourne House, chatting about nothing in particular, Rafe's eyes wandered to the servant's entrance and the window he knew to be Alix's. It was time, he reflected, to pay another late night call on his wife.

Rafe was helping Alix to dismount when a footman came hurrying down the stairs towards them. "Madame la Comtesse has a visitor and she would like mademoiselle and your lordship to join her in the sitting room as soon possible."

Rafe looked over to Louisa and Elizabeth, still mounted on their horses. "Would you mind terribly, Louisa," he called over to her, "if I didn't accompany you back to Moreham House?"

Louisa smiled. "I wouldn't mind at all my dear. I have some business to attend to and Elizabeth needs to change her gown. James Dinsmore is coming by to take her round to a poetry reading."

A whisper of concern crossed Rafe's mind; he didn't generally associate James Dinsmore with poetry readings.

He reminded himself to discuss it with Elizabeth later that evening as he turned back to the footman. "Will you ask Morris to arrange for a groom to accompany my mother and sister home?"

The footman rushed off as Rafe and Alix went up into the house. When they reached the sitting room, Rafe saw Madeleine, in her customary black, seated on the edge of a brocade armchair. Directly across from her was a slight figure in an old-fashioned bagwig and a plain brown suit. As the man turned his pale face and watery blue eyes to meet them, Rafe realized with a shock that his suspicions had been correct. Sitting with the comtesse was the man he had struck with the candlestick and left unconscious in her apartments in Paris.

The man rose, his eyes flickering quickly over Rafe's face, and Rafe understood that he, too, recalled their last meeting.

Madeleine waved her hand in Alix and Rafe's direction. "I've asked my daughter and Lord Moreham to join us, Lamartine."

Lamartine gave a slight bow of his head. "As you wish, madame." He fixed his watery gaze on Rafe. "If I am not mistaken, His Lordship and I have met before."

Madeleine looked confused. "I beg your pardon, how can that be?"

Rafe moved swiftly, anxious to avoid having to explain to Madeleine that he'd encountered Lamartine while breaking into her apartments with Alix dressed as a man. Drawing himself up so that he towered over the little man, he said in a dismissive tone. "I am certain he is mistaken. It is simply not possible for our paths to have crossed before."

Lamartine's face was expressionless, his only movement a slight flaring of his thin nostrils, as the earl's words reminded him of the difference in their stations. He was uncertain whether the long-nosed Englishman was a fool and had failed to recognize him, or whether he was simply a liar. He smiled, fool or liar, either explanation might work to his advantage. "My apologies, Your Lordship, I thought your features seemed familiar."

Rafe waved a careless hand in Lamartine's direction as he took a seat. "It is of no matter."

Alix remained standing, her eyes taking in every inch of the steward's form. She'd never particularly liked Lamartine, but now he represented everything familiar that she'd known and lost. She moved closer to him and took both his smooth white hands in hers. "Robert, it is so good to see you again, and simply astonishing to see you here in London. How ever did you get here?"

"Yes, how did you find your way here?" Rafe asked, his pleasant tone belying his intense interest in what the man would say.

Lamartine folded his hands together. "It was after the peasants stormed the château, after . . ." He paused and dropped his eyes. "The death of my good master. I was endeavoring to clean up some of the destruction when I came across some of His Lordship's papers scattered about. Among them was a letter from Madame la Comtesse, explaining that she was leaving France and hoping to stay with Lady Melbourne."

Alix frowned as she settled into a chair. She hadn't known her father knew Madeleine had left the country. Usually he would have railed about such a thing, but perhaps knowing she would have argued that they join her mother, he had decided not to make an issue of it. She leaned forward, anxious to hear what else Lamartine had to say. "You were in the château when the mob attacked?" she prompted.

"Ah, yes," he said in a dolorous voice. "I was reviewing some accounts when I heard them coming up the drive." He wrung his hands. "So often I had begged Monsieur le

Comte to prepare for such an event, but he had such faith in his people."

Alix nodded.

Lamartine continued. "When I was certain the mob had left, I made my way to where I thought the comte might be."

"How very brave of you," Rafe interjected dryly.

Arrogant oaf, Lamartine thought as he said in an apologetic whine, "There were so many of them, my lord, it was so very frightening and I knew there was nothing I could do."

"Go on, Robert," Alix said gently.

"I found him in his study. It was gruesome . . . what they had done to him. . . ." He shook his bewigged head, and Rafe caught a whiff of an expensive Oxford Street cologne that seemed at odds with Lamartine's modest appearance. "I will not distress the ladies with the details. Suffice it to say when I reached his side the comte was valiantly clinging to life. I cradled his noble head in my arms." Lamartine stopped as if overcome.

Rafe looked over at Alix and saw tears pooling along her lower lashes. He restrained a grimace. He didn't believe Lamartine's story any more than he had that night in Madeleine's grand salon. He waited, certain that Lamartine was nearing the purpose of his visit.

"I begged Monsieur le Comte to tell me what I could do to comfort him in his last moments. He looked up at me, his hand locked in mine, and whispered that there was something I could do to protect his wife and child, and his beloved Valcour." Lamartine cast a quick glance around, judging his audience, wondering if he'd struck the right note of drama. Madeleine looked composed, but pale, and silent tears slipped down Alix's cheeks. It was going well, he thought.

"The comte told me that he'd taken the precaution of

transferring his property titles into my name to prevent
them from falling into the hands of the Revolutionary government. He wanted me to take the titles, along with his
notarized letter and make certain the transfer was registered with the district authorities. I promised him that I
would see it done, and I think . . . I pray to the good Lord
that he died in peace."

Lamartine spread his hands and looked appealingly at
the de La Brou women. "But I have failed in my promise.
Though I searched through all my master's papers, I could
not find the titles. And now time is running out. In a
month's time the authorities will claim Valcour." He allowed his shoulders to slump. "They have already come
round to chain the gates."

Rafe heard Alix inhale sharply and wished he'd struck
Lamartine with something heavier than a candlestick.

Lamartine raised his head and looked straight at
Madeleine. "Madame knows that I was raised by the village priest after my family perished." She nodded. "Father
Bonheur taught me that there is nothing more sacred than
a deathbed oath. And so I have made my way here to see if
perhaps you, or Mademoiselle Alix, have the papers that
will enable me to save Valcour."

He saw Madeleine cast a questioning look at Alix, and
a feeling of deep satisfaction washed over him.

So, he had guessed correctly.

The little fool *had* slipped away with the titles.

For the finishing touch, he pretended to fumble about
his coat pockets. "I have a letter here that will prove the
truth of what I have told you."

Madeleine took the letter from his outstretched hand
and perused it quickly. Wordlessly she passed it to Alix.
When Alix finished reading the letter, Madeleine finally
spoke. "Valcour is Alix's inheritance. It will be part of her
dowry and her legacy to her children." Glancing at Rafe as

though she thought he might raise a challenge, she said, "I think the decision about what should be done should be left up to her."

Alix sat very still for several moments, then raised her chin, her eyes now dry and her lips set.

"Thank you mother for allowing me to decide. Valcour meant more to my father than any of his other estates. He used to say that de La Brou blood had been mixed into the mortar of its walls, and that was what made them so strong." She looked over at Lamartine and her voice softened. "Robert I cannot thank you enough for comforting my father in his final hours, and for making your way here so that we might know how he died."

Lamartine gave Alix a slight smile.

"But," she continued, "I cannot bring myself to give the titles over to you. They have been in de La Brou hands for nearly four hundred years, and they will remain so, no matter what that rabble government in Paris might say."

"But mademoiselle—" Lamartine began.

"No Robert. Who can say what might happen in France? There is still a chance that the king and queen might be rescued and restored to the throne, or that the dauphin might live to see his parents avenged. And the king's brothers still live safe from the reach of the revolutionaries."

She looked at Madeleine and Rafe. "I, too, swore an oath on my father's soul. That I would keep the titles safe, and that someday I or my offspring would return to Valcour."

She handed the letter back to Lamartine. "In the name of my father, I thank you again and I release you from your promise. You have done as much as you can, Robert. My mother and I shall always be grateful. If you let us know where you are staying, we shall have some money sent over to cover your expenses and to help you make a new start."

Madeleine rose, tugging a small, embroidered bell pull by her chair to summon a footman, and Lamartine understood their meeting was over. He resisted the urge to throw their offer of money back into their simpering faces as he made his farewell. He'd be back for the titles. The silly bitches, he thought as he smiled and bowed his way out of the room.

If they thought they'd seen the last of Robert Lamartine, they were sadly mistaken.

Chapter Twenty-four

"Well," Madeleine said after a moment, "that was quite a peculiar visit." She made as if to pick up her embroidery, but then let it lie. "I must admit I never liked that man, but Paul thought the world of him." No one else spoke, and she seemed to want to fill the silence. "It is truly astonishing that he would make his way to England on Paul's behalf." A slight frown appeared between her arched brows. "But then I must say I am equally astonished that Paul would have made arrangements to have the estates transferred into Lamartine's name." She turned to look at Alix. "You were closest to your father in those final days. Did he ever mention such a thing to you?"

Alix shook her head. "Never. Indeed, when I tried to discuss with him how we might prepare for the worst, he was completely dismissive, saying that I worried too much." She sighed. "It doesn't matter. I have no intention of giving over the de La Brou titles. I meant what I said about returning some day."

"I'm sure you made the right decision, Alix," Madeleine said soothingly.

Something didn't fit, Rafe thought. Lamartine had tracked Alix through Paris, followed her here for the titles, then gone away peaceful as you please when she refused to give them to him? He looked over at Alix, considering whether to raise his concerns. Seeing how pale and drawn she looked, he decided not to burden her. He'd discuss it with Jervis, he decided, as he rose to take his leave.

"Alix," he said. "I agree with your mother, I think you did the right thing." He didn't add that in a month's time, if the state chose to take the estates, it would not matter what she did with the titles. Let her keep her pride. "I can see that Lamartine's visit has disturbed you both," he continued, "so I think it best if I leave now."

Alix rose to see him out, and he held her hand tightly for a moment, disliking the pain he saw in her eyes. Tonight, he told himself as he raised her hand and kissed it softly, tonight he would find his way to her and see if he couldn't set things right.

"He's a good man," Madeleine said, as the door closed behind Rafe. Alix nodded, her lower lip beginning to tremble. Madeleine eyed her sharply. "No, no, *ma petite*, I am not going to let you begin to brood again simply because that horrid little man showed up on our doorstep with his awful tales of what's past and can't be helped."

Alix looked at her in surprise as Madeleine continued. "I know you must think I am a terrible, shallow woman to speak to you so. But I have lived longer than you, *chérie*, I know what it is to be parted from the ones you love, to suffer and to feel powerless. And I know that railing against fate and wallowing in your tears might feel good for a while but it solves nothing. *Nothing*. You must learn to make the best of what you have, Alix. You are young, you are pretty, and you have a man who looks at you as if he has discovered a rare treasure."

Alix's eyes were filling with tears.

"I see that you do not believe me," Madeleine said, shaking her head. "Come out with me tonight," she added suddenly. "Let us find a moment to enjoy. We shall put on our dominoes so no one will know who we are, go to Vauxhall for a light supper, and listen to some Handel under the stars. No men, no women eyeing you as if you were some foreign interloper looking to steal the crown jewels, no idle chatter, just good food, good music, and the pleasure of being alive." Madeleine looked eagerly over at her and Alix thought how young her mother still was.

"Very well," she agreed, taking a deep breath. "Vauxhall it shall be."

Vauxhall, Rafe thought, as he fumbled a shilling for the entrance fee.

"That'll be another shilling, Your Lordship, price's gone up since September."

Rafe reached into his pocket for another shilling and dropped it into the man's outstretched hand. "Thankee sir, and have a lovely evening," the man called after him as he strode down the grand walk, gravel spitting beneath his boots.

He'd been worrying about her state of mind, picturing her alone in her room, wracked with grief, only to discover that Alix and her mother were dining at Vauxhall Gardens! Unbelievable, he'd thought as he glanced at the clusters of people strolling beneath the globe lights, laughing and talking. He scanned the faces briefly spotlighted by the lights strung among the trees, frowning as he noted the flushed faces of drunken young bloods, heavily made-up demi-reps, and several coarse-looking characters seeded among the crowds. Hadn't Lady Melbourne thought to warn her guests that the gardens were full of drunken libertines out for a quick thrill, pickpockets, ladies of the evening and lord knew what else? As he headed toward sounds of music drifting from the grove, he hoped they had the good sense to bring some sturdy footmen with them.

It took him nearly half of an hour to find Madeleine and Alix.

Leaning against the trunk of a thickly leafed tree, Rafe lit a cheroot and watched the two women, seated alone in a small box toward the back of the grove. He was pleased to see two burly footmen at the entrance warding off the occasional young blood who tried to join the solitary ladies. As the smoke rose through the shadowy branches, he mused that even if he lived to be one hundred and three he'd never understand women, particularly de La Brou women. They were laughing and clinking their champagne glasses together, whispering into each other's ear. What could they be talking about? he wondered as he caught the silvery sound of Alix's laughter.

Her mother was right. Food, wine, and glorious music *was* the remedy for the shock of seeing Lamartine and thinking about how her father had died. Alix leaned her head back against the mural painted on the curved wall of the box, staring past the glittering strings of lights that hung between the trees into the velvety night sky. As the music of the orchestra reached a crescendo, she imagined great black notes floating skyward, with her troubles somehow attached to their staffs. She gave a tipsy giggle.

"Alix," Madeleine asked, "what is it that you find so amusing?"

"I feel, I feel totally irresponsible." She turned her velvet-hooded head toward her mother. "Is that wicked of me?"

"No, that is exactly what I've sought to achieve this

evening," her mother responded, satisfaction sounding in her voice. "I don't know what happened at Valcour, or how you managed to reach London." She paused for a moment, casting an inquisitive glance at Alix, but when her daughter did not respond, Madeleine continued. She waved a dark gloved hand. "Whatever occurred, you have come through and survived. You mustn't throw that away."

"You're certain I shouldn't have entrusted the titles to Lamartine?"

"I doubt there's anything he could do to protect our interests in France." Her voice softened. "I doubt very much we shall see France any time soon."

"*Maman*, do you think we shall ever return to Valcour?"

Madeleine's voice was intense as she answered. "Forget Valcour, it is nothing but an old pile of stones."

Alix was shocked at her mother's response. "But *Maman*, Valcour is who we are."

"*Non, ma petite*, Valcour is not who we are. Haven't you learned that yet? Who we are is in here." She tapped Alix gently on the chest with her fan. "In the choices we make, in the way that we live our lives. It's not determined by a name, or a château, or even a man, no matter how noble." She laughed lightly. "If it were, your father would have been much more content with our marriage."

Alix couldn't resist asking. "Was it so very bad?"

"The marriage bed or the marriage?" Madeleine responded, motioning for the waiter to bring another bottle of champagne.

They both fell silent as the waiter refilled their glasses.

"Bad enough," Madeleine continued. "I didn't know what to expect, I was just so desperate to get out from under my grandmother's thumb and to stop being so poor. As for Paul, he simply misjudged. I tried, but I could never be the submissive, passionless wife he desired.

"Still," she said in a more cheerful tone, "you came out

of the marriage, and that was definitely something good."
She lifted her glass. "But we are not here to mourn the past.
Let us drink to the future, to making our own choices, and
to making the best of our new lives in England."

Alix sipped thoughtfully at her glass. A smile played at
the corners of her mouth, and she felt the wine warming
her skin, like Rafe's hands and his mouth. She had chosen
Rafe, she mused, and so far the choice had not been bad,
not bad at all.

After several hours, Rafe watched the two velvet-draped
figures leave their box and make their way to the line of
coaches for hire. He noted with amusement that the taller
of the two women wobbled a bit as she walked. His Alix,
he mused, had no head for liquor, though Madeleine, who
stepped gracefully into the carriage, seemed none the
worse for wear. He heard her instruct the coachman to take
them round to Lady Melbourne's. He made sure the hackney set off in the right direction before turning to order his
coach brought around.

From across the street, Rafe observed as the ladies dis-
embarked and drifted gaily up the stairs into the well-lit ro-
tunda of the duchess's home. He chuckled softly as he
thought about how much champagne Alix had consumed,
wondering what sort of company she'd be tomorrow when
he met her to go riding in the park, and whether he ought
to make her suffer by taking the long way round.

His smile spread as he recollected the last time he'd
been with Alix when she'd had too much wine. She'd been
in a fine passion then, recalling the wineglass that had just
missed his ear. It had been the first time he'd kissed her, really kissed her, and he felt his blood begin to heat as more
than his mind remembered her passionate response. He felt
himself grow hard as images of Alix's lithe body flooded
his mind. He needed to be with her. He was tired of watch-

ing her from across crowded rooms and from the distance of windows. He'd been too long without the taste of her mouth and the silken touch of her skin.

She was his wife, damn it all, she belonged with him, in his arms and in his bed.

He leaned out the coach window, told his coachman to take him a bit farther up the street, and then to let him out. "You needn't wait, Harris," he said as he climbed out. "You may take the horses back to Moreham House." He watched until his coach had disappeared, then turned and began to walk purposefully towards the back of Melbourne House. He'd agreed they would live apart for two months, he reasoned with himself, but he'd said nothing about how they would spend their nights. And if his little hoyden chose to start tossing glasses at his head, well then, he had a fair idea of how to distract her.

Dropping her domino on the floor, kicking off her shoes, and beginning to pull the pins from her hair, it struck Alix that Ginny had left precious few candles burning this evening. Two branches of candles burned on the mantelpiece of her the sitting room, but her bedchamber was completely dark. Ginny, she thought, and a hiccup escaped her, was no doubt distracted by Jervis again. Should she ring for more light and help with her stays? Or leave the lovebirds to themselves? Suddenly, she heard a rustling noise in her bedchamber.

"Ginny?" she called softly, peering into the bedroom. The curtains near her desk had been drawn open slightly, and moonlight spilled across its cluttered surface and onto the floor. She didn't recall leaving it such a mess, she thought hazily when she realized there was a man standing quite close to her bed. She caught a whiff of musk that was teasingly familiar. She stood at the threshold, with a pricking sense that she should go no farther, and then her visitor moved swiftly forward, grabbing her by the arm and yanking her into the room. She stumbled and the grip around her wrist tightened. The stranger dragged her back, against his chest, twisting her arm high behind her back, and hissed into her ear.

"The *titles*, Mademoiselle de La Brou, where are the *titles*?"

She flung up an arm and raked her nails down the man's face. She heard him snarl as he wrenched her arm up and pushed her sharply in the shoulder blades, propelling her against the marble fireplace. Her cheek hit the carved edge of the mantle and she slid to the floor.

Pain careened through her face and arm and back. She shifted her limbs, wincing with the effort, trying to determine if anything was broken. As she did so, her attacker stepped closer and knelt on her outspread skirts. She felt something cool and sharp press against the exposed flesh of her neck. Arching away from the knife, she found herself looking up into the pallid face of Robert Lamartine.

"You?" she whispered in stunned confusion.

"You are surprised to see me, mademoiselle? As surprised as I was to discover you had made it safely out of France?" She saw his small teeth glitter in the moonlight as his lips parted in a faint smile. "I should have known when I saw your arrogant friend at your mother's apartments in Paris that you had found a way to save yourself. Such a shame your father didn't live to see his aristocratic daughter turned whore. Not that he should have been surprised with a mother like yours." A faint puff of disgust escaped his nostrils. "After all, he was the one who said breeding always told."

Lamartine turned the knife gently so the edge made firmer contact with her skin. "Alix," he purred, "I have come a long way for those titles, and I would like them now."

As if sensing the resistance in her body, he slid the knife ever so slightly forward and Alix felt the wetness of blood on her neck. "I killed your father for those titles, Alix. Don't think for a moment I won't do the same to you."

Her mind raced frantically, she needed time, just a fragment of time to think what to do.

"The peasants killed my father," she croaked against the blade.

A look of contempt flickered over his pallid features. "The peasants may have done the deed, but where do you think the idea came from?" His watery eyes lit with satisfaction. "I was the one who created the rumors that your father was sending money to the Royalists, and it was my hirelings who raised the mob and encouraged them to attack Valcour."

A shudder of revulsion swept through Alix.

"You were supposed to die with him, but you escaped. You've proven quite an annoyance, mademoiselle." He gazed down upon her neck fondly. "Perhaps I should kill you anyway." He slid the knife again. "The peasants cut off your father's head, you know. Quite the stain on the Aubusson carpet."

"But then you wouldn't have the titles," Alix managed to gasp.

"Quite true," he agreed, "so now tell me where they are."

"In the desk."

Lamartine's eyes narrowed and Alix felt the razor's edge of the knife. "Don't play me for a fool, mademoiselle. I've already searched your desk."

"No," she managed to gasp, "there's a secret drawer in the desk, at the bottom, the engraved base slides out."

"How does it work?" he snapped.

"There's a catch but it's too difficult to describe. If you let me up, I'll open it for you."

Alix felt the pressure of the knife ease. Lamartine rose from his knees then and motioned with his knife. "Show me, mademoiselle."

Alix rose shakily to her feet, resisting the urge to touch her throat, sensing it would only bring Lamartine pleasure and heighten her fear if she touched the blood she knew to be there.

Walking slowly to the desk she scanned the top, desperate for something to fight him with, her eyes racing over so many useless items, paper, wax seals, a delicate china bud vase, quills set in a glass holder with matching ink bottles in an ornate marble tray. Her eyes flew to a heavy candelabra, which Lamartine swept out of her reach as she reached the desk. She heard him set it on a table behind her as he whispered softly in her ear, "Get the titles, Alix; don't think of trying to fight me."

She slid her hands along the elaborately carved garlands at the base of the desk. "I won't," she lied, her voice strained and thin. "I'm just trying to find the right rosette." She made a show of fumbling her hands along the woodwork. "It's back here somewhere," she muttered bending to one side and placing one hand on the desk.

Lamartine peered around to see where Alix was looking as her hand connected with the marble inkstand. Grasping the cool, heavy stone, she swung around and slammed it hard against his head.

There was a sickening crack, a splatter and crackle of shattering glass.

The bottles and quills fell away and an outraged cry escaped from Lamartine. Alix swung again, this time with all the force and rage she could muster and Lamartine went down. She stood over him, her breath coming fast, waiting to see if he would move, trying to find the voice to scream. She stared at his prostrate body, saw his chest rise and fall in the moonlight, but his limbs were mercifully still.

And then she heard another set of footsteps coming across her sitting room.

She whirled around, the marble tray still clutched in her hand, and in the dim candlelight saw the familiar tawny hair and tall frame of Rafe Harcrest. The tray slid from her grasp as she ran across the room, hurling herself against his chest, her arms wrapping tightly around his neck. She clung to him, her body shaking with tremors of delayed fear.

"Hush, sweetheart," she heard him chuckle against her hair, as his arms solidly enfolded her. "I hoped you'd be pleased to see me, but I never thought your greeting would be so enthusiastic." He gently tilted her head back to kiss her, then froze as he caught sight of the swollen bruise on her cheek and the smeary line of blood against her neck. An unintelligible oath escaped him as he stared at her, then caught her face close in his hands. "God in heaven Alix, what's happened to you?"

Still shivering, Alix slid from his grasp and turned, pointing wordlessly to the bedroom and the still form crumpled by the desk.

Chapter Twenty-five

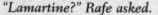

"Lamartine?" Rafe asked.

Alix nodded.

He knelt by the body; his fingers pressed against the Frenchman's neck and he was relieved to feel a slow but steady pulse. Moving quickly about the room, Rafe lit several candles, then pulled the cord from the window curtains. Looping it around Lamartine's neck, he tied his hands and then his feet together. "There," he said rising as he finished, "that should take care of Monsieur Lamartine, at least for the present. If he regains consciousness and tries to move, he'll find the rope around his throat a major inconvenience. Now," he continued, casting his eyes around the room for the washbasin and towels, "let's see about fixing you up."

Rafe settled next to Alix on the bed and began gently dabbing at the blood on her neck. "It looks a mess," he said more to himself than to her. "But underneath it all there's not much more than a scratch." He brushed her swollen cheek. "But you're going to have quite the shiner there.

Major Harris and Lord Minton may have to do without your company for a week or so." His tone grew serious as he looked her over. "Are you hurt anywhere else love?"

Alix shook her head. Rafe brushed her hair back from her face. "I want to know everything that happened here, but first I think we'd better decide what to do about your unwanted visitor."

Alix nodded slowly. "If I call for a footman and they send for the authorities, what will happen?"

Rafe considered. "They'll take him to Old Bailey where he'll rest uncomfortably for a few months until his trial and then in all likelihood he'll hang for attempted murder."

Alix pursed her lips. "The broadsheets will cover it, won't they? It'll be quite a scandal."

"There'll be a great deal of noise about it, no doubt, but I'll be there for you and there's no one who'll blame you."

Alix's eyes were cloudy and her fingers played at the painful line across her throat. "He said he arranged to have my father killed. He seemed so proud of himself. I can just see him boasting about it at a trial." She shook her head. "I don't care about the scandal, but I couldn't bear that, couldn't bear to keep reliving the nightmare of Valcour, and this night over and over till he's dead." Her eyes cleared and she looked up at Rafe, her tone suddenly fierce. "I hear London is a dangerous city. Couldn't you take him somewhere and dump him?"

Rafe took her hands, they were unnaturally cold, and he worried that she might be slipping into shock. He began to rub them between his own large, warm ones. "I won't just dump him, Alix. I want to know that when we are rid of him there will be no chance of him returning to harm you or anyone else in your family." She gave an involuntary shudder and he fell silent. He had an idea but he knew she would oppose it; still, if she trusted him, he felt certain it would work.

"Alix," he began carefully. "I want to give Lamartine the titles and send him back to France."

She pulled her hands free of his and stared at him aghast. "You what? You want me to *give* him the titles? And send him back to claim my lands? Are you mad?"

"Alix, listen to me," Rafe said urgently, "if we send him back with the titles and the letter from your father, I can promise you he will be denounced as soon as he sets foot in France."

She leapt off the bed glaring at him. "I think not!"

"Alix," Rafe tried to interject, "I have certain connections. I can make sure that Lamartine will never walk free and that the titles . . ."

She turned on him, incredulity rampant in her face and in her voice. "You would have me surrender the last scrap of my heritage, the last bit of who I am, to this . . . animal, this filth!"

"You don't understand, let me explain—"

"No," she said coldly, "you don't understand."

He did understand, he wanted to say, but he was over-whelmed by the sight of her, her hair streaming, her face bruised, the angry red line across her throat. He'd come so close to losing her. Lamartine might have *killed* her. She'd risked her life for titles that in a month's time would be worthless. Even now, with Alix and her mother in England, the titles were already as good as worthless.

"I do understand, Alix," he said sharply. "I understand that you are determined to have your way, no matter what the costs, no matter what the consequences." The words began to tumble out, to gain speed as his pent up anxiety, frustration, and anger over their separation spilled over. "You might have been safe with me, living in my home, surrounded by my servants, but you chose instead to stay with a stranger." He raked his hands with his hair. "You flirt with Major Harris, Lord Minton, lord knows who else . . . You wander about Vauxhall at night unattended—"

"I beg your pardon? *I* flirt? I socialize with respectable gentleman while you, you . . ." she said stepping closer her voice filled with outrage. "You traipse about London with *Anne Dinsmore* draped all over you—"

"Lady Anne Dinsmore is nothing more than a friend," he replied angrily.

"A friend who thinks to slip in your bed."

"A bed that should be filled with my wife."

"Why Rafe Harcrest," she said sarcastically, "I had no idea you were so particular about your bedmates."

He stepped closer, looming over her, his eyes and hair seem to flare golden in the candlelight. "When it comes to you, madame, I am most particular."

She stared defiantly up at him. "Why?" she demanded.

"Because I love you, you infuriating little hoyden."

Alix felt as if she were standing on a ledge that had suddenly given way. Her mouth fell open in silent shock.

"That's right, sweetheart," he continued savagely, "I've fallen in love with you. I've offered you my name and my protection, and now, heaven help me, I'm offering you my heart so that you can throw that back at me, too. Go ahead." He taunted her. "Then wrap yourself in your titles and see if they keep you as warm as I can."

Rafe seized her upper arms and pulled her unresisting against his chest. Bending his head he took her mouth in a kiss that seared, leaving one thought like a standard flapping fiercely in the breeze: He loved her.

Rafe Harcrest loved her.

Alix struggled to free her mouth, to tell him that she loved him, too, but his lips offered no quarter. Instead, they pressed more deeply against hers, his tongue plundering hers, carrying away all thoughts of resistance.

Her arms locked in his hands, Alix strained upwards on

her toes, trying to reach him, trying to tell him with her lips and tongue, and all the body she could lay against his, that she loved him, too.

A strangled groan from the floor, caused Rafe to push her away, not harshly but resolutely.

"Send for Ginny," he said hoarsely, "and tell her to bring her home remedies with her."

Alix cast him a quizzical look, but did as he asked.

Several moments later Ginny appeared, disheveled as if she had just jumped out of bed, a mobcap hastily thrown over her curls. She was accompanied by an oddly dressed footman. Even in her distracted state, Alix couldn't help noticing that his jacket was too large and his britches were too tight. When he stepped into the candlelight, she realized the footman was Jervis.

"But how?" she began.

"I have had you followed," Rafe said curtly. "Ever since Jervis recognized Lamartine as the man who was waiting for you that night we broke into your mother's apartments in Paris." Rafe nodded toward the figure on the floor. "Jervis noticed him skulking about Lady Melbourne's several days ago. We figured he was up to something, but we weren't sure what until this afternoon." His eyes moved to her swollen cheek and neck. "I didn't think he'd go away easily."

Alix sank down onto the bed. *Wandering about Vauxhall at night unattended,* he'd said earlier and she understood that he'd been there tonight. It occurred to her that she might have raged against him for spying on her, but the fight had gone out of her. "You recognized him," she said quietly.

"I didn't know his name until today, but yes I recognized him. I didn't tell you because I didn't want to frighten you with my speculations." He paused. "Perhaps I was wrong."

Alix knew it was as close as he would get to an apology. "It doesn't matter now," she answered.

"Alix," he said sharply, and she looked up at him. "Jervis and I are going to take Lamartine with us. Ginny will help you into bed.

"Ginny," he continued, "perhaps you should tell the household that your mistress is ill and does not wish to be disturbed." His eyes flickered to Alix's cheek. "You might say that she fainted and struck her cheek on the desk."

Jervis, who'd bound Lamartine's mouth with a soiled handkerchief, untied his legs and pulled the battered Frenchman up on his feet. Retrieving a hat from the floor, Jervis placed it atop Lamartine's lopsided bagwig. "Shoo, Monsieur," he said. "Now I understand why you wear that awful excuse for a wig." He chortled. "If I went around getting hit on the head with candlesticks and inkstands and the like, I just might get me one for protection, too." Grasping Lamartine firmly by the arm, Jervis turned to Rafe. "Ready, Captain," he said, and he pushed Lamartine out the door into the hall. Rafe took one more look at Alix, then followed.

"Rafe wait." Alix rose and went to an armoire across the room. Throwing open the painted doors, she began rifling through the drawers until she found a familiar set of satin stays. "The titles are still sewn in them," she said holding them out to him. She looked him straight in the eyes. "I want you to take them." She nodded towards the door. "So that he won't bother us again."

"Are you sure, Alix?" Rafe asked softly.

"I'm sure," she said. "I understand now that they are not the most important thing I possess."

A curious light flared in Rafe's hazel eyes. "Do you trust me Alix?" he asked.

"I do, Rafe."

He grasped the stays. "I'll be back in a day or two. Take

good care of my wife, Ginny." And then Rafe and Jervis left, dragging Lamartine along with them. "You're in luck, my friend," Alix heard Jervis's cheerful voice drift back to her. "We're sending you back to France."

"Okay, up with you, and let's get that dress and them stays off," Ginny ordered. Alix stood unresisting as the bright-haired maid bustled about, removing her dress and chemise, slipping a crisp clean nightdress over her head. "Now you just lay back here," she said, patting a space in the bed where she'd drawn back the covers. "I'll go down to the kitchen and see if I can't get something for your cheek."

Alix sat for a time after Ginny had gone, her knees drawn up under her chin, her eyes staring unfocused at the fire Ginny had stoked before leaving. Images from the night's events kept replaying unbidden in her head. Lamartine standing next to her bed, Lamartine kneeling beside her boasting about killing her father, his knife edging into her neck. And over and over the words, "You were supposed to die with your father . . . perhaps I should kill you." She'd sent Lamartine to his death she knew and that haunted her, too.

Alix rubbed her temples, pulling inadvertently at the skin across her cheek and sending a fresh wave of pain through her swollen face. Lamartine had wanted to kill her and she'd stopped him, and then Rafe had appeared. It was a wonder how he kept showing up just when she needed him most. She closed her eyes, recalling the relief she'd felt when she'd seen him standing in her bedchamber tonight, when his arms had closed around her, when he'd kissed her and told her he loved her. She hadn't had a chance to tell him she loved him, too, so she'd given him the one thing that meant as much to her as her own soul, the titles to Valcour.

Had he understood what she had not been able to say?

She heard her sitting room door open, then Ginny's voice, "I've brought a nice piece of raw meat with a bit of salt and lemon on it. Should take that swelling down, though it might sting a bit." As Ginny arranged the meat on Alix's face, she explained, "I took His Lordship's suggestion and told 'em all downstairs that you fainted and that you're shivering abed with the fever. That ought to keep them all away till you're ready to face the world again. As for your neck, we can wrap a bit of ribbon around it; I hear it's actually becoming the fashion in Paris, mocking the guillotine, they say." She shook her strawberry curls. "It's grisly, I think. But then there's no accounting for taste." Ginny stood back, admiring her handiwork. "Will you be needing anything else, mademoiselle? A bit of tea, or something stronger?"

Alix shook her head. "Thank you, Ginny, you've been wonderful. Jervis, too. Give him my thanks when you see him next. I'm sure I'll be asleep before my head hits the pillow," she lied. "It's been a long night. Why don't you go on back to your bed now?"

As soon as the maid departed, Alix got out of bed, tossed the beef into the farthest trash bin, then washed her stinging cheek off with the most heavily scented soap she could find. She was climbing back into bed when she heard her bedroom door opening. The scent of lilacs and the swish of skirts alerted her to her mother's presence, even before she caught sight of Madeleine's peach floral dressing gown.

"So," Madeleine said as she seated herself on the end of Alix's bed and smoothed her brightly colored skirts into a neat arrangement. "Your maid says you are unwell, but I don't believe it." She gave a knowing smile. "Really, my dear, if you are going to have your lover visit you late at night, you might at least be a bit more quiet. I could hear you and Moreham shouting at one another all the way down the hall."

Alix had the grace to blush.

Madeleine gasped. *"Mon dieu!* What has happened to your beautiful face? Did that English beast strike you? If so, you may not marry him. No matter what you think, my dear, wife beaters never change."

Alix raised a hand to stem the flow of her mother's tirade. *"Non, Maman,* he didn't hit me. Lamartine did." She ran her hand down the length of her throat and saw Madeleine's eyes widen as she saw the evidence of Lamartine's knife. "He wanted the titles for Valcour. He killed Papa for them and he would have killed me."

"Moreham saved you?"

"I saved myself," Alix responded. "But Rafe has promised to see to it that Lamartine never threatens us again."

"But then why were you fighting with his lordship?" Madeleine asked, confusion plain in her dark eyes.

Alix gave a tired laugh. "A misunderstanding, Mother, that is all."

Madeleine nodded, then gave her a serious look. "You understand that if I heard you two shouting, others did, too." She pursed her lips. "I have always suspected there was something more between the two of you than either of you let on. It wouldn't surprise me if the earl were somehow involved in your sudden arrival on Lady Melbourne's doorstep." She shrugged. "You have chosen not to confide in me, and this I understand."

Alix attempted to interrupt, but Madeleine waved her into silence. "I could overlook Moreham's previous visit, even if he did stay rather close to dawn, since you were both quite discreet. But this time, *ma petite*,"—she shook her head—"I'm afraid I will have to insist that he marry you."

"Oh, Mother . . ." Alix managed to get a few words in edgewise. "Oh, Mother, we're already married."

Chapter Twenty-six

❧

Rafe stood on the dock at Dover, listening to the creak of the great masted ships as they rocked at anchor and the waves beating against the shore. Somewhere out in the velvet darkness a ship was carrying Lamartine and Jervis back to France. Rafe closed his eyes, feeling the cool breeze wash over his face and tug at his hair. He was so tired, but he'd done what he needed to do to keep Alix safe. He, Jervis, and Lamartine—tied upright in the saddle of his horse—had ridden all night in order to reach port.

Rafe thought back to his discussion with the de La Brou's former steward. Sitting at a small table in the taproom of the King's Arms, the titles to Valcour and the other de La Brou estates piled in the middle of the table, Jervis had untied Lamartine. The little Frenchman sat stiffly at the table between them. Rafe speculated the tension in Lamartine's body had less to do with fear of what they might do to him than the strain of keeping himself from reaching out and grabbing up the titles. His eyes looked like those of a drowning man who sees a long boat drifting just out of reach.

"You'd like to have those, wouldn't you, monsieur?" Rafe had said, his long fingers tapping gently on the edge of the papers.

Lamartine nodded.

Rafe leaned back in his chair, his fingers still resting on the titles. "I don't want them. I have no interest in property in France; it's all going to hell there. And I don't wish my wife to have any interest in France."

Lamartine looked momentarily confused, then his watery eyes narrowed with understanding.

"That's right, monsieur," Rafe continued. "Alexandre de Rabec de La Brou is my wife. So you understand the titles are now mine to do with as I please. And what pleases me is to have my wife concentrate on providing me with an heir to the Moreham title, not mewl about some pile of stones in the middle of France. Do you understand, monsieur?"

Lamartine nodded, his expressionless face betrayed by the hunger that flared in his eyes. "Oh yes, my lord, women are so easily distracted."

"If I give you these titles, you will never return to England, will you?" Rafe said evenly.

"I give you my word," Lamartine responded.

"Good, monsieur." Rafe leaned forward, his hand spread on the paper and his eyes flat and cold. "Because if I ever hear that you have returned to these shores, I will have you killed. And rest assured, I have the power and the connections to carry out such a threat." He slid the papers over to Lamartine. "Take these. I will tell Alix that you escaped with them."

Lamartine grasped the papers and tucked them hastily into his waistcoat pocket, "Thank you, my lord, and if there is ever anything else I can do for you . . ."

"You can leave for France tonight," Rafe said sharply, finishing the sentence in his mind: and die just the way you planned for Alix. "My manservant Jervis will accompany you, to ensure that you disembark in Calais."

Lamartine stared at Rafe. "My pardon for questioning Your Lordship, but how do I know that he will not kill me and take the papers?"

"Don't be a fool, Lamartine," Rafe spat disgustedly. "If I wanted you dead, why would I give you the papers? Why wouldn't I slit your gullet now and dump your body in a ditch?"

Lamartine looked confused as he tried to work his way through this answer. Finally he nodded. "Forgive me, Your Lordship, for questioning you."

Rafe gave him a disinterested look and, glancing over at Jervis, said, "Take Monsieur Lamartine to the ship, and when you have completed your business in France, return immediately. I don't want you spending my money drinking and whoring in Calais."

He had watched from the shadows as Jervis had Lamartine bundled into a rowboat and taken out to board the packet *Cerebrus*. Jervis, he knew, would alert their contacts in Calais and make sure Lamartine was arrested as soon as he stepped foot on French soil. The letter from the comte, detailing how he was depending on his faithful steward to protect the family fortunes until the de La Brou's could return to claim them, would be all that was necessary to condemn the little man as a traitor. And in the uproar of Lamartine's arrest, the titles to the de La Brou estates would somehow mysteriously disappear. He smiled grimly. There were times when having a light-fingered colonial on one's staff was an invaluable asset.

Rafe rubbed his temples. It was perhaps an unnecessarily elaborate plan, but he wanted Lamartine to taste the fear and suffering he'd inflicted on Alix. Moreover, there was a certain poetic justice to the fact that it would be Lamartine's own twisted machinations that would bring about his downfall. Rafe wondered how Lamartine had forced the comte to write the letter, or indeed, whether the Comte de La Brou had written it at all. He shook his head. It made no difference.

All that mattered now was to make sure that Alix was safe and that the de La Brou legacy was safe. An image of Alix's face when she'd handed him the stays wavered in his mind. She hadn't said she loved him, but she'd entrusted him with the titles. Rafe thought he understood the depth of that gesture, and he wouldn't let her down. The sound of a ship's bells tolling the change of the watch reminded him of the time. He wanted to get a few hours of sleep, he thought, before he took care of the other tasks he'd set for himself. He yawned, wondering groggily how he would explain to his cousin, the bishop, that he needed a special license to remarry his wife.

Alix sat up in bed, the book on her knees sliding to the floor with a resounding thump. She stared at the bright sunshine pouring through her open curtains. She was bored—bored, and frustrated with keeping to her room, pretending to be sick. She picked up a silver hand mirror lying on her bedside table. Turning her head, she examined the bruise on her cheek from different angles, a bit green around the purple edges, but most of the swelling had gone down. The cut on her neck had faded to a thin line of red.

"I'm tired of just sitting about," she announced to the room.

"Alix, don't be so impatient," Madeleine tutted as she examined the stitches she'd finished in her needlepoint. "It's only been two days. One more and I think we can cover that nasty mark on your face with a bit of powder and paint." She glanced over at her daughter. "You don't want people gossiping over your face, *ma petite*."

She didn't care, Alix thought, she just wanted to get up and out of her room. She frowned. No, it wasn't just that she wanted to escape her bedchamber; she wanted to see Rafe, to talk to him. Two days and she'd heard nothing from him. Well, not exactly nothing, she thought examining the ring on her left hand. She wiggled her fingers, admiring the way the gemstones threw off sparks of light. The ring had arrived by messenger yesterday, accompanied by a short note.

> *Sweetheart,*
> *Thought this would keep the gossips quiet until I returned. R*

Not a particularly loverlike note, she reflected, no words of courtship or love. Still, he had *said* he loved her, she reminded herself fiercely. She regretted that she hadn't had the chance to tell him that she loved him, too. Did he understand why she had given him the titles? she wondered. Did he understand it had been like surrendering the deepest part of herself? She wanted him to know that she was committing to a future with him, in England.

Where was he? she wondered. Two days and no word. She'd even pumped Ginny on Jervis's whereabouts, but the maid had heard nothing and had seen no sign of the men since they'd dragged Lamartine out of the duchess's house. Alix thought about Lamartine and a cold chill swept across her skin. What if Lamartine had escaped, what if he'd harmed Rafe in some way? She knew now how dangerous he was.

"Alexandre Charlotte stop frowning," Madeleine said reprovingly. "It will give you wrinkles. Men like women with skin like fresh peaches, not like dried apples. Of course," she added with a smile. "I guess I don't have to tell you how to go about catching a man. You've done quite well for yourself, *chèrie*. Lady Melbourne says the earl has several estates and that he's managed them so well he's brought the family back from the brink of ruination. Indeed, he's rumored to be quite plump in the pocket. And quite handsome, too, I might add. If I hadn't seen how he looked at you that first night we met, I might have pursued him myself.

"Of course," Madeleine paused and then gave a sparkling laugh. "I never would have guessed you two were married. It's quite unfashionable for a husband and wife to be in love, you know. Spoils all the fun of flirtation. Your admirers will be most disappointed." Madeleine looked over at her. "Lady Melbourne's small salon has been besieged by messengers delivering flowers and cards wishing you better health. Lord Rothwell paid rather a lengthy call yesterday inquiring after you."

A speculative look crossed Madeleine's face. "He's a nice man and nice to look at, too. Lady Melbourne says he's looking for a mother for his six children. What do you think, Alix? Could you see me with a brood of little ones trailing after me?" Her voice was wistful. "I think I might have been a good mother, if I'd been given the chance."

Alix looked over at Madeleine's dark head, suddenly intent on her needlework. "I think if you set your mind to it, you could be a wonderful mother for Lord Rothwell's little ones." Her voice softened. "I think they'd be quite lucky."

Madeleine smiled warmly. "Perhaps I shall think on it then. Lord Rothwell has offered to take me riding tomorrow."

The room fell comfortably silent, and Alix glanced down at her fallen book wondering if she should reach down and pick it up. The trouble was she didn't feel like reading.

Madeleine started another conversation. "So," she said, snipping off a thread. "What do you think of the earl's sister?"

"Elizabeth?" Alix answered absently. "I think she's lively and fun."

"Hmm," Madeleine said, as she threaded a new color into her needle. "Lady Melbourne says she's getting a bit of a reputation. Been dashing around the park with James Dinsmore. Just imagine if they were to marry, you'd have Anne Dinsmore as a sort of sister-in-law. How uncomfortable."

"I don't think Elizabeth is serious about James," Alix said. "I think she's just curious."

"Some ladies think that just because they are young, nothing can harm them; their mistakes can just be chalked up to youthful high jinx." She shook her head knowingly. "A breath, a whisper of scandal can do irreparable harm. I'm glad you and the earl have been so discreet. Perhaps after you're married, you might speak with Elizabeth."

Alix nodded, as her mother continued on with some cautionary tale of a young girl at Versailles who'd dallied with a notorious rake. She couldn't focus her mind on Elizabeth, not when it was so full of Rafe. It occurred to her that she was tired of being discreet, tired of waiting for him to return. Madeleine's story reached its shocking crescendo. "And so they caught the girl dressed in a footman's livery climbing out the window to meet her lover!"

Alix made the appropriate noises to reassure her mother that she was listening to the story and understood its intent.

Madeleine finished with a flourish. "And she died an old woman locked away in a convent." She sighed dramatically. "But we should not be speaking of such sad subjects. We should be talking of happier things, such as your wedding. Have you thought about what you might like to wear?"

Alix hadn't. Wedding dresses had been among the furthest thoughts from her mind.

"*I won't do* it, mademoiselle," Ginny blustered later that afternoon when she'd finished setting up Alix's tea and the two of them were alone. "That's scandalous behavior and I could lose my job if you were caught and anyone found out I'd helped you.

"And sure as anything you would be caught," she added indignantly.

"Oh Ginny, it's not scandalous, he's my husband. And besides, I traveled halfway across France without getting caught, I can certainly make a few blocks across town."

Ginny dug her meaty hands into her hips and glared obstinately.

"Oh come now, Ginny. You've snuck Jervis in and out the back stairs dozens of times and no one's been the wiser."

"That's different, no one cares what a maid servant does, so long as she's quiet about it and don't get herself in a family way."

"Well, that's my point, who's going to notice what a maid and a footman accompanying her are about?"

Ginny frowned. "I still don't like it."

"It'll be a quick trip. I'll be back before anyone even notices I've been gone," Alix cajoled. "You do still have the footman's livery you borrowed for Jervis?"

Ginny nodded reluctantly.

Alix laughed. "It won't be the first time I've borrowed Jervis's things. Besides, I have a notion those britches will fit me far better."

Ginny gave a scandalized gasp. "I don't like it, mademoiselle, and if I were a betting woman I'd wager his lordship won't either."

A mischievous look came over Alix's face and her eyes

glinted like polished silver. "You let me worry about his lordship, Ginny. I've a fair idea how to change his mind."

The next day Alix refused to let her curtains be opened, bemoaning the effects of a murderous headache. When her mother came to sit with her, she complained that the slightest light or sound in the room sent spasms through her head, and begged to be left alone. Madeleine wondered aloud whether a doctor should be sent for, but Alix assured her she'd often suffered through such migraines, and that when it passed, probably by the next day, she'd be right as rain again. All she needed, Alix said in a weak voice, was a bit of tea, a dose of laudanum, and to be left undisturbed.

As Alix had hoped, Madeleine instructed Ginny to fetch some laudanum and to make sure that Mademoiselle was left in peace. As soon as her mother had left the room, Alix was up and out of the bed.

"Very good, Ginny, let me see what you've got," she said eagerly, pulling her chemise over her head.

"It's disgraceful, that's what it is," Ginny muttered, as she began pulling clothes out of a pillowcase she'd tucked under Alix's bed. "Lying to Lady Melbourne and your poor mother like that. I'll be sacked for sure."

"You won't, Ginny," Alix declared as she pulled on a pair of men's drawers, stockings, and white wool britches.

"That's what you say," her maid responded. "Here, let me tie your stock for you, it looks all crooked."

Alix buttoned up her white waistcoat and then raised her head so Ginny could arrange her stock properly.

"And your hair, mademoiselle. How are we going to hide all that hair?"

"We twist it into one long plait, tuck it down the back of this great oversized coat and then put the wig on top."

Ginny cast her a dubious look, then turned her around

and began braiding, pulling the hair tight to communicate her disapproval.

"If anything shows, I can toss a muffler around my neck to cover it. It is getting a bit cold out these days anyway."

Ginny was still wondering how her mistress had talked her into such a mad scheme when she left the house a short time later, accompanied by a slight footman in a too-large jacket and a muffler.

Chapter Twenty-seven

✤

Rafe Moreham sat alone in his study the following afternoon, trying to focus on his business correspondence, but his mind kept wandering. He'd always loved this room; the deep greens of the walls, curtains, and carpet, and the dark wood of the furniture had always made him feel as if he had escaped to some hidden forest. It was at the back of the house, away from the busy front rooms and the street, and the thick velvet curtains and plush wool carpet quickly absorbed any sound that managed to permeate the heavy paneled door. The only sound was the ticking of an ornate clock on the mantle, reminding him that time was passing and that he still had not attended to his work.

He forced his eyes back down to the pile of papers on his desk and exhaled deeply. He had been so many places and done so many things in the last three days, and yet it felt as though important details were slipping through his hands. He'd seen Lamartine safely dispatched to France, convinced his cousin to grant him a special marriage license, found what he hoped was the perfect ring for Alix and even visited with Anne Dinsmore to let her know about the wedding announcement that would appear in the papers.

His jaw tensed as he thought about his meeting with Anne. She'd greeted him with a warm smile as he'd been ushered into her cream and yellow sitting room. Gesturing gracefully to a comfortable seat by the fire, she'd poured him some tea and served him, talking easily of the most recent goings on of the ton. When he'd indicated his need to speak seriously with her, she'd sat with her back straight and her head held as still and precise as an egret. She'd been polite and pleasant throughout, and when he'd finished, she'd wished him a happy future with Alix.

And yet, as he'd left he'd had the sense that he'd behaved like a cad.

He couldn't put his finger on what she'd said or done that had made him feel that way. He tugged at his stock, loosening the knot. Perhaps it had been her knowing smile as she'd hinted that he'd lost his head over a younger woman and was being ruled by passion rather than thoughtful planning. Or how she'd cast him a sympathetic look through her pale lashes as she'd said she hoped everything would turn out for the best. As if, he thought with some annoyance, just beneath the surface she believed he and Alix hadn't a chance in hell.

He reached again for the pile of invoices on his desk. Anne had played to his deepest fears. He realized he was doing all these things for Alix, rearranging his life, and he still was uncertain about how she felt. He'd even told her he loved her, and she'd said nothing in return. He was placing a lot of faith, he thought, in how their bodies seemed to fuse whenever they were together. Damn Cole Davenport and his talk of impulses.

There was a light knock on the door, and Rafe heard the ever-polite tones of his butler.

"Come," he said, more gruffly than he meant.

The door opened and Ferguson, a tall, dark-haired man with a face that looked as if it had been carved from limestone, stepped into the room. "There is a footman from Lady Melbourne's who insists upon seeing you, sir." He paused, then continued in an apologetic tone. "He claims he has words for your ears alone and insisted I give you this." Ferguson held out a gloved hand, and Rafe could see his ruby signet ring stark against the white cotton.

He held his hand out for the band, wondering what excuses Alix had sent now to delay accepting her position as his wife. As he felt the heavy metal slip into his hand, he felt the anger and frustration of the past few days began to fuse into a white heat. She might return the ring, he thought bitterly, but she was going to find that it was not so easy to break the ties that bound them.

"Send the man in, Ferguson," he said sharply.

Rafe sat turning the signet ring about in his hands when the footman dressed in Melbourne livery entered the room. He heard the man's footfalls step slowly across the thick green carpet, but he didn't bother to look up. "Go ahead," he muttered, "deliver your message." There was no answer. Annoyed, Rafe ceased toying with the ring, and glanced up. Lady Melbourne's butler must be getting slack, he thought critically, eyeing the slight frame in the ill-fitting clothes.

The footman cleared his throat nervously, and Rafe focused an impatient gaze on the man. Or was it a man? he wondered, his mind slowly registering the familiar features beneath the white wig. "Alix," he murmured in disbelief, as he rose, moving in front of the desk to get a better look.

She stepped uncertainly back. "You left so abruptly the other night, you didn't give me a chance to say a word."

"Did you come across town in that get up?" he demanded, pulling the white wig off and dropping it to the floor.

She pulled herself up defiantly. "Well, it's been three days, and I haven't heard a word from you."

"I sent you a ring," he said defensively.

"With a note that said nothing more than that you hoped it fit."

"And does it?"

"Yes," she said, annoyance sounding in her voice. "And it's beautiful."

"But?" he queried, leaning back against the edge of his desk and eyeing her expectantly. "What is the problem *this* time?" He paused and, as his anger got the better of him, resumed speaking without waiting for her answer. "No, let me guess. You don't love me, you don't trust me, you don't want to spend your life with me. Is that what you've come to tell me?" His voice gained momentum. "Well, Alexandre Charlotte de Rabec de La Brou," he said, "it doesn't matter. You're my wife and that's how it's going to stay, no annulments, no divorces, no separate residences."

He crossed his arms over his chest, warming to his theme. "After December you are going to live with me, have my children, and God willing, grow old with me. And if you don't love me, well, it's too damn bad, because I love you. I love your hair and your eyes, every inch of your delectable body. I love the way we never run out of things to talk and laugh and even fight about. God help me, I even love you when you stand in front of me ready to protest that our marriage is some colossal mistake."

"Are you quite finished?" she asked.

"Yes," he said resolutely.

"Well, then, Rafe Harcrest, it's my turn to speak and this time," she said pointing a slim finger at him. "You will listen."

Rafe stood unmoving as Alix eyed him with an odd mixture of annoyance and affection. "Rafe Harcrest, you are the most arrogant, overbearing man I have ever met. You sweep into my life and turn everything upside down. And then, to top it off, you never, never, let me have the last word."

"I promise, you have my full attention."

"When I gave you those titles—" she began, her voice growing stronger.

"The titles are—" he interrupted, but she hushed him with a finger to his lips.

"Giving you those titles was one of the hardest things I've ever done. The de La Brou lands meant everything to my father. He was always telling me stories about how our ancestors had fought and died for those lands. The mortar, he'd say, was mixed with more de La Brou blood than water."

She shook her head. "I knew he was disappointed that I was not a son. He never said those words to me precisely, but when my mother had done something to annoy him, he'd rant about what weak and useless vessels women were. Then he'd turn to me and say since I couldn't protect the de La Brou heritage with my wits or the strength of my arms, the least I could do was to preserve it through my body with an heir."

Rafe nodded for her to continue.

"After my first betrothal fell through, I don't know why he didn't arrange another for me." She shrugged. "I think he thought he had plenty of time, that he'd live forever. He refused to consider death the same way he refused to consider the consequences of the overthrow of the king."

"When the troubles started, I began to think that maybe there was something more I could do to protect Valcour, more than just marrying and having babies. At first I tried to keep my father informed of what was happening in

France and in the village. I hoped it might rouse him to action."

She frowned. "And then, when I heard that the mob was coming, I stole the titles from his desk. I suppose it sounds ridiculous, but I felt like the guardian of my family's past and future. Those papers were what kept me going when I was trying to escape France." Her hands curled unconsciously around her waist as if the papers were still sewn into her stays. "They were like a sacred trust."

She paused, struggling for the words and Rafe resisted the urge to enfold her in his arms. "And then I met you, and you were like one of those knights who comes charging up, defeats the dragon, and carries the lady off. Only I didn't want to be carried off. I wanted to, I don't know, do everything on my own and make my father proud." She looked up at him, the pain drawn on her face as if with a thin knife. "As if I could prove that a woman had something more to offer than her body. And there you were . . ."

"So eager for your body," he breathed.

"Yes," she admitted softly, "I do seem unnaturally conscious of your body and mine when we are together."

Rafe smiled.

"But there was more," she continued firmly, "you were so ready to fix everything, to change my name and my life . . ."

"I wanted to give you a chance to put the nightmare behind you, to start over."

"I know," Alix said, "but starting over seemed like abandoning my father and Valcour."

Rafe's reached out a hand and swept a tousled strand of hair from her face. Alix looked up at him.

"When I left you and found my mother, I thought I'd feel . . . I don't know . . . triumphant, fulfilled. But all I felt was lost and empty. And my mother." Alix again struggled for words. "She was glad that I had escaped, but the titles . . ." She paused. "She looked upon them as ghosts from the past. She was insistent that we not look back, that we concentrate on moving forward and building a new life. For the first time, she said, we had a chance to make our own choices. We didn't have to look to a man to decide every detail of our lives, from what we should wear to whom we should marry."

Alix looked at him, her eyes clear. "During the time we were apart, I thought a lot about what my mother said. I tried to see myself in different lights, as your wife, as Major Harris's wife, or Lord Minton's, or no one's at all."

Rafe stiffened and she saw his fingers clench the edge of the desk. This was hard, she thought, but she knew that she needed to finish what she'd come to say. "When Lamartine showed up . . ."

"Lamartine will never hurt you again, sweetheart, I promise," he cut in, all the while a voice inside his head reassuring himself that if she chose to stay with him out of fear, he would accept even that to have her with him always.

"I'm not afraid of Lamartine," Alix insisted. "It's just when he broke into my room, I realized what he'd . . . *become* . . . in pursuit of those titles. Even if he'd gotten away with them and claimed the estates, what would he have had?" She answered her own question, a note of bitterness creeping into her voice. "Trappings, empty trappings."

Her tone softened. "When I didn't hear from you for days, and I thought he might have killed you, too, I realized I'd very nearly made the same choice."

"So that's why you came across town dressed like a footman?"

"I wasn't going to wait another day, I wasn't going to waste any more time. I want to be with you Rafe, now, in December, for always." She traced a hand along his neck, feeling the bristles of his beard rasp against her fingertips, amazed, as always, by the thousand tiny differences between men and women. "All these conventions that make us noble lords and ladies, that bind us up into a pretty package, counting the number of dances we can share, the amount of time we can speak, and the chaperones."

She took his face between her hands. "I wanted you to know before we are *officially* married, that you aren't browbeating me into this."

"And?" he prompted, understanding her answer, but wanting to hear the words.

"I'm making my own choice, Lord Moreham, being your wife is what *I* want."

Rafe kissed her softly. "I couldn't browbeat you if I tried, Alix," he chuckled softly. "Though I will admit I may have tried a little." He slid her heavy footman's coat off her shoulders and onto the floor. "Good lord, woman, I can't even prevent you from traipsing about Paris and London in men's britches." His hands moved around her waist and his fingers searching for the buttons at her waistband, and as he found them he murmured huskily. "Perhaps they do present some advantages."

Rafe unlaced the men's drawers beneath the britches and pushed both garments down around Alix's ankles. She stepped out of them and closer to him, her arms reaching to close the distance remaining between them.

"God, you're beautiful," she murmured as she stretched on her toes to kiss him.

"Isn't that the gentleman's line?" he inquired in an amused voice before bending to take her lips.

Alix paused for the briefest moment, her hand slipping to his chest to hold him off. "It's my choice, my lord, and I say you're beautiful."

With a laugh, he swooped down and covered her mouth, his hands sliding under the loose shirt and waistcoat, which were all that remained of her footman's garb. "A most shocking abuse of Lady Melbourne's livery, Alix," he whispered nipping at her ear.

"Then perhaps," she said, as her fingers began to work the buttons on his waistcoat, "You should remove them to avoid giving further offense."

"An excellent decision, my love," he murmured as he swept the remaining garments over her head. Smiling at her, he pulled off his own shirt and waistcoat and tossed them to the floor.

A wave of desire swept through Alix, and she placed both hands on his chest and pushed him back against his mahogany desk, sending his work fluttering to the floor like a fall of bleached leaves. Rafe leaned back on his elbows, a wicked gleam in his eyes as he gazed expectantly up at her.

She leaned over him and began to unfasten his britches and drawers, yanking them down over his tapered hips. As they fell against the thick carpet, her hands began stroking their way up the columns of his thighs. She heard Rafe's breath quicken and he reached down and lifted her over him, straddling his hips, mahogany hair falling like a silken net around them.

Crouching over his taut body, Alix took Rafe's face in her hands and explored his features with her mouth, dropping kisses on his nose, his eyelids, the crease between his eyebrows before settling on his mouth. "I love you, Rafe Harcrest," she whispered glorying in the feel of him beneath her.

"I love you, Alexandre Charlotte de Rabec de La Brou Harcrest." Rafe reached up and caught her around the hips, his thumbs trailing urgently over the lines of her waist and ribs, moving to cup her breasts. His circling caresses sent spiraling waves of sensation through her. She moaned softly, her body pulsing under his touch, the heat beginning to burn between her thighs.

He thrust his hips up at her, his erection pressed against the curve of her bottom. She reached down and caught him in her hand, her fingers stroking the heated length of him, and he whispered hoarsely, "Alix, what are you doing to me?"

"Making my own decisions, my lord," she whispered.

She heard his breath quicken, then the sharp tug of his mouth on her nipples and she released him, and began stroking his body with her hips, brushing her damp curls against his belly and his thighs, circling, then settling gently against the length of his pulsing member. Slowly she slid against it, letting him feel the slick heat of her arousal. Rafe's hands caught at her hips, urging her down on him.

Alix resisted, though as the waves of pleasure rippled through her, she knew it would not be for long. She dipped and rose against him, feeling him strain to follow her, like a stallion fighting the bit. She kissed him deeply and he thrust upward, catching her and entering her. She sank down against him, and he slid deeply within her. And suddenly it didn't matter who was in control, who was leading and who was following, only that they were making love together.

Alix stretched herself against the length of him; he felt like home, she thought as the scent of his body and the warmth of his skin enveloped her. She felt one hand slide along her hip to press her firmly down, and another slip between her thighs to caress the sensitive folds between her legs. His thumb found the delicate tip of flesh, and with each gentle stroke sent searing streams of pleasure throughout her body. She arched against him, her hips shuddering with need.

"Fill me, Rafe," she cried in an agonized whisper, "complete me." His eyes grew dark and his breathing came in broken gasps that matched her own. She felt his muscles tighten as he arched upward, and she closed her eyes as red flowers blossomed behind her lids. Alix felt as if she'd been swept into something swirling and molten that did not burn, but only consumed. And as he bucked against her, crying out her name, she was certain that Rafe felt it, too. In that brief instant before it seemed they must surely be turned to ash and smoke, she opened her eyes and saw him looking at her with such passion and love that she knew if she could have this man forever it would be enough.

Chapter Twenty-eight

~

Rafe watched Elizabeth dancing with James Dinsmore at Lord and Lady Landsdownes's ball. The whole world, it seemed, knew he and Alexandre de La Brou would be wed in one month's time. The ceremony, after much discussion, was to be at Lady Melbourne's, though he would have preferred Moreham House. Still, the important thing was that everyone knew Alexandre de La Brou belonged with him. All evening he'd had his hand shaken and his back slapped by well-wishers, though he noticed with a bit of amusement that Lord Minton and Major Harris had been rather slow to offer their congratulations. He'd heard a rumor that Minton had composed a mournful ode bemoaning his loss, entitled *Silver Tears*. Thinking of it, Rafe couldn't help a snort of laughter.

"You're in fine spirits," Cole Davenport remarked, strolling up beside him. "Understandably, considering you've managed to find your way back into your wife's good graces. Though how such a lovely lady succumbed to your cantankerous charms, has much of London mystified." He raised his glass in a mock salute. "Still, my winnings from the betting at White's will be a generous contribution towards your wedding gift. Seems the odds had begun to tip in favor of the dashing Major Harris."

Rafe snorted again.

"Pity," Cole continued between sips of wine, "that Major Harris was unfamiliar with the motto on the Harcrest coat of arms."

"What I claim is mine," Rafe said glancing down with a smile at the ruby signet ring that once again adorned his right hand. Alix had no need for it now that she was wearing the betrothal ring he'd given her.

"Though I must admit the ton is quite buzzing with the haste of your nuptials."

"Let them talk," Rafe replied, "in a few months they'll find some new bit of nonsense to chatter about."

"No doubt fed to them by Anne Dinsmore," Cole noted.

Rafe shook his head. "You misjudge Anne. She's received the news that I intended to wed Alix quite gracefully."

Cole frowned. "I'd still keep an eye out for that rock in the back of the head."

The dance drew to a close and Cole and Rafe watched as James Dinsmore bent to whisper something in Elizabeth's ear. She laughed and motioned with her fan in the direction of Rafe and Cole.

Cole's eyes narrowed. "Did you ever consider that young James might be the rock?"

"James Dinsmore is a rattlebrain, too busy playing hazard and betting on the horses to cause anyone but his family trouble."

"Word is that he's mightily disappointed he won't be having your money to pay his gambling debts."

Their conversation was cut short as Elizabeth and James

drew up in front of them, Elizabeth laughing, a light flush spreading across her face.

"James was telling me the most shocking story," she said smiling mischievously at her escort.

"A tale that no doubt would hold little interest for your brother and Lord Davenport." James interjected a bit hastily, Rafe thought.

"Quite so, I'm sure," Rafe said coolly.

James flushed darkly and after exchanging a few obligatory pleasantries, hurriedly made his excuses.

"Well, that was rather rude," Elizabeth said as soon as he was out of earshot.

"There's something about that young man I don't care for," Rafe responded, his eyes still fixed on the powdered blond head as it wove through the crowd to join a cluster of dandies near the door.

Elizabeth frowned, a stubborn look on her face that bore a remarkable likeness to her brother's. "So Lady Anne's a paragon and James is the devil?" she inquired.

"A very keen observation, Lizzie," Cole said flashing her a smile.

Rafe frowned, aware he was caught in a trap of his own making. "It's different," he muttered searching for a way out. "The man sets the tone for a relationship."

"I see," Elizabeth said slowly, "a lady is uplifted or dragged down by the man's moral stance?"

"Something like that."

She pressed her lips together and gave him a thoughtful look. "And that's how it happens that Mademoiselle de La Brou has been dragged into a scandalously brief betrothal with you?"

Cole gave a bark of laughter. "If you only knew . . ."

Rafe shot him a searing glance, and Cole closed his mouth on the rest of the sentence, his dark eyes dancing. "Look, Lizzie," he began instead, "Rafe and I are just a bit concerned about James's intentions. Are you developing a *tendresse* for the fellow?"

Elizabeth threw him a fond but exasperated look. "Lud, no! He's just good fun. But then I suppose at your age," she batted her fan, "you've both forgotten what that is."

Cole sighed and pulled a long face. "That's us, my girl, the souls of staid propriety."

Elizabeth laughed. "I appreciate your and my brother's concerns, but I can take care of myself, you know, I'm not a child."

"If you were, I could safely send you back to the nursery," Rafe grumbled.

"Are you sure you wish to marry my brother?" Elizabeth asked Alix, who had appeared just then with Phoebe.

Alix linked her arm through Rafe's. "I'm afraid only he will suit."

Elizabeth eyed Alix's elegant gray and lavender patterned gown and shook her head in dismay. "And your taste seems so refined otherwise."

"Incorrigible brat," Rafe growled.

Cole nodded sagely. "The considered response of older brothers everywhere."

As Ginny slid the pale pink satin wedding dress over her head and began fastening up the back, Alix realized with a sense of wonder that she was not in the least nervous. Standing in front of the long mirror in her dressing room, smoothing down her three-quarter-length net sleeves, it struck her that all she felt was a sense of impatience. She'd spent so much time over the past few weeks pulling apart her feelings for Rafe and worrying about his feelings for her. That confusion was behind her now, she thought as Ginny arranged the floor-length veil over her hair. She knew without a doubt that she loved Rafe and that he

loved her, and that she was more than ready to spend the
rest of her life with him.

"Lordy, mademoiselle, if you don't look just like a fairy
princess," Ginny breathed in admiration.

Alix smiled, touching the sweep of lace at the bodice of
her dress, then smoothing the satin underskirt. She felt a bit
like a fairy princess. "Well, Ginny," she said, "I think it's
time to go downstairs and show off your handiwork."

Ginny gave Alix's veil a final pat, then pulled a handkerchief out of her sleeve and noisily blew her nose.
"Sorry, mademoiselle, but weddings always choke me up.
Don't know why, guess it's just the feelings of promise in
the air."

Alix gave her a quick hug. "Are you sure you won't
change your mind and come to Moreham House with me?"

Ginny shook her mobcapped head. "I thank you, mademoiselle, for the offer, but I guess I'm just stuck in my
ways. We Potters have been part of the Melbourne household for generations. It just wouldn't feel right, picking up
and moving somewhere else."

Alix took a last look at the rose-colored bedchamber
and went downstairs to marry Rafe Harcrest, Earl of Moreham.

The ceremony passed in a blur, not a blur of gray as she
remembered their first wedding at the Place de la Grève,
but it seemed to Alix, a blur of gold. Candles blazed everywhere, in the great glass chandelier overhead, in candelabras and candlestands, their starry light reflected in the
mirrors and long dark windows of the grand salon. Lady
Melbourne had decorated the room with swathes of amber
satin and bowls of late blooming foliage. Rafe, too, seemed
to glow, Alix thought, as the candlelight played about his
hair and eyes and the rich dark velvet of his wedding
clothes.

The words of the ceremony were lost in sensations, the

gleam in the depths of his hazel eyes as she walked toward him, the softness of his smile, the warmth of his hand as it closed around hers. When the last muted words had been spoken, she felt his kiss, firm and sweet against her mouth.

"I love you, Lady Moreham," he whispered as they turned to walk hand in hand, man and wife, through the rows of guests.

She smiled up at him. "And I love you Lord Moreham."

Alix clasped Rafe's hand tightly through the supper party Lady Melbourne had arranged for them, barely tasting the dazzling array of dishes the servants standing behind her chair offered. The air was loud with the sounds of conversation, the clink of glassware, and rounds of toasts. Listening to the wishes for health, happiness, a long life together, and children, Alix found herself nodding, thinking yes, this was what she wanted from her life with Rafe. And when he squeezed her hand, she knew that it was all that he desired, too.

As they danced their first "officially" married dance together, Rafe leaned close and said, "I want to take you home, Alix." She felt a delicious shiver, both at the desire vibrating deep and low in his voice, and the word *home*. She nodded in assent.

She wasn't certain how he managed it, but a short time later she found herself wrapped in his arms in a coach heading toward Moreham House.

"It was lovely," she sighed, leaning into the solid warmth of his body and listening with contentment to the tick of snowflakes against the coach windows.

"Any ceremony with you at its center can't help but be lovely," he said kissing the top of her head.

Alix laughed softly. "Even a gray and dreary ceremony at the Place de la Grève?"

Rafe's voice grew serious. "I think I knew even then when I saw you standing among the crowd of brides in your navy gown that I was falling in love with you." He caressed her cheek. "But I think this ceremony was a bit nicer, don't you?"

Alix nodded. "Though, after the Place de la Grève, I swore when I married again it would be in the summer in a garden full of flowers."

"That's what Louisa said we should have done, but I'm afraid, my love, I couldn't leave the Silver Siren wandering loose about London any longer." He chuckled, then started abruptly. "What do you mean, when you married again?"

Alix laughed. "Oh yes, I also decided that my next husband would be kind and undemanding, and not so disconcertingly handsome."

Rafe smiled. "Well, Lady Moreham, suitable or no, I believe you are well and truly stuck with me. I shall endeavor to be kind, but I make no promises about being undemanding." His eyes took on a very demanding gleam as he tilted up her chin. "And I hope that I shall never fail to disconcert."

As his lips took hers and Alix felt her senses begin to thrum in response, she doubted very much that he would ever fail to do so.

The lurch of the carriage and the jangling sounds of the harness as the horse came to a stop signaled their arrival at Moreham House. Rafe reluctantly released Alix. A moment later there was a thump on the carriage door, the door swung open, and Jervis peered anxiously into the interior of the coach. Seeing Alix, his face split into a wide grin. "So you've finally brought your lady home. Good for you, sir." He winked at Rafe. "Most of the staff's been sent on their way. The cook wants you to know she's left out some cold meats, some sweets, and a bit of champagne should you need it."

Alix and Rafe made their way up the stairs to Moreham

House, the snow crunching thickly underfoot. As they reached the top, Jervis swung the front door open for them and offered Alix an extravagant imitation of a courtier's bow. "Welcome to Moreham House, my lady."

"Welcome home, Alix," Rafe murmured in her ear as he slipped her cloak off and handed it to Jervis. Handing over his own great coat and hat as well, he nodded to the grinning little man. "Thank you, Jones, I think I can handle it from here."

As Jervis disappeared, cloaks piled high around his head, Rafe pulled a silken scarf from out of his pocket. To Alix's surprise, he tied it over her eyes. She moved to pull it off, but he stopped her. "I've been waiting a long time for this, Alix," he said. "One more promise to you I swore I'd keep."

Alix felt his arms sweep around her waist and under her knees, heard his heart beating beneath her ears as he began to carry her through the great house and up the stairs. She sensed they were moving down long corridors, turning corners, and moving up another flight of stairs. Excitement, but no fear, streaked through her body as she heard him turn a handle, felt him push a door open with his shoulder. He stopped in what Alix judged to be the middle of a room and slid her slowly to her feet. Turning her away from him, he whispered, "For you, my love," and untied the silken blindfold.

As it fluttered to her feet, Alix gasped, unbelieving.

It was a bedroom, but unlike any she had ever seen before. On the floor was a dark green carpet, woven with flowers, and on the walls had been painted a garden, the most magnificent she had ever seen. Thick trellises of ivy hung over arched pathways, the weathered stone painted so realistically, she felt sure that if she touched it she would feel the warm sun of southern France beneath her fingertips. Daisies and zinnias and a half dozen other kinds of flowers she recognized but could not name spilled over pebbled pathways, leading to fountains splashing with silver blue water and sculptures of nymphs.

She felt Rafe's hands gently touch her shoulders, his cheek graze her hair. "Do you like it? Louisa assures me it's authentic."

"It's a French garden," she breathed, "a real French garden."

"It's my promise to you," he said softly, "that someday you and our children will return to France." Alix heard a rustle of papers, and when she turned to face him, she saw that he was holding out a pile of creased and stained, but still familiar papers. "The titles to the de La Brou estates," he said simply. "My wedding gift to you."

Alix wrapped her arms around his neck and kissed him fiercely, communicating with her lips and tongue the words that were too overwhelming to say. Rafe felt wetness against his cheeks, and when Alix pulled away, he tasted her tears.

"I'm sorry, love, I didn't mean to make you cry."

Alix gave a watery laugh as she buried her face against his neck, her hands beginning to make their way down the mother of pearl buttons of his waistcoat. "Rafe Moreham, you sweet idiot, I'm not crying because I'm sad, but because I'm happy. Happier than I ever thought I could be."

"And always will be, my love," he whispered as he carried her to the bed. "And always will be."